Praise for John Banville's

Mrs. Osmond

"Banville is one of the best novelists in English. . . . *Mrs. Osmond* is both a remarkable novel in its own right and a superb pastiche." —Edmund White, *The Guardian*

"[A] modern classic . . . a striking imagined follow-up to *The Portrait of a Lady*." —*Entertainment Weekly*

"A brilliant feat of literary ventriloquism. . . . Richly enjoyable and enthralling, this exercise in creative empathy is a sequel of very high finish." —*The Sunday Times* (London)

"An audacious sequel." —*O, The Oprah Magazine*

"Fusing the essence of James's style with his own signature wit and irony, Banville crafts a story that will delight and inspire classicists." —*Harper's Bazaar*

"Less a sequel to *Portrait* than a kind of recapitulation of it, a filtering of its events through a different novelistic consciousness. . . . There's something inherently fun about being reintroduced, in a changed context, to all these half-familiar characters." —*Financial Times*

"Banville does an impeccable job of re-creating James's prose style and moving his characters forward in believable ways. As *Mrs. Osmond* progresses, his wicked sense of humor emerges more, and he adds twists to the plot James would have cloaked in reticence."　　　　　—*Tampa Bay Times*

"[Written] with wit, daring, vivid description and a sense of fun."　　　　　—*The Irish Times*

"[An] act of literary ventriloquism and imagination."
　　　　　—*The Independent* (London)

"A great storyteller. [Banville's] book is not only an impressive re-creation of James's atmospheres and pacing, but also full of minor cliffhangers and page-turning suspenses that keep you guessing."　　　　　—*The Observer* (London)

"[Banville] pulls off [*Mrs. Osmond*] with vigor and style. It's hard to say no to a second helping of Isabel Archer."
　　　　　—*The Seattle Times*

"So successful it felt like discovering a new Henry James novel."　　　　　—Lara Feigel, *The Guardian*

"Banville's ventriloquism is word-perfect."　　　　　—*Vulture*

John Banville

Mrs. Osmond

John Banville, the author of seventeen novels, has been the recipient of the Man Booker Prize, the James Tait Black Memorial Prize, the Guardian Fiction Award, the Franz Kafka Prize, a Lannan Literary Award for Fiction, and the Prince of Asturias Award for Literature. He lives in Dublin.

www.john-banville.com

VINTAGE

INTERNATIONAL

Mrs. Osmond

Mrs. Osmond

JOHN BANVILLE

Vintage International

VINTAGE BOOKS

A DIVISION OF PENGUIN RANDOM HOUSE LLC

NEW YORK

FIRST VINTAGE INTERNATIONAL EDITION, OCTOBER 2018

The Library of Congress has cataloged the Knopf edition as follows:
Names: Banville, John, author.
Title: Mrs. Osmond : a novel / John Banville.
Description: First American edition. | New York : Alfred A. Knopf, 2017.
Identifiers: LCCN 2017027401
Subjects: LCSH: Young women—Fiction. | Americans—Italy—Fiction. | Inheritance and succession—Fiction. | Married people—Fiction. | Triangles (Interpersonal relations)—Fiction. | Psychological fiction. | BISAC: FICTION / Literary. | FICTION / Historical. | FICTION / Classics. | GSAFD: Love stories.
Classification: LCC PR6052.A57 M78 2017 | DDC 823/.914—dc23
LC record available at https://lccn.loc.gov/2017027401

Vintage International Trade Paperback ISBN: 978-1-101-97289-2
eBook ISBN: 978-0-451-49343-9

Book design by Soonyoung Kwon

www.vintagebooks.com

Printed in the United States of America
10 9 8 7 6 5 4 3 2 1

Deep in her soul—deeper than any appetite for renunciation—was the sense that life would be her business for a long time to come.

—*The Portrait of a Lady*

I

I

It had been a day of agitations and alarms, of smoke and steam
and grit. Even yet she felt, did Mrs. Osmond, the awful surge and
rhythm of the train's wheels, beating on and on within her. It was
as if she were still seated at the carriage window, as she had sat for
what seemed impossibly many hours, gazing with unseeing eyes
upon the placid English countryside flowing away from her endlessly in all the soft-green splendour of the early-summer afternoon. Her thoughts had sped along with the speeding train but,
unlike the train, to no end. Indeed, she had never registered so
acutely the mind's unstoppable senseless headlong rush as she
had since leaving Gardencourt. The great snorting and smoking
brute that had paused with brusque impatience at the meek little
village station and suffered her to take her place in one of its lat-
termost compartments—her fingertips still retained the impression of hot plush and greasy leather—now stood gasping after its
mighty efforts under the high, soot-blackened glass canopy of the
throbbing terminus, disgorging on to the platform its complement of dazed, bedraggled travellers and their jumbles of baggage. Well, she told herself, she had arrived somewhere, at least.

Staines, her maid, had hardly stepped down from the train
before she flew into an altercation with a red-faced railway porter.

Had she not been a female it might have been said of Staines that she was a fellow with a heart of oak. She was tall and gaunt, a person all of angles, with long wrists and large feet, and a jaw that put one in mind of the blade of a primitive axe. In the years that she had been in Mrs. Osmond's employ, or, given how closely they were conjoined, better say in the years that they had been together, Staines's devotion to her mistress had not wavered by a jot. In their long period of exile in the south her forbearance had extended to putting up with the Italian market and the Italian kitchen, and, which required an even more saintly fortitude, with Italian plumbing. Indeed, such was her steadfastness that on occasion Mrs. Osmond—Isabel—found herself longing wistfully for even half a day's respite from her servant's unrelenting, stone-hard solicitude. In their recent travels together the chief token and proof of Staines's loyalty had been a permanently maintained state of vexedness, not only in face of the impudence of porters, cab-drivers, boot-boys and the like, but also against what she considered her mistress's wilful credulousness, deplorable gullibility and incurably soft heart. Now, as the maid, her bonnet fairly wagging from the force of her indignation, stood berating the porter for unspecified shortcomings—as a Londoner she was exercising her right to quarrel with her own kind, in her own city—Isabel moved away with that wide-eyed blandness of manner she had perfected over the years at the scenes of so many similar confrontations between Staines's will and the world's recalcitrance.

She longed for the hotel and its stilly-breathing cool and shadowed spaces, in which she might sit perfectly immobile for a long time and let her reeling mind run down of its own accord. She would rest if only she could stop thinking, but how to effect that marvellous trick? The death of her cousin Ralph Touchett on a recent eve in his mother's house at Gardencourt—extraordinary to reflect that there had been an exact, measurable moment, marked by a click on the clock, when for him eternity had begun—had left her with a hard task to solve, like an exercise in geometry or algebra. The solution she was required to derive was no more or less than to find a fit mode by which to mourn the young man's passing. In truth, her cousin could no longer have been described as young, but that was how she thought of him, and no doubt how she would think of him always. Perhaps that was the main part of her difficulty, that it seemed a scandal to shed tears for a person whose life had been so marked by the slow vastation of a wasting illness that he could hardly have been said to have had a life at all. Thinking this, she at once chided herself. Who was she to judge the quality of any life, however brief or burdened? Behind the chidden thought, however, lay a darker, irrepressible formulation, which was, that the intensest living Ralph had done he had done through her, by way of a passionate vicariousness, watching in smiling wonderment from his seat at the ringside her breathtaking flights, her spangled swoopings, to and fro in the powdery light high up, oh, so high up, under the big, the tremendous, top. To have lived through someone else, even someone he professed to adore, that had been the height of Ralph's triumph, and the depth of his failure. How she wished now she had been capable of that greatness he had hoped for in her, those loftier leaps, those ever more graceful pirouettes in mid-air, those weightless landings on one braced toe, those sweeping bows with swan's-neck arms widespread. If she had lifted him up, she had also let him down. What he could not have expected, what he could not have imagined possible for one so firmly balanced as she, was the great, the catastrophic plunge from airy heights that had been precipitated by her marrying the perfectly wrong person.

Behind her now she heard an unmistakably solid step, and a

moment later Staines loomed at her shoulder, her scant plumage ruffled and crackling, and she readied herself for the inevitable rebuke.

"Why, there you are, ma'am!" the maid said loudly, for she had a voice as large and forceful as the rest of her. "I was looking for you everywheres among all this pushing and pulling crowd."

"I merely walked on," Isabel mildly protested, offering a mitigating smile. Staines, however, was in no mood to be mollified, and her mistress waited, almost with interest, to know how she herself should be implicated in that recent struggle on the platform, of which she had experienced no more than a hard glare from the porter's soiled eye and a muffled oath directed at her departing back.

"The gall of that fellow!" the maid said now, puffing out her cheeks in the way she did when she was wroth. "Well, he got a piece of my mind, I can tell you." Here she made a marked pause, as she notched the barb to her bow-string, and when she resumed it was in a tone seemingly more of regret than reproval. "Of course, if he'd have known you was in mourning I have no doubt he would have presented a very different attitude."

This time Isabel reserved her smile to herself. The maid's veiled yet pointed reference was to the dispute she and her mistress had engaged in, before departing Gardencourt, over the matter of a mourning band, a dispute in which, unusually, the more determined of the two combatants had been forced to concede. It was to all intents a perfectly acceptable circlet of black crape that the servant had proffered, with a matchingly solemn mien, and it was a question as to which of them had been the more surprised when Isabel had declined, politely but firmly, to allow it to be pinned high up about the sleeve of her travelling coat. After a second of shocked silence the maid had begun to remonstrate, but her remonstrances proved to no avail; it was one of those instances, few but momentous, when the mistress showed her steel and the maid prudently stepped back. Mrs. Osmond would not wear a mourning band, and that, incontestably, was that. Staines had sulked, of course, and had bided her time, until now, when her mistress's flashing blade was safely back in its scabbard and she could risk a retributive shot. "Yes, I'm sure," she said, with a sort of toss of the head in her tone, "I'm sure even a ruffian of his sort would have shown a bit of respect for a person's loss, if he'd only of been able to see the evidence of it."

To this Isabel did not respond; she had found, over the years, that a remote and unemphatic silence was often the most effective counter to her maid's insinuative provocations. In truth, she was not certain herself why she had refused, to the point of vehemence, to have the thing on her sleeve. Perhaps it was that to her it would have been somehow to claim too much to make such publicity of her sorrow; that it would have been a breach of common decency—a breach, even, of common modesty. On the other hand, she was sure Ralph himself would be only too delighted to behold her draped from top to toe in black bombazine, complete with jet veil and broad sash, but only so that he could tease her and laugh at her in his fond, ironical fashion. So perhaps, after all, she thought now, she should have consented to the harmless convention of the band, if only to afford Ralph's spirit a moment of amusement in the place he dwelt in now, that realm of shades where surely he would welcome the opportunity for even the most wan of smiles. He had given her so much, and had asked so little in return.

Coming out at last from the cinder-smelling confines of the station, she felt as if she had dived into some clear light vaporous medium that was at once more and less than air. She had lived for so long amid southern harshnesses that London looked to her almost immaterial, with no sharp edges to it at all. Even in sunlight, as now, the city had a pearly sheen, and its shadows were the deepest shade of mauve. The crowds, too, weaving their endlessly shifting tapestry to and fro before her, had to her eye a quality of dreamy vagueness, as if all these people, despite the determination of their step and the fixity of their forward gaze, were not entirely certain of their destination, as likewise they could not quite remember their setting-off place, and yet minded not at all, in either case. Already she felt smoothed down and soothed; she had not been aware, before arriving in it, how achingly she had yearned for the strangely tender accommodations of this great metropolis of the north. She did not know London, not with any intimacy; she had spent time here, on visits, but for the most part she had viewed it not through her own eyes but through the eyes of others—those of her husband, of Ralph Touchett and his mother, of her friend Henrietta Stackpole; of painters, too, and of poets and novelists—so many!—the Dickenses and Thackerays, the Byrons and the Brownings, all the bards who had sung to her, in the far-off city of Albany where she had passed the years of her youth, of this magically distant Land of Cockaigne.

Before she discerned the man himself her ear was caught by the sound of his weeping. It was a strange, unhuman sound, and at first she looked about for some wounded creature nearby, a fledgling gull, perhaps, fallen from the edge of some high parapet and mewling for its mother. But, no, it was a man. He was burly and broad but not at all strong-looking, with a big box-shaped head and hair of a fiery ginger shade and curly ginger whiskers. He had positioned himself at the corner of the wide thoroughfare that led the way out of the station precincts. She did not think she had ever seen or heard a grown man crying like this, copiously, helplessly, unstaunchably. His washed-blue eyes were red-rimmed, and his swollen and glistening nether lip trembled like a baby's. He wore a collarless shirt, an ancient pair of moleskin trousers shiny with grime, and a jacket of rusty serge that was much too small for him and pinched him under the arms and left his frail white wrists defencelessly exposed. He stood in one spot but kept turning his body first in one direction and then the other, caught it seemed in a trance of convulsive indecision. Beside him on the pavement was a shapeless bundle of something tied up in a knotted rag. It had seemed at first he was wearing shoes, but now that Isabel looked more closely she saw that his feet were bare but thoroughly caked with black, tar-like dirt. The coppery bright-ness of his whiskers, through which dark glinting rivulets of tears were coursing, and the pulpy paleness of his lightly freckled skin, somehow added to and intensified, for her, the sorrow and abjec-tion of the spectacle he made; it was as if he had been flayed of a protective integument, and his flaming hair were blushing for him to be so nakedly and shamefully on show.

"Oh, look, that poor creature!" she breathed, laying a hand on her maid's arm to stay her. "We must do something to help him."

Staines, however, was unimpressed, and barely cast a glance in the direction of the weeping man where he stood sobbing and shaking and rocking. "There's no helping them as can't help themselves," she said, with a sniff, and went resolutely on, despite her mistress's restraining touch. Isabel, after a moment's hesita-tion, had no alternative but to follow her, albeit with a troubled heart. It was strange—surely Staines, who most likely had sprung from the same depths of society as had the weeping man, was the one in whom the urge to render him succour should have been strongest, instead of which she had turned her face against him, with lips compressed into a white line. And yet it was understandable, after all: the maid's instincts were those of a still uninfected person spurning a doomed victim of the plague. To Isabel, however, whose store of bullion in the bank guaranteed her immunity, it was plain that her duty lay precisely in helping such as he, the unfortunate and fallen ones of the world. But the rules were the rules: they applied in both directions, downwards as well as upwards, and she knew the impossibility of disobeying her servant and going to the weeping man even if it were for no more than to press a coin shamefacedly into his hand.

In the hansom cab, the choosing of which was a right Staines naturally arrogated to herself, Isabel sat hard by the open window to have the benefit of what freshness the city air could offer. After her moment of mild exaltation on exiting the station she had relapsed once more into her former state of diminished numbness. The lingering rhythm of the train was replaced by the harshing of the cab's steel-rimmed wheels on the metalled roadway. She viewed the panorama of the city passing in the window as if it were a running series of exhibits under glass. She felt dulled and dazed, like one who after a long illness is taken out for a supposedly invigorating "spin." They had crossed the park and come out into the cacophonous bustle of Knightsbridge. She glanced at Staines sitting opposite her, stiffly upright with her big jaw stolidly set and her sceptical gaze fixed upon the passage of brightly bedecked shop-fronts. "Are you happy to be amid familiar sights?" she asked. "I mean, are you happy to be home, even if only briefly?"

The maid turned upon her a stare as stony as adamant. "What, you mean London?" she said. She gave herself a scornful sort of twitch, bridling her bony shoulders. "This"—directing the tip of her sharp nose at the fashionable parade of parasols and silk hats along the busy pavement—"this is not *my* London, ma'am."

To this rebuff Isabel responded with her smile of practised vagueness, and once again retreated into herself, as into the folds of a capacious, all-covering cape. She could never be annoyed with Staines, not fully; she knew that what appeared in the young woman a large, unremitting and ill-tempered disdain was no more than a mask for an incapacity to show her ever-marvelling appreciation of Isabel's tolerance and loyalty. For the maid loved her mistress, incoherently, inexpressibly, and would be willing, as she might say herself, to walk barefoot over burning coals, if thereby she might strike up for Isabel a spark of needed warmth. Acknowledging this fact to herself for the thousandth time, Isabel found her thoughts turning back to the somehow related matter of the weeping man. It was true, she had never witnessed a grown-up human being display in public such helplessness, such haplessness, such raw infantile grief, yet now it occurred to her, who had lately suffered so many blows to the spirit, to wonder why it was not more common, why it was not an everyday occurrence, to be witnessed at any time at any street corner—why were we not all given to periodic outbursts of public wailings? For in the scale of things, she was sure, the weight of the world's sorrow would sink the balance so sharply that the pan on that side would make a brassy bang on the counter-top. Indeed, she felt at this moment that she might direct the cab to stop, and leap down and run back and take her place beside that poor soul and pour out her own distress upon the commonplace air; but of course she did not.

How had the man arrived at such a sorry pass? From the intense manner of his weeping it might have newly dawned on him how desperate were his circumstances, yet it was not lately he had stumbled into such wretched straits, that much was plain. Perhaps some fresh misfortune had just befallen him. It seemed to Isabel that he was bewailing not the particular but the general, as if today at last all of his misfortunate and bedevilled life, if it merited to be called a life, had come to a head somehow and overwhelmed him. Should she have defied Staines and offered him, if nothing else, at least a word or two of comfort? She suspected there would be no comforting a sorrow such as his, yet that suspicion, however strong it might be, did not exonerate her. Was it not her duty, from her place of vantage, to reach down a hand to the crushed and helpless, to the ones who might have soared but instead had plummeted from the sky and lay now with broken wing, flailing and twitching on the pavement at her feet? Her spirit, the better part of her, moaned in sympathy with the weeping man, yet in another cold and calculating region of her consciousness the necessary defences were already being erected. What, after all, could she have done for the poor wretch? What comfort would a word of hers have brought to him? Money, yes, she might have given him money, and a large portion of it, at that; but even her silver would not have saved him, for surely he was beyond saving. No: as well hope to help the lost souls in Hades. And yet.

II

At the hotel in Dover Street she declined the suite of rooms that had been prepared for her, requesting instead only a single chamber for herself, and a bed for her maid. This caused a consternated flurry, and the manager himself was called in to deal with the matter. He was a plump smooth person with waxed moustaches, wearing a frock-coat and sporting a rich dove-grey cravat stuck with a diamond pin. He assured the "dear madam" it was a suite that had been ordered: the command had come from Gardencourt by telegraph that morning. Isabel detected the hand of Ralph's mother—Mrs. Touchett, practical lady though she was, would not be capable of imagining anyone putting up in anything less than a fleet of hotel rooms—but insisted nevertheless on her own preference. There followed an ostentatious consultation of the register, accompanied by frowns and sighs and a rapid twirling of moustaches, and at last she was led to a pleasant first-floor room, where chintz reigned in flowery triumph, and two tall windows, curtained with gauze, gave on to the narrow busy street below. Isabel, despite the manager's lingering air of mild affront, said this would do very nicely, and went and stood at one of the windows with her back turned, savouring the evocative fragrance of dusty muslin, until the man, murmuring politenesses, consented to withdraw. Meanwhile Staines took charge of the delivery of the luggage—the only tangible outcome of her clash with the station porter, Isabel noted, was a broken clasp on a pigskin dressing-case and a bad dent in a hat-box—and the disposition of her mistress's "things."

In the street outside the sun was shining, for the afternoon still lingered—the seemingly endless journey from Gardencourt, first by dog-cart along by the Thames, with their luggage piled on a four-wheeler behind them, and then on the hurrying train from Pangbourne, had in reality taken somewhat less than two hours in total. Isabel, parting the faintly crepitant curtains, stepped into the bay of the window and leaned her forehead against the glass to bathe a moment in its sharp chill smoothness. Staines had completed the unpacking and stowing, and now withdrew to her own quarters, and stillness descended upon the room like a fall of dew. Letting her eyes close, Isabel dipped into the dark behind her lids as if into the mossy coolness of a forest pool. Yet she could not linger long, for in that darkness she was sure to meet the padding, yellow-eyed, implacable creature that was her conscience. Strange: she it was who had been wronged, grievously wronged, by her husband, and by a woman whom she had considered, if not her ally, then not her enemy either, yet it was she herself who felt the shame of the thing. Or was her failure to live up to her cousin Ralph's hopes and expectations—reasonable hopes, legitimate expectations—was that the thing the trace of which the beast from the forest was following? She did not know, she could not think: so many things were interpenetrated and beyond her strength to separate and assess singly, on their own merits, their own demerits. She felt within her all the shrinkings of a sinner, only she could not identify the sin.

But if a particular sin could not be singled out, she had plenty of possibilities at her disposal nonetheless. There was pride, yes indeed, pride, and vanity, and complacent self-absorption, though goodness knew she had been dragged away from the looking-glass roughly enough by Gilbert Osmond and Serena Merle, her husband and his—but Isabel could not find a term that might suitably be applied to the ineffable Madame Merle. Isabel was well aware of the danger of succumbing to the sinner's secret love of self that glories in the sackcloth and under the soft fall of ashes. "Adored" was the last word the dying Ralph Touchett had uttered in her hearing, and it came to her now that she had taken it for granted that she would always be adored by someone, without having to adore in return—*that* was complacency, *that* was vanity, *that* was pride, all of which affects had gone a long way to sustain her notion of herself as a singular figure, and a force in the world, or at least her miniaturised version of the world. And so she had been allowed to live along, happily, in the house of herself, which, as she acknowledged now, was no more substantial in dimensions than a doll's house.

Happily? The word caught her up, and brought her back sharply to the reality surrounding her, the reality of sunlight, of street, of passers-by, of the whole strange busy transaction of being alive. She had lived long years with her husband—they had not been many, the years, but they had been long—crouched in the cramped confines of the little model dwelling that she had so handily fashioned. Had she been happy? At first, perhaps; but that contented first had soon given way to a lamentable second, which state had itself lately ended with such violent abruptness that her nerves still vibrated from the blow, like the tines of a tuning fork. Now she posed again the question she had been asking herself since she had departed from Italy to come and be at her cousin's deathbed, the question of how much of the truth about the real nature and circumstances of her marriage she had known all along without letting herself know she knew it. If she had committed a great wrong, against herself and others, perhaps that was precisely it, that she had willed her own ignorance. But how, she inwardly cried, how could she have avoided it, with her husband and Madame Merle so actively abetting her in her purblind state, holding the veil firmly drawn over her eyes, the wonderfully scented, silken veil? And the fact was, of course, that her husband had not been with her in that little house, but had been outside it all along, standing upright and at his leisure, with his hands in his pockets, and only leaning down to peep in at her amusedly now and then where she sat huddled with her arms circled about her knees and her head so sharply inclined she could see little more than the tips of her toes.

She sighed, there at the window. She was weary. She put up her hands and pressed her fingertips to her brow. "Headache" seemed nowadays for her the name of a permanent state of being. She turned and walked back into the room and stood vaguely at a loss at the foot of the vast high slightly frightening bed. Would she be able to sleep upon such an expanse of feathers and springs, of ticking and wool, of linen and satin? Should she summon Staines to fetch her a sedative? There was bound to be a chemist's shop nearby that would be open. No, she must not come to depend on artificial palliatives, but must get by on the exertions of her will alone. If she could not force herself to sleep she could at least command rest. Yet the thought of lying here for hour upon hour gazing upwards sightlessly into a depthless dark filled her suddenly with a sort of anguish. She set a hand to the bedpost and gripped it tightly and bade herself be calm. Tonight would be only another night among nights; it would pass, and another day would come. She went and drew open the wardrobe, instinctively avoiding her own eye in the mirror set into an inner panel of the door, and chose an evening-gown at random. Not five minutes later she was downstairs, enquiring for directions to the dining room. Yes, she would have a table; no, there would be no one joining her.

It was early, and she thought at first the small dim room was empty. How expectant the chairs and tables seemed, bedecked with silver and crystal and linen and carefully arranged in ranks, like so many dancers ready to plunge into a waltz and tensely awaiting the first crashing chord from the orchestra. The maître d' appeared—another frock-coat, another grey cravat plumped up like a pigeon's chest—and she was murmuringly led to a place in the corner and deftly seated, although, despite the man's soft obsequiousness of manner, she had momentarily the sense of having been screwed down into her chair, like a cork forced into the neck of a bottle. Restaurants always reminded her a little of the schoolroom, if an unusually democratic and well-appointed one, where she had been sent to receive lessons in some of the finer and more venerable social disciplines. She was handed the menu, and glancing about, as one does when this small ceremony is being enacted, she spied at a table in the corner diagonally across from hers a gentleman of somewhat stout appearance, bearded and balding, who was reading a newspaper with the aid of a pair of pince-nez. He was, she judged, on the brink of his middle years, though still displaying an aspect of youthful vigour, despite the marked rotundity that strained the buttons of the lower half of his waistcoat. This waistcoat was the sole slightly remarkable aspect of himself that he presented to the world's inspection, for while his jacket and his flowing bow tie were mutely black, and his starched collar was a pillar of pristine whiteness, his gaily sported vest—which is what it would be called at home—was composed of alternating vertical stripes of sky-blue and buttercup-yellow satin. Such a splash of colours set her to wondering what he might be—a man of the theatre, perhaps, an actor-manager, or even a playwright? She could see from the skill with which he had folded his newspaper for ease of propping against the water jug that he was well accustomed to dining alone. Feeling her eye on him now he lifted his head and regarded her with cool directness over the steel rims of the nippers clipped to the bridge of his nose. She essayed a small smile, which he did not return, not out of coldness or unfriendliness, it seemed, but as if he considered a reciprocal gesture of politeness on his part would be superfluous. He went on looking at her for some moments, quite still and calm and not at all intrusively, but taking her in, merely, as she immediately was. Did he know her, had they met at some time, somewhere? He seemed in a way familiar, but she had come to a stage in her life when everyone seemed so who stepped out of the passing crowd for long enough to be held steady and fixed upon for a moment. Yet she had the impression, caught there in the unblinking beam of those preternaturally wide-open, glossy-grey and somewhat protuberant organs, that she was being checked and assessed—no, reassessed; she might have been a portrait that he, the portraitist, had come upon unexpectedly, hanging on the wall of a gallery he had chanced to wander into, and in front of which he had paused, looking to see how his composition had weathered with the years, and what time had done to the quality of the pigment.

At home—that was how it had come to her, that the man's waistcoat would be called a vest *at home*. She sat back on her chair, marvelling at herself. It seemed to her she had long since ceased to think of that foundered behemoth on the far side of the Atlantic as anything like home. But is it not to there, to home, that the injured child runs, for safety and solace? And what was she once

more, if not a child, and injured?—no matter what indignant protests might be lodged by the side of her that was grown-up and
healthily sound. Injured, yes, injured and—she was compelled to
confess it—homeless.

The waiter came and she gave her order, and had forgotten
what it was before the young man had turned away with the
retrieved menu in his white-gloved hand. Her mind was upon the
morrow, and now she realised that there was a telegram she had
forgotten to send. She summoned what she thought was the original waiter, although he turned out to be a different one—there
seemed to be so many of them, and all seemed to look alike—and
requested him to bring to the table a telegraph form and a pencil. Her first appointment next day was to be at the bank, and at
lunchtime she hoped to see her friend—or, rather, she should say,
her acquaintance, since she had no more right to intimacy with
the lady than that—Miss Florence Janeway, at her home in Fulham. The call to the bank would be tedious at most, with the usual
flutterings and flummeries, but Miss Janeway was an altogether
different prospect, even though it was Isabel herself who had proposed the visit, which the telegram she was about to write would
reconfirm. It appeared she needed to talk to someone, a thing she
had never needed before, if by talk was meant a laying out of facts
and feelings so that they might be considered with the benefit of
an additional pair of eyes, another instrument of measuring and
placing and judging. Was that what she anticipated, was that what
she hoped for, of Miss Janeway? There were others in this city
she could turn to, one of whom was her friend—and she verily
was her friend, by any standards—namely Henrietta Stackpole,
with whom she was to put up tomorrow night, at her lodgings in
Welbeck Street, before setting out on her return journey to Rome.
Miss Stackpole, however, the good, the decent, the ever-sensible

Henrietta, was too much vexed at Isabel over too many things for Isabel to think of employing her as a sounding board. No, Henrietta would have to be left to "cool" for at least another day. What Isabel needed was the long, indeed the remote, perspective of Miss Janeway, who, she expected, would neither accuse her nor let her off. And yet, for all that, the question remained why she must have *anyone* either to lay a charge against her or pronounce her innocent. If she felt in need of a confessor, the naves of numerous of the churches in London were lined with confessionals.

She knew very well, of course, that it was herself she wished to converse with, only her voice had gone so weak and her hearing so faint that she would have to do so through the open channel of some other, if need be, even if that other were not very much more than a blank stranger. It was a risk, it was a perilous risk, but one she had to take.

Now the two indistinguishable waiters appeared simultaneously at her table, one with the telegraph form and the other with her fish. She scribbled a message to Miss Janeway, then turned her attention to her plate. The morsel laid across it was grey in hue, and smeared over with a beige sauce upon which a firm yet shivery skin had already formed. The hermits of the desert could hardly have been less the gourmand than Isabel Osmond, but all the same she never ceased to wonder at the inventiveness of English chefs in transforming perfectly presentable produce into messes of a kind that a French or Italian schoolboy would descend to sampling only on a dare. She probed the fish cautiously with her fork and separated off a flake of flesh uncontaminated by sauce and chewed upon it with the gloomy resignation of a ruminant. Looking to that other table across the way, perhaps with the intention of exchanging an empathetic glance with her fellow-suffering fellow-diner, she found to her surprise that the portly gentleman had vacated his table. She could not understand how he had managed to depart without her noticing. He seemed to have consumed nothing, and the only proof of his having been there at all was the folded newspaper he had left behind him, still expertly propped against the jug. She felt an obscure sense of disappointment at being so curtly abandoned to the solitude of the sombre room. Yet what had she hoped for, what did she imagine she had missed? She would hardly have entertained the friendly advances of a man she did not know, however considerate or courtly he might have proved to be, while seated all alone at a hotel dining table. Yet the way he had looked at her, with that calmly candid, undeflected gaze, had seemed to offer—what? Not sympathy, certainly, which anyway she would have rebuffed; some form of sustenance, then? The word came to her, but she was not at all sure what it meant, in the context of the two of them sitting here isolated from each other and as far from direct contact or communication as the dimensions of the room would allow. But definitely, mysteriously, she did miss him, now that he was gone. It was as if she were an invalid making her feeble way over difficult terrain, who had found suddenly that a hand that had been sustaining her for so long she had ceased to notice its support had suddenly been withdrawn, leaving her to totter on alone. Absurd, absurd, she told herself. What a fantasy to weave about a person she had never seen before, and would most likely never see again!

The waiter came and took away her plate.

III

The great grey stone edifice seemed to look down upon the sunlit street with its nostrils flared in pained reprehension and disdain. The tall doors admitted her willingly enough, however. Inside, there was a cathedral hush, and high-collared pale young men in black tended their desks with a positively priestly intentness and devotion. Having given her name, she was shown into an oak-panelled waiting room, where after a matter of moments there appeared a lofty person of wintry aspect with a very long and very sharp white nose, who announced himself as Mr. Goresby. Although his title, as she half heard him say, was under-manager for something or other, it was apparent from the measured stateliness of his carriage that he was keenly aware of himself as possessed of a large authority. He shook Isabel's gloved hand gravely and made a stiff bow. He offered his condolences on the sad demise of "young Mr. Touchett," then cleared his throat and remarked the clemency of the weather. Behind the chill blandness of his look she detected a faint but lively gleam—*So this,* she imagined him saying to himself, *this is the famous young heiress of whom we have heard so many words spoken and so much exclaimed.*

They sat down at a small circular table, and tea was brought. She had not been offered this refreshment, and had she been she would have declined it, for she did not wish to spend more of her morning in this distinctly oppressive pantheon than she could help. It was only a bank, she knew, as impersonal and detached as an institution could be, yet it brought to her mind certain things she would rather not have been reminded of, such as the burdensomeness of her wealth, which by an intricate web of connections made the burden of her sorrow for her cousin Ralph's death harder still to bear. Mr. Goresby, stirring his tea, was now enquiring politely as to her immediate plans: Would she be travelling back to Rome, where he understood she had her principal residence, or were there further business affairs she must attend to in London? She replied that she would set out for Rome the following evening, then was surprised to hear herself add that she might stop in Paris for a day or two on the way. She frowned, and glanced aside; she could not think from where had come the idea of Paris—it had popped into her head at just that moment—and wondered at herself for it. What was there in Paris to detain her? Was it merely a ruse to delay her return to Rome and all that awaited her there? If so, she would not lack for cities along the way that would be more than happy to offer hospitality to a moneyed young woman—"widow," she realised with surprise, indeed with shock, was the word that had first occurred to her; it was an absent-minded tribute to her late cousin, as she supposed, but also perhaps, in a frightening way, a pointer to a darker thought, a darker wish, at the very possibility of which she felt herself begin guiltily to blush.

Now she set down her cup and, with a firmness which, as she was aware, verged on the rude, brought the talk abruptly round to the piece of business that was the reason for her being there. She wished, she announced, to withdraw a sum of money, in cash. Mr. Goresby raised his eyebrows calmly and said that of course he would be happy to facilitate the transaction—he would attend to it personally. However, when Isabel mentioned the sum she intended to withdraw, he flinched in a manner that caused the cup and saucer he was holding to make a brief but definite rattle.

"My dear Mrs. Osmond," he breathed, "that is a very large sum, to be taken out, *in cash*."

This gave her pause, and she experienced a flash of misgiving, so that now it was her turn to flinch. The truth was that she had no object in mind in making the withdrawal, and had fixed upon the amount by a whim. In fact, it was only now, seeing the bank official's startlement, that she asked herself why she should wish to take upon herself, upon her very person, such a tangible store of money—what did she intend to do with it? She did not know. Had the impulse, which she had not questioned until now, sprung from a primitive urge for safety and assurance by way of amassing and hoarding? She was surprised at herself, but her sense of sheepishness only compelled her to put on a bolder, even a more brazen, front, and she looked Mr. Goresby firmly in the eye and repeated her request, and reaffirmed the amazing amount. He swallowed with some difficulty—she saw the wobble of his Adam's apple—and with the ghost of a queasy smile excused himself and rose, and creaked his way to the door, where he paused a second and glanced back at her over his shoulder, still with that uneasy spectral smile, then made a soundless exit.

This time she was left unattended for some minutes in the room's faintly ticking, surreptitious silence. She sat very straight on the chair, both hands resting on the clasp of the black silk reticule that she held balanced on her knees, and tried to think of nothing at all. She felt very light, almost weightless, as if she were levitating somehow a fraction of an inch above the chair on which she was seated. She thought of her schooldays, and of waiting in a cold room to face the wrath of authority over some misdemeanour committed unwittingly yet unamenable to being explained away. Why had she been so foolish as to come here today—what child-ish compulsion had she thought to appease? Well, she was paying for her rashness now.

And she would have to go on paying for some time yet. Pres-ently Mr. Goresby returned, accompanied by a second official, in morning dress and spats, whose name was Grimes. Where Mr. Goresby was tall and thin, Mr. Grimes was short and stout, though it was clear the latter stood upon a higher rung of the fiscal hierarchy than his gaunt colleague. He approached Isabel with a curiously springing, one might almost say a bouncing, step, chaf-ing his hands together in a washing motion, a broad but decidedly nervous smile puckering his bewhiskered chubby cheeks. He said that Mr. Goresby had informed him of her desire to make a with-drawal, *in cash;* he mentioned the sum she had specified; he pursed his lips. That was a large and, dared he say it, a potentially perilous quantity of banknotes for a lady to be carrying with her through the city's busy streets. He cast a dubious look at the silken purse on which her hands rested. Did she have someone waiting for her outside the bank, preferably in a private carriage, a relative, per-haps, a *male* relative, or even a servant, one whom she could trust and whose protection, whose strength and protection—in fine, whose brawn, although he did not use so brash a word—she could depend on? She had not? Ah. Mr. Grimes exchanged a glance with Mr. Goresby. They both displayed the marks not only of anxiety but of embarrassed discomfiture. Isabel rose to her feet. For how much longer would she have to endure this absurd torment, a torment that was all the more acute by virtue of the fact that the painful yet faintly comical predicament she had blundered into was of her own making?

"Please, gentlemen, you mustn't concern yourselves," she said, producing, from a hitherto unsuspected histrionic capacity within her, a brilliant smile. Then, continuing to play the player and desperately improvising, she went on to declare that her husband awaited her at a lawyer's office not three minutes' walk from the bank. The fact was—she widened that theatrically mendacious smile another notch—a house, a delightful little place in Dover Street, yes, Dover Street, had unexpectedly come up for sale, and they must fairly snatch at it, while the chance was there. "The owner is going abroad at once, and we have been given until midday today to agree the purchase and make a down payment as a mark of our intent. So you see why I am here."

She looked from one to the other of the worried faces before her; it would have been impossible to say on which of the two visages was registered the deeper doubt. Nevertheless, there she was before them, a smiling customer, and a highly valued one at that, with every right to withdraw however large a portion of her own substantial fund she wished, and in whatever form she cared to specify. So, after a whispered exchange between the two officials, Mr. Goresby departed, leaving Mr. Grimes to escort Isabel out of the waiting room, across the building's nave-like floor, up a broad marble staircase resembling a frozen waterfall, and into his unexpectedly poky little office, which smelt of candle grease and stale tobacco smoke. There the two of them waited for ten of the longest minutes it seemed to Isabel she had ever endured, until at last Mr. Goresby reappeared, bearing before him in both hands, as if it were the Grail itself, a leather case containing a big white crackling bundle of legal tender. A document was produced and laid on Mr. Grimes's desk, and Isabel was handed a pen with which to inscribe her signature. In the hush while she signed she could hear, above the scratching of the pen, the stertorous breathing of Mr. Grimes and Mr. Goresby's lighter and therefore somehow more anxious-sounding aspirations. Now came another moment of awkwardness, when she enquired as to the provenance of the attaché-case in which the notes were stored, and was informed that it was Mr. Goresby's personal property. Oh, but then, she exclaimed, how was she to repay him for the sacrifice? Would he allow her to recompense him the value of the case, so that he might replace it with a new one? This brought on a prolonged clearing of throats and a casting down of eyes, and Isabel felt herself flush in the shaming realisation of having committed a gaffe. Mr. Goresby said that perhaps she would find an opportunity to return the case to him at some future date, but that in the meantime she must accept it as a token of the bank's concern for her safety and peace of mind—here he demonstrated how securely the flap of the case could be fastened—and also as a gesture of appreciation and goodwill on his own part, a gesture in which of course he would include Mr. Grimes, his superior, as he generously, and no doubt advisedly, added. Then both men bowed to her, smiling as if in pain, and walked her between them out of the office, down the staircase and across the echoing marble hall to the tall front door. She felt, with the case under her arm, like a once-favoured niece being sent out into an unwelcoming world by two sadly disappointed, disapproving uncles. Once outside and released, she paused for a moment on the top step and took in a slow deep draught of the morning's mild air. How lucky it was, she suddenly thought, that Staines had not been with her—there was that, at least.

IV

Yet as she walked along in the still tentative sunlight of the early-summer day her agitation began to abate and she found herself able to think back over the past hour with only the faintest after-shudder of shame. And, indeed, why should she be at all ashamed of having allowed herself so harmless an adventure? If she had lied, about the purchase of the fictitious house in Dover Street, her lie had been one of convenience, and had hurt no one; if she had been frivolous, her frivolity had not been without a dash of daring; if she had been irresponsible, her irresponsibility had been in some sense an affirmation of the fact of her freedom. And freedom, for Isabel, was and always had been a significant quality, perhaps for her the most significant of all, for how was life to be in any way tolerable if one were trapped and trammelled on all sides? In the implications of that question lay the reason, or at least part of the reason, for her being here, on this hazy London morning, with a satchel stuffed full of legal tender under her arm. The conditions in which she had lived these past years, the years, that is, of her marriage—so surprisingly, so shockingly few!—had made it imperative that something of hers, something exclusively her own, should be affirmed, and its latitudes exercised, however narrow such latitudes might be. She was not of so coarse a cast of mind as to imagine that mere money constituted the temple of liberty, although it was perhaps one of its pillars, but such were the restrictions within which she had been struggling, like a lamb caught up in a hedge of thorns, that even the little gambol she had indulged in at the bank could seem a wild dance of ecstatic vernal release.

The air was so still that she heard faintly afar the chimes of Big Ben: it was midday already, and she was due to take luncheon at Miss Janeway's house in a little less than an hour. She had intended to return to Dover Street and request that the attaché-case be stored securely in the hotel safe, but there would not be time for that now. She found a cab rank and, having named her destination, which lay in the depths of Fulham's maze of back-streets running out to the river, she mounted the high seat of the hansom and settled herself with the case clutched tightly to her side. Her bravado was diminishing by the moment; she no longer conceived herself a gay corsair bounding off upon the main with her bag of booty, but acknowledged instead how reckless and fool-hardy she had been in imagining that she could blithely entrust herself and her treasure to the dangerous shoals and reefs of the city's public thoroughfares. She pictured an eye-patched brigand of the streets leaping up at her with a flashing blade held fast in his teeth and snatching the case out of her grasp and plunging back into the passing crowd as swiftly as he had come. And would it not serve her right to be thus set upon and piratically robbed?

However, here was the broad calm vista of the Mall, and the Palace nobly presiding off at the end of it, and then Constitution Hill flanked on both sides by ample trees powdered with young June's tender foliage in a score or more shades of gauzy green. Lulled by the softness of the scene and the whir and warble of the cab-wheels on this smooth straight stretch of roadway, Isabel felt her heart, which had been struggling within her like a cat in a bag, settling back to its accustomed muted beat. Her thoughts winged their way idly here and there, alighting at last on Miss Janeway. Isabel had first encountered this admirable lady at a meeting in a somewhat dingy hall in Wigmore Street to which she had gone, not entirely willingly, in the company of her friend Henrietta Stackpole. She could not now remember what the purpose or the topic of the meeting had been—it was years ago, when she was still unmarried—but she retained the impression of an atmosphere of muted ardency, and of a passionate glister in the eyes of the preponderantly female audience rustling excitedly all about her. Miss Stackpole, dear Henrietta, was a journalist of a particular American stamp, in that she judged it incumbent on the people and places she proposed to write about to convince her of their worthiness before she would so much as dip her pen in the inkpot. She had only a slightly exaggerated notion of her status as a commentator on the ways, and wiles, of the English at large, although there were some unkind natives of the realm who had been heard to mutter that she was no more than a purveyor of social tittle-tattle to the ever-avid ears of leisured ladies in New York, Boston and San Francisco; and certainly it was nothing less than the truth that she did often supply copy to the less intellectually high-toned of the American monthlies, for a body had to live, after all, as she would remark with a sigh.

At the close of the meeting the pair had come out into the darkness and drizzle of the late-autumn evening, and on the pavement under the glass awning there was such a flexing and ballooning of black umbrellas that it seemed a flock of night-winged birds was about to take flight and flap away over the rooftops. In the midst of the twittering crush Henrietta's eye had fallen on Miss Janeway. The two greeted each other with measured warmth—

Henrietta "was not the kissing kind," as the saying has it, and neither, decidedly, was Miss Janeway—and Isabel was drawn forward and introduced as "Miss Isabel Archer of Albany," rather like, as she forgivingly thought, a prize exhibit at a rural fair. Miss Janeway's smile was friendly enough, but the hand she offered Isabel was cool outside with an impression of brittleness within, like a bundle of twigs bound up in a vine leaf. She was a dry neat person, lean and tall, as tall as Isabel herself, with prematurely silvered hair, which, along with the powdery-pink smoothness of her skin, gave to her an ageless aspect. She spoke with a firm light voice, and was, as Isabel soon detected, slightly hard of hearing.

Isabel and Miss Stackpole were staying during that earlier visit to the city—Isabel had come up from Gardencourt then, too, but in far happier circumstances—at a funny little hotel on Cavendish Square, and since by now the rain had given way to fog, Henrietta would not hear but that Miss Janeway should accompany them thither and partake of a glass of hot port to dispel the evening's autumnal vapours, before setting out on her long homeward journey to Fulham. So they had proceeded to the Portland Palace, as the little hotel grandly styled itself, and sat for half an hour, the three of them, in the cramped downstairs parlour, where they were ministered to by an elderly, rheumatical and tremulous night waiter, who stumbled on the mat and spilled port over his knuckles and shook his head and sighed in deprecation of his own unhandiness. Miss Janeway—it was rumoured that in her youth she had gone under the sobriquet of "Florrie," but this Isabel found impossible to credit—was, as quickly became clear, a person of pamphlets and polemics, of parades and protests: in a word, a member of that species, still rare at the time, known as the New Woman. However, she had none of the fearsomeness of which this novel and partly mythical phenomenon, this latter-day Amazon, is so often accused; she was not shrill, she was not strident, and as for argumentativeness, no one could have been more measured, more downright placid, in the expression of her opinions than this somewhat distant, drily humorous, middle-aged silver-haired bluestocking. Isabel had long ago forgotten what it was they had talked about that night, as the fire hissed and muttered in the hearth and the fog came up and rolled itself against the windows, like so many thick wads of steel shavings. The conversation, whatever it concerned, had been brief, for Miss Janeway had soon put aside her glass, from which she had taken no more than the merest sip, and rose, saying she must not miss her omnibus, for it would be the last one of the night. As she was leaving, standing in the hotel doorway and struggling to unfurl a refractory umbrella, she had half turned back to Isabel and said something that the girl—for she could still be thought a girl in those days—was to remember in aftertime with a pang that had never lost its point.

"You seem to me, Miss Archer," said the lady, "a person possessed of a large potential; do be careful not to under-spend your resource."

Henrietta had gone back to the parlour to fetch a pair of gloves that Miss Janeway had forgotten, and so had not been present to hear this piece of advice, if that was what it was, delivered. And, indeed, it was in her absence that her two friends had exchanged between them a look that would not have been allowed them, Isabel considered, had they not been alone. It was a look, on Miss Janeway's side, of more force and penetration that the shared moment and the words spoken seemed to warrant, although Isabel had returned it with an equal force, and, she believed, an equal candour. Afterwards, when Miss Janeway had been swallowed in what was rapidly turning into that dense variety of fog known, mysteriously, as a "London particular," and Henrietta had retired to her room to apply a final polish to an article on the English sport of beagling for the New York *Interviewer,* Isabel had returned to the parlour and sat in solitude for a good half of an hour beside the dreamily diminishing fire. Her thoughts moved, as thoughts do, in large loose loops, but at least once in every round they revisited, like a planet at its perihelion, the question of what precisely Miss Janeway's portentous remark might have been meant to mean. The words themselves were perfectly plain and clear, but was the formulation into which she had set them intended as advice or admonition, as challenge or condescension, as encouragement or the expression of a deep doubt? Whichever it was, Isabel had never forgotten the moment, there in the hotel's flickeringly lighted vestibule, on the threshold of night and fog, with the woman's calmly piercing eye fixed on her. She suspected, she strongly suspected, that the way in which she had conducted her life in the intervening years would represent a serious falling short of the expectations, however tentative and circumspect, that had seemed implied by Miss Janeway's injunction. She felt she had overspent herself, to the point of emotional and spiritual bankruptcy—but was it so? Had she not, on the contrary, withheld and hoarded the resources she should have lavished on others? She tried to recall the Biblical lesson of the talents and its exact purport, but it became confused in her mind with the parable of the camel and the needle's eye, and in the end she gave it up. The air was so mild, and the leafing trees so lovely, as they passed by Hyde Park Corner, that the darkness of her thoughts could not but be lightened.

Miss Janeway's house proved hard to find. The narrow streets between Fulham Palace Road and the waterside, although pleasantly appointed with handsome bow windows and lilac trees in lavish tender blue blossom, all appeared much alike, and her driver, whom she had hired for his experienced and confident aspect—his whiskers were particularly impressive—was plainly unfamiliar with the area. He had to stop frequently to ask for assistance from such denizens of the neighbourhood as would deign to be thus accosted, and whose help in every case somehow turned out to be singularly unhelpful. As they went blunderingly along, Isabel could hear the fellow muttering to himself on his high perch behind her, and it occurred to her to wonder if he might not have a secret bottle up there that he had been resorting to for comfort and fortification in the toils of this trying odyssey they were bound upon. At last there came into sight a policeman, in a tall helmet and a broad belt, stationed on a corner by a red pillar box and rocking himself pensively on the balls of his notably extensive feet, who, having paused to give his moustaches a flourishing wipe to right and left with the side of a thumb, pointed them with ponderous assurance in the direction of Cedar Street. When they pulled up at last at number seven, Isabel realised that her long sojourn abroad had left her incapable of dealing with the baffling intricacies of shillings and pence, and she could not be sure if the fare being demanded of her was as grossly inflated as she suspected it to be. She thought to delay paying, so as to consult Miss Janeway in the matter, but instead surrendered utterly, and on the spot fumbled the coins out of her purse—oh dear, was that a florin or a half crown?—and handed up, with face averted, what she judged to be more or less the demanded amount of jingling silver and copper. She dearly wished Staines had been with her—Staines would have known exactly how to deal with a bibulous cabman—but the maid had requested the morning free in order to visit her sister, her only surviving relative, at her abode in Hackney. Mrs. Gilhooley, for such was the sister's name, was mar-

ried to an Irishman, a hod-carrier by trade, although Isabel was
not entirely sure what the carrying of hods entailed, or, indeed,
what a hod itself was, exactly. There had come into existence, during the years when Staines and her mistress were residing abroad,
a numerous brood of little Gilhooleys, although Cissy—Mrs. G.—
loved them all as if, according to her sister, "they was each of them
but the one and only." Isabel had insisted the darlings must have
a coin apiece as a token of her warm if necessarily distant regard,
but when the money was proffered to her, Staines, inevitably, had
set her face and hidden her hands firmly behind her back, saying
in a loud voice, with her gaze fixed on a spot an inch above the
top of Isabel's head, that Madam should not think of frittering her
wealth away upon "them little scallywags." This kind of tussle,
which was commonplace between the two, amused Isabel as often
as it irritated her. Today, however, she had been startled when, the
contest having barely been joined, the maid had suddenly abandoned her stance of defiance and, with a moan of apology and distress, had made as if to embrace her, saying, in a thickened voice,
"Oh, but, *ma'am!*" It was only then, taking a small step backwards,
that Isabel became aware of the warm spots of moisture speckling
her cheeks, and realised that she had, unknowingly and all unaccountably, begun to weep.

V

The house, which smelt of dried lavender and silver polish, was as neat and pleasingly plain as its occupant. On all sides the predominant shade was grey—warm-grey walls, silver-grey floorboards, even lively-grey air—in the midst of which Miss Janeway appeared like an emanation of the place itself. To Isabel's eye she seemed hardly altered from their last encounter, which had also been their first, at the Portland Palace Hotel that long-ago foggy night after the Wigmore Street meeting, except that she looked, not thinner, but as if hollowed out somehow, and there was a knot of tension in the space between her eyebrows that suggested she was, as Isabel had become in recent times, a semi-permanent dweller in the land of the megrims. She wore a straight-sided taupe dress, with a narrow froth of lace at collar and wrists that was her sole concession to the notion of self-adornment.

She received Isabel with a show of muted welcome, managing the trick of coming forward while at the same time seeming to draw back, with a twist to her lips that was nearly but not quite a smile; the restraint of her demeanour was a pointed invitation for both of them to acknowledge that any more vigorous display of sentiment was not to be indulged in by grown-up persons such as they were—or such as Miss Janeway indubitably was, for Isabel was not at all certain the lady before her would ever be able to bring herself fully to accept her, or anyone else, for that matter, as an intellectual coeval.

"You look hot, my dear," Miss Janeway said, with an all but imperceptible intensification of that not-quite smile. "Would you care for something cooling? A glass of lemonade, perhaps?"

Isabel in fact had not been aware of the level of her temperature, but under the force of Miss Janeway's steely solicitude it seemed she must be bright-red and positively glistening all over. She said that a glass of plain water would be a welcome balm, and a maid was summoned. This was a petite and pretty girl, whose complexion and eyes made a nice contrast of pink and blue—she was not at all of the fellowship of the sturdy Staineses—and who faced the visitor with an air of openness and assurance that was, Isabel privately conceded, a credit to the egalitarian tenets of the house.

"Some water, please, Daisy, for Mrs. Osmond," Miss Janeway said. "And tell Cook luncheon at half past, yes?"

"Certainly, ma'am," Daisy said, and departed, casting another easy, smiling glance in Isabel's direction.

The two ladies, with Miss Janeway going ahead, entered a pleasant little drawing room and seated themselves at a square table of waxed deal placed, just so, in what was surely the dead centre of the floor. They sat opposite each other, on upright chairs, as if, Isabel thought, she were here to be interviewed by a potential employer. Then she noticed how Miss Janeway strained her head forward a little at the left side, and remembered that she had been slightly deaf, which must be why she had placed herself so as to have a direct view of her visitor's face. But had the poor woman's hearing declined so drastically that she was reduced to lip-reading? At this thought Isabel experienced a small sharp stab of pity, which in turn made her feel obscurely ashamed.

"Your stay in London will be brief?" Miss Janeway enquired.

"Yes, tomorrow I set out for Rome," Isabel answered, trying not to seem to shout, "or perhaps Paris, first. I have not decided."

"My goodness, such freedom!" Miss Janeway pleasantly exclaimed, bringing her long-fingered ivory-pale hands together in front of her in a single, soundless clap.

Ah, Isabel thought, if you only knew!

Daisy returned then, bearing on a little tin tray Isabel's by now sacral-seeming cooling glass. The sun in the window had assembled a complicated shape, like a broken birdcage made of old gold, and thrown it down on the floor, where it lay partly athwart the legs of the deal table. Isabel's fat bag of banknotes was wedged awkwardly between her hip and the rungs of the chair-back. She had seen, when she first arrived, Miss Janeway take in the bulging satchel with a discreet, swiftly sliding glance. Now she felt again acutely how childish she had been to cause such a deal of money to be materialised in front of her; yes, childish, for she was like the spoilt child at a magic show whose rich daddy has bribed the magician to turn his top hat inside out and show her the tawdry mechanism by which the poor dazed rabbit is made to pop up. "But money is not money, my dear!" Ralph Touchett's elderly father had said to her, with one of his gentle, feathery laughs, sitting in his chair on the lawn at Gardencourt to take the last of the sunlight on a summer evening that now seemed to her impossibly far off in the past. "That is," he had continued, "it's not what the good plain folk of this world imagine it to be. That stuff, the stuff with which they feed and clothe themselves and their children, putting away what little surplus they can keep of it against that famous and much-feared rainy day—well, I say, child, that's not money: that's small change."

But what, then, *was* money? She had pressed this question on the wise old man, who in his days as a banker had amassed a fabulous fortune by shrewd manipulations of the mysterious commodity of which they were now speaking, but he had only laughed again, shaking his head at her naivety. Left therefore to make it out for herself, she had figured money, real money and not "that stuff," to be as an underground river, a vast dark unseen rushing force sweeping along with it rattling shoals of stones and the torn-off roots of plants and trees and endlessly replenishing from below the secret springs of power. What had she to do with this unstoppable, elemental surge? What was she, despite the airs and graces she had been required to put on over the years, but one of the "plain folk" whom Mr. Touchett had so lightly spoken of in his characteristic and kindly condescending fashion? The satchel at her back seemed all at once a horribly burdensome extrusion of herself, something along the lines of a hunchback's hump.

"I gather from our dear friend Henrietta Stackpole," Miss Janeway said, directing her careful gaze at the table-top now, "that the welcome awaiting you on your return to Rome may not be as warm as one might expect of that sun-blest city?"

Isabel sat very still, like a fox, she thought, who has heard the blare of the huntsman's horn sound frighteningly close to the covert. But for how long, she asked herself ruefully, and aware of mixing her sporting metaphors, had she imagined the bush could reasonably be beaten about? Miss Janeway, it seemed, was as plain in her speech as she was in everything else. Was it not exactly in hope of just this quality that Isabel had made her meandering way here to the riverside reaches of the city? She had come to talk and, more importantly, to be talked to. Now that the moment had arrived, however, the moment of being pitched precipitately into just that "talk," something within her, some sulkily resentful and, once again, childish version of herself, resisted. Miss Janeway, who obviously had an eye for such things, at once perceived her visitor stubbornly hesitate, and smiled, and setting her palms flat on the table before her suggested briskly that, although the half-hour was still a good ten minutes short, they might run the risk of Mrs. Pullan's wrath—this person, Isabel surmised, must be the cook—and venture into the dining room to demand their luncheon.

The main course of this predictably modest repast consisted of boiled broccoli, boiled beans and boiled spinach, garnished all over with a light sprinkling of chopped almonds. At least the nuts, Isabel noted, had been spared the ordeal of the ebullient cauldron. She was aware of Miss Janeway's eye bent discreetly upon her. Was the frugality of the fare meant as a test of her spiritual mettle? She was certainly no trencher-woman—she nursed a positive aversion to the celebrated roast beef of old England—but the expanse of steaming greenery confronting her, even with the amelioration of the pretty tan-and-cream particles of almond, she found peculiarly daunting.

"I eat no flesh," Miss Janeway observed, in a tone not at all apologetic, and even added, with what seemed a hint of reproach, that she hoped her guest "would not feel the want of meat."

Isabel, with forgivable fraudulence, hastened to assert her total contentment with what had been put before her, and stalwartly took up her knife and fork. Her hostess, however, continued to observe her.

"I have it as a moral principle," she said, "that any living thing possessed of facial features should not be converted into food."

To this Isabel could find no commensurate rejoinder, and

therefore said nothing, and instead raised to her mouth a floret of broccoli not much smaller than, and of much the same texture as, so it seemed to her, a miniature shrub.

For some little time the two ladies ate together in silence save for irrepressible herbivoral crunchings. Daisy the maid came and went, attending with deft cheerfulness to the modest needs of the table, now re-stocking the bread-plate, now topping up the water jug, all the time sustaining a rosy-cheeked smile and distributing freely her self-contented glances. It seemed, all in all, Isabel reflected, a notably peaceable household, with an easy-going way to it that belied its directress's faint though definite frostiness. Did the chill of her demeanour betoken a particular disapproval of her visitor, perhaps? The possibility was there, and Isabel had to acknowledge it, and, if she decided it was more than a possibility, modulate her behaviour accordingly. But what should such a modulation consist in, short of finishing up her greens and making her excuses and departing, as speedily and with as much politeness as she could muster? Meanwhile she was distracted by an inability to stop herself enumerating in her mind the varieties of creatures possessed of some sort of face whose flesh she had thoughtlessly partaken of over the years.

It occurred to her, as surely it should have done long before this, that perhaps her silence in response to Miss Janeway's frank question about Rome had seemed rude, if not indeed offensive. When this notion dropped inside her, like a suddenly plunging plumb-line, she at once set down her knife and fork and turned up her face to the lady before her and spoke out in perfect unpreparedness.

"Yes," she heard herself say, or blurt, more like, "it is a cold welcome that awaits me in Rome."

Miss Janeway's eyebrows, which had so far been as straight as pen-strokes, rose up now in two steep arches, while in the places where her cheekbones were most prominent there appeared two round bright patches of pink.

"My dear," she murmured, holding her own knife and fork suspended in mid-air, "oh, my dear!"

This abrupt show of sympathy left Isabel more than anything uncertain and confused. It was not that she was unappreciative, only the effect on her was curious. The warmth of Miss Janeway's response, which was like a sudden glow of sunlight on the crazed surface of a frozen pond, sent the young woman skimming back through the years to a certain time, that seemed to her now immemorial, and to a certain moment of that time, when on a damp and, to her, not unpleasantly doleful spring afternoon she had sat on a sagging horsehair sofa in a funny old room in her grandmother's house in Albany, with a book open on her lap, a formidable work tracing in overly intricate detail the immense history of German philosophy, doggedly concentrating on the dense text and attempting frowningly to shut her ears to the clamour of many small children at their "play hour" in a little school on the other side of the street. She had lately, herself, become an orphan, following the death of her father, and she was not sure what to make of this novel state she had suddenly found herself in. Up to now, in her lazy conception of the thing, she had thought of an orphan largely as a barefoot waif in a sentimental novel, and certainly not such as she herself was, a strapping and perfectly well-shod person in her twentieth year. She mourned her father, naturally—her mother had died a long time before—but she could not deny that his passing had left her in a position that was, at least in one of its effects, interesting: that is, the effect of her having been set free. Oh, it was a circumscribed freedom she had entered upon, certainly—her father had left very little money, and the bulk of it had of course to go to her two older, married sisters—and the horizons of her life seemed not markedly broader than they had been. All the same, she was aware of an inner lightness, a buoyancy, even, that she was sure she should be, yet was not, ashamed of. The dead make a space for the living, she told herself by way of self-exculpation; it is the natural order of things. She felt, that rainy afternoon in Albany, as she struggled diligently to stay in step with Herr Professor Hegel's tracking of the undeviating forward march of the Spirit of History, that she herself, in her newly lightened state, was surely on the way somewhere too, even if she had no more control of her direction than a hot-air balloon that had slipped its tethers and must drift where the wind listeth.

It was there in her dim little reading room, and in that heightened though formless mood, that she had been chanced upon by her Aunt Lydia, Ralph Touchett's mother. This forceful lady, remote in manner yet startlingly direct in address, lived mainly in Italy, and was visiting America to check the state of her investments, which she kept strictly separate from her husband's widely encompassing financial sphere—not that Daniel Touchett had the least urge to meddle in his formidable wife's business affairs—and had come up from New York to pay a rare visit to her late sister's family, her two married daughters, and this one, who as yet was contentedly single. They spent an hour and more together, Isabel and Mrs. Touchett, while the rough rain spattered on the roof and the noisy young students across the way straggled back to their lessons, and by the time they parted it had been agreed between them that Isabel, to whom the undemonstrative elderly lady had decidedly "taken a shine," should accompany her aunt when in the summer she returned to Europe. By then the Albany house would be sold—Isabel's brother-in-law was to handle the matter with his accustomed brisk dependability—and the girl should have her modest portion of the proceeds, with which to maintain at least the aspect of independence.

Now, sitting at Miss Janeway's table, and drawn within the strangely discomfiting ambit of that lady's concern, Isabel acknowledged to herself, not for the first time but with an unprecedented pang of what was almost anger, that it was in that rainy hour her downfall had begun. Downfall, yes: the word was not too large for what, in her case, it encompassed. Yet had she refused Aunt Lydia's handsome invitation—although it had been less invitation than directive—and stayed in Albany, what would have become of her? How long would it have taken for the airy balloon bearing her aloft to come fizzling back to earth? She seemed to hear again the racket of children's voices from the Dutch House school across the street, and pictured herself, older than she was now, standing by a blackboard, with a ruler in her hand and chalk-dust in her hair, dully paying out the reels of rote that years of repetition had robbed even of what little interest or purpose they might once have possessed for her. Yes, that would have been her fate: a teacher at a provincial school for fractious tots, or otherwise a governess, perhaps; perhaps even—dear heavens!—the paid companion of a person such as her Aunt Lydia was bound one day, quite soon, to become.

It was a fact that, for Isabel, Europe had been unavoidable; Europe had been her fate, and so it was still. Yet she should not have allowed her aunt to thrust her upon that fabled continent so precipitately, as a free-trader's posse might snatch from the door-way of a dockside tavern some poor young hearty fuddled on rum and press him into a captive life upon the roiling ocean; indeed, she should not have allowed it. Her aunt was not to blame that she was lashed by unbreakable bonds to Europe's mast. The girl had lived her Albany life offhandedly, as it might be, without due regard; impatient of being young, of being merely young, she had struck out strongly where she should have lingered, at least for a while, and in eager haste had covered leagues, of land and sea, to arrive in a place that had seemed the place itself of pure possibility, pure potential. She had, if not willed it, then acquiesced to it, all this, with haughty enthusiasm, taking it as her due. What was it she had once said to someone as a definition of her ideal of happiness? Something about being in a coach and four of a pitch-dark night rattling over unseen roads. Ah, she thought, the innocence of it—the arrogance! The creature she imagined in that coach now was not herself, but a captive child, baffled and frightened and in dread of whatever destination lay ahead, while up on the driving seat, in the darkness of the rushing night, a wordless fiend rattled the reins and mercilessly plied the whip.

They had reached the end of the course of uncompromising greens—Isabel had called up the knack, which we all learned in the nursery, of arranging a nearly full plate so as to make it seem half-empty—and now the cheerful maid, having cleared the table, carried in two small porcelain bowls of lemon syllabub and an open tin of little hard brown biscuits. As on many another exclusively female occasion, Isabel found herself hankering after the male dispensations of decanter and cigar, if only for the glistening look of the brandy glass and the humid savour of scented smoke; a drink of plain water, refreshing though it was, did not encourage one to settle down and delve deep into intimate matters. In this regard, however, Miss Janeway was made of sterner stuff than her guest, and, obviously considering sufficient time had elapsed for the earlier awkwardness to have dissipated, set her elbows firmly on the table and folded together her slender, pale, though not unwrinkled hands and once more plunged straight in.

"The good Henrietta hinted," she said, "that your domestic

circumstances—in Rome, I mean—set a definite hindrance to your attending at your cousin's deathbed."

Isabel managed the feat of nodding and shrugging simultaneously. "By 'domestic circumstances,'" she said drily, "you mean of course my husband."

Miss Janeway glanced into her bowl of syllabub like a scryer looking to her crystal globe for guidance. "Mr. Osmond, I understand," she said, "is not, was not, an admirer of the deceased young man."

Isabel in response was still more dry. "There are not many people Mr. Osmond does admire, among my circle, such as it is, or in the world at large, for that matter. Our friend Miss Stackpole, for instance, inspires in him the liveliest disdain; he would have set Ralph Touchett hardly a step above her in esteem. The term it pleased him most often to apply to Ralph was 'that long jackanapes'—my cousin was very tall, and very spare. He suffered from consumption throughout his short life, and died of it in the end. He was also, I have discovered," she went on, feeling anew the wonder of it, "the person who in the world loved me most dearly, and whom I loved most dearly in return."

At this her hostess made a cautious pause, and for a moment the silence seemed to press about them both, as if they were trapped inside a tremulous and steadily swelling bubble. Isabel ate a spoonful of her dessert, assuming a placidly blank expression; it was imperative to maintain the quotidian appearance of things—the niceties of a shared table, polite manners, a tone of calm discourse—otherwise everything at any moment might burst in a cascade of soap-suds and miniature rainbows, for the skin of the bubble in which they were held was exceedingly fine.

"He loved you," Miss Janeway ventured at last, in a voice perfectly, deliberately, flat, and without the faintest shade of an interrogation mark, "and you loved him."

"Yes," Isabel answered, with a matching lack of emphasis, "but it was not the kind of love to trouble a husband. Or not a normal husband, at least," she added.

Miss Janeway was gazing at her over the peak of her clasped hands, projecting forward slightly the side of her head where her good ear was.

"Do you consider Mr. Osmond to be an *ab*normal husband, then?" she asked, with what Isabel thought might even be the faintest flicker of humour.

She should counter the question by quashing it at once, Isabel knew, yet instead she paused to reflect upon it. What, in a husband, would constitute normality? She was not sure that it was "normal" to be a husband at all, or, even more, a wife. From what she had learned of the married state—and she had learned much, and at much cost to her sense both of herself and of society's arrangements—it seemed to her nothing but a throwback to a prehistoric time, a codification of far more casual, rough rituals of seizure and subjugation. She gave due regard to the civilising moral principle of the marriage vow, yet still she could not stifle the sense she had of how strange a thing it was to be required to commit oneself body and soul to another human being for the entire length of a life. For a long time she had been content to accept what all the laws and all the religions assured her was the case, namely that marriage was the natural state for men and women to live and thrive in, but then, gradually at first and more recently with a quickening conviction, she had come to see what the thing really entailed, and had come to recognise the vast anachronism of it, as vast as the fact of life itself; as vast as the fact of death.

She wondered, with a quaver of alarm, what the lean lady seated opposite her would make of such heresies, were she to hear them voiced aloud, and raising her eyes cautiously now from her dessert she saw by Miss Janeway's look that she had more than an inkling of the thoughts that had been skittering through her guest's troubled consciousness.

"I take it you have not come here in the expectation of advice," the lady said in a measured tone. "Spinsters," she went on, with a wide-eyed blankness of expression that might have been the surrogate for a smile, "tend not to be called upon to arbitrate in the kind of predicament in which I suspect you are"—her hesitation was of the briefest—"trapped."

"Oh, of course," Isabel responded quickly, stumbling a little in awkwardness and confusion, "I would not dream—that is, I would not presume to burden you with my troubles. Only—" Here her voice trailed off into an agitated silence. She saw herself now, from a distance and yet with a strange and frightening clarity, not as a passenger in a careering carriage, but as a floundering animal crushed under the iron of the vehicle's wheels, and she felt for herself the same remote compassion that she would extend to any such poor maimed victim. She cast an unseeing glance here and there about the bright little room, striving to gather her thoughts. "I have a choice, you see," she said quietly, looking aside still and directing her words more at herself than towards her hospitable companion.

"A choice?" Miss Janeway prompted, and when Isabel, seeming lost in herself, failed to respond, went on: "All choices are always difficult, in my experience. However, I'm sure my experience stops far short of the kinds of alternatives that you, my dear, find yourself caught between at the present moment."

It was apparent, however, that Isabel had not been listening fully, and now she fairly burst out again: "I have not one choice," she said, "but a number! The first, which is clear and simple, is to return to Rome—simple and clear, but momentous too, of course. When that decision is made, then, *then* I shall know how difficult are the others that present themselves."

Miss Janeway sat through a lengthy pause, and at last enquired, with all the tact and gentleness of tone that surely she was capable of: "Does your husband expect you to return? I mean, has he allowed for it?"

Here Isabel gave herself a sort of rough shake, as if reproving herself for her recent inattention, then drew a deep breath that made her lift up her shoulders and raise high her chin. "I no longer know what my husband expects," she said, and then, with a woeful smile, "I suspect I no longer know my husband at all—if I ever did."

VI

The maid reappeared—by now Isabel had come to think of her as one of those minor but necessary characters in a drawing-room drama, who pop out from the wings to interrupt the action so that the audience may have an opportunity to shuffle their feet and lean back in their seats and cough—carrying before her reverently, as if it were a ciborium, an antique silver teapot, authentically dented, and giving off a sharp grassy odour that provoked in Isabel a glum sense of foreboding. There were more biscuits, less brown, less hard and ever so slightly sweeter than their predecessors, and a small slab of cheese on a wooden board.

"Mrs. Pullan says to tell you," the girl informed her mistress, "that she's going off now, if that's all right, as Mr. Pullan is at home today with his bad leg, and requires tending."

"Very well, Daisy," Miss Janeway said. "But please make sure she understands that she must be back in time to prepare dinner—Miss Woolson is coming, and she does not care to dine late."

"Yes'm," Daisy said, and departed, casting another friendly smile in Isabel's direction. The maid was of such a warm and easy disposition, Isabel noted wistfully, that her appearances in the room, however fleeting, seemed at once to intensify and soften the sunlight falling in at the window. Had she herself ever been thus, the burdened young woman wondered, that she could light up a room simply by stepping into it? Ralph Touchett would have answered her with a ringing affirmative, and there were others, a couple, at least, of not inconsiderable gentlemen, and perhaps even a lady or two, who would have seconded him in his certainty, but for herself she had her doubts. She suspected the light that Ralph and the others had detected shining from her was no more than the outward glow of an inner self-regard. She had always too assured and lofty an opinion of herself, she saw that now—oh, how she saw it, and with such starkness!—but was it required that she should cast herself altogether from that high perch to plummet down and flutter helplessly in the dust? Surely no one expected total abjection of her, not even her husband—not even the infinitely subtle Serena Merle. It was possible, Isabel knew, that she was her own harshest critic, for whom the aforementioned sackcloth and ashes were what would be as a bed of roses for those less inclined than she to self-laceration.

"I wish," she said, looking towards that light-filled window, "I wish to be free."

"To see?" Miss Janeway responded, with a startled and uncertain frown. "What is it you wish to see?"

For a moment they gazed at each other helplessly, until it came to Isabel that she had been misheard.

"Ah, no," she exclaimed, again striving not to seem to yell, "*free* is what I said—free, not see." She looked away quickly from those splotches high on Miss Janeway's cheekbones as they intensified from rose to flame. "You marvelled a little while ago at what you seemed to think the almost indecent breadth of freedom at my command," Isabel said, conscious of "hurrying on" so as to cover an awkwardness, "I mean when I spoke of perhaps stopping a while in Paris on my way to Rome; but that is not the kind of freedom to which I am referring."

"You mean, then," Miss Janeway said, fingering the base of her emptied dessert dish, "that you wish to be free of your husband."

Her tone seemed one of prim deprecation, but Isabel guessed the lady had spoken rather out of that access of irritation and chagrin into which the hard of hearing must be plunged many times every day, when yet another mistaken response provokes yet another flurry of earnestly ignored potential comedy.

"I think," Isabel said, with a smile betokening misery, "that it is myself I wish to be free of."

She had meant, with that smile, to placate and disarm; Miss Janeway, however, still smarting from what had been, after all, a trivial display of infirmity, was relentless. "But your husband must be, of course," she said, "a part of the self of which you chafe to be free."

The atmosphere in the room had markedly altered—what had gone wrong had gone momentously wrong—and even the sunlight seemed to have taken on a sort of creeping chill. In her hostess too Isabel detected a gelid glint of an intensity she had not registered hitherto, if indeed it had been there, if indeed it was there now and she were not imagining it. But no, it was not her imagining: looking more closely, and testing the air, as it were, with the most delicate feelers she was capable of extending, she understood that behind her mask of measured sympathy Miss Janeway was, not to put too fine a point on it—not to put a point on it of any fineness at all—quite simply, if faintly, gratified. She had watched Isabel since her arrival, had watched, and studied, and, for all her defective hearing, had listened, too, oh, had listened with the keenest attention. And now Isabel saw herself as she was being seen, as a wife, merely, young and spoilt and discontented, bored with the grandeurs of her Roman life, and wishing to be rid of an ageing, dull husband. Well, what else could she have expected? She had as good as invited herself here, had descended, like some great ruddy-faced raucous girl, on the home of a woman with whom she was barely acquainted, thinking to be understood and sympathised with and indulged, while she prattled of freedom, and choices, and Paris. And all the while Miss Janeway had observed her, taking note of everything and recording it all, in all its satisfyingly dismal detail, with the clever little cold steel-pen of her intellect. There was a word—Isabel tried to recall it now—a German word that her husband often used, with a delectatory and spiteful smacking of the lips. What was it, the word? No; it would not come.

Miss Janeway had poured out for her a cup of formidably aromatic tea, and it was upon the gently steaming surface of this blameless beverage that Isabel now fixed her gaze. She should not have come here; no, she should not have come.

There was a light tap upon the door, and a young woman entered. She wore a dark dress so severely lacking in any hint of frill or furbelow as to bespeak the conventual. Her hair was braided and coiled into a tight round and held in a net at the nape of her neck. Her features were as plain as her gown. She bore in her hands a large sheet of stiff cardboard, on one side of which Isabel glimpsed some tall stark letters printed in a violent shade of scarlet. Miss Janeway addressed the young woman as Mary Anne, and rose and went to her, seeming to regard it superfluous to introduce her to her guest. The two moved nearer to the window, and Miss Janeway took the sheet of cardboard and held it at arm's length up to the light and studied it in silence. Then she nodded, and returned it to the girl, who withdrew as quietly as she had entered; her brief presence had made hardly a ripple upon the air.

"We have a little printing press here," Miss Janeway explained, returning to the table and seating herself as before. "I had one of the back bedrooms converted to accommodate it. We are to make a demonstration tomorrow at the Houses of Parliament. Mary— Miss Evans—is overseeing the printing of the banners."

"A demonstration?" Isabel vaguely enquired.

Miss Janeway bent on her a faintly ironical look. "You spoke just now of wishing to be free. But freedom is first and foremost a practical matter."

"Ah, I see," Isabel said, returning the lady's look with a hint of irony of her own. "You are suffragettes."

"We," Miss Janeway gently corrected her, "are *suffragists*. It was the gentlemen of the press who invented the word 'suffragette,' as a term of derision." She paused. "I hardly imagine news of our movement has reached as far as the gates of the Eternal City?"

Isabel shook her head. "Not yet, alas. I fear the women of Italy know their place very well. Certainly the men know it, and keep them firmly to it."

"But you are not a 'woman of Italy'—you are an American. And your husband too, I believe, is a native of the New World?"

"Yes, he is. Or was. He was born in Baltimore, but has lived so long in Europe, and has so mastered its ways, that he has raised himself to a position from which he considers himself perfectly at liberty to patronise the natives."

On this Miss Janeway settled grimly. "And one of the ways of old Europe he has mastered is the subjugation of Woman?"

She had sought to mitigate the harshness of her words with a tight-lipped smile, yet Isabel was startled by the lady's vehemence nonetheless. "I have not come here to disparage my husband," she said quietly, directing her eyes at the table-top. She was aware of the question suspended in the air between them, the altogether pertinent question as to why she *had* come, but she was content to let it hang there unaddressed. "I would not have him thought some kind of conventional monster. Indeed, I know of no man less brutish, if we are to speak of such things as subjugation, and none more alive to the nuances of what it is to be free."

"And unfree?" Miss Janeway pursued, still keeping in place that polite pinched smile; the lady had, Isabel acknowledged, her own rules of tolerance and urbanity, or of the appearance of such, at least.

The maid came then to ask if there was anything else required. Miss Janeway said there was not, and the smiling girl bobbed out again. Her mistress turned to Isabel. "Forgive me, my dear," she said, "I am remiss—perhaps there *is* something else you'd like? We do not drink coffee, I'm afraid, and"—her smile softened— "I should not dare to ask what is surely by now a thoroughly Italianated palate to risk the sampling of one of our less than Dionysian fruit cordials."

Isabel was aware of being mocked, albeit without malice, and in response stoutly declared that there was not a thing more in the world she required at this moment, which was true, insofar as beverages were concerned. Then the two put aside their napkins—they were made of calico, not linen, in keeping with the general frugality and modesty of the house—and rose from the table. Miss Janeway seated herself at one end of a small sofa upholstered in dark-green fustian that was shiny along the tops of the armrests, while Isabel wandered to the window. As she stood there, viewing through sun-bright panes the nascent hollyhocks and the flowering lilac blossom in the narrow strip of front garden outside, she suddenly found the word that she had been searching for earlier, the German word of which her husband was so fond. It was *Schadenfreude,* which meant, as she knew all too well, the taking of pleasure in the misfortunes of others. Trust the precise and finical Teutons, she thought, to compress so broad a concept into a single handy term. But what was it now that had caused the elusive word to alight so promptly in her consciousness? She had no sooner posed the question than the answer came flying at her with the violent swiftness of a seabird plunging after its prey. It was that the disposition of herself and Miss Janeway in the room, she standing while her hostess sat, had brought to mind a similar but far less casual arrangement witnessed elsewhere, and in what seemed to her already another life. One day at the Palazzo Roccanera, her grand but incurably oppressive house in Rome that she shared with her husband and his daughter, she had entered one of the drawing rooms and, stopping just past the threshold, had seen, in the second before she was noticed by them, her husband and their friend—their friend!—Madame Merle there together, quite still, regarding each other silently in what must be a pause in a conversation that had been going on for some time. There was nothing untoward in their being thus engaged in familiar colloquy—Gilbert Osmond of Baltimore had known Brooklyn's Serena Merle for many years before Isabel had made an appearance in either of their lives—yet Isabel had been struck not only by the absorbed yet easy fashion in which they regarded each other, but by the fact that Madame Merle was standing, her large fair head held aloft as usual, while Osmond was seated in a deep armchair, looking up at her, with his legs extended and his hands loosely in his trouser pockets, in somewhat the way, as Isabel fondly remembered, that Ralph Touchett used to sit, or lounge, rather, but in such lazy relaxation as Isabel's husband would never permit himself to be seen enjoying. Catching sight of his wife, Osmond had hurriedly gathered himself up and, fairly scrambling to his feet, had as good as fled the room, mumbling of the need of a walk. Madame Merle, on the other hand, had remained as she had been, bravely erect and calm of gaze, and with the same small sharp light in her eye that some few minutes earlier Isabel believed she had detected in Miss Janeway's look, the light of secret gratification before the spectacle of another's distress, perplexity and general helplessness. Helpless, perplexed and in distress Isabel had not been that day, amid the gloomy splendours of the Roman palazzo that was her home, hers and her husband's, but sooner or later she would be, oh, certainly she would, as who should know better than this same Madame Merle?

"We were speaking of freedom, and of what it is to be free," Isabel said now to Miss Janeway, without turning from the window. "I fear I speak of these concepts in such a general fashion that you hardly recognise them as what you know. I mean, freedom for you, I should imagine, is a matter of immediate and graspable practicalities."

"And what is it for *you*?" Miss Janeway, behind her, enquired. "Is it not a practical matter, for instance, as to whether or not to stop off at Paris on your way to Italy and home?"

About that word, "home," Isabel had clearly discerned the imprint of quotation marks, and once more she was aware of being mocked, although this time she felt distinctly the sting of it; Miss Janeway, she divined, was, for all the calm certitudes of her position and opinions, not immune to the smarting effect of plain envy. Isabel regretted having spoken of Paris, regretted the large liberalities, as well as the bottomless depths of her pocket, that mention of that city, that place of grand possibilities, had implied. She decided she must meet the matter directly. She turned from the window and, approaching the sofa, requested leave to be seated. Taking her place on a worn and decidedly unaccommodating cushion, she realised, too late, that she had made a mistake,

for the proximity to her hostess in which she had placed herself—
it really was a very small sofa—created an unwilling and awkward condition of intimacy, like that between two young ladies
at a debutantes' ball who find themselves thrown together on the
periphery of the dance floor for no other reason than a want of
partners. And yet she pressed on.

"Money," she said, "that is, the having of it, is of course an
aspect of freedom, if not, at certain times and in certain circumstances, freedom itself."

"It certainly allows of wider aspects," Miss Janeway observed,
after a pause; it was plain she was puzzled by and somewhat wary
of the candidly, even the brazenly, mercenary turn the conversation had taken.

"The money which I possess," Isabel went on, gazing before
her with a musing frown, "was left to me by my uncle—an uncle
by marriage, my aunt's husband—but recently I discovered that
in fact it came to me, clandestinely, from my cousin, the one who
has just died."

"That would be young Mr. Touchett," Miss Janeway gently
offered. "Henrietta spoke of him to me."

"Charitably, I hope," Isabel said, and smiled. "She claimed
to disapprove of him as an idler and a cynic, while he for his part
liked nothing better than to feed her disapproval by endlessly teas-
ing her. She never quite believed him to be as ill as he was."

"And now that he has proved it, she feels guilty?"

"Oh, don't say so!" Isabel smilingly cried. "Ralph would be
horrified to think he should have caused her the faintest prickings
of remorse. Whatever she thought of him, or pretended to think,
he saw the point of *her,* as few others did, or do."

They fell silent, as if out of respect for the passage of something, an acknowledging sigh, perhaps, from the land of the shades. Miss Janeway was the first to stir.

"May I be permitted to enquire," she tentatively resumed, leaning forward a little, "how it came about that your cousin made an heiress of you, and without your knowing of it until recently?"

Miss Janeway saw, from the blurred look Isabel had taken on, that she was no longer fully there, that the livelier part of her consciousness was somewhere else, back at the side of her cousin's deathbed, no doubt. When she spoke, her voice, too, seemed to come from a distant place.

"He separated off half of his own inheritance—more than half, perhaps, I don't know—and persuaded his father to settle it on me instead, swearing him to secrecy. He wanted, Ralph wanted, to see my sails filled out as I set off on the voyage of my life. In return he desired only to have dispatches now and then, to hear word of the wonders I encountered, and the fabulous ports I should stop at along the way. I'm afraid I proved to be no Marco Polo or Vasco da Gama. I no sooner set out than my frail bark struck upon the rocks."

Again there fell between them a brief resounding silence, and again it was Miss Janeway who broke it. "You married, you mean," she said, in a voice as flat as the air about them.

"I married," Isabel said, and her tone was equally subdued, pressed upon by a weight of resignation. "Or perhaps I should say I was *led into* marriage"—she turned her face fully towards her hostess where she sat so straight at the other corner of the sofa—"that is, to put it at its plainest and most vulgar, I was married for my money."

She rose now and crossed again to stand with her face to the window. Sunlight glowed in the soft auburn ringlets at her temples. She was so young, Miss Janeway reflected—she was, in truth, not even thirty yet!—a young woman whom disenchantment had already made to seem almost middle-aged.

"Was there so much of it, your money?"

Isabel turned again to face her questioner. "Well, there was enough of it to make me an asset worth acquiring. And by now there is a great deal more. Whatever my husband may not be, he is shrewd. With my blessing he made himself trusted at the bank—my bank, here in London—and succeeded in turning my modest fortune into—"

She hesitated. Miss Janeway coolly twinkled. "An immodest one?" she murmured.

"Modest or immodest," Isabel declared, a little surprised at the almost belligerent force of her own voice, "my fortune has for now become the central fact of my life, the mountain that blocks out all the rest of the view before me."

To this Miss Janeway returned a dry stare. She was silent for a moment, and when she spoke it was as if she were distracted by some other thought unconnected with what she was saying. "I have always been struck by the ambiguity of the word 'fortune' in the context in which you use it," she vaguely murmured.

However, Isabel as good as brushed this aside. "I intend to use it, my fortune—my money—to buy my freedom."

A new light had sprung up in her eye, a light that illumined her entire countenance—her entire being, as it seemed. Miss Janeway regarded her with a startled interest, drawing back a little way on the sofa. It was as if a new person had come sweeping into the room, a figure all fortitude and determination, with metaphorical sleeves rolled, to replace by some transformative magic the uncertain and troubled young woman who had been there until a moment ago.

"You mean to make your money over to your husband," the older lady shrewdly ventured.

Isabel, with nostrils flared, glowed at her like a veritable beacon.

"I mean," she said, "to purchase my emancipation—my suffrage, if you like!"

VII

She worried, afterwards, that her departure should have appeared rudely precipitate. Immediately following her grand statement of intent as to the purchasing of her freedom, and feeling somewhat abashed for what must have seemed the baldly pecuniary tone of it, she had snatched up her gloves and her bonnet, uttered hurried thanks for a delightful luncheon, added a brisk farewell, and made for the front door with such haste that her hostess had been compelled almost to scramble to be first at the latch. Outside, the sunlight dazzled her eyes. Her only thought was how she was to procure a cab in what on her journey hither had proved itself to be a suburban wilderness. She stood on the pavement turning her head this way and that with bird-like urgency. Miss Janeway was able to tell her that there was a rank but two short streets away, and even offered to escort her there, to be sure she did not miss the spot, but Isabel said no, no, she would not hear of it, for she knew her hostess had much to attend to, and she would find her own way with ease. She was flushed and agitated, and wished for nothing more dearly than to be on her way back to Dover Street. But plain mannerliness, such as had been dinned into her over the years when she was a little girl in Albany, forced her to hesitate. Miss Janeway stood beside the hollyhocks with her hands folded at her waist, watching her with what appeared to be a certain bemusement. There was, Isabel realised, the question of whether to offer the exchange of a kiss, again if only for the sake of being polite. But Miss Janeway seemed to see her thinking of it, and drew back with an infinitesimal yet significant movement, twisting her lips in the same peculiar fashion as she had done when greeting Isabel on her arrival at the house, a facial gesture that was not so much a smile as the mark of a smile withheld; no doubt the lady considered kissing and such carrying-on as not the kind of thing to be indulged in by serious people, and Miss Janeway, if she was nothing else, was categorically serious.

As it turned out, Isabel succeeded in making her way to the rank directly and with ease. There was a single cab waiting, as if specially for her; it looked very shinily black and somewhat funereal, standing so still there in the gay spring sunshine. The driver, unlike the earlier one, was briskly young, and eager to the point of unctuousness. When with much fussing and balletic skipping about he helped her to negotiate the not very perilous step, she settled back against the sun-warmed cushioned seat and gave herself up to basking in the luxury of having so bravely and conclusively made up her mind. This, she realised, was what she had set herself, on the neutral ground of Miss Janeway's house, to do: to come to a decision, or at least to consolidate what, without realising it, she had already decided. Her husband would get the money, or a sufficient portion of it, anyway, and in return she should have what she would stoutly continue to call, striking inwardly a defiant stance against Miss Janeway's half-suppressed scepticism, her liberty.

As the cab negotiated its way along the tree-lined streets, wheeling in a sharp right-angle at every other corner, her mind was, as it might be, jolted into relaxedness, and in a state of wakeful reverie she allowed her thoughts to return to the lady whose Spartan hospitality she had, if not enjoyed, then at least appreciated. Isabel considered herself to be as contemporary-minded and as "up" with the vital matters of the day as her years as an expatriate in a southern land should allow, but Miss Janeway seemed so radical a being as to belong to a different species from the one of which she was herself a member. However, as she came now to see, in reflecting upon it, the older lady's radicalism was not necessarily of a modern or progressive kind. In fact she seemed to Isabel a primordial figure, something out of the ancient drama, one of those shroud-clad anonymous Cassandras who step forward from the chorus calmly to prophesy the sacked city, the toppling towers and the errant king expiring in a welter of his own blood. Miss Janeway, in her quiet and considered fashion, would bring crashing down into the dust the entire world as it was at present constituted, if only she could print sufficient placards, and mount enough parades. And yet was she not precisely what was required, if there was to be any change at all in society? She was not nice, nor meant to be; she was not accommodating; she had sharp edges, awkward corners; any man attempting to lay a patronising hand upon her would quickly draw back, his flesh pierced by the bristling spines of her conviction, her zealot's self-sustaining *réssentiment*.

The hotel, when Isabel gained the sanctuary of it, was cool and quiet, as it always somehow managed to be, or at least to seem. The corridors were empty, save for the odd furtive porter or scurrying maid, and the reception rooms that she glanced into were suffused with a grainy radiance so mild and still and self-absorbed that she was almost loath to disturb it. She wandered about for a while, charmed by the unwonted solitude of the place; she felt like a child given the run of a delightfully deserted house. She had spoken to Miss Janeway of freedom—she rather feared she had spoken to her of little else—and now, in these unpeopled, dreaming spaces, she was being given a sample of the thing itself, as a seamstress might press upon her without charge a sample of fine silk. She consulted the timepiece suspended on a gold chain about her neck, and sighed to see how early the hour was; her appetite had not been at all satisfied by the unglimpsed Mrs. Pullan's boiled greens, and she was looking forward to her dinner with an almost vengeful keenness. She felt it her duty, after that blameless viridescent luncheon, to fly the flag of the carnivore, and she determined to take herself to Wilton's restaurant in Jermyn Street and order a rare steak and a glass of claret, followed by something unhealthily sweet and rich, the entire great feast to be rounded off with a pot of wickedly strong coffee. But then she recalled where she was, and sighed again: in London it was "not the done thing" for a lady to dare to dine alone in the public glare of a restaurant.

She went up to her room and drew one of the chintz-covered armchairs to the window and sat there placidly for a while, listening to the early-evening noises in the street below. All over the city the telegraph wires would be humming with last-minute invitations, and ladies would be already instructing their maids as to which gowns to lay out, and in the clubs the gentlemen would be sighingly consulting their timepieces and folding their newspapers and requesting that their cabs be ordered up. Indeed, as she recalled now, Isabel herself had been invited forth, for had not Henrietta Stackpole informed her that she would be at her usual lodging in Wimpole Street, and since Isabel was to stay the night there, she might think of coming early and joining her friend for supper. Perhaps she would do so; she did not have to decide quite yet, and it was pleasant to sit here quiet and calm in the soft light of the summer evening.

She wondered at what time Miss Janeway's dinner guest would arrive in Fulham. What was the name she had said? Wilson? Walston? Whoever she was, Isabel hoped the lady knew what to expect of Mrs. Pullan's culinary skills and had fortified herself accordingly in advance.

Thinking of Miss Janeway now, Isabel could not but see in this neat dry sharp-eyed person an image of what she might herself have become had she not ventured out into the world, the world as it was and not as Miss Janeway was convinced it would be, off in the hazy future when universal right should have been established at last. She had taken personal risks, the like of which she suspected Miss Janeway would disdain precisely because they were personal and not shouldered for the sake of the general good. Without doubt the greatest of those risks had been her consenting to marry Gilbert Osmond; the risk, however, as she was obliged to acknowledge, was apparent only in hindsight, and it would be self-deception to congratulate herself for her courage and daring. When he had proposed their union to her, a thing he had done with an application of delicacy and consummate, if calculated, charm that she could even still only admire, it had seemed to her the safest and most sensible arrangement she could enter upon— But here her thoughts stopped short, and she sat up as straight as the yielding amplitude of the armchair would allow. An arrangement: the word had slipped into her mind in sideways fashion, but there it was, in all its baleful neutrality. Was that how she had thought of her marriage to that clever and immensely cultivated man, as a mere arrangement, like the repositioning of an item of furniture, such as a chair, a table—a bed? But no, no: there was a limit to the lengths to which she might go in excoriating herself. She had loved Gilbert Osmond, as much as her youth and want of experience had allowed. That the world at large had considered her to be throwing herself away on an arid dilettante—even Ralph, especially Ralph, had been against the match, although he had refrained from saying so in so many words until after she had sealed her fate and accepted Osmond—had served only to make her more certain of the rightness of her choice. Oh, there had been an arrangement, from the first there had been an arrangement, of that there was no doubt; it was not she who had done the arranging, however, nor had it been entirely the work of Gilbert Osmond, although he would not have been other than wholly acquiescent in the planning of it. No, it was Serena Merle, Osmond's confidante and confederate of old, who had conceived and put up the entire thing, once it came out that Isabel was to have a plump portion of old Mr. Touchett's money.

Isabel closed her eyes and sat so still, there at the window in the seemingly endless twilight's glow, that an observer in the room would have sworn she had stopped breathing and had turned into an effigy of herself. The money: she felt befouled each time she thought of it and the disasters it had wrought in her life. For her, the alchemical process had been reversed, and gold had been turned into dross. Money was like one of the products of those fundamental operations of the physical life that must not be mentioned, that must be passed over in the strictest silence, if the necessary norms of civilised society were to be maintained and preserved intact; but it was always there, something we must not seem to know yet cannot not know, something that must be disavowed, save in the secret closet of the self.

Now suddenly she opened wide her eyes, and sat up, and then jumped up, clasping her hands before her. She had at that moment remembered the satchel of banknotes—what had become of it? She must have left it at Miss Janeway's house. Yes, yes, that was what had happened: she had left it wedged against the back of the bent-wood chair when she and Miss Janeway had stood up from the table, she crossing to the window to look out at the garden while her hostess settled herself on the faded green sofa. Perhaps it was still there, unnoticed by anyone. But the maid—what was her name?—surely she would have discovered it when she was clearing the table and setting the room to rights in preparation for dinner? At this thought Isabel flushed, flushed twice, in fact, first in fright and then in self-recriminating shame. Why should she imagine the maid—Daisy! That was her name—why should she imagine that Daisy would be any less honest than Miss Janeway herself? Yet it was a great deal of money, probably more than the girl herself would earn in a lifetime of service. Oh, what to do? What to *do*? She paced back and forth at the window with her hands clasped at her mouth and the knuckles of both thumbs pressed so hard against her nether lip that she could feel behind the soft flesh the sharp contours of her teeth.

And then the answer came to her, the answer to her dilemma, clear and compact as one of those telegraphed messages that she had thought of a little while ago, humming through the wires. In fact it would involve the dispatching of a telegram, and she was about to ring for a pad and pencil, such as she had employed in confirming to Miss Janeway her presence in London and reconfirming that they were to lunch together, but as her fingertip was approaching the bell she stopped herself, and again consulted her watch. A telegram would not do it, a telegram would not do it at all; what she had in mind called for the more generous breadth, the wider margins, of a proper letter. Staines was due back from her sister's at any moment, and before she had even removed her bonnet could be redirected to Fulham. It was true, the evening was latening, but if the cab was a fast one, and the driver competent enough not to get himself and his passenger lost in that warren of riverside streets, the errand could be run in little more than an hour.

She went to the bureau that was set against the wall to one side of the bed—which now seemed less lofty and less alarming than it had at first sight the previous day—and sat down, feeling light-hearted almost to the point of frivolity. There was notepaper aplenty, each sheet embossed at the head with the hotel's crest. She took up the pen from where it lay in a groove above the blotter, opened the lid of the inkwell, dipped in the nib, and began to write. What was freedom, she thought, other than the right to exercise one's choices?

VIII

The smoke-blue twilight was deepening at last into night and she was again in a carriage with her maid, travelling through the quiet of the city northwards towards Wimpole Street. In the end she had decided she could not face again the hotel's tenebrous dining room, and instead of going down to dinner had ordered eggs and toast and tea to be brought to her in her chamber. By the time she had finished her supper, which she took at a little table by the window above the by now shadowed street, Staines had fulfilled her errand and returned from Fulham. The hotel would later send on their baggage to Miss Stackpole's lodgings, for there the two were to stay the night. Isabel had so arranged it that she should be with her friend at an hour when it would be too late for dinner, but not so late that there would not be time for a talk—Henrietta would expect, would demand, a talk, and not a brief one, either. Isabel was dreading this ordeal—she could think of it as nothing other than that—and she was drawing up in her mind a list of possible innocuous topics she might introduce, or throw down, more like, as a series of stumbling blocks in the way of Henrietta's relentless onward drive.

Two weeks previously, on her journey down to Gardencourt, Isabel had paused briefly here in London and allowed herself to be interrogated by her friend on the circumstances in which she had left Rome to come and share with Ralph Touchett his final days and hours. She had given only the sparest account of the tumultuous emotional events that had preceded her departure from the Eternal City—the common cognomen nowadays gave her an inward shudder, with its Dantesque suggestion of a place of endless incarceration, endless suffering—but now the time had come for her to take her friend fully into her confidence, or as fully as she deemed advisable; she owed this act of confession to Henrietta, and to herself. Yet she had no doubt but that the revelation of so many painful and pernicious matters would cost her dear. One of the many terrible things she had recently been made to learn was that there were no limits to the depths of private disgrace and abjection to which one could plummet. Her husband and Serena Merle had together pushed her from the plaster pedestal upon which, she now realised, she had set herself so long ago, even as early as in her girlhood, that she had ceased to be aware of it under her feet; now, still tumbling and turning in precipitous fall, she would, by displaying her wounds and woes to her friend, emerge from the concealing clouds and appear in plain air, in the sight of all who cared to look. Oh, she had no doubt her friend would keep her secrets safe—there was none more decent or discreet than Henrietta Stackpole—but to have told even one person was tantamount, for the teller, to having told the multitude.

Now Staines spoke, for the first time since they had quitted the hotel; she too, as it would prove, had been brooding upon a grave matter.

"I talked to your friend's cook," she said, her voice sounding strangely disembodied in the extreme dimness within the carriage.

"Oh, yes?" Isabel responded. "Mrs. Pullan."

The maid sniffed. "I wasn't told her name."

"Well, that's it, that's what she's called: Mrs. Pullan."

"Right, then. She didn't say."

There was another sniff.

"I did not encounter her," Isabel offered apologetically, although she was not at all sure what there was to apologise for. "I only heard her spoken of, and in hushed tones. Is she so very fierce?"

This the maid took as a rhetorical question, and did not grace it with a reply. There was a brief silence. They heard a bell in some nearby belfry solemnly tolling the half-hour. In the hushed gloaming through which they were progressing the wheels of the carriage made upon the roadway a distinctly loud and grating noise.

"She's free in her talk, whatever she's called," the maid said, and now she too sounded exaggeratedly loud, in the manner of one "breaking out."

"Is she?" Isabel responded cautiously, and felt an inner coldness, as if something icy had touched her heart.

"She told me a thing about her mistress which I reckons she shouldn't of," Staines said, in the same aggrievedly censorious tone. To Isabel's ear it was uncertain who it was that was being censured, Mrs. Pullan *in absentia,* or herself, although she did not know of any way in which she could be held at fault in the present instance; but then, no matter at what target Staines's arrows were ostensibly aimed, once in flight they tended inevitably to bend, by a magnetic force acting mysteriously on them, in her mistress's direction.

"And what was it she told you?" Isabel had to ask, since it was clear Staines had no intention of volunteering the information without being prompted. Having asked the question, however, Isabel realised she was not certain she wished to hear the answer.

The maid was seated in such a way that the glow of the intermittent streetlamps did not reach as far as her face, and Isabel found it unnerving to crouch like this—she felt herself to be crouching forward anxiously—and be spoken to out of the darkness by this eerily sourceless, harsh and recriminatory voice.

"Maybe you knows already," Staines said, with a continuing sullenness of tone.

"Say what it is and I shall tell you if I know it or not," Isabel replied, permitting herself a finely measured hint of impatience; dealing with Staines, she reflected, was like having repeatedly to coax and cajole some needy and not entirely tamed creature to come forward sufficiently in its lair to be seen and tended to.

"It's that she's not well, the lady."

"Miss Janeway?" Isabel redundantly enquired.

"She's not well at all," Staines replied, "not at all at all. Leastways that's what the Pulling woman said."

"Ah." Isabel let herself sink back slowly against the taut leather of the seat behind her. "So she's ill, then."

"Six months, the doctor give her."

"Oh, as little as that," Isabel said faintly. She looked out of the window at the darkling street and the indistinct buildings passing by; the carriage, the dusky air, her own voice and the maid's, all had taken on suddenly a funerary weight. "Heavens, the poor dear thing!"

"So you wasn't aware, then," the maid said, softening markedly, if not entirely willingly. "Maybe I shouldn't of said."

"No, no," Isabel hastened to reply, "I'm glad you told me, I'm glad to know. Well, not *glad*—"

"Only I thought as maybe that was why you made the particular effort to go that far to see her," the maid said, rekindling a mildly resentful note. "And then sending me to her with the letter, and all."

"Did you meet her? Did you talk to her, to Miss Janeway?"

"No, I give the letter to the maid—a saucy manner that one has. I was going out by the back door when the cook appeared, with her hat on, and wouldn't hear of me leaving until I'd had a cup of tea—two cups, as it turned out—and a slice of her plum cake, seeing as I'd missed my supper and was facing all that long way in the cab back up to Piccadilly."

The accusatory tone of this last Isabel disregarded; her thoughts were dashing here and there, like a wild bird trapped in a room, seeking escape or shelter.

"But how could she, the cook, make such a delicate and tragic revelation," she asked, "when she had not even told you her own name?"

"Well, you see, she'll be in want of a position, soon," the maid said.

The simple statement sounded to Isabel callously, almost brutally matter-of-fact, until she reflected that after all she had never known what it was to be without "a position" in the world; even when her father had drunk and gambled away the family's scant fortune, and then had wrought the ultimate dereliction by dying early, she had not doubted that there was a place—a placement, if you like—awaiting her that would sooner or later present itself, if she would only bide her time and be patient. And had she not been justified in her assurance, however complacent, even presumptuous, her waiting might have seemed to an observing stranger? Daniel Touchett's beneficence, though it had come to her through the covert agency of his son, Ralph, had set her up, as they say, had set her up magnificently. That subsequently she had been brought low did not invalidate her initial confidence. Despite all that she had suffered in these recent, these catastrophic times, when the roof of her world had collapsed upon her, she could not find it in herself, bruised and battered as she might be, to regret stepping forward into that world once its portals had been opened to her. She had been offered much—she had been proposed to by two suitors, one of them a peer of the realm, master of myriads of acres and who knew how many great houses—and much she had spurned. She had observed, and thought, and hung fire, making patience her watchword. If in the end the step she had taken into the world's wideness had been disastrously misdirected, it was she who had taken it, asking no guidance, assisted by no one's hand. She had made a monstrous mistake, but she could say, triumphantly, that she had lived, and would live yet, richly, deeply, to the broadest stretch of her being. To this conviction she clung, as fiercely, and at times as desperately, as a shipwrecked mariner clinging to a spar.

Miss Stackpole's first-floor lodgings consisted mainly and most forcefully of a large lofty brown drawing room with a big bay window that goggled out in seeming wonderment upon a portion of the innocent and undistinguished frontage of the opposite side of Wimpole Street. She had preserved the place largely as it had been when she had first taken it, for she was impatient of those women who insist upon applying a feminine gloss to whatever quarters they happened to be placed in for any appreciable period of time. It was Mr. Robert Bantling, to whom not long before she had become affianced, who had directed her towards the apartments when their owner, an old chum of his, for so he figured his friend, had given them up and decamped with his regiment to India. Her first glance about the gaunt rooms had seemed to her fiancé reprehending, and had provoked in him a nervous laugh. Over the years of their acquaintanceship, and there had been a good many years before the pair had reached the point of the plighting of troths, Mr. Bantling had developed a wide repertory of laughs, from the indulgent to the frankly frightened, in dealing with, in negotiating his way round, his not always predictable and often downright baffling beloved. "I imagine, my dear," he had said, touching the tips of a finger and a thumb nervously to his moustache, "you'll be wanting the painters and decorators in to brighten things up and dispel the bachelor blight left behind by old Horace, eh?" Horace, Major Horace Henry, was the friend who had taken himself off to the great subcontinent.

"I don't know why you should think that," Henrietta had replied, with a bright sharpness, giving him what he thought of as one of her large looks, opening wide her lively eyes and drawing her head far back as if to take a broader measure of him. "Your friend's taste in furnishings and fittings is perfectly acceptable to me. Mahogany is a restful shade, and the lingering odour of pipe tobacco puts me in mind of my late Uncle Winslow, of whom I was very fond. So, you see, I shall be quite content." And so she had been, and so she had remained, to Bob Bantling's grateful relief.

Henrietta was fair of complexion and short in stature, and where once she had been plump she tended now to a definite stoutness, as Isabel again noted, upon her arrival at Wimpole Street that summer night along with her baggage and her maid. Although it was scarcely more than a fortnight since the two friends had last encountered each other, on the morning when Isabel was passing through London on her way to Gardencourt, somehow the intervening death of Ralph Touchett had caused his cousin to look at everything around her, no matter how familiar, with a new and keener discernment. And it was with the aid of this enhanced faculty that now she saw how Henrietta, even as she was on the point of exchanging maidenhood for marriage, had already entered prematurely upon middle age, at least as far as appearances went. She stooped, ever so slightly, and a gathering of light-brown curls at the back of her neck, oddly but definitely reminiscent of a bunch of grapes, betrayed here and there a fine seam of silver. The bright light of her eye had not dimmed, but the peculiar stillness and fixedness of gaze, which she had always been wont intermittently to fall into, was now a more frequent and more marked, more worrying, phenomenon. Her arbitrarily stopping like this and staring, seeming to look inwards rather than out, had the effect on those around her of making them feel suddenly and strangely isolated, of having been abandoned to their own agitatedly self-conscious devices. Henrietta herself seemed unaware of these brief cataleptic absences, and would emerge from them instantaneously and pick up without the least effort, in mid-sentence, in mid-word, even, the thread of what she had been saying.

She had come down herself in response to Staines's vigorous plying of the brass knocker—the maid's manner of signalling her mistress's arrival at their doors had been likened by more than one among Isabel's small circle of acquaintances to the summons of the Last Trump—and brushed aside Isabel's apologies for the lateness of the hour. She greeted her friend not with a smile of welcome, Isabel grimly noted, but with instead a sharp and searching look. Thus was fore-signalled, even as the door was opening, the interrogation Isabel dreaded, but knew was inescapable, and which she had avoided for a day by the expedient of putting up at Pratt's Hotel on her return from Gardencourt, rather than coming straight here to Wimpole Street.

"You are exhausted, I see," Henrietta said, with what, had Isabel not known her better, would have sounded more like severity than sympathy.

"I'm somewhat tired, I confess," Isabel replied. "Yesterday's journey was uncommonly long, although I suppose simply it was that the train was uncommonly slow."

There was a deal of business to be attended to immediately— the coachman had borne in the baggage and now Staines was directed to show him to the back stairs—and it was not until the two friends were themselves ascending towards Henrietta's parlour that the lady of the house spoke again. "Was it very terrible, at the end?" she asked. This time there was no mistaking the sincere and tender concern in her tone, yet for a moment Isabel imagined confusedly that she was still speaking of the rigours of the train journey, but then understood that the subject in fact was the circumstances of her cousin's death.

"No," she said, "not terrible. Peaceful, rather, though melancholy in the extreme, of course."

Henrietta gave her another searching look, and they resumed their ascent.

Mr. Bantling, substantial, smooth and smiling, was waiting to greet them in the doorway at the top of the stairs. He was without a jacket, Isabel saw with some surprise; it was a mark, she supposed, of a new access of ease between the happy couple as the day of their nuptials drew near. She had also taken note of Henrietta's gown of coruscating brittle blue satin, obviously of recent purchase, and the product, if she was not mistaken, and she was sure she was not, of one of the more discreet and exclusive of the Paris houses. Henrietta had never been a "dresser," and in the uncharacteristic sumptuousness of her costume this night Isabel felt certain she detected the influence of Mr. Bantling, who, although an unlikely arbiter of fashion, would be eager that his intended bride should be properly "kitted out."

"My dear Mrs. Osmond," this gentleman said now, moulding

his smile to a graver frame, "how sad a circumstance it is that we see you nowadays only at sad times."

On the previous occasion, when Isabel was on her hurried way down to be with her dying cousin, Henrietta had contrived to leave her alone for the space of some minutes with Mr. Bantling, and that gentleman, despite a soldierly awkwardness of expression, had found the words, simple and kindly, in which to speak of his old friend Ralph's unfailing good nature, and of his patience and fortitude in face of his final illness, and despite all her woes she had been comforted.

The three of them now entered together the high dim room, where despite the years of Henrietta's occupancy there still lingered a faint trace, the very faintest, of Major Horace Henry's pipe tobacco.

"We held dinner," Henrietta said, "in hopes that you might still come, but then this great hungry beast"—she cast a mock scowl in the direction of her fiancé where he hovered jacketless behind her—"had to be fed, and so you find us in our dishevelled post-prandial state."

Isabel glanced with veiled amusement at her friend; Henrietta, who for so long had been a self-appointed scourge of the British and their, to her, maddeningly complacent ways, had moved so far as to take on, surely under osmotic pressure attendant upon extended proximity to Mr. Bantling, something of her lately adopted country's hearty archness of tone.

They stood in silence, Mr. Bantling and his soon-to-be bride, and gazed upon their friend—for surely by now she was friend to both of them, and well-nigh equally—with an easy fond regard. Then Mr. Bantling looked to Henrietta and delicately cleared his throat in what was patently a pre-agreed signal.

"Robert begs to be excused," Henrietta said, turning to Isabel and folding her hands before her. "It seems there is a card game at his club that simply cannot proceed without him."

Bob Bantling blushed and loudly laughed—it had always been his way to treat his companion's utterances, even at their most inconsequential, as the very acme of cleverness and subtle wit—and in hardly more than the blinking of an eye had donned his jacket and taken up his hat and cane and dived off into the night. Henrietta and her guest allowed a moment for the flurry of his departure to subside, smiling, yet aware, to their surprise, of being a little shy of each other and the contiguous intimacy to which they had been so abruptly abandoned.

IX

Henrietta summoned her maid, a sallow, sleepy-eyed girl, and bade her bring coffee and cakes. When she had gone the two women remained standing in the middle of the room, held there by a curious indecisiveness; it was as if they were waiting for someone of larger authority to come and direct them as to how they should dispose themselves. The night, slate-blue and shining, pressed against the panes of the bow window on which the curtains had not been drawn; the air in the room seemed unwontedly warm and constricting.

"I suspect," Isabel said gently, "that your fiancé has become a little frightened of me."

Henrietta stared. "Frightened?—my Robert?" she said. "Why ever would he be frightened of you?" Then she saw the idea of it. "You mean, because you are in mourning? You think him afraid of your grief? Then you underestimate him. He is a soldier, remember, or was, at least. He is not unacquainted with death and its distressful consequences."

"You're right, of course," Isabel said, with a placating shrug. "No doubt I'm being fanciful. I hardly know my own mind, these days."

"Should you imagine," her friend persisted, her voice rising and broadening in pitch—here was a flash of the Henrietta of old—"that his admittedly abrupt departure was due to wariness of you, then certainly you are mistaken. If he fears anyone, my dear, it is myself."

"Oh, yes," Isabel responded lightly, "I can see how with whip and chair you keep him in check."

She stopped. Henrietta regarded her in silence for a moment: Had she in her irreverence gone too far? What she had confessed a moment ago was true: in these woeful and turbulent times she hardly knew herself. Yet since she had left Rome to be with Ralph at the end, and especially in the days that had elapsed since his death, she had, when she was among people, the sense of having herself passed over an ultimate boundary, into some other bourne, and that her presence here in the world was as a phantom, a sort of ghastly revenant, whose touch would freeze, whose look would terrify. It was fancy, all fancy, she knew it. Yet try as she might she could not rid herself of the notion of being somehow beyond nature. That was how she framed it, that she had become denatured, although she was not at all sure what she meant by it.

Henrietta had turned away, and was repositioning one of the cushions that sat in a row, like so many plump, self-satisfied pets—pug-dogs, say, or large soft colourful cats—along the deep back of a rather lumpy-looking sofa.

"The fact is," she said, "the good man and I had agreed beforehand that he would absent himself—'slope off' was the term he employed—once you had arrived and he had said a civil word to you. He knew, of course, that you and I would wish to be alone."

At this last Isabel felt rise in her an impulse of protest. It might be Henrietta's wish to be alone with her—indeed, she was sure it was—but the wish was far from mutual. She knew what awaited her. First there would be the litany of questions, sympathetic, to be sure, but probing and relentless too, followed by the familiar homily, urging upon her what she should and must do, in order to—in order to what? Save herself? That, the saving of herself, or something like it, would be what Henrietta would proclaim her friend's first duty, now that, as it seemed, her marriage had come to a crisis, a crisis that appeared likely to prove terminal. The idea of self-rescue, so aspirational and lofty, struck Isabel as almost comical, and she almost laughed. It was true, there was something to be saved, something of life itself, precious and essential, but she felt, strangely, that this act of preservation, of redemption, need not necessarily involve *her*. She might perform the ceremony of preserving and redeeming, while at the same time standing back, or to one side. It was what the priests did: in Rome she often went on a Sunday morning to watch them do it, the ritual conjuring of invisible flesh and blood upon the altar.

Now the maid returned with coffee and macaroons, and the two women, released from their spell of indecision, seated themselves opposite each other in deep armchairs at either side of the window. Henrietta, never one to recline, held herself upright with her left hand laid along the arm of her chair, a pose that gave to her the aspect of an heraldic figure, representing the spirit of Justice, as it might be, or Retribution. Once again Isabel felt within her a stirring of rebellious protest; she had not come to Wimpole Street to be judged, much less to have a sentence handed down upon her. Which of course begged the question of what it was, then, that she *had* come here for. At this, she checked herself: Henrietta Stackpole was one of her oldest, and certainly one of her truest friends, and she would do well, she told herself severely, to keep this steadily in mind during the course of the cross-questioning— and, oh, how cross it would be!—that she knew was now about to begin. Sure enough, Henrietta's first enquiry, though it sounded innocent enough, addressed itself straight to the heart of what had been for a very long time a contentious matter between these two insistently independent spirits. "Did you speak to Lord Warburton after the funeral?"

"Well, *he* spoke to *me*," Isabel mildly replied.

Henrietta refused to smile.

"I understand that is not, of course, the same thing at all," she said, with a hint of cold rebuke.

"No, I suppose it isn't," Isabel murmured, taking a sip of coffee and lowering her eyelashes over the cup. "He is to be married, you know."

It had occurred to her to wonder if Staines had managed to find a place for herself in the dim far reaches of the house. Could Miss Stackpole's sleepy-eyed servant be counted upon to show the maid to a corner where she might lay her head for the night? But then, Staines would be capable of improvising a lair for herself on the floor, among her mistress's half-unpacked bags, if she were put to it.

Henrietta was gazing at her friend with eyes that seemed to bulge brightly in their sockets. "May one ask who it is His Lordship"—the honorific was sarcastically pronounced—"has chosen for a bride?"

"Oh, Lady somebody," Isabel said, with all the signs of distractedness. "An heiress, I believe, from one of the great families. Mrs. Touchett told me of it—she could not recall the name. The thing has been announced—I'm surprised you haven't heard of it."

"I do not follow with any interest the doings of the aristocracy," Henrietta said stiffly.

Isabel looked to the window. "Strange, I don't think of him as an aristocrat. He seems too amply liberal in his views."

Lord Warburton, of Lockleigh Hall, it should be said, was one of the premier peers of the land, heir to a fabled fortune and, unlike others of that ilk—not that there were many as favoured as he with the riches and talents of this world—deeply immersed in the politics and policies of his time. That Isabel had hardly set foot upon English soil before this formidable gentleman had proposed marriage to her, and that she had rejected him with an almost equal alacrity, still left Henrietta perplexed—though not displeased—even at this remove of years.

"He asked me to come to Lockleigh," Isabel went on, with an air of inconsequence, which, although her friend wondered at it, seemed not at all assumed but wholly genuine. "He said his sisters would be there at Whitsuntide and would be glad to see me. I confess I too should be glad to see them, for they're very sweet and kind."

"Yes," Henrietta responded flatly. "I have met them."

"Oh, of course, I was forgetting that you were at Gardencourt once when they came to call."

A brief silence ensued. Lord Warburton's sisters, the Misses Molyneux, were precisely the kind of women—meek, placid, ever accommodating—for whom Henrietta, sharing her friend Miss Janeway's opinions in the matter of female suffrage, reserved her strongest disapproval and disdain.

"And did he say," Isabel's friend now enquired, with honeyed irony, "if his fiancée, 'Lady somebody,' would be there also, at Whitsuntide, should you come to call?"

Isabel, for her part, nodded an ironical acknowledgement, dimly smiling. "That was my thought, too. But I did not ask. It hardly mattered, as I had no intention of visiting Lockleigh."

"I should think not!" Henrietta fairly burst out. "The wonder is he dared to ask."

Isabel, with deliberation, put her coffee cup aside. "He was merely being polite," she said. "Or perhaps a little more than that. The invitation was meant, or so at any rate I took it, as a seal of closure upon"—she hesitated—"upon what might have been and never was." She glanced at Henrietta and saw her formulating a question and not being sure if she dared pose it. "Do I regret rejecting him?" she said softly, sparing her friend the daring choice. "No, I don't. I regret nothing—that is to say, I regret everything, which amounts to the same thing."

"Oh, Isabel!" her friend said, in what was hardly more than a whisper, yet a whisper fraught with feeling.

Isabel slowly shook her head. "You must not pity me, you know, dear Henrietta. That would be the unkindest thing. I do not pity myself—I blame myself, yes, I accuse, I excoriate, but I do not pity; I shall never sink that low."

She looked again to the window and glimpsed down in the street, by the light of the gas lamp, a man in a black hat walking past on the far pavement. His carriage was so erect and his step so firmly determined that her heart skipped a beat, though a single beat only, at the possibility that he was someone whom she knew. But now it took only a closer look for her to see that he was not the one she had thought he might be; the world, after all, can boast of many tall hard stubborn straight-backed gentlemen.

"You haven't asked," she said, turning away from the window, "of Mr. Goodwood. That bespeaks admirable forbearance on your part." How, she wondered, out of what callous resource, could she find it in her to tease her friend at such a moment, on such a topic? "He also returned to Gardencourt," she went on, "a week after the funeral, and on the same day as Lord Warburton—practically, indeed, on that nobleman's heels. It was a day of comings and goings, of entrances and exits, rather like a comedy act in the music-hall."

She paused, struck by something that had come into her friend's expression, a ripple, merely the faintest, of pain, as it seemed, the mute pain of one who hears carelessly dismissed as of no worth a thing she would have deemed herself blessed to have been offered. And seeing it, seeing that pang of muffled suffering, Isabel herself experienced a hot spasm of mortification and shame. She, the ever-sought-after Isabel Archer, she might scoff at the mournful persistence of her numerous admirers, but what did that leave to others? Bob Bantling was good enough, and more than good, he was precious, he was peerless, in his way, but that was not the way of Lord Warburton and his millions, of Ralph Touchett and his abiding lonely passion, of Caspar Goodwood, even, and his stern New England lean brown look.

"And did *he* speak to you, Mr. Goodwood?" Henrietta asked, with a definite note of sourness.

"He did, yes," Isabel somewhat wearily replied. "He always does. He can be markedly loquacious, for one who puts such store by the virtues of a masculine reticence and restraint."

"Perhaps he thinks you do not hear him properly—"

"That I do not listen, you mean?"

"—and is impelled therefore to repeat himself."

Isabel rose and again faced the window and the summer night's blued darkness beyond the glass. She did not wish Henrietta to witness her expression when she said what she was about to say, for she could feel her cheeks begin to flush already.

"He kissed me."

"Ah," Henrietta exclaimed, though without emphasis, merely marking the beat while she waited.

"It was evening," Isabel went on. "I was walking on the lawn, under the oaks—you recall the oaks at Gardencourt, how their shadows stretch so far and so sharply across the grass when the sun begins to set? I came upon a bench, wreathed in ivy. It was a spot I remembered." She spoke in a low voice, reflectively, as if recounting the thing for her own benefit, not to experience it again in recollection, but to inscribe it on her memory, recording it for a future time, for that special form of posterity she imagined the remainder of her life would be. "I had sat there, on that very bench, six years previously, not long after my arrival in England, when a letter was brought to me from the house, to say that Caspar Goodwood had followed me from America. This time I would not sit down, at first—I was afraid, afraid that if I did I would somehow call up the past to stand before me again. But I was tired, and gave in. I should have heeded my instincts. I can't say how much time had passed, but the twilight had come on, when I looked up and—"

"And Mr. Goodwood was there?" Henrietta, behind her, offered helpingly.

Isabel, still with her face to the window, sighed. "Yes, he was there, so eager, so ardent, so filled with hopeful resolution, as only he can be, in his stiff way."

"I don't know why you call him stiff," Henrietta said, with a marked stiffness of her own. "He is a New Englander, he observes the proprieties. If that's to be stiff, then I approve it."

Henrietta had backed Mr. Goodwood's cause with Isabel from the start, even though she was indeed, as Isabel could plainly see now, a little in love with him herself, for all that she was pledged to Mr. Bantling. Isabel's conscience, in regard to Caspar Goodwood, suffered even yet a residual soreness, for in Albany she had encouraged him, seeing only when she came to Europe how impossible he would be for her. To have married him, she acknowledged, would have been to elect to live between seasons, neither in summer nor in winter, neither in spring nor in fall; together, they would have inhabited a weatherless world.

"He had been given new hope, you see," Isabel said. "My cousin had spoken to him, Ralph on his deathbed had spoken to him, and told him—told him—"

"Told him what?" Henrietta impatiently prompted.

Now on a sudden Isabel turned almost violently from the window and sat herself down again, and crouched there in the armchair with a fist pressed to her mouth, her gaze fixed desperately upon nothing. Henrietta put out a hand instinctively to touch her, but then withdrew it slowly.

"He told him," Isabel muttered, her voice distorted behind her knuckles, "he told him of how my life is—my life in Rome."

There was silence. Henrietta rose, the satin of her gown rustling, and crossed quickly the small space that separated the two armchairs, with a hand again extended, which this time she did not withdraw, but laid instead on Isabel's tense, hunched shoulder. "And will you now tell *me*," she softly urged, "how it is, your life in Rome?"

"I've told you—"

"My dear, you told me, two weeks ago, in this very room, before you set out for Gardencourt, that your coming away from Italy, to see your cousin before he died, had caused a break—"

"I spoke of no break!" Isabel cried out. "You did not hear me say the word 'break.'"

"I did not have to hear it, it was there in everything you did not say, a yawning chasm."

Isabel, crouching there, sank lower again into the deep recess of the chair, as if to make herself so small and hidden that she should quite disappear, never be found again. Henrietta, her fingers on her friend's shoulder still, felt the tension in her suddenly relax, to be replaced with something far worse, a limpness, a laxity, that seemed the very token of a general surrender. Now Isabel, without lifting her head, reached up blindly and fumbled for her comforter's wrist and pressed it briefly. "Go back, now," she murmured, "go back and sit down, do." Henrietta hesitated, and then returned reluctantly to her chair. Isabel, bethinking herself, hurriedly consulted the watch that hung on its chain at her bosom. "But look at the hour!" she cried. "Poor Mr. Bantling, by now he will have lost every penny he owns at the card table!"

"Don't trouble yourself," Henrietta said drily. "Mr. Bantling, I can tell you, is more than he looks. He's the very devil at bridge, and comes home with banknotes spilling out of every pocket and sometimes from under his hat." Isabel, despite herself, had to smile at the notion of her friend's fiancé as a card-sharp at once cunning and dashing. "Besides, you don't think he stays here, do you? My Bob is too jealous of his reputation to allow anyone to imagine such a thing. He keeps a room at the club—his billet, as he calls it. No, my dear, we shall not be disturbed, not this night."

Isabel's heart, not half an hour previously, would have sunk at such a prospect, but the time had come, she realised, for an unburdening.

X

Yet in the event it felt to her less like a sharing of confidences than a continuation of that process of self-communing she had set in train at Miss Janeway's table earlier in the day. Henrietta's attendance on her was as a shell she had picked up and put to her ear, not to catch the susurrations of the sea but the sound of herself confessing to foolishness and arrogance, willed blindness, failure and defeat. For it seemed to her now that she *had* failed, that she *had* been defeated. The passionate pledge she had made to life but a short while ago, in the carriage on the way here to Wimpole Street, suddenly seemed to her as hollow as—yes!—as the echoing inner chamber of a seashell.

They conversed, the two friends, late into the night, if it truly was a conversing. Isabel spoke again of the ivied bench at Gardencourt on which she had been seated that recent eve when Caspar Goodwood had surprised her. "It was the same spot where, half a dozen years ago, on that day when I received Mr. Goodwood's notice of his arrival in England, I looked up and spied Lord Warburton bearing down upon me with his proposal of marriage." She gave a little wondering laugh. "In a world as wide as ours is, how can it be that so much that was momentous in my life should converge on such a tiny scrap of turf?"

They had become mingled in her mind, those repeated occasions in that same small corner. She thought of her suitors now not as a comic duo in a slapstick show—she was ashamed for having thought of them so in the first place—but like the mechanical figures in a medieval clock tower, who come trundling round at their appointed intervals, vividly limned and fixed of aspect, ever new and ever the same. Or that is how she would have conceived of them, had it not been for the fact that Caspar Goodwood, this time, had broken the round and seized her in his arms and sent a flash of fire coursing through her being the like of which she had never experienced before. He had kissed her, but what, after all, was a kiss? She had been kissed before—or had she? In the meeting of their lips, his upon hers and hers yielding to his, it was as if some process of chemical melding had taken place, a fusing of essences, hers with his and his with hers, after which surely she could never again be quite herself, separate and solitary, one and alone. Yet what did it signify, this mysterious merging? Caspar Goodwood, with all the force of his appreciable being, had conjoined the two of them in his embrace, had combined their othernesses into one, and yet she felt as isolated as ever, set far off upon a dark and desolate plain. She could not judge which had done her more damage: the subtle anathema her husband had laid upon her in Rome when he saw she would defy him and hurry to be with her dying cousin, or the possibility of a radiant instauration that Caspar Goodwood's kiss had opened before her, a possibility she knew would never be fulfilled yet could never be denied. Having been struck by the lightning flash of his love, could she ever entirely be again what she had been before?

"And what," Henrietta asked, "did you say to him, to Mr. Goodwood?"

The flat, the prosaic practicality of the question summoned

Isabel back from the wastes of desolation where she had been wandering. Henrietta always had been for her a friendly flame before which to warm her hands.

"I fear I said nothing that was not harsh," she answered, offering to the other a small wan smile of apologetic pleading. "I told him that he frightened me—he thought I meant it literally, that I had been scared by his looming up at me out of the twilight."

"Yes," her friend conceded, "he tends towards literalness, I grant you that."

"I told him I wanted nothing more than that he should leave me alone and let me be. He demanded to know why I would even think of returning to Rome and all that awaited me there, and I said I would do it if only to get away from *him*. Oh, I was horrible, horrible."

"You sound as if you're proud of yourself for it."

"Do I? Perhaps I am. *There's* horror for you."

Henrietta in her armchair was sitting even further forward now than she had before—she was, as they have it in the theatre, "on the edge of her seat," only actually as well as figuratively.

"And yet you say for all your horribleness he—"

Here the mature maiden faltered before the word, so that Isabel was compelled to fill it in for her. "Kissed me? Yes. He kissed me."

"And may I ask how you responded?" Henrietta enquired, with a heightening of colour at her throat and over her cheek-bones that was, despite herself, a clear testimony as to what her own response would have been, had she been the favoured one, not Isabel. Mr. Caspar Goodwood was a man of substance, a former athlete and the present owner of a successful cotton-mill, a man of whose kisses, bestowed in no matter what circumstances, most women would feel it not only an excitement but a privilege to be the beneficiary. But in most women Mr. Goodwood had no interest. In Albany, six years previously, young Isabel Archer, over the space of the few seasons during which he had assiduously courted her, had made him no promise, but nor had she forbidden him to have an expectation of her. He had followed her to England to press his case, and she had rejected him, as she had rejected Lord Warburton; but now, this half-dozen years later, having heard from Ralph Touchett how her marriage had proved a bitter match, he had come to her once more, only to be once more rebuffed.

"I left him there," Isabel said simply, "at the bench, and ran to the house. When I looked back, I could no longer see him for the darkness."

The silence that followed this did not fall, but rose up between them, rather, like a welling of cold yet insubstantial water. They heard footfalls in the street below, they heard the gas lamps hissing on the walls above them. It was Isabel at last who broke the brimming surface of the pool in which they had been briefly immersed.

"You asked me what happened in Rome," she said.

"I think I can guess."

"Ah, no, my dear. Your mind is too fine and clean for such guessing."

"Can it have been so dreadful?"

"More so than you can imagine," Isabel murmured, and her voice, by virtue of its very softness, made the dimness lurking in the corners of the room seem to shrink back further still. She looked aside, in that way she had, frowning, as if in search of some firm support upon which to set her gaze and let it rest there a while before embarking on her tale. "It begins so far back," she said, "so far." Now she turned her head and fixed her eyes almost fiercely on her friend. "I must tell you first that it was not the idea of Mr. Touchett senior to leave me a fortune in his will—the seed of that idea was planted by the son in his father's consciousness. It is thanks to Ralph that I have my riches." She paused. "You seem not at all surprised."

Henrietta gave the merest shrug. "I had thought something of the sort must be the case. You see? There *are* things I am capable of guessing."

"Indeed, indeed," Isabel said, smiling and nodding. "Forgive me for seeming to underestimate you."

"There is no seeming to it," Henrietta responded calmly, without a hint of rancour. "You do underestimate me, you always have, in the matter of my grasp of life's intricacies."

"But *how* did you—?"

"Guess? How would I not? Your cousin was determined to do something for you, to 'set you up.' That Ralph Touchett loved you, that you were the passion of his life, was the plainest fact about that anything but plain, that deeply subtle person."

Isabel opened her eyes wide. "And I thought you held him in such low regard!"

"My dear, my dear, have you not grasped even yet how deplorably, how dismayingly, how endearingly wrong you have been about so many things?"

"Of course I have—I have known for years of my mistakes, my catastrophic misapprehensions, only I did not know that everyone else knew of them too." She lifted the coffee cup to her lips, and finding the coffee cold she peered at her watch. "What is the time? Heavens, it's midnight! I didn't notice the tolling of the hour."

"We have till dawn, if that's what it takes," Henrietta said.

"Shall I call for more coffee? No? But let us turn out the lamps—they give me such an ache behind the eyes. Will you be content with candles?"

"Of course. That's all we have, in Rome. We're very backward there, as you know. I think you wrote about it once, our Roman backwardness, for the New York papers."

"No," Henrietta corrected, smiling, "it was for the Boston *Atlantic,* and for a far more substantial fee than ever I would have got from the New York *Interviewer!*"

The maid was summoned to renew the candles in a big brass candelabrum, majestically suggestive of the synagogue, that stood on the mantelpiece in exotic splendour. Isabel enquired of the by now positively somnolent maid, as she applied flame to wicks, how Staines was faring, and was informed that the person in question was happily set up in a very nice little room behind the scullery, complete with cot and candle, and had retired all of an hour ago; the faintly resentful tone in which this information was imparted bore the implication that the visiting servant enjoyed a position of pampered privilege unheard-of below stairs in this establishment. "I can rouse her, if Madam wishes," the girl said, with a discernibly vindictive glint, but Isabel said no, no, there was nothing that she needed. The flaring candles sent shadows leaping up the walls, and the window-panes became gleamingly opaque again.

Isabel felt at once exhausted and agitated. The matters she had been made to face before her daring departure from Rome—she had the sense of having been grasped at the back of the neck and thrust hard up against them—jostled before her now, like so many monstrous chunks of the tumbling masonry of her life. She wished to relate the painful tale of her misfortunes, indeed she would sit up until dawn to do it, as Henrietta had suggested she might, but there was too much of it for her to know which jagged block to fix on first. It was Henrietta, however, who impelled the narrative on its way by reverting to the topic of what she considered, as would soon show, to have been the keystone of the entire edifice. "I wonder," she said, "how well-advised your cousin was in his magnanimity towards you."

"Well-advised?" Isabel frowningly responded. "I believe Ralph was his own adviser, and took scant account of the counsel of others."

"Oh, I have no doubt that was the case."

The ironical emphasis Henrietta laid upon her words served to deepen Isabel's frown.

"I don't understand what you mean," she said.

"What I mean, my dear Isabel, is simply—simply!—that your greatest troubles, your greatest *trouble,* I should say, since I deem you singularly misfortunate, sprang like a rank flower out of the heap of money that the Touchetts, father and son, so freely, so cavalierly, laid at your feet."

Isabel, marvelling briefly, not without amusement, at Henrietta's unwonted rhetorical flourishes—it was not for nothing indeed that she had been long among the English!—shrugged in dismissive acquiescence. "What you say is true, in part at least, but you can hardly blame my *trouble,* as you call it, on my cousin's generosity of spirit."

"Are you sure his generosity was entirely spiritual?"

Isabel sat back in her chair, as if to take the benefit of a longer view, and gazed at her friend in perplexity. "Are you suggesting my cousin was driven by some base motive to persuade his father to leave me a portion of his fortune?"

"I don't believe your cousin was capable of the least baseness," Miss Stackpole hastened to declare, "and I should say so even if he were not lately dead and deserving of all respect. He loved you, as we have agreed, and wished to see you thrive in the world. You are the kind of young woman, daring, agile, supremely self-composed—"

"Oh, come!" Isabel cried, with a deprecating laugh. Her friend, however, would not be balked.

"—the kind of young woman," she went on, "whom people watch, and envy, and inwardly urge on, even when they see clearly, which you do not, the precipice towards which your bounding stride is taking you."

Here Isabel thought to enter a renewed plea of protest, but paused. Had she not acknowledged, herself, the degree to which her frail and ailing cousin had lived, or sought to live, through a vicarious participation in her life? He had tacitly approved when she rejected Caspar Goodwood, and had stood back in breathless awe at her refusal of Lord Warburton; that a girl in her position—for this was in the time before she had any prospect of a fortune—should spurn a man of Warburton's wealth and stature in the world surely betokened a spirit that nothing could prevent from achieving the very pinnacle of its potential. But perhaps that was the trouble: Ralph had wanted wonders of her. That he had it in his power to fund her fearless ascent of the sheer rock-face of her—of his!—ambitions must have seemed to him the justification, the compensation, for his having to bide below, in the shadowed valley, while she scaled the radiant heights. And what a drab disappointment it must have been for him that instead of pressing onwards to the peak she had lost her footing and plunged headlong down the sheer cliff that Henrietta had spoken of just now.

"We all had a hand in urging you on," her friend said, and gave a quick little sigh. "I certainly don't hold myself innocent in the disastrous course you took—"

"Disastrous?" Isabel pleaded almost piteously, in a small weak voice.

"You seemed to us whatever is the female version of a 'parfit gentil knight.' When you were about we smiled at each other in the secret hooded way that parents do when their child is independently brilliant in front of a class of worthy dullards. We bragged of you. I depicted you—anonymously, don't worry—in articles I knew you would never stoop to read, as the very epitome of young American womanhood comporting itself beautifully, oh, beautifully, before the wondering eyes of fusty old Europe. You were our blazon!"

Here she stopped, and turned her face determinedly away, whether in impatience, anger or regret, Isabel could not tell.

"What a sad let-down I must have been for you all, in that case," she miserably said.

Henrietta whirled upon her in an outburst of passion. "We were furious at you, furious! You had so much, and you exchanged it for"—she scrabbled after a formulation that would match the enormity of the case, but fixed instead on a desiccated puniness— "a pinch of dry dust that would fall through your fingers and leave not a trace!"

This made Isabel wince. Was she not, in her torments, to be afforded even a touch of the tragic? But Henrietta's image was apt, after all: she was in a dry place, in a parched season, with not a sign of fructifying rains.

"I'm sorry," Henrietta said, curbing her outrage with a visible effort and looking to left and right of her with bird-like twitches. "I have no right to speak to you in this way. You never asked us to have expectations of you. It is for you to live your life according to your convictions. I grieve that you're unhappy now, and only wish that you may be happy again in the future."

To this Isabel could but bow her head. Henrietta rose from her chair, disturbing the candle flames and causing the phantom shadows around her on the walls to prance and plunge. As Isabel had done earlier, she now set herself at the window above the deserted street. "Oh, look at the moon," she inconsequently murmured, craning forward to peer up between the houses into the summer night's humid, deep-violet sky. "What will happen," she asked, without turning, "when you return to Rome?"

"Ah, I cannot think of that now," Isabel said, with weary dismissiveness. "It's what happened before I left that is taking all of my thoughts."

"You told me before you went down to Gardencourt that if you go back—"

"*When* I go back," Isabel dully intoned.

"—that your husband will not make a scene, at least not in the ordinary sense."

What Isabel had said was that Osmond would make a scene that would continue relentlessly for the rest of her life. But she saw no sense in iterating that insight now. "What will happen will happen, as my stoical Italian neighbours say. I have little influence in the matter."

Now Henrietta did turn her head, and, looking back over her shoulder, studied her friend for a moment in silence. "But you have intentions?" she said. "You have a plan, surely."

"Yes, I have a plan, of a sort. It is a consequence of a number of things I learned before I came away. It all fell upon me in a tearing rush."

"All?"

"Yes, there was much of it. Though it came in segments, it felt all of a piece. It was as if a wardrobe had toppled over on one—

a large part of it was witnessing one's own image in the door-mirror smashing into shards."

Henrietta moved from the window and resumed her seat. The candles the maid had lighted, Isabel noticed, had already burned some way down, and as yet she had done not much more than tug at the fringes of her tale to straighten them.

"There must be somewhere for you to begin," Henrietta said, in her practical way.

"Begin to tell you all that happened, you mean? It was not so much a matter of things happening, as of things—coming out."

"Secrets, you mean? Revelations?"

Isabel reflected. "Well, there was one deliberate act. My husband banished his daughter to a convent. She had been there before, and now he sent her back for another taste of confinement. It was tantamount to condemning her to a penal colony."

"Dear Lord!" Henrietta indignantly exclaimed. "What on earth had the child done to merit such correction?"

"She fell in love with the wrong man—wrong in the eyes of her father, that is. He was an inoffensive poor fellow, her swain, but Pansy would have him and no other."

"So her father had her incarcerated! It's like something out of the Middle Ages. Your husband has been so long in Europe he has lost the last traces of American egalitarianism. People over here think they're so civilised, but they're savages compared to—why, to a hall full of New Jersey teamsters!"

Isabel was pulling absent-mindedly with the fingers of her right hand at a loose filament in the lace at her left wrist. "Her father," she said quietly, and as if distracted, "wished her to marry Lord Warburton."

"Lord—?" Miss Stackpole could not summon the name for

outrage, and her eyes bulged with the force of it. "Tell me it's not so."

"Well, it's not—but it might have been. The gentleman indicated an interest."

"Why, the thing is unnatural—he must be near thrice times the girl's age!"

"Oh, not so much as that. But there would have been a not inconsiderable gap, I grant you."

"Did he—did he ask for her hand? I mean, did he utter the words?"

"It did not get that far. Pansy loves, or loved, Mr. Rosier—Ned Rosier, I think you met him, in Rome?—and Lord Warburton, being the man he is, saw that he was not favoured, and withdrew. He conducted himself throughout with the greatest delicacy and discretion. Only my husband fixed upon it that I had interfered—"

"Interfered?"

"Yes; that I had put Lord Warburton off, so to say, out of jealousy, or vindictiveness, or the simple pleasure of thwarting my husband's fine and subtle scheme. From this if nothing else you will see how little he knows me, despite the years he has had in which to observe me." She paused; Henrietta, she saw, was looking at her with what appeared a faint shade of doubt. "Please say," Isabel went on, with almost a hint of playfulness, "please say, Henrietta Stackpole, that *you* do not suspect me capable of such meddling."

XI

The candles had consumed another inch of wax when Isabel gave in to her fatigue at last and announced that she must, she simply must, go to her bed. Beyond the large gaunt parlour Henrietta's lodgings broke up into a seemingly endless warren of what were little more than cells, and Isabel was reminded of the convent of San Marco in Florence, where Fra Angelico's murals adorn the walls of so many similar little square low-ceilinged chambers. The quarters she had been allotted were a sort of cabinet-with-bed that she guessed must be not much bigger than Staines's lair behind the scullery. She undressed and lay down on the narrow cot and composed herself for sleep. Henrietta had sent her off with a fresh candle, and when she had extinguished it, the smoky impenetrable darkness seemed to press in from all sides and crowd about her menacingly. For all that her aching mind yearned for blessed oblivion, she could not sleep, and at last she got up and sat on a rickety, rush-bottomed chair by the window with her chin resting on her fist. Above the darkly gleaming rooftops with their deep-shadowed chimney pots hung the same full moon that Henrietta had exclaimed at earlier. To Isabel it had the look of a big round lumpy clay-coloured face peering at her askance, with a gloating smirk.

In the long interval that they had sat together, Isabel had related to her friend no more than a fraction of the tale she had to tell. She wondered now if perhaps that had been for the best— what was to be gained by undoing all at once the stiffened rags in which her wounds were wrapped? She had concealed those wounds for so long, for years and years, thinking it her duty to suffer in silence, but what if that reticence were only another mark of her arrogance, her overweening self-regard? Once, somewhere in the vast ornate barn of the Vatican, she had come upon a statue of St. Sebastian, not quite life-sized, as is so often the case with the figures in that great basilica—it was as if for the Church of Rome the majority of her saints had stopped short at adolescence— which, when her eye fell on it, set up in her a small shiver of revulsion. It seemed plain from the appearance of the martyr, with his creamy flesh, his upturned and passionately anguished eyes, his slackly parted crimson lips that found a repeated echo in the bleeding slits where the arrow shafts were embedded, that his suffering was in fact a form of ecstasy. She feared that was how she would appear to others should she make public her pain. But she was no sanguinate martyr; nor did she intend to seem to be.

All at once she gave a start—she had fallen without noticing it into a kind of sleep and her fist had slipped from under her chin—and she rose from the chair now and got into bed quickly, so as to exploit the onset of drowsiness, and firmly closed her eyes. For a little while her mind resisted the Lethean pull upon it, but soon the current of sleep caught her up and swept her away.

She woke in daylight and did not know where she was, which for some seconds caused in her a muffled panic. It was early, for the sunlight coming in at the mean little window beside the bed was brittle and lacked warmth. In these latitudes at this time of year there was hardly any night to speak of, only an intensified glimmering twilight that lasted the few hours between the final going down of the sun and its hurried coming up again. She lay motionless, gazing up blankly at the mottled ceiling, where damp-stains, long dried, resembled a map of a world different from this one yet perfectly plausible in itself, complete with oceans and continents, islands and archipelagos, shorelines and lakes and mountain ranges. She hoped it was not so early that she would have to bide here long alone: she felt an unaccustomed yearning for the everyday human concourse. Usually she was content with her own company, but this morning she wanted, yes, she eagerly looked forward to the mindless bustle and business of the matutinal hour. In the end she had slept well enough, for however short a time. It did not seem to matter where she laid her head nowadays, since there was no longer a bed anywhere that she could properly call her own.

Presently, to her relief, Staines appeared, starched and brisk as always, bringing tea and toast on a silver tray, along with a copy of *The Times*, folded as firmly as an Englishman's umbrella and smelling, so it distinctly seemed to Isabel, of the smoothing-iron. If the journal had been pressed before being offered to her it would be the sallow-faced maid, and certainly not Staines, who had wielded the iron; nor surely had the vital service been carried out at the behest of a mistress as democratically minded as Henri-etta; no, it would have been done at the direction of Mr. Bantling, surely, in whose family this little ritual was probably a tradition stretching back to the first invention of the daily news-sheet.

Staines nodded dourly towards the steadily burgeoning sun-light in the window. "Going to be a scorcher," she intoned, as of one announcing the imminence of the Apocalypse.

"That will be nice," Isabel murmured distractedly, drawing herself up in the bed and arranging the pillows into a plump support for her back. "There's a thing," she went on, "that I wish you to do, without delay."

"Yes, madam," Staines said, and sniffed. Staines's day was strictly demarcated along the lines of her own regulations and precepts, and breakfast time, according to her scheme, was the time for breakfast and nothing else, certainly not for the giving and receiving of directives of a practical nature. This morning, however, Isabel was disinclined to abide by her maid's rules.

"Please reserve two seats on an early train at Charing Cross," she said, "connecting with the first manageable ferry to Calais."

"*Calais?*" the maid as good as yelped—the destination her mistress had named might as well have been Timbuctoo.

"Yes, and then please book for the express onwards to Paris."

Here the maid hesitated: she did not care for surprises, and the announcement that they were to be on their way again so precipitately certainly had surprised her; on the other hand, the news that they were to go to Paris was not unwelcome, for Paris she *did* like, despite the persistent presence there of French people. And so, on balance, she was willing, insofar as she could ever permit herself to enter upon such an uncontentious state of mind.

The reason for Isabel's haste in setting forth was a thing that Henrietta had told her in the early hours of the morning, when they had parted in candlelight at the door of Isabel's cellular little room; the thing imparted was that Caspar Goodwood had telegraphed to ask if he might call here at Wimpole Street this morning, and if the hour of eleven o'clock would be a suitable time for him to appear on Henrietta's doorstep. "And what did you say?" Isabel had cried. "What did you tell him?" Why, that he would be more than welcome, Henrietta had calmly answered, while Isabel had stared at her dumbly, shaking her head in a kind of frenzy of denial. She wondered again now how her friend could have done such a thing, how she could have invited that good man, of all men, to present himself at these lodgings when she knew Isabel would be here. The only observation Henrietta had offered, as they stood by the light of the candle, like a pair of carven busts facing each other in a gallery at night, was that she had not known that Mr. Goodwood's ardour had been rekindled—she had assumed that flame had long since died, for want of fuel—or that he had actively renewed his passionate pursuit of a lady who had refused him more than once and was, into the bargain, married. Isabel was not at all sure she had believed this account, delivered as it was with such wide-eyed candour that it seemed it must be a mask of disingenuousness. Had Henrietta apprised Mr. Goodwood of the fact that Isabel would be here? No, Henrietta airily replied, she had not thought it any concern of the gentleman as to who should or should not be in the house when he called. This only served to deepen Isabel's suspicions. Her friend was a person of the highest probity but, as we have already noted, she had been an energetic promoter of Mr. Goodwood's cause in the days when Isabel's hand was still for the having, and as recently as two weeks ago she had openly urged Isabel to break with her husband and lay claim once more to her independence, to the extent that such a condition was represented in the person of Mr. Goodwood. Was it impossible that Henrietta should have stifled temporarily her commitment to strict honesty and frankness for the possibility of a happier future for her at present unhappy friend, under the care of a man who, by tenacity of purpose if nothing else, had demonstrated that he genuinely valued and truly loved her? But Isabel, having lately learned how drastically her fate had been tampered with by people pretending to want only the best for her, was in no mood to accept another piece of interference in her affairs, no matter how well-intentioned. She had not, last night, pressed

Henrietta further on the matter of Mr. Goodwood's promised, or better say threatened, visit this morning, not least because she had no wish to catch out her friend in a falsehood, albeit a benign one—benign, that is to say, according to Henrietta's lights—but had determined simply to be gone from Wimpole Street with the greatest possible dispatch, even if it did make her feel a little like a financially embarrassed hotel guest engaging in a "flit."

Now as she sat leaning back against the pile of pillows and sipped her tea and nibbled at a slice of toast, deriving from neither the least savour, she could not prevent her thoughts from returning speculatively to the possibility Henrietta had brought to her mind, that her cousin Ralph, by arranging without her knowledge that a fortune should be settled upon her, had all unintentionally done her a grave disservice. It was a notion that Ralph himself had raised, when on his deathbed he had wondered aloud, in an access of anguish, if he had not ruined her—"ruined" was the very term he had used, but at the time Isabel had not understood, or had not wished to understand, what he might mean by it. That he had intended the money to make her happy and free she did not doubt by a whit; but had he had the right, she wondered now, so to interfere—there was that word again, she could not resist it—in the course and conditions of her life? She had always set a great store by the concept of personal independence: each life is given once, with no possibility of repetition or revision, and the individual actor on whom the vivifying gift is bestowed must play his hour upon the stage with unflagging conviction and in the full realisation that there will be only an opening night, with no "run" to follow. What justification had anyone to leave his seat and step on to the stage and seek to redirect the action?

She put away her cup and closed her eyes and covered them with a hand. These were wicked thoughts to think of a person so recently dead, a person, moreover, who had loved her unreservedly, without hope of having anything of her for himself, save the harmless pleasure of murmuring *"Brava!"* and casting a rose at her feet, before the interval curtain came down, to encourage her performance in the second half. And yet, she reflected, life is not a metaphor, is not a dramatic monologue or a dazzling circus act. It is a mundane project, carried out not in powdered air or on burnished boards, but upon plain ground, without the transfiguring touch of art, without transports of any kind, except on those occasions, rare and precious, when in ordinary daylight, and impelled by mysterious powers larger than ourselves, we seem to see the world before us burst into unearthly radiance. It was in expectation of knowing such moments, as many of them as she could bear, that Isabel had come to Europe. But Europe had proved a much more muted place than her fancy had made it into before ever she had landed on its shores. Experiences had come to her here, experiences rich and full, but from none of them had there flashed a fire sufficiently strong to sear her soul—not until, so recently, so unexpectedly, so incomprehensibly, she had found herself burning in Caspar Goodwood's embrace, when in the lush blue twilight at Gardencourt, beside the old stone bench, he had grasped her in his electric embrace and branded her with a kiss. Before all else, before the revelations in Rome and her flight from that city, before the treachery of Serena Merle and the unmasking of her husband, before even—God forgive her!—before even the death of her beloved cousin, the fact of that kiss, and the heaped pyre of possibilities it had set alight inside her, took all precedence, consumed all oxygen, and set her staggering backwards, clutching at her throat and gasping for breath. That was the reason she was so soon in flight again. It was not Caspar Goodwood's unwanted attentions that had caused her to flee, but the fear of being touched again by that transforming fire. Nor was it the man himself she was frightened of, but the disembodied menace he represented: he was a form of infernal paraclete.

A half-hour later she found Henrietta in the parlour, standing at the bay window with her back to the room. She did not turn at the sound of Isabel's step, although Isabel was sure she had heard it. From the stiffness of her stance it was plain that she was cross, and more than cross.

"I'm told you are to leave straight away," she said, without turning.

"Yes," Isabel murmured. "I sent Staines to make the bookings. Has she returned yet, do you know?"

"Hardly—Thomas Cook's is not so near as that."

"Of course, of course." The silence stretched itself between them, like a fine elastic cord. "Won't you at least look at me?" Isabel pleaded. "I feel very badly, to spurn your hospitality in this way."

"Oh, a fig for my hospitality!" Henrietta said, and turned about with such rapidity she might have spun on a pivot. "It's not my hospitality you should feel badly for, but something and someone else entirely."

"Yes, I know," Isabel responded meekly, and bowed her head. Then she gave herself a sort of hopeless shake. "You don't understand, Henrietta," she softly wailed. "I cannot face him— I cannot!"

"Cannot, or dare not?" her friend unrelentingly returned.

"Oh, what is the difference!"

"You're running away, like a frightened rabbit," Henrietta pronounced, with a narrow glare. "I should have expected better of you, Isabel Archer."

"Ah, you call me by my old name," Isabel said, with an attempt at a mollifying smile.

"It's your true and only name, in my mind," Henrietta said implacably. "Since you will not rid yourself of the dreadful man who took it from you in the first place, I reserve the right to restore it to you, if only for my own satisfaction."

Isabel, fatigued suddenly although she was not long risen from rest, went and sat down on the unwelcoming sofa, and folded her hands in her lap. Henrietta remained standing with her back to the window, fixed upon her despairingly. "Mr. Goodwood is due at eleven; it is now"—she consulted her watch—"very nearly nine-thirty, and your maid has not returned. Shall I telegraph, and see if I can put him off? He is at a hotel in Piccadilly."

Isabel shook her head. "If necessary I shall go and wait in some square, until it's time for the train. The day is sunny, I should welcome the open air for a while."

Henrietta sighed exasperatedly. In the old days she had found it hard to remain vexed at her friend for any extended time, and it was no different now. "Come and take one of these armchairs," she said, "that sofa is impossible—even Robert refuses to sit on it."

"Oh, Mr. Bantling!" Isabel exclaimed vaguely. "I had quite forgot about him. Have you spoken to him this morning? Did he do well at his card game?"

This enquiry Henrietta set aside as unworthy of reply. "It would be distressing for all concerned," she said, "were we to encounter Mr. Goodwood just as you're in the act of taking to your heels."

"Oh, Henrietta!" Isabel murmured, shaking her head. "I see I have made you very angry. I'm sorry." She looked again to the window where her friend stood, and to the light of the summer morning sparkling on the glass. "I really should like to go outside. Is there a grassy spot with a bench? In London one is never far from a park, I certainly remember that. We can leave a note for Staines, to tell her where I am."

Henrietta delivered herself of a distinctly unladylike snort. "I must say I am surprised at you, wanting to run and hide like this. It's not the behaviour of the person I thought I knew in former days."

"I'm afraid that person is no more," Isabel sadly responded. "She finally expired some weeks ago, in Rome, at the end of what might be said to have been a wasting illness—I have that much in common with my cousin."

Henrietta, forgetting her anger for the moment, looked at her friend in frank dismay. "You shock me, Isabel, but you worry me more. I knew your life had taken a turn for the worse—"

"That's what they say of the mortally ill," Isabel interposed, with a smile expressive of gallows gaiety.

"—but I did not realise," Henrietta pressed on, content to sustain the morbid note, "the gravity of your condition. I think you're right: that man you insisted on marrying had near killed you. Mark, I say *near:* you are not beyond saving, not by a long way, my girl, if I, and others of a like mind to me, have anything to do with it!"

On the strength of this stoutly affirming pledge the two friends left the room together, in an unaccountably lightened mood, and descended to the hall. There Isabel pressed a sovereign into the damp palm of the sleepy maid and instructed her to tell Staines to summon a hansom and come with the luggage and look for her at— She turned questioningly to Henrietta, who named Cavendish Square as being but a short walk away. Then the ladies donned their straw hats and, equipped with a pair of lace parasols, sallied forth into the morning.

The day was not quite as fresh as it had seemed when it was shining in at the panes of Henrietta's bay window. There was dust in the air, and a dull brown smell of carriage horses, and the sunlight had a dingy cast, so that Isabel was surprised to find in herself a sudden longing for the pellucid air of Italy. Perhaps that country, the glory of the south, was more of home to her than she had realised. The possibility struck at her with an edge of cold steel. She had conceived of her return to Rome as a matter of grim duty; it would be nothing less than a scandal if she were to get something out of it, something for herself, even if it were to be no more than the sense of a sweet homecoming. The matters she would have to attend to there would leave her bruised and bleeding, or, to figure it less heroically, would smear her with slime from top to toe. She would rather not to have to go back, much rather; at first she had thought of fleeing Europe altogether and returning to her native shores, and might have gone, indeed almost certainly would have gone, save that the final remark Madame Merle had made to her at their last meeting was that she herself would "go to America," a thing that for Isabel would have been tantamount to the sowing of that great good land with salt. Besides, it was not in her nature to shirk her duty and shrink from the things that must be dealt with. Always it had been a prominent part of her idea of herself that in life one may preserve the shreds of honour only by facing up squarely to one's misdeeds and gross misprisions—facing up to them was the only way of facing them down. But of the sins that had been committed in the unhappy and less than Edenic fields to which she had lately been forced to say farewell, even such a passionate penitent as she was could make out no sins of her own that were more than venial, compared at least to the enormities committed by others. She had examined her conscience thoroughly in this matter and, wont as she was to blame herself before others, she failed to see how she could be held the first accountable for the fall into those retributive flames in which she, and Madame Merle, and even Madame Merle's daughter—that precious and misfortunate innocent!—were now being consumed. Yes, she had given in to pride, that pride indeed which cometh before the fall; yes, she had wilfully ignored the counsels of those who loved and revered her; yes, she had married Gilbert Osmond out of—was it mere stubbornness? Yes, yes, yes, she had done these things, but surely she could say, and not for any effort at self-exoneration, that worse, far worse, had been done to her.

XII

Cavendish Square Gardens proved to be, in the endearingly eccentric way that London has of arranging these things, perfectly circular. There had been a long drought, and the grass was crisp underfoot, and the trees looked decidedly dejected, their foliage being more grey than green. The densely moted air occluded the morning sun's vigorous rays, and the traffic grinding its way around the square, like a malfunctioning carousel, seemed unnaturally clamorous. Isabel and her friend found a shaded bench and arranged themselves upon it as comfortably as the hard slats beneath and behind them would allow. Already their footwear was uniformly hazed over with a fine film of beige dust. Isabel remarked idly on the daintiness of the parasols they had carried out with them—one was pink, the other a translucent shade of baby-blue—and Henrietta was quick to observe that they had been left behind by successive and now forgotten summer visitors, for surely no one would imagine for a moment that *she* would have stooped to the purchasing of anything so frivolously feminine. Isabel suppressed a smile; she was always struck by the number and variety of social solecisms her dear friend was afraid the world would suspect her capable of. She had never forgotten, although she dearly wished she could, the occasion at table during

an overnight stay at the abode of Lord Warburton and his sisters—
Lord W. was one of the not very numerous Englishmen of whom
it could be said with perfect accuracy that his home was indeed
his castle—she had noted how, as each new course was laid before
her, Henrietta would hesitate and cast a sharp but covert glance
about her to see which implement the other diners should choose
from the gleaming array laid out to right and left of their plates,
before daring to pick up knife or fork or spoon herself.

"I *am* sorry, you know," Isabel said now, with friendly emphasis, "to be compelled to leave you so soon and so abruptly."

" 'Compelled'?" Henrietta responded sonorously, her sarcasm
mitigated by a smile. "I say again, you seem deplorably changed
from the person I knew you to be hitherto. *That* person would
have bowed to no one's, and certainly no man's, compulsion."

"And I say again," Isabel, also smiling, insisted, "that the person you speak of, *that* version of me, is no more."

"Pshaw!" Henrietta vulgarly exclaimed; it was one of her most
favoured expletives. "That 'version' of you, as you call it, is cra-
venly in hiding, and nothing more."

"Well, if so, I wonder whom it could be that I am in hiding
from."

Henrietta turned upon her another of those looks Mr. Bantling
would admiringly characterise as "large." "Why, from yourself!"
she pronounced. "Whom else, in the world, are you so frightened
of? Oh, I know you, Isabel Archer. The most monstrous ghouls
might parade before you, clanking their chains and keening, and
not a hair on your head will turn, but set you square in front of a
looking-glass and you will start back from your own image with
piercing cries of fright."

"But is that not true of all of us?" Isabel proposed, after a moment's cogitation. "Nothing is as uncanny as the look of one's own eyes peering out of a glass."

"That's only so for those who spend overly much time reflecting on their own reflections."

"You are unkind, dear Henrietta, to harp so on my vanity!" Isabel said with a light laugh. "It is only one, after all, among my many besetting sins."

"It's not your vanity I am thinking of," her friend complacently returned, "although you are vain, I grant you."

Despite the mildness with which these words were uttered, they struck a sharp note.

"What is it then you *are* thinking of?" Isabel demanded, with equal measures of impatience, humour and misgiving.

For a long moment Henrietta said no word, only sat very straight on the bench and gazed at her friend with tightened lips and a kind of grimly speculating air. Then abruptly she clapped her palms on her knees and stood up. "Come, let us make a circuit in the sun—you'll be trapped for long enough in railway carriages, smothered amid smoke and cinders."

The sunshine had intensified even in the short interval while they were seated, although its fieriness was somewhat tempered by an intrepid little breeze that was making a muttering in the leaves of the tall trees above them. As they set off along the perimeter path Henrietta linked her arm in Isabel's in a token of easy friendliness. Isabel turned her head to cast a glance behind her; she was wondering how long it would be before Staines would come for her with the carriage. Since the decision to leave had been forced on her, by the prospect of Caspar Goodwood's imminent appearance, she was anxious to be on her way.

"You must find me a frightful scold," Henrietta said, without, however, the slightest note of apology or remorse. "But I hope you know how I care about you and worry for your welfare." She allowed a brief pause, then pressed Isabel's arm more tightly to her side. "I wish, my dear, you would tell me what happened in Rome. I know it was bad, and I cannot bear for you to go off and leave me to speculate. I shall imagine the most monstrous things."

Isabel smiled a little to herself; she doubted so fine and decent an imaginative faculty as her friend possessed would be capable of generating a concept of wickednesses commensurate with those that had been visited upon her in Rome.

"Well, then, if only to spare you sleepless nights of wasted speculation, I shall tell you all—or as much as I know, for such is the web of deceit in which I'm caught up I cannot be sure there are not more predators readying themselves to spring out at me."

"Heavens," Henrietta breathed. "Is it really so heinous?"

A black-clad nurse passed them by on the dusty pathway, pushing before her a perambulator as shiny and glidingly buoyant as a truncated gondola, from the white satin depths of which a somewhat mottled tiny pink face peered out, with that expression of dazed astonishment, eyes wide and soft lips formed into a tiny round, with which babies regard the brightly lit and unaccountably populous place they have so recently arrived in. Catching Isabel's glance, the creature lifted higher still its invisible brows and drew in its extensible neck in what seemed a deepened access of alarm. Isabel thought of her own child, who had been so frail and had died so soon he could hardly be said to have been fully born at all. Gilberto, the creature was called, a pallid speck of failing life that had flickered out after a mere six months upon this earth. Sometimes, especially in her increasingly sleepless nights, she tormented herself with the thought that the child might have lived if she had loved him more.

"Do you remember," she asked, "my husband's sister Amy, the Countess Gemini?"

Henrietta delivered herself of another of those snorts of hers that were rarely noticed "at home" but that had temporarily silenced many a dinner table on this side of the great dividing ocean. "I should think I do!" she said animatedly. "Who could forget such a person?" She stopped and stared. "Don't say it is *she* who has gotten her talons into you?"

"No no," Isabel answered. "In fact she did me a service, though whether it was intended to be in my best interest or not I cannot say." They walked on. Isabel had begun to suffer from the dusty heat, but she did not wish to sit down again, finding the slow, deliberate pace conducive to the baring of her heart, to the shedding of her secrets. "She told me something, my sister-in-law, something I had not known, that had been kept hidden from me for—oh, for years."

She was silent for some paces, made speechless by the thought of the scale of the thing.

"Kept from you by whom?" Henrietta enquired, with a gentleness expressive of the keenness of the sympathy she felt for her suffering friend. It might be supposed that a person of Miss Stackpole's profession, an assiduous observer of the world's ways, the crooked as well as the straight, and a colourful reporter on them to her distant and numerous readers, would have been avid that there should be disclosed to her in all their awful detail the hidden horrors of a society into which this dearest of her friends had allowed herself to be lured for the capture. Henrietta, however, awaited Isabel's confession with nothing but the deepest dread, and wished only that what she was about to hear might prove laughably innocuous, the account of a few trifling troubles grossly inflated by a mind fantastically at odds with itself. But the look of

Isabel's drawn features, which were of a shade of grey against the bounding green of summer, told her unmistakably what she was "in for."

"It was a thing," Isabel said, in a low, urgent voice, with her gaze fixed fiercely on the path before her, "that the countess had known of for years—that she had known of from the start, but had been too afraid to tell me, until the time came when even she could no longer countenance my being left in the dark."

"Afraid—?"

"Of her brother, my husband, of course; of him, and of Serena Merle."

Henrietta frowned. Madame Merle's was not a name she had expected to hear mentioned in the tale that at last was beginning to be unfolded before her, but now, when she did hear it, she was surprised to find herself unsurprised. She had seen little of this lady, and knew less, but what she had seen, and what she did know, left her in no doubt as to what such a person would be capable of, and the lengths she would go to in achieving her ends. And despite the warmth of the sun on her back, the staunch young woman felt a chill shiver along her spine.

They had progressed sufficiently far around the circle of greenery for them now to encounter once more the dark-suited nurse and her tiny charge. This time Isabel carefully avoided looking at the startled pink face framed in satin within the hood, and passed on quickly. When she began to speak again the words tumbled out of her in a sullen, low monotone.

"Amy told me many things, of which the most remarkable, to say the least, was that my husband's first wife had no child. Yes, yes, there is Pansy, I know, and she is Osmond's daughter. Until the time when she was born he was living in Naples, although he and his wife were elsewhere—in Piedmont, if I have it right—

when the poor woman supposedly died in childbirth. He was fortunate in the way the dates fell out—he was always fortunate in such things, I see that now; the luck of the devil, you may say." She gave a brief laugh, which sounded, however, more like a harsh sigh. "He returned from Piedmont, and thereafter left Naples, a widower with a little daughter, and settled in Florence, in rented apartments on the hill of Bellosguardo. As to where Madame Merle made off to, I do not know."

Henrietta as good as gaped. "Where she 'made off to'?"

"Yes. She must have gone somewhere, to recover herself. The lady has always a place to go to, a place that will accommodate her in return for the pleasure of her company and of her many social gifts, and I'm sure she had then, as well."

Once more Henrietta stopped in her tracks, although this time Isabel did not stop with her, but went on, with her head down, her gait, dull and determined, resembling that of an automaton.

"You mean," Henrietta said to her retreating back, and set off hurriedly and soon caught her up, "you mean Madame Merle—?"

"Yes," Isabel said, with a pursed vehemence, and this time it was her turn to halt. "Yes, Serena Merle is Pansy Osmond's mother."

XIII

Henrietta could not decide which she found the more shocking: the things she was being told or the effect the telling of them had upon her friend. In the space of but a few minutes Isabel seemed to have grown older by many years, indeed by many decades. It was as if the young woman that she was had been replaced by the hunched and desiccated crone that she might be expected to turn into only in the far-off reaches of the future. If Henrietta had not been thoroughly convinced already of the weight and extent of her friend's misery, this sudden transformation, the spectacle of which shook her to her solid core, would have banished all doubt. At a point in their long talk of the previous night Isabel had recalled that when she first came to Europe she had looked about at so much softly abraded antiquity and had become on the spot impatient of her own lack of years. Untried and rough-edged, as she appeared to herself, she had felt acutely the want of a finish that only time and the accumulation of experience could effect. But might it not be, she wondered, that in her impetuousness she had raced where she should have sauntered, pounced where she should have paused? Had she robbed herself of her own youth? Isabel's companion, in the stillness of the summer midnight, had listened to these rueful musings and tactfully kept her counsel; in her view of the constitution of things it was a flouting of the fundamental laws of life to seek to be something other than one was. She was aware of the moral questions such a prescription begged were it to be applied to, say, the Emperor Caligula, or King Richard III or, for that matter, Gilbert Osmond and his malign familiar Madame Merle; but for Henrietta such creatures existed in an altogether other dimension, a cool crystalline place of the damned, sealed off by a pane of thick and impenetrable plate-glass from the sphere inhabited by herself and Isabel and others like them, such as Mr. Bantling, and Caspar Goodwood, and, oh, a host of decent fair right-thinking people. If to Henrietta's eye her friend had a fault, it was that, like the stern-faced Germanic thinkers whose works she claimed to revere, she devoted an unconscionable degree of speculation to questions entirely incapable of solution. Philosophy, in the opinion of the correspondent of the New York *Interviewer*, was a harmless diversion from the true brisk business of being human, which was nothing more and nothing less than to live a harmonious, fulfilled and useful life.

"Forgive me," she said now, "if I seem to be pressing upon an open wound, but I need to be clear in my mind as to the details of this matter: You are saying, are you not, that your husband's daughter is the child not of the late Mrs. Osmond, but one that he and the Merle woman had together?"

Hearing herself say it, she felt she should apologise for the bluntness of her words, but Isabel took the question plain and straight, which was how it had been delivered, and did not shy from it.

"Yes, that is the secret the Countess Gemini revealed to me, but a few weeks ago, in my house, in Rome."

Henrietta said nothing for a time, turning the thing over in wonderment, breathless before the thought of such a studiedly sustained and horrible subterfuge.

"And the daughter, Pansy," she asked at last, "is she aware of her true origins?"

"No, of course not. They kept it hidden from her—they kept it hidden from everyone, so clever were they, so circumspect."

"But the sister, the countess—?"

"Oh, she knew, of course."

"But how? Had her brother confided in her?" This possibility was posed in an extreme of incredulity.

"I don't know how she knew," Isabel calmly replied. "I did not ask." She smiled despite herself. "There is not much that can be kept from Amy Osmond, and I feel sure it was ever thus, especially in the case of a suppressed scandal as deliciously well-seasoned as this one."

Henrietta, struggling to encompass and absorb all that she had so far heard, walked along with a pace as dully automatic as her friend's had been a minute previously, putting down her feet one after the other with a heaviness indicative of the difficulty she had in coming to terms with a state of affairs entirely incommensurate with her conception of how people should comport themselves in regard to, in regard *for*, their fellow human beings. It must be remarked also, though in a whisper, that in another, baser, part of her mind she was demanding furiously to know how someone who took such pride in her own acuity as an observer of human behaviour and as an unresting reporter thereon—herself, that is—could have "missed out" on so glaring an instance of deceitfulness, mendacity and outrageous brazenness. It was true that the conspiracy, and it was nothing less than a conspiracy, had been carried on in cloistral quiet by two masterly practitioners of the art of the surreptitious, yet she could not but ruefully acknowledge that it was a poor sort of a newshound who should have failed to nose out so strongly odoriferous a truffle. Not that readers would tolerate the recounting of such a scandal in the pages of the *Interviewer,* or at least not without a vaguening veil of decency being interposed between the bald facts and the purity of their gaze.

In favour of Henrietta the compassionate person, if not in that of the disconcerted journalist that she also was, we must point out that her chagrin at having lost a "story" made her blush for her own perhaps too hard-baked and sometimes unshameable professionalism. It was partly to still or at least to push aside these turbid and discomforting thoughts that she turned once more to her friend with almost a howl of renewed outrage and incredulity.

"But why," she demanded, "why did your sister-in-law wait so long before telling you? And why tell you *now?*"

Isabel in reply sounded almost placid. "As to the first part of your question, I have already answered it: she was afraid of her brother, and of his—his consort—"

"And all of a sudden she had ceased to fear them?"

"No, I'm sure not. But for all that she may seem to be of no more substance than a gadfly, the countess is not without spirit— she was born in Baltimore, remember. She recognised that something of moment had occurred between her brother and me, that we had entered upon a darker and more perilous, more painful passage than anything she had known of or guessed at heretofore, and that the time had come when she must speak out. And, of course"—here Isabel smiled—"there was also a small sharp pleasure to be derived from being the one to dash the scales from my eyes at last. She was simply irritated by me—she said so herself— by me and my self-willed ignorance, although she was considerate enough to call it my 'innocent ignorance.' She was irritated by the way I had kept myself blinded for so long, and appeared set to continue to do for the rest of my life. She was bored—that was her word—with my not knowing, and bored with herself for not enlightening me." Here she paused, and when she resumed, she spoke in a tone of reflective realisation. "I do think, you know, that we do not sufficiently acknowledge the force of boredom in human affairs. Or, rather, I should say, the terror human beings have of *being* bored."

In the course of these somewhat aimless animadversions, an observer of the pair of friends as they circumambulated the dusty outer fringe of the little pleasure garden might have been forgiven for thinking that one of them, namely Miss Stackpole, had herself drifted into that very state of unappreciated potential upon which Isabel had just been musing. However, such an assumption, on the part of a speculative faun, say, peeping out from his hiding place among the verdure skirting the path, would have been mistaken. Far from having given way to boredom, as her slackly frowning expression might have suggested, Henrietta instead was intently occupied in gathering various loose strands of specula-tion into a cohesive and concentrated unity, and now she turned to her friend with the suddenness and fluttering force of an eagle swooping down out of the sky.

"I have remembered," she exclaimed, breathless before the fact of it, "that it was Madame Merle who introduced you to the man you would marry—it was she who put you in the way of him. Oho!"—this a kind of verbal grim clapping of the hands—"I see it now, I see the entire thing. She was his John the Baptist, but he was no Redeemer—quite the opposite, in fact. And between the two of them they ensnared you. What chance had you of elud-ing them, innocent that you certainly were? Once you had old

Mr. Touchett's money, you became an object of desire, to both of them. You couldn't see what was afoot. Fortune-hunters we imagine as young and bright, with glossy teeth and soft moustaches and a winning smile, not a grizzled widower twice your age with a ready-made daughter of fifteen years old. That woman had her work cut out for her, to bring you round without your noticing. Ah, but what a wicked scheming witch she is!"

"I choose to believe," Isabel said, in a small thin voice, "it was for the sake of her daughter that she acted as she did."

"Ha! It was, I'll wager, because they were penniless, Osmond and your Madame Merle, so-called—what, by the way, of Monsieur Merle, if there ever was such a person in the first place?"

"There was. A Swiss, of some kind. No one ever spoke of him. He died, although he was living still at the time of Pansy's birth. So, you see, the fact of her true parentage had to be kept hidden on all sides."

A little girl in a dark-blue pinafore came towards them on the pathway, running lightly along and concentratedly bowling a hoop that in its circumference was taller than herself. Isabel watched her, half in delight and half in trepidation, as if the vivid little creature were the ghost of the past itself, flickering there amid the dappled sunlight of summer.

"Well, at least she seems to have got little out of it for herself," Henrietta said, with satisfaction, "for still she has to wander about Europe living off rich acquaintances of the likes of your Mrs. Touchett. I trust *you* didn't take her in? Although I suppose you did, since you imagined her to be your friend. Did you confront her, when you learned of her perfidy?"

"It was rather she who confronted me," Isabel said measuredly. "She it was who told me Ralph Touchett was the one who persuaded his father to make me an heiress."

"Did she now! No doubt she enjoyed it."

"Yes, I suppose it must have given her some shred of satisfaction. Such an irony, there: I had thought if anyone had spoken for me to Mr. Touchett it would have been she."

"That woman," Henrietta declared, with a deep throb of indignation, "that woman would be incapable of speaking for anyone but herself, for she recognises no one else's existence in the world, except perhaps that of your husband, her erstwhile—" She stopped, and pressed her lips tight shut, for she would not allow herself to say the word, the scandalous word. "When did he cast her off, I wonder? As soon as the child was born, I suppose, and the story fabricated, and he knew himself safe, the heartless ruffian."

For some minutes Isabel had been on the point of protest, of turning to her friend and pleading with her to say no more. She could not stretch to the level of anger against her husband and Madame Merle that Henrietta had so plainly reached. There was the shrillness of excess in it, and a vehement self-righteousness, which Isabel considered—she could not avoid acknowledging it— just the tiniest shade vulgar. However grievously he had wronged her, she owed a duty to her husband not to hear him maligned and mocked for a scoundrel and a fortune-hunter—nay, for a common embezzler! Nor had she the freedom to turn on Serena Merle and present her as one of Macbeth's witches, if not indeed as the king's murderous wife herself, thrusting incarnadined hands towards a cold heaven and calling out to be cursed. If only life were as simple as a play, with heroes and villains, and clowns and songs and the clash of unseen battles, and a curtain at the close of each night's performance! Certainly she had ample cause to castigate Gilbert Osmond and his subtle co-conspirator, but she could indulge herself in hating them only if she were prepared to pronounce worthless and excise from the drama of her life, from the actual drama of her real life, one of its richest and most intricately woven acts.

By now Henrietta had added Mrs. Touchett to the line of targets against which to propel the arrows of her indignation, and was criticising that lady for a gross dereliction of responsibility towards her niece; but Isabel turned and interrupted her with what in other circumstances would have been blank rudeness.

"They have both suffered injury, you know, Madame Merle more seriously than my husband, of course. She is, I can assure you, a most unhappy woman. She has lost everything, including her child—"

"The child," Henrietta asserted loudly, swivelling her bent bow towards a previous mark, "which was never more to her, it seems, than an inconvenience, and which she disowned to save her reputation!"

"Yet I cannot believe her so lacking in maternal care that such a renunciation, even though she made it willingly, would not have caused her pain. There is no mother who will not weep for the loss of a child." She smiled. "Medea is the invention of a man."

Henrietta, flushed of cheek and with a riposte ready prepared, nevertheless held back. Isabel, she reminded herself, had in her time shed salt tears over an emptied cradle. "I'm sorry," she said, in a voice tight with restraint, "I've said too much, I always do."

"My dear—"

"No, you're right to rebuke me. Enough that you have to bear such a burden of woe without my adding to your load with my hectoring."

Isabel was ready to apply further assuagement to the dents she feared she had inflicted upon her friend's *amour-propre*, but at that moment she caught sight of Staines, her bonnet set square on the crown of her head—no one else had Staines's ability to turn a scrap of felt and feathers into the simulacrum of a Vandal's horned helmet—advancing determinedly towards her from the roadway, where a hansom cab was parked, with, directly behind it, another carriage, a four-wheeler, on which were loaded a steamer trunk along with various bags and bandboxes, all of which she recognised as her own. The maid, as she informed her mistress, with a vexed waggling of the head, had already been three times round the square in search of her and her friend. The boat train would leave from Charing Cross in less than an hour, and if they were to be on it they must set off without delay—without *further* delay, as Staines pointedly emphasised, with another accusatory twitch of the head.

There followed then that passage of awkwardness inevitably entailed in a hurried parting precedent to what is likely to be a lengthy separation between old friends, and more than one feint at final departure was cancelled by a breathless running back for another pressing of hands, another exchange of kisses, another plea, another promise, so that when Isabel had finally climbed to her seat in the impatiently waiting cab she felt hot and flustered and not a little foolish for allowing herself to be caught up in such a deal of, for her, unwonted fuss. However, when she looked back she experienced a pang of tender sadness at the sight of Henrietta, standing there on the pathway against the towering mass of what, despite the steady sunshine, now seemed sombre trees. How they dwarfed and isolated her, those indifferent and restlessly stirring giants! We are so small, Isabel thought, and the world is so vast. Then the driver flicked his whip and the cab gave a little lurch and rolled away from the kerb, out into the blare and bustle of the traffic. Staines was saying something to her but she was not listening. She had glimpsed a person making his way through the endlessly intermeshing crowd of pedestrians on the far side of the street, a tall figure, in a grey coat and a grey hat, lean and brown and with a gait of an unmistakable stiffness, his jaw set square and his eye fixed firmly before him. It was Caspar Goodwood, bound, surely, for Wimpole Street, in hope of finding her there, at her friend's lodgings. As she watched the last of him receding from her—the cab was moving swiftly now and she had to turn her head sharply back to keep him in view—the thought came to her that she would never see him again, and for a second it was as if a great gust of hot and stifling wind had sprung up and engulfed her.

XIV

Once more there was the clacking and crashing of steel wheels on steel rails, then the lurch of arrival, and the crush of the embarking crowd, then a brief gliding respite amid salt air and a gaiety of breezes, then the swaying gangplank again, and the clamour of the Customs hall, and then, oh, then, the sulphurous travelling inferno of yet another train. In these recent days of disruption and hectic travel Isabel seemed to herself an unnatural point of stillness at the centre of an implacable riot of commotion and chaos. The stillness that she seemed to embody was not the stillness of one at rest. She too was moving, she too was being borne forward, inexorably, towards a destination she did not wish to reach. Sometimes she felt that she was part of a funeral cortège, and that she was in the hearse—no, that she *was* the hearse, somehow, carrying inside her some small expired thing, the cold little corpse of her own heart, her own self, her own life. Perhaps when she reached Paris she should go direct to Père Lachaise and have the final rites performed over herself. To die, yes, to die would solve so much, so very much. But she would not die, she had no intention of dying. Death, the possibility of death, was a fantasy only, not even a nightmare but a daydream, in which she allowed herself now and then to indulge, as a person lost in chronic melancholy might betake herself to the churchyard of a Sunday eve and pace the cindered walkways and be comforted, a little, by being for a while in the company of those whose sorrows were for ever at an end.

By the time they arrived at the Gare du Nord night had fallen, the deep-violet night of Paris in summer that has no hint of the Stygian to it, that seems not night at all, but only a pause, generally agreed upon, like the interval of an opera, but an interval during which the lights do not go up but down. Isabel, at Staines's command, sat on a bench in the station's vast resounding central hall while the maid issued directives, very loudly, in English, to various puzzled porters, glaring at them for what she considered their insolence and all-round laziness and guile. A fiacre was found that would accommodate the two passengers inside, with their luggage piled on a little supplementary cart attached behind, and shortly thereafter they found themselves being transported pleasantly down the rue du Faubourg Saint-Martin, towards one of the sparkling centres of that perpetually illumined city.

Telegraph messages had been sent ahead, to the Hôtel des Étoiles, near the Tuileries, and Isabel's suite awaited her, lamp-lit and aired, to the extent that any space may be said to be aired in Paris, in June. The Étoiles was a modest little place, hardly more than a *pension,* but Isabel often stayed there—she had a horror of those overstuffed establishments that designate themselves as "grand" and made her feel like a great dull overstuffed doll—for it was comfortable and, as even Staines conceded, admirably well-kept and clean. Additionally, a select and highly demanding coterie of epicureans were of the opinion, an opinion they shared with few outside their own charmed circle, that the dining room at the Étoiles, however humble the aspect it presented to a world in want of its dinner, was one of the more delectable treasures of a city that could hardly be said to lack for notable eating places. And indeed no sooner had Isabel been settled in her quarters—which included a delightful miniature drawing room the walls of which were painted all over in Provençal-blue—than she instructed Staines to go down and speak to the *patron* about the securing of a dinner table. It surprised and even shocked her somewhat to realise how hungry she was. No matter how troubled the spirit, she thought, the body will persist in its wilful ways, demanding its food and its drink, its rest and its exercise, and all those little ordinary attentions of the day, those pamperings and pettings, that it never for a moment doubted were its due. Since she had left Italy and set off on her travels, wading, as it seemed, through a mire of misery, her physical self had accompanied her like a single-mindedly demanding child that had been thrust into her less than willing care. Still, the faint fragrances wafting up from the kitchen were as imperative in their insidious way as a trumpeter's clarion sounding from the door of the mess-hall, and she was, she had to admit, as eager for her victuals as any trooper just in from an afternoon spent tramping up and down in the dust of the parade ground.

The maid had hardly reached the door when Isabel bade her tarry. Staines stopped with her hand on the doorknob and turned back enquiringly. Isabel hesitated, looking down and biting her lip. When she raised her eyes again she was smiling abashedly.

"Why don't you," she began, "that's to say, perhaps you would—" She stopped, and lifted her hands in a helpless gesture; her cheeks had gone quite pink. "Please come and have dinner with me!" she got out at last, all in a rush.

The maid stood, still with her hand on the porcelain knob, and gazed at her without expression. They both registered how quiet the room had suddenly become.

"I'm sorry, ma'am, I don't understand," the maid said, and the truth of her words was apparent from the blankness of her look.

"Well, it's quite simple," Isabel exclaimed lightly, but with a nervous laugh. "I wish you to accompany me to dinner, as my"—she stopped, swallowed, then lifted high her chin and spoke it out firmly—"as my guest."

She felt, for a moment, as dizzy as when, she did not know how many hours earlier, she had tottered down the berthed ferry's swaying gangplank. The gap that had opened beneath her now was in its way deeper and more dangerous than the few yards of the English Channel she had walked over before stepping lightly on to the quayside at Calais. Staines, for her part, was even more distressed than her mistress, and at a far more elevated level. There she stood at the doorway, mute, unmoving, like a climber of high places who in a moment of lapsed concentration glances into the limitless chasm below his feet and, seeing it for what it really is, becomes on the instant frozen to the ledge where he is perched. At last she summoned up the power of speech.

"But how could I, ma'am?" she said, or pleaded, rather. "They wouldn't let me in!"

"Nonsense!" Isabel said stoutly, as much to encourage herself as to impress the maid. "Of course they'll 'let you in.' We are not in England now, and no one knows us. Why, pray, should not two ladies sit down and dine together, here in this capital of civilisation?"

The maid's eyes widened. *"Ladies,"* she breathed, as if she had heard a gross blasphemy casually uttered.

"You can tell me about your family," Isabel blithely went on. "I should like to hear more about your sister—in Hackney, is it?—and her husband and his work, and the little ones, your nephews and nieces." She could not, she realised, remember Staines's sister's married name. "There is so much we do not know about each other."

But Staines was still stuck upon that word "ladies," as if it were a pin and she a butterfly fixed by it to a board. "Two ladies, at dinner," she murmured, gazing before her, entranced, as if the impossible scene were there in front of her eyes, shimmering on the air of the little blue room. Then she came back to herself and looked at Isabel and shook her head. "I couldn't, ma'am," she said, slowly, sadly. "I *couldn't*."

Isabel sighed. She was beginning to lose patience, although she knew very well her exasperation was only another ploy to quell her sense of having set out upon a great transgression. And yet, after all, she put it to herself crossly, after all why should not she, why should not they, the two of them together, flout an absurd convention? What was to stop them swinging the blade and breaking the shackles society had bound them in?—she was aware of her figurings slipping out of focus and mixing themselves together. And who anyhow was to attempt to bar their path to freedom, except some popinjay in a greasy frock-coat with a dyed moustache and a napkin over his sleeve? Here she had to stop and make herself dismount from her high horse. Distinctly to her mind came an image of Miss Janeway, looking at her directly with a puckered parched little smile and one sceptical eyebrow arched. But no, all the same, no, she would not be diverted from the course she had set herself upon, no matter where it should take her.

"Please, now, do as I say," she said to the maid, closing her eyes and holding up a peremptory palm. "Go down at once and instruct the manager to reserve a table for two—for two, mind—at nine o'clock. Then you may lay out a gown for me, and"—she wavered, but only for an instant—"and choose something that you should like to borrow for yourself, my blue shawl, for example, or that lace wrap I know you admire, or—or—well, whatever you wish. You may take your pick!"

She had finished with a gay little flourish, like the parting flick of a dancer's fan, but then, returning her full attention to the woman before her at the door, she saw that the poor creature was still frozen to the spot high up on the narrow ledge of her own vertiginous fright.

"Oh, ma'am!" the maid whispered. She was even yet clutching the doorknob—Isabel saw how white her knuckles were—not with any intention of opening the door, it seemed, but rather as if to stop herself from falling. "Oh, ma'am!"

"What?" Isabel asked softly, struggling to keep out of her voice any hint of the wave of weariness that had washed over her suddenly. "What is it you're afraid of?"

"Oh, ma'am," the maid said yet again, but this time with a tremor of passionate entreaty, so that for a moment Isabel feared that the terrified girl—and what was she, only a grown-up girl, for all her fierceness, largeness and mannish angularity?—might fall to her knees like a suffering captive and hold out clasped and quivering hands and plead for release. "You don't understand—you couldn't. If I was to go into that dining room and sit down with you at table, why, they'd—they'd all know, you see, they'd know who I am, and *what* I am, and"—her voice grew faint—"and they'd laugh at me."

XV

_____

And so it was that half an hour later Isabel was seated in the dining room at a table by herself, picking listlessly at an exquisitely prepared _confit de canard_. The recent tussle with Staines, which had concluded with pain and humiliation on both sides, had quite robbed her of her appetite. What had she been thinking of, to urge the timid creature towards an impossible breach of an ancient code—what madness had taken hold of her? If Staines had been French the thing might have been carried off as a harmless _blague_, although Isabel was inclined to suspect that the reputation of French maids for coquetry and merry _diablerie_ was largely the work of the Comédie-Française. In Italy, of course, one's personal maid might sit down to dinner with one every night of the week, at home or in the _trattoria_, and think it merely one of the more pleasant of the duties required of her by her mistress. But Staines was English, and a Cockney at that, and the English were the People of the Law. And, besides, what would they have talked about, really? Accounts of Staines's sister Mrs. Gilhooley—that was the name!—and her hod-carrying husband and their ever-expanding brood of "nippers" would soon be exhausted, and what gulfs would open between them then, there at the table, while the smirking waiters came and went, treating Staines with elaborate deference and addressing her as *chère Madame* and flapping the menu at her as if to shoo her back to her rightful place among the lowly.

Names, she realised, names were so important: they were the lubricant of the social round, and she was bad with names, she "had no head" for them, as the saying is—look how she had forgotten Mrs. Gilhooley's name, even though a passing mention of it might have opened up a little avenue of intimacy and gone some way towards soothing Staines's alarm at the prospect of dining, in public, with her mistress. And Staines herself had a name—it was Elsie, Isabel knew, although she was not sure what it was a diminutive of—so why had she not taken the risk, a small risk, surely, and addressed her by it? *Elsie,* she should have said, *my dear Elsie, I wish you to come and dine with me as my guest here in the Hôtel des Étoiles, by the Tuileries Garden, on the banks of the Seine, on this softly lovely summer night.* Surely even so dour and doughty a person as poor Miss Elsie Staines could not have resisted an offer as direct, as simple and as personal as that. But even as she was formulating these thoughts, in another part of her mind she was laughing in mockery of herself and her sentimental delusions. The world is as it is, she thought, and even one so wilful as I—she was still laughing at herself—will not change it by inviting my personal maid to dinner. She picked up her knife and fork; the duck had gone somewhat cold, but it would be a shame to let go to waste such a masterpiece of culinary art.

As she ate, her thoughts drifted back to the topic of names and naming and their talismanic significance. It occurred to her, on the spot, and with a little shock that was strong enough to make her pause with her fork lifted halfway to her mouth, that she had never heard Gilbert Osmond and Serena Merle address each other directly by their proper names. Surely that, if nothing else, should have given her pause, as it was giving her pause now, and made her consider carefully, as carefully as a police investigator turning over the circumstances of a crime—and had there not been a crime? and was she not investigating it?—the peculiar nature of the relation that existed, and had existed for so many years, between these two people, as it could be made out from the graceful, elaborate and fiendishly subtle dance they were engaged in together. It was what they did not do, the words they did not speak, the looks they did not exchange, the accidental contacts they so scrupulously avoided, that should have pricked her suspicions and woken them up.

She put down her cutlery and leaned back on her chair and closed her eyes. What was the good of going over it all again like this? The stable door was smashed and the bolting horse was a dot in the distance. She signalled to the waiter to bring *l'addition* for her to sign. She had travelled so long a journey, and she was tired.

Yet for most of the night she slept badly. After falling into an uneasy doze she woke suddenly into that state of stark clarity that sweeps sleep away like a hanging veil of cobwebs to reveal a depthless and unyielding dark. She rose and went to the window and drew back the curtain and stood looking out at the silver and gilt lights of Saint-Germain reflected in the river. The same fat moon that had attended her midnight exchanges with Henrietta Stackpole in her parlour in Wimpole Street was here suspended on the tip of a slender spire standing up between the bulking burly shoulders of Notre Dame; last night—could it really be so recent as that?—it had looked to her like a gloating face, but now it seemed a severed head stuck upon a pike. Strange to think of its coldly polished radiance touching so many places that she knew: the house and street where she had grown up in Albany; the ghostly grey lawns of Gardencourt and the bench where over the years she had sat through—"endured" seemed to her the better word—such a number of momentous encounters; the Hôtel des Étoiles and this window where she was standing, and all the silvered roofs of Paris; the old, old house perched on the hill of Bellosguardo, with its enchanting vista over the Val d'Arno, where in the late spring evenings countless nightingales draped the darkness for miles with their exquisite, pained and plaintive calls; the Palazzo Crescentini, in Florence, in one of whose lofty apartments Gilbert Osmond had first taken her hand in his. It comforted her a little to think how all things must submit themselves together equally *sub specie aeternitatis.*

Her mind, haul on its reins though she would, returned once more by its own will to that shaming passage earlier with the maid. Over the course of the past weeks it had more than once occurred to Isabel to wonder exactly how much Staines knew of her mistress's present predicament. One of the things she had learned since coming to Europe, and in England especially, was the startling extent to which the denizens of "below stairs" were aware of even the most secret matters going on in the supposedly sealed world above their heads. More remarkable than the range of knowledge they were privy to, however, was how little store the servants seemed to put by such knowledge, and how little it seemed to interest them. *"Prenez garde!"* the master of the house might murmur, up at the far end of his dining table, touching a finger lightly to his lips, unaware that the scandalous topic his guests have launched upon has already been considered, and dismissed, by the uniformed shadowy figures moving unseen on quiet feet here and there behind their chairs. They might be, those ministering shades, the inhabitants of a village nestled under Mount Olympus, who hear the thunder rumbling high above them, as the gods dispute, hear clearly, and pause to ponder the runic import of each peal, only to move on a moment later about their mundane business. Staines surely knew, could not but know, that Isabel's life in general and her marriage in particular were in a state of deep crisis—why else would they be hurrying like this hither and thither about Europe, from Rome to Gardencourt, from Gardencourt to London, and now from London, so precipitately as practically to constitute a scandal, to Paris, as if pursued by demons? Yet never once, by even the flicker of an eye, much less the uttering of a word, had the maid sought to question what their travels were prompted by or what they entailed or where or when they might culminate. Her task was to keep a tally of her mistress's baggage, to put porters in their place, to purchase train tickets and make certain the ferries had a first-class lounge, to tick off cabmen and browbeat hotel waiters and tweak the ears, if necessary, of slovenly chambermaids. What she might think of Gilbert Osmond, or—great heavens!—of Serena Merle, poor floundering Isabel would not even attempt to fathom. Those two, of course, behaved towards the maid as if convinced they would pass straight through the lowly creature without noticing, should she be foolhardy enough to stray into the path of their imperial progress. Surprisingly, it was Pansy, and Pansy alone, with whom Staines had over the years formed a secretive and mysterious pact of intimacy. There was little, in years, between the pair, and on occasion they might be glimpsed, in one or other of the many chambers that comprised the Palazzo Roccanera, the home, such as it was, in Rome, of the Osmonds, seated together in conspiratorial quiet, their heads bent over their separate bits of embroidery; always at such times the atmosphere between them, superficially placid, seemed to vibrate at a deep level with what might be suppressed mirth, or some intensity of shared knowing, or mutual expectancy. Madame Merle had spoken once to Pansy's father, in

Isabel's hearing, remonstrating with him softly, smilingly, on the inappropriateness of this strange relation between girl and servant, but Osmond had only laughed, and remarked lightly that it was "the Italian way."

"I suppose it is," Madame Merle had replied evenly, but had gone on to press her point, ever so gently yet with a palpable firmness of touch. "However, the maid is not Italian, and neither, for that matter, is Pansy."

Osmond, standing before an easel and dabbing a fine sable brush at one of his clever but undeniably insipid little watercolours, had paused for a second and glanced over his shoulder in response to the lady's lightly veiled challenge.

"And for that matter, my dear woman, neither are you!"

This sally, bland and, so far as Isabel was concerned, inscrutable, seemed nevertheless to please him greatly, and he turned back to his damp sketch with that smile, the one Isabel had come to know so well, which exposed, at either extremity of his thin dry mouth, the fine sharp tip of a gleaming eye-tooth. This easy mutual intimacy between her husband and his friend of long-standing, which the pair often entered upon when the three of them were together, was supposed to betoken a wider happy communality in which Isabel was included, and for a long time, for an unconscionably long time, Isabel had taken it as such; now, however, she realised that in reality it was a private place, a little closed chamber into which the pair would retire to partake together of the sweetmeats of shared memories, familiar jokes, choice snippets of past gossip that for them was still current, still polished, still precious.

Isabel, tired of gazing at the bone-white moon, which by now had succeeded in freeing itself from impalement on that incongruously slender spire, lay down on her bed again, sure she was facing into a night of wakefulness, and almost at once and without noticing it fell asleep, and remained so until a splinter of early sunlight entered at a gap in the curtains and struck at her eyes and made her open them.

Later, downstairs, she was presented at the reception desk with a small embossed envelope on which her name was inscribed with a curlicued solemnity that she thought of as the very mark, the very seal, of the Parisian *gratin*. As she opened the flap and extracted the small rectangle of pasteboard she noticed the manager beaming upon her with a pink-faced intensification of respect; the envelope, it seemed, had been carried hither by a liveried footman in a coach with a coat of arms emblazoned on its lacquered door and drawn by a proudly prancing plumed white horse. Isabel smiled, examining the card; it had slipped her mind that she had sent ahead, before leaving Gardencourt, to inform the Princess d'Attrait that in the coming days she might happen to be in the French capital, and enquiring, should she indeed find herself here, if she might call to the Château Vivier and visit her old friend. And now, with typically calculated aplomb, and as a result of that omniscience for which the princess was justly renowned— how in Heaven's name, Isabel asked herself, had Lorelei known that she had arrived?—here was a printed invitation to a soirée at six of the clock at the château, which was conspicuously hidden in an unexpectedly bosky little *place* off the rue Saint-Honoré. On the back of the card was scrawled, in a hand that could not have been more dissimilar from the one on the envelope, the jauntily imperious command, *Come, or I shall FOR EVER hate you. L.*

XVI

On the morrow the city wore a summer haze, like a fine muslin hanging, through which high up at the level of tall windows and rooftops of polished slate there showed numerous jewel-like silvery gleams and hot little glints of gold. Isabel, after her morning coffee and croissant, had decided to avail herself of the somewhat marshalled freedom of the Tuileries. She strolled down the long central *allée* between the two circular ponds, the larger and the smaller, idly noting the manners and costumes of the dallying *flâneurs* among whom she passed, the fortunate ones who, like her, had time to waste in the middle of a workday morning. She purchased a spray of lily of the valley tightly wrapped in paper from a stall tended by an elderly blind lady in a black lace bonnet. What was the French name for this flower? She could not remember it. She sat down on a bench and watched a band of noisy little boys—why were they not at school?—playing some arcane game that involved much running and hiding among the groves of so many orderly and exquisitely barbered trees. Avid sparrows came and hopped and fluttered about her feet in the dust; she was sorry not to have a crumb to give to them, thinking how they would savour the flakes of pastry she had left on her breakfast plate at the hotel. She listened to the muffled tolling of the bell of the great church of Our Lady on the far side of the river, and thought how the sound seemed, to her fancy, to be of the same old-gold hue as the hazy air out of which the peals came rolling, like a succession of ponderous, reverberant spheres. She lifted the posy of flowers to her face and inhaled deeply their almost fleshly fragrance. She tried again to recall the name of the blossom, it was on the tip of her tongue. Then suddenly she remembered: *muguet*—that was it. Yes, *muguet,* which was also the word for the thrush. Ah, yes. She closed her eyes, shrinking inwardly from the approach of the next thought, trying to fend it off, but in vain. And the blackbird? her mind all innocently enquired of her. What was the French appellation for that proud songster? And despite herself her mind promptly and mercilessly replied: why, *merle,* of course. She let fall the flowers into the dust and rose swiftly to her feet and strode away. Behind her, the cries of the boys at play might have been a cacophony of jeers flung at her retreating back.

Coming out from the gardens she crossed quickly the place du Carrousel, paying scant heed to the traffic. The shadowy arcades of the Louvre rose before her, seeming, in the veiled air, curiously insubstantial despite their stony massedness, and suddenly she could think of nothing more inviting to her agitated spirit than the prospect of the museum's cool and echoing galleries. She hurried forward, yearning towards those glades of peace and sequestered solace, narrowly missing, as she went, being run over by a phaeton that came bounding down upon her like a speeding ostrich.

What she encountered, of course, was the antithesis of the balm of quietude towards which she had so desperately panted. The Parisian tourist season was in what the booking agencies, gleefully rubbing their hands, would have said was "full swing," and the noble palace of art was fairly a-bulge with crowds and clamour. The spectacle of so many childishly exclaimant people scurrying from one masterpiece to the next gave Isabel the impression of one of those *grands lycées* of which the French were so self-satisfiedly proud, wherein, on the morning of yet another national insurrection, the pupils had murdered their monitors with happy enthusiasm and now were running riot through the school's spacious corridors and ornate high halls. She thought of fleeing the place but felt that first she must sit down in coolness, if only for a brief spell, in order to catch her breath and decide what to do with the rest of her morning—for she felt, herself, a little like a student who had been unexpectedly set free from her lessons and urged to go outside and glory in the largeness of the day and partake in Nature's lightsome and airy beneficence. At length, having negotiated her way through the throng by a series of deft sideways insinuations of her person among its throbbing mass, she at last attained that sanctuary she sought, in a vast cool hushed gallery where, as she had remembered, few visitors ventured, and none tarried, discouraged no less by its mean-windowed gloom than by the series of very tall and very broad canvases which, one could not help suspecting, had been discreetly hidden away here by the museum's embarrassed curators. For to Isabel's eye, and according to her husband's scoffing dismissals, they were, however earnestly executed and sumptuously framed, very bad pictures, by, if she recalled correctly, some of the less promising apprentices of a minor school of Peter Paul Rubens. She found a little brocaded chair cowering in a corner, which besides its appealingly forlorn aspect attracted her by occupying what seemed precisely the spot that would afford a view of the least number of the room's treasures, with their curiously unimpassioned representations of tumult, dissolution and mass ravishment. The chair was, she sur-

mised, that of the custode, and the fact of this sentinel's dereliction was an indirect attestation of the value the museum put upon
the objects of his watch. Here she sat herself down to bide quietly
for a while with nothing more to disturb her other than her own
thoughts. Presently, however, her meditations were borne in upon
by the sound of approaching male footsteps. So quiet were they
and ever so discreet that she might not have registered them at
all had not one of the gentleman's boots had a squeak in the sole.
She looked to the doorway and recognised, at once, the exquisitely cut pale-grey suit, the single eyeglass and soft moustache,
of Mr. Edward Rosier. They came into each other's view at the
same instant, and Isabel noted with a sort of inward sigh of sad
amusement how at sight of her the young man wavered momentarily, as if he had felt upon his face a gust of not entirely fresh or
fragrant air. Nevertheless he came on resolutely, or as resolutely
as Mr. Rosier ever did anything, and even managed to summon
up for the sake of politeness a faint, strained smile. They greeted
each other, and he took Isabel's proffered hand and made over it
one of his stiff little Gallic bows.

"Goodness," Isabel said, "it seems one cannot put one's face
inside the doors of this delightful place without encountering
someone whom one knows."

A wrinkle appeared above the eye in the socket of which
Mr. Rosier's single glass was gripped, but already Isabel was
regretting her choice of words and the tone in which she had
framed them. It had not been her intention to sound anything
other than light and friendly, since after all they were, if not old
friends, then certainly of long acquaintance, but she could see the
poor man had taken the form of her greeting as at best a piece
of heartless raillery and at worst as a calculated rebuff. She rose
quickly from her chair, as if by doing so she might mitigate what-

ever he thought had been her ill-intention, and smiled into his face with as much of apologetic warmth as she could manage.

"I rarely come here," Mr. Rosier said, with disdainful coolness. "The crowds—well! But there is a Titian I wish to look at, in which there is a certain combination of lapis-lazuli blue and terracotta that I believe matches exactly a little Venetian piece I am negotiating for."

"Ah, I see," Isabel said, as if she understood exactly the significance of the young man's quest. "Perhaps I might—perhaps you might permit me to accompany you? I'm very fond of Titian."

Mr. Rosier said nothing for a moment, but one corner of his mouth twitched almost imperceptibly, in a way that made Isabel think at once of her husband, and how he would look at her should she so far forget herself as to express the fatuous notion that a person could be "fond" of one of the most transcendently magnificent Old Masters. Ned Rosier, as she saw now, had not failed to learn from his few and far from pleasant encounters with Gilbert Osmond, a master himself in his own line of art, that of deprecation and withering contempt. Indeed, as she studied the young man now, standing before her with his cane and his gloves in one hand and his silk hat in the other, the thought came to her, a thought from which had she been another sort of person she would have squeezed a zestful drop of bitter satisfaction, that in dismissing Edward Rosier's application for his daughter's hand in marriage he had passed up the opportunity of bringing into his family— an institution that, Isabel knew now, from the start had hardly included her—a young man who despite appearances of softness and a delicate spirit would likely have become in time a worthy successor to him in his carefully fashioned and punctiliously maintained pose as a contemnor of the world and all but a few, a very few, exceptions to the general mass of mere people who had the effrontery to inhabit it. Yes, she thought, little Ned Rosier might yet draw himself to his full height and take his place beside her husband as one of the lords of condescension.

He said now that of course she should go along with him to view the great Venetian's picture, adding smoothly that he would always and in whatever circumstances welcome her company. At this she looked at him sidelong, but his gaze was set straight ahead and his expression betrayed no hint that he was not sincere. She had known Ned Rosier since they were children. Once, in Switzerland, her father had taken himself away on one of his mysterious adventures, and abandoned her and her sisters to the care of a *gouvernante* who had read too many French novels and under their influence ran off with a person representing himself as a Russian prince. The waifs were rescued by Mr. Rosier senior, an old friend of her father's, since he happened to be in Neufchâtel with his little boy, who was Isabel's age, and with whom for some days she felt herself to be solemnly in love. At the time he had been a precious little person, ever careful of his footwear and his linen, and over the intervening years he had not altered by very much, except that he had amassed a great deal of knowledge of Limoges china and Louis Quatorze enamels, of rare books and rare vintages, and a deal of other fine old things besides. He had set his collector's eye on Pansy Osmond, and in the process of seeking to acquire her had found himself, to his considerable confusion, falling in love with the child. Pansy's father had spurned him as a candidate for son-in-law, considering the notion preposterous for more reasons than he would bother to ponder, the main one of which, however, was that Lord Warburton himself, on a visit to Rome, had hovered for a time in the vicinity of the sweet little blossom, and might well have made an offer had not Isabel, so her husband believed, conspired against the match and sent the peer on his way. Rosier had persisted, however, swept off his daintily shod feet, for the first time in his life, by the gusts of a genuine passion, and had even gone so far as to auction off his famous collection of bibelots—holding back only his enamels, the forfeiture of which he feared might literally kill him—and having realised fifty thousand dollars on the sale had marched up in triumph to the great carved doors of Palazzo Roccanera and as good as brandished a bundle of banknotes in the face of his beloved's father, certain this time of being accepted for the formidable fellow he had proved to be, and acknowledged as a fit partner even for a daughter of the great Gilbert Osmond. It was not to be, of course: in Lord Warburton, he of the half-dozen castles and the tens of thousands of acres, Osmond had seen the reflected flash of purple fall upon his daughter and for a moment make her radiant, and even if this time that noble flame had turned out to be a case of *feu follet*, there would be other opportunities in abundance, for was there not in England a whole House overflowing with lords, and had not his daughter, his poor little slip of a hothouse blossom, proved that she was capable of drawing in her direction the intensest rays of aristocratic attention?

"You have quit Rome," Isabel said.

"I have quit Rome," Mr. Rosier answered. "There is nothing there for me any longer."

Again she fixed on him keenly. She never ceased to marvel at the swift neat way young men such as this one went about the mending of a broken heart. On the occasion of her most recent view of him, after Osmond had finished kicking to pieces the last vestiges of his hopes and calmly stepped back, brushing his hands, she had come close to tears for the piteousness of the poor creature's plight; yet here he was, hard of eye and firm of step, bent already upon the restoration of his collection of precious *objets*—

his enamels, remember, were intact and safe, and a sound base on which to build—with no thought in his head, as it seemed, for that most precious treasure he had so recently lost.

"And you," he asked, "are you on the way from Rome to somewhere else, or returning there?" She told him of her sad pilgrimage to Gardencourt and of her cousin's death. "I'm sorry to hear of it," he said, and added vaguely, "I believe I met him, at the Palazzo Roccanera."

"You probably did. But, then, when you were at our house you had eyes for one person and one person only."

She smiled while he, on the contrary, frowned, and made her no reply. Something had happened, she decided; something had intervened to make him put the past behind him and turn with a set and steady gaze towards the future. It surprised her to find that she wished to know what it could be that had so bucked him up.

"Do you remember," she gently enquired, "at that ball in Rome, when you asked my permission to pluck and keep one flower from the little bunch I was minding for Pansy while she was away at the *galop*?"

She felt rather than saw his frown deepen.

"Of course," he said.

"They were pansies—I mean, all the flowers in the posy were—"

"Yes, yes, I know; I remember."

There was a note of agitation in his voice—or was it merely impatience? She could not decide.

"Did you keep it, I wonder, the blossom?" she asked.

Instead of answering, he propelled himself forward suddenly and strode ahead of her, like a racehorse making its final dash towards the winning-post, so that she had to lift the hem of her gown and skip along hurriedly to keep up. It was not a display of rudeness on his part, she knew; she regretted having posed the question, in fact regretted having mentioned the matter at all; perhaps, indeed, it had been nothing less than coarse of her to do so.

They came at last to the picture that was the object of Mr. Rosier's quest. It was a portrait of a young man seated, or perhaps standing loosely, with his left arm supported on a pillar, and looking off somewhat tentatively to the side. He wore a grey glove and held its fellow in the same hand. Under a jet-black jerkin there was amply visible a glowing white shirt with small frills at the throat and wrists. His black hair, as black as his coat, was cut low in a straight line across his forehead, and his upper lip was adorned with what might be termed an undecided moustache. He reminded Isabel of no one so much as Mr. Rosier himself; it was not that the two young men, one on the canvas before her and the other standing by her side, resembled each other in any strong manner; but there was something in the way the painter's subject held himself, at a slight angle to the perpendicular, in a pose pensive yet tense, that was her companion to the life. She remarked the touch of melancholy in his look, and Rosier lifted his nose a fraction of an inch and sniffed. He was leaning forward from the waist with his face almost pressed up against the pigment.

"All his men are sad-eyed," he said, quietly and vaguely, as if he were alone and communing with himself. "Even his kings and his generals, all seem to be looking in sorrow towards something distant and terrible."

He was still bent upon the painting, his eyeglass held a little away from his eye, in that attitude of uncanny stillness she knew so well—how often had she seen her husband stand rapt like this before a coveted masterpiece?—examining intently the small locket that hung about the young man's neck on a string of amber beads. The locket was made of some stone the colour of sealing wax, with a single pearl pendent from it and a small square blue stone set at its centre. Mr. Rosier sighed contentedly and stepped back from the canvas, screwing the eyeglass tight again into its socket.

"Yes," he murmured, "yes, that's it."

"What?" Isabel exclaimed. "You mean this is a picture of the thing you are negotiating the purchase of, the very thing itself?"

Mr. Rosier's cheek turned pink, and he bit his lip to stop a smile; but his *embarras,* as she realised at once, was not for anything he had said or done himself, but for her *naïveté* and want of knowledge of the world of rare things.

"No, no," he said, stammering a little, "only the colours, the tints, are the same. That is a sapphire, you see, and as for the red stone, well, it might be anything, for I cannot identify it."

Isabel could only nod, and follow dutifully with her eyes where his finger pointed; he might have been a lecturer tapping with his ferrule upon a chalkboard, illustrating all the points of her ignorance. Of course, the ornament in the picture was only a painted bauble, which the artist would keep in a drawer among a jumble of other "props" with which to bedeck a sitter in need of a touch of jewelled interest, of vivid colour. No doubt, she thought, half in sadness and half in amusement, Mr. Rosier must consider her hopelessly provincial, despite the position she held as a *grande signora* in an ancient palace at the heart of the capital of Christendom. They were both Americans, but from childhood he had lived among the splendours of old Europe, while she was still pent in Albany, like a clay pigeon in its sprung cage, awaiting the moment when she should be released to soar gloriously high into the highest blue. And she had soared, until she heard the booming of the guns. That the two people who had brought her low were Americans did not lead her to look more forgivingly upon

Europe; indeed, in those moments, surprisingly rare, when she could not but give in to raging indignation, it seemed to her that the continent had lured that pair separately to its shores and purposely corrupted them and joined them together and laid them down, like poisoned bait, in the certain knowledge that one day she would chance upon them.

She let her gaze rest once more on the painting of the anxious-eyed youth in his black coat. Perhaps Osmond himself had been like this once, tentative, irresolute, a little fearful, even. Had she not, in the early days of their marriage, glimpsed a vulnerability in him he tried so hard to hide, an almost boyish defencelessness before a world that he dared to show, that he gloried in showing, how deeply he despised it? There must have been, when he was young, moments of doubt? Yes, even Gilbert Osmond must at times have had his tremors in the dark. It could not have been at all easy for a young man from Baltimore with nothing to his name save a modest allowance from his family, some learning, and a great belief in his own superiority in taste, spirit and intellect, to storm single-handedly the citadel of European society, to storm it, and breach its walls, and ride triumphant into its central square, and then deliver the conqueror's *coup de grâce* by seeming to retreat from the tiresome fripperies of public life and immure himself in his own citadel, the fortress of his self-regard.

Yes, he had done much, he had achieved much, but she was wrong, Isabel realised, to think that he had done it single-handedly. Had not Serena Merle been by his side, and more than by his side—oh, much more!—to stiffen his sword arm and hold up the hem of his cloak? Isabel could not conceive of two people more unalike than Madame Merle and little Ned Rosier. Nevertheless when just now the young man had let slip his little smile at her *faux-pas*, there had risen before her on the spot, not only the memory of her husband's deprecating smirk, but also that of Madame Merle's own smile, bland, slow, insinuative, that drew up her lips at the left side, like the corner of a curtain being lifted on something that had better not be seen— But here Isabel stopped herself, and laid a restraining hand, as it were, on her more vengeful impulses, impulses which, as she had ruefully to acknowledge, she had not known herself capable of until these recent weeks. In the particular hell to which they were condemned, herself, her husband and Madame Merle, no one escaped the flames, except perhaps her husband, for it was ice that he was being burned by, although the numbness that had set in so long ago prevented him from knowing himself to be already seared to the bone.

Now the two accidental companions turned aside from Titian's immortal young man and walked back along the way they had come. Soon they were plunged once more in the midst of the pullulating throng. There was the question of locating a site of egress, but beyond that there was the trickier problem of finding a mode by which they might, in the politest and most civilised manner, separate and go their ways. Isabel had the notion that Mr. Rosier would happily have parted from her some time ago, and she did mean to release him very soon; however, there was something she needed to settle between them, if for no other than the selfish reason of putting her mind at rest, although she was not certain this was not an elevated way of saying that she wished to satisfy her curiosity. She was thinking of the sudden acceleration of pace that Mr. Rosier had put on, pulling ahead of her as surgingly as any thoroughbred in the last length at Longchamps, when she had made so bold—perhaps far too bold—as to remind him of the flower he had plucked from Pansy's bouquet that night of the party at Gloriani's house in Rome. Now she had to marshal all her courage, or, if you like, to summon up all her shamelessness—of which, it pleased her to think, she had had much less heretofore than lately she had acquired—in order to be far more forward than so far she had dared. It was in her mind to tell him, to risk telling him, how well aware she was that any help she had afforded him in his siege of Palazzo Roccanera and his fruitless attempt to rescue the damsel sequestered within its forbiddingly massive walls had been wholly of a negative nature—she had confined herself to doing nothing to hinder him or damage his case for the winning of Pansy's hand—but that in the meantime many things had changed, such that now, should he still be as devoted to the girl as before, she might easily find it within herself to come down, with all the force at her disposal, on the positive side. It was not, as in her mind she clearly acknowledged, that she wished particularly to see Pansy wedded to Mr. Rosier, but such an outcome would have the merit, the large, the illimitable merit, of meaning that her stepdaughter could not be married to a person of Gilbert Osmond's choosing. And so, when they had come out into the welcome shade and quiet under the arcades, she turned to him with the bright intention of taking him into her confidence; he, however, on his side, somehow anticipated the nature of what she was about to say, and hastened himself to speak before she could get out so much as a word.

"The rather fine piece I am negotiating for," he said, "the piece resembling the one in the picture, is intended as a gift for a young lady."

"Ah," Isabel murmured, on a long and falling breath, "ah, I see."

There followed a silence, eloquently expressive of the whole width of what it was she saw.

"Her name," Mr. Rosier confided, touching a finger to his moustache, "is Rothstein—Leah Rothstein. Her father is one of the leading dealers at the Hôtel Drouot."

Isabel nodded. "And may I be so bold as to ask if it is in order for me to—to congratulate you?"

Her companion reddened, and looked down. "We have an understanding, she and I. I have spoken to her father."

So, Isabel thought, the deed is as good as done. Her friend would have, along with his saved enamels, a rich man's daughter for a wife, and for a father-in-law a person through whose agency and insider's expertise he would amass, in hardly any time at all, a new collection of precious "things" that would outdo in magnificence and lustre the one he had forfeited for the sake of Pansy Osmond. How neatly the thing had been effected! Isabel had known the young man as careful and shrewd, but she had greatly underestimated his swiftness in action. Hardly had the tears shed for one loved object dried on his cheeks than he had set about securing a replacement, this one with a father infinitely more amenable than Gilbert Osmond would ever be to the importunate Ned Rosiers of this world.

"Then I do congratulate you!" Isabel cried, surprised to find that she almost meant it. "I wish you and Miss Rothstein all the happiness you deserve."

The young man raised his eyes and looked at her somewhat sheepishly; he made her think of a schoolboy who had been caught stealing apples only to be let off by the orchard-keeper with nothing more than an indulgent smile.

"I mean to try to be happy," he said, with a throb of anxious sincerity that softened her heart. "I think it is the duty of all of us to seek happiness—don't you?"

"Oh, yes, of course," she agreed, though more in a tone of wistfulness than affirmation.

Mr. Rosier gave her a look at once sharp and somehow commiserating, so that she asked herself if he might have heard a word from Rome of the circumstances of her departure some weeks ago from that city. It was a cause of wonderment to her that she seemed incapable of lifting her little finger without the world knowing of it, while yet her husband and his erstwhile lover had managed to keep hidden for so long, for so very long, their nothing less than gigantic secret. She had struggled to hold at bay the thought that she might have been the only one, in the concentric circles of society in which she moved, who was ignorant of what had been going on for years under her nose, but now it sprang upon her with all its claws bared. She had to admit it was perfectly possible that she had been living in a fool's paradise, except, of course, there was little about her life with Gilbert Osmond, after the first few prelapsarian months of their marriage, that was in any way paradisal. But that everyone should have known! Oh, that was not to be borne.

She had said her farewells to Mr. Rosier under the shade of the honey-tinted stones of the arcades, and had almost made her way in the misted sunlight to the other side of the immense courtyard, when she heard a quick light step behind her, and there was the young man again, a little out of breath after his pursuit of her.

"Pardonnez-moi, Madame," he panted, lapsing into that tongue in which he was most accustomed to converse, *"je voulais dire —"* He stopped. "That is to say, I wanted to answer the question you asked me when we were inside, and which I could not reply to, out of—out of—" He stopped again, lost in confusion and tensely turning the brim of his silk hat between his fingertips. Then he

took a deep breath and looked direct into her face. "The answer," he said, "is, yes, I did keep the blossom you let me take from the little bunch you were holding that night for—for your step-daughter. I pressed it between the leaves of a volume of the letters of Abelard and Héloïse—a first edition, very rare."

"And have you got it still?" Isabel asked. "The blossom, I mean, not the book." Despite the pathos of the young man's confession she was aware of the temptation to laugh at his inability not to mention the volume's priceless rarity.

"No. I didn't think I could keep it, not when—"

"Not when you had plighted yourself to Miss Rothstein."

"Ah, you understand," he said, smiling his relief.

"Yes," Isabel said, returning his smile, "yes, I understand."

XVII

Château Vivier was an exquisite small mansion built for one of the less conspicuous paramours of Louis XIV. Its rather low-set frontage of pale and pitted sandstone somehow contrived to seem always to be smiling, in happy contemplation, as it might be, of its own venerable yet ever fresh loveliness. It had been in Prince d'Attrait's family for countless generations— indeed it was whispered, half in malice and half in awe, that the original prince of that line had been one of the Sun King's numerous unacknowledged offspring, a rumour that the present prince's wife, Isabel's friend, took every opportunity to disseminate to as wide an audience as she could reach, and her reach was wide indeed. Princess d'Attrait, the former Lorelei Bird of Philadelphia, a large loud cheerful woman *d'un certain âge,* was the heiress to a coal-mining fortune of such stupendous magnitude as to place by comparison Mr. Touchett's bequest to Isabel in value somewhat slightly above the level of the widow's mite. The princess wore her riches lightly, and was known for her largesse in general, and in particular for the lavishness of her regular "occasions." Isabel, having descended from her cab, was greeted in the glow of the pillared front portal by a gorgeous personage in scarlet and gold livery and a powdered periwig, who with regal tread conducted her to a vast, mirrored *salle de dessin,* which seemed to her at first sight to be on fire, so dazzling was the illumination—there were no fewer than three grand and shimmering chandeliers, suspended in a row— and so intense the hum and crackle of the medleyed voices of the company, gathered there under a magnificent vaulted ceiling with classical scenes of unbridled romping from the bright, perhaps too bright, brush of Le Brun. As she moved through the room, catching occasional and hardly recognisable glimpses of herself in the mirrored walls, she saw numerous faces of people whom she knew, or used to know, none well enough, or happily enough, to cause her to do more than offer a polite, wordless greeting and pass on. There was Mr. Rosier, in a corner, bent slightly forward from the waist, in a pose so habitual with him that Isabel worried for the state of his spine when he was older, examining with the aid of his eyeglass a cabinet of majolica figurines. When he chanced to glance up and saw her reflected in the glass, where she had paused some way behind him, he took on the look of a startled hare, and for a moment she thought he would duck down and scurry away into the crush so as to avoid having to speak to her for the second time in one day. However, she spared him a humiliating flight by herself turning away, with nothing more than a vague smile and a nod.

Almost at once she was swooped down upon by her friend the princess, whose ample form was enclosed in an empire gown of pale-green silk, the skirt of which was overly voluminous and the bodice far too tight—Lorelei was a famously inattentive dresser, a reputation she was fully aware of, and was often heard to laugh at. Her costume tonight was topped off by a mighty headdress stuck with a bristling spray of brightly painted feathers, an ornament that would not have shamed a Red Indian chieftain, and that sat above her large plain pleasant face as if it had sprouted there. The two ladies kissed and exclaimed, as long acquaintance and the present occasion required, but then the princess took Isabel firmly by both shoulders and held her in place while she leaned her own head far back and examined the young woman with a hard and searching stare. "My dear," she said, in that loud, twanging voice of hers, "you look like you've seen a graveyard-full of ghosts. Whatever is the matter with you?"

Isabel dipped her eyes to escape her friend's good-natured but unrelenting scrutiny. She was glad of one thing: if Lorelei, whose ear was never far from the ground, had not heard of the nature and cause of her abrupt departure from Rome, then it was likely no one else had, either.

"You're right," she said, smiling, "but it's only one ghost I have to deal with. I was in England, to be with my dying cousin, who is now dead."

"Ah, yes," the princess said. "That poor fellow, Lydia Touchett's boy. I saw the notice in the papers. Very sad. But come, let's find some nook where we can hear ourselves speak."

They found, but not until they had made almost a circuit of the room, an empty alcove half hidden by a curtain of crimson velvet gathered at the middle and tied back by a silken rope. Here they seated themselves.

"How has Lydia taken her son's death?" the princess asked, plying her fan and keeping an eye on the throng of guests, which seemed much more numerous than it was by virtue of the many tall mirrors all round. "Much as she takes everything else in life, whether good or ill, I suppose?"

"No," Isabel said, "this time is different. The loss has hit her hard."

"I'm sorry to hear it. I've always admired her—*admired*, mark you, for that's about the limit of it. Lydia Touchett is not an easy woman to love, or even to tolerate, for that matter."

"But if you had seen her, as I last saw her, you would have been moved to embrace her."

"You intend that in the sense of a metaphor, I take it? I cannot imagine Lydia submitting to anyone's embrace, no matter how sad the circumstances. I hear she insisted recently in taking herself off to America for her annual visit to her stocks and shares, even when her son was hovering at death's door."

"Yes, she is committed to her habits," Isabel gently responded.

"Ha! She's a self-willed old woman who never bothered to learn how to comport herself among human beings!"

Isabel regarded her friend for a moment with keen concentration. It was not like good-humoured Lorelei to sound so harsh a note, or to display such ire in her look; there must be, she decided, some secret history of strife between her and Mrs. Touchett. She would have preferred to let the subject drop—certainly that seemed the safest course—but she owed it to her aunt to enter one last plea.

"She's a woman whom life has disappointed," she said. "That would make one hard."

Now it was her friend's turn to regard her with a sharply penetrating stare. "You say that, my dear, in the manner of one who knows whereof she speaks. Have *you* been disappointed?"

"Ah, but what life does not have its shadowed corners?" Isabel lightly countered, and dropped her eyes and picked a speck of loose thread from the front of her gown.

The princess, all unsmiling now, continued to watch her. "I have always had a motherly feeling for you," she said. "Though we don't meet as often as I'd like, I think of you frequently, and fondly." She paused. "And tell me," she went on then, in a changed manner, bland on the surface and brittle underneath, "how does Mr. Gilbert Osmond fare, these days?"

Isabel would not look at her. "He's very well," she said, in a tone as much a mixture of the bland and brittle as her friend's.

The princess nodded, with tightened lips. "I dare say *he*'s not disappointed, at any rate."

"No, I should think he's not," Isabel answered calmly, choosing to dodge the sharp tip of her companion's pointed sarcasm. "He lives as he always has, very content and quiet."

"Well, he has much to be quiet about."

There was a silence, as in the moment after something fragile has fallen to the floor and smashed. This remark of Lorelei's was too far, too free, even for her, and she had the grace to blush a little and sit back and re-set her shoulders under the tautened green silk of her gown. What had she meant? Isabel wondered, with a deep stirring of unease. Had it been merely a clumsy, and, for the princess, an uncharacteristically tasteless reference to the fact that Osmond had married a rich wife, in consequence of which it behoved him to hold his peace and count his gold, or was there, perhaps, a darker implication? Had rumours come from Rome, after all, rumours of things her husband had better keep quiet about, other than his good fortune? It was a question Isabel did not wish to address, did not wish to at all, and she felt a flash of resentment against her friend for forcing her to pose it in the first place.

It was fortunate that at that moment the princess's husband chanced upon them in their partly curtained nook. The nobleman, who had a good many years on his wife, seemed to Isabel far more frail and shrunken than the last time she had seen him. He was of a fascinatingly reptilian aspect, his head especially, with its smooth, bony brow, and ancient eyes tapering at the corners, resembling that of a venerable tortoise. He was wonderfully delicately made, with skin as palely translucent as crêpe paper, and impossibly spindly legs, on which even when he was standing still he seemed to totter and waver. He wore a frock-coat and knee-breeches and silk stockings gartered just under the knee; the front of his coat was bedizened over the heart with a panoply of vari-coloured squares of ribbon and bits of metal and twists of braid, betokening a surely foolhardy frequency of instances of valour on the battlefields of yesteryear. To Isabel he made a deep though not quite steady bow, and smiled, and mumbled some words of politeness; it was clear he had no notion of her precise identity, despite the fact that they had met many times before. Then he turned to his wife.

"*Ma chère,*" he said, in so soft a voice it hardly registered on the air, "*le duc d'Orléans a demandé sa voiture.*"

The princess rose at once in a hurried silken flounce, the feathers of her headdress quivering, and requested of Isabel to excuse her, as she must say a word of farewell to her illustrious guest. Then she was gone, with more haste and urgency, Isabel judged, than the moment would seem to require. The old prince bowed to Isabel again, mouthing some more soft and indistinguishable words, and followed after his wife. Isabel wondered if she had become one of those mysteriously marked persons, the carriers of an obscure hurt, whose company others found awkward to sustain?

She sat alone for a while, vacant of eye, with her hands folded in her lap, her thoughts wandering in aimless circles, like a breath of a breeze trapped at the end of a blind alley. She returned once more to the question of what had prompted Lorelei's remark regarding Osmond and the much that he should keep silent about; but it was a fruitless interrogation, and she soon gave it up. She had come to a stage of her life, had been hauled to it, like one condemned to the guillotine, when such questions were best left unasked, the answers being at once too obscure and potentially destructive. She had only to think of Rome to know the sentence she was under, and as she sat there in the little yellow-painted alcove behind the angle of the crimson curtain, she seemed to hear the big steel blade being winched steadily higher and higher above her.

Presently, since it was clear the princess was not to come back to her, she rose and wandered among the busily chattering guests; it was, she reflected, like moving in the midst of a flock of flamingos, for the talk around her might have been the calling and crying of some such exotic creatures. No one stopped her to address her, no one called for her attention, and she did not pause or speak to anyone. It was a restful kind of anonymity she was being afforded, and she was grateful for it. She had noticed already in these past weeks how being in places where she was not known granted her a peculiar sense of security, and even brought her a grain of solace; it was as if her hidden troubles, clamouring within her for the attention of those who were close to her—but who were they?—settled down in sulky silence when there were only strangers about. But did this somehow mean, in the contrary and furtive way by which the mind works, that far from being content to be a public cipher for so much of the time, these days, she was in fact, without knowing it, going in hope of encountering someone with whom she was deeply and peculiarly acquainted, whom her anxious and troubled heart could jump up at, like a long-neglected pet, panting in eager recognition? If that were the case, her secret wish was about to be granted, but in a fashion that even her most ardent longings would find excessive, not to say grotesque, and that would elicit no happy barks or waggings of the tail.

XVIII

Her wanderings led her to a small salon oddly wedged into a corner between two much larger rooms, on to both of which it gave by way of two identical, tall and elaborately ornamented oaken doorways set at a right angle to each other. On one of the thresholds Isabel paused, with a cat-like softness of step. The walls of the delightful little space before her were decorated from floor to ceiling with watercolour frescos, delicately faded, in which courtly gentlemen and pink-cheeked young ladies disported themselves among sylvan settings. As to furnishings, there was nothing except two oddly innocent-seeming chairs upholstered in brocade, also faded, and a tall table with tapered legs and a marble top, on which there sat an excessively decorated clock, which showed the time, with complacent inaccuracy, as ten minutes after three. The company occupying the room consisted of two young gallants in black coats and narrow trousers with black satin stripes down the outer side of each leg. Isabel thought one of them was wearing spurs, but her recollection of the scene afterwards was too blurred for her to trust anything in it for accuracy. The identity of the third person, a woman, on whom the young men appeared to be attending with a more than usual intensity of interest, was at first obscured from Isabel, and she was about to turn away from the doorway and leave the three to their conversation—grouped there so picturesquely, they might have stepped out of the *fête galante* depicted on the wall above them, except that they were far more vivid than the painted figures could ever have been, even in the freshest, brightest hues of their heyday—but at that moment one of the gentlemen, laughing at something under discussion, inclined his head to one side, and in the space thus opened there appeared, as if borne aloft on a platter, which was how Isabel instantly thought of it, the seemingly slightly larger than life-sized, handsome head of Serena Merle.

In revisiting the scene later in her mind, as she would frequently find herself doing, Isabel for the life of her could not account for the disappearance of the two gentlemen. One moment they were there, and the next they were gone, as if they had simply melted away on the spot. It was a trick of memory, of course, but she found it remarkable for all that. Madame Merle was dressed in pale silvery-blue satin, the shade she favoured most—it set off very well the fairness of her complexion and her hair, which was the colour of rain-wet corn—and was holding a painted fan fully opened and resting against her bosom. She was tall, and broad of shoulder, in looks impressive rather than handsome, and wore her years well—she had for an unconscionable time been "somewhat over forty." Now, when she first beheld Isabel standing in the doorway, there was no change in her expression of agreeable tolerance, assumed for the sake of the young men and still in place although they had gone; only a sort of fine fast tremor seemed to run through her, as if she were a statue of some deity registering, on her plinth, the deep and the terrible reverberation of a far-off earthquake. For a moment, too, Isabel plainly saw the woman before her resist the urge to whip the fan up to her face to hide herself. Instead she managed, of all things, a smile, which involved, as always, the slight lifting of her lips at the left corner.

"Why, Mrs. Osmond!" she exclaimed. "I must say, you are the last person I expected to meet here this evening. Are you a friend of our dear, redoubtable Lorelei? I cannot imagine the prince would count you among his circle of acquaintances."

Isabel had to admit it, the woman's cool air of self-possession was nothing but admirable. The only real sign of inner agitation she continued to evince was a slightly raised tone of voice, allied to a certain over-rapidity in the delivery of her words.

"I thought you had gone to America," Isabel said, putting aside as of no consequence to the moment the question Madame Merle had so smoothly put to her. "You said you would."

"I did say it, and I meant it. I am on my way there—I have booked my passage from Southampton in a week's time. We do not all move with your enviable decisiveness and speed."

"I would have preferred not to meet you."

"My dear lady, the feeling is more than mutual, if I may put it so."

"Indeed, I hoped never to see you again."

"Yet here we are, by unhappy accident. Do you wish me to go?"

"If either of us is to be gone, it should be I."

"Why, pray? I fail to see the logic of it."

As did Isabel herself, when she gave it a moment's thought. She wanted to be gone, and yet she was held. Something had flared up in her mind, like a tiny spot of light shining in the distance on a dark night. Was it the flame of a lantern, to lead her forward? For the moment she could not tell exactly what it was—the glow was so faint and the darkness so large—but if it was a guiding light, this meeting in this painted room with the

woman who had done so much to damage her was the thing that
had applied the spark to the wick. Madame Merle, who had quite
recovered her accustomed composure, was watching her with a
quizzical eye. She seemed almost amused by the unlikelihood of
their encountering each other in this grotesquely accidental fashion. But then, Isabel reflected, this was a woman who had lived
for years among grotesqueries—for how else to characterise her
pretences, her subterfuges, her so calmly calculated lies?—and
perhaps a kind of infernal laughter was by now her only defence
against the onslaughts of her conscience, if she might be said to
possess such a faculty.

"Well, since I am not to be required to remove myself, and
you seem inclined to tarry, shall we avail ourselves of this suspiciously convenient pair of chairs and at least be comfortable? I
declare, I must be growing old, for I find the demands these occasions impose upon the feet increasingly hard to sustain."

Here, Isabel realised, was her last chance to quit this room, to
be gone from Château Vivier itself and the sight of her deceiver's
large, calm and by now entirely settled presence, a presence which
declared with unmistakable complacency that, of the two of them,
she, Madame Merle, with all the authority of her assiduously oiled
and polished social armourage, was the one who had the greater
right to be here, even if the Princess d'Attrait was Isabel's firmest
friend in Paris. But that light burning in the back of Isabel's mind
was steadily advancing and becoming brighter, to the point that
she was held fast in its glare; it was neither a comforting nor a
sustaining radiance, but it did illuminate, however garishly, a path
that had been before her since she had departed from Gardencourt and the fresh-filled grave of her cousin. Crossing to one of
the chairs she sat down quickly, like an obedient pupil taking her
place in a class that was to begin that moment. Madame Merle too

seated herself, with a far more majestic deliberateness, and after the briefest hesitation—she seemed not yet entirely convinced that Isabel would not change her mind and jump up and scamper from the room in terror of her—folded her fan and settled the rustling skirts of her blue gown about her knees.

"I take it I am not mistaken in assuming that you hate me?" she said, in the politely affectless tone of one offering the opening gambit of what would be a scrupulously undemanding *conversazione*. "Certainly I know that if our positions were reversed, *I* should certainly hate *you*—indeed, I suspect I should regard the abhorring of you as a duty to myself."

Isabel considered for a moment, then lifted her eyes to meet those of her interlocutor. "You said to me, at our last encounter, that you knew I must be very unhappy, but that you were more so. I believe it's true, and therefore I cannot find it in myself to hate you."

"You think me heartless, all the same. Yet I say to you that if I had a heart, then it was broken, and the pieces torn out of me, by—well, you know by what, without my saying." They were both silent for a time, both gazing fixedly before them now, as if they were looking upon the settled scene of a recent catastrophe in which all they held dear had been lost. Then Madame Merle resumed, her voice softened by a sort of weary curiosity. "Did you not know, all along? Surely you must have, even if only at some unreachable level. Think back; tell me the truth."

Isabel turned and looked level upon her. "Did you believe I knew?"

"Ah, my dear woman," Madame Merle exclaimed, with a cold little peal of laughter, "it's clear you've led a blameless life. You know nothing of the ease, the tormented ease, with which the sinner can avoid putting awkward questions to himself." Now it was she who turned her head, and looked on her hapless *compagnon de douleur*. "Tell me," she said, again with that air of one who seeks only enlightenment, "why do you sit here like this, with me? Do you hope to see me weep, do you wish me to fall to my knees and beg your forgiveness? Is it revenge you want? If so, I can hardly resent you for it—but I think it would be vulgar of you, and whatever you might have been, you were never vulgar."

Once again Isabel gave the question some moments of thought.

"Not revenge," she at length replied. "What I wish for is an accounting, but I don't expect to have it." She paused, casting about her a little in aimless agitation. "I've written to—to my husband," she said, and for a second seemed a child confessing to some impossibly rash, adult action.

"Oh, yes? And may one make so bold as to enquire what the subject was, in particular? I take it that since you have mentioned having written, you're not averse to my knowing what you wrote."

"I'll tell you another time," Isabel murmured, shaking her head.

" 'Another time'?" Madame Merle said, with a look of large surprise. "Is there to be another time, for us two?"

Instead of answering, Isabel posed a question of her own. "Tell me," she said, "what shall you do in America?"

This enquiry, so unexpected and so at odds with the circumstances, caused Madame Merle again to open wider her already wide grey eyes. "What shall I do? I confess I don't quite know. I have people there, in Brooklyn—cousins, and a very elderly aunt." She shrugged her handsome broad shoulders and gave a sort of laugh. "Perhaps I shall throw myself upon their mercy. They're my relatives, after all, of however tenuous a connection—they're bound by common decency to take me in."

Now Isabel turned herself halfway round on the chair to face her neighbour fully. "Don't go," she said, in a loud clear ringing voice, as if she were calling across a chasm.

Again Madame Merle had cause for staring. "Not go?" she said. "Pray tell me, whatever else should I do?"

"Come back."

" 'Back'? To where, may I ask?"

"Come back, go back, to Rome," Isabel said, in a breathless rush. "Arrange to arrive in a week—no, in two weeks' time. I shall be there; I shall see you."

"I don't understand—what do you mean?"

"I mean that I want you to come back and live in Rome."

"How can I do that? I have no house."

"You shall have a house, and an allowance to keep it up. I shall help you. This is my promise."

Madame Merle could only stare. "But—?"

The remains of the question the lady meant to ask were to remain unasked, however, for Isabel had risen abruptly from her chair, and now swept swiftly from the room, as if her heels had wings.

II

XIX

The valley was immersed in a gauze of glittering gold sunlight, in which the city, looked down on from the vantage of the familiar old hill, was the merest vagueness of domes and towers and sharply angled russet roofs, while the meandering river appeared a shining seam of molten yellow ore. If there was birdsong it was muffled under the throbbing canopy of sound thrown out upon the air by an unseen multitude of crickets about their ceaseless and monotonously vibrant labour. On the height of the hill, on a rose-entangled terrace, a man of middling years, wearing a broad-brimmed straw hat, stood leaning with the palms of both his hands set upon a mossy parapet, registering with abstracted pleasure the friendly warmth of the ancient stone. Before him the sloping hillside was an untidy but picturesque quilt of olive groves and vineyards, and there was a heady fragrance of old roses and cypress trees and dust. He was watching the road that led up from the direction of the city's Roman Gate. He had always fancied himself a person misplaced in time; his was a sensibility more attuned, he was convinced, to a grander, more garlanded age, an age in which his talents would have shone with a more vivid flame than ever they could be fanned to by the vapid breezes of the prosaic present day. He did not see himself among the Caesars: that world of conquest and cruelty was too grossly primitive for his taste; his was a spirit that would have been best suited, so he considered, to the civilities and exquisite subtleties of the Quattrocento. Today he felt somewhat akin to one of the nobler *condottieri* from those days, but sadly fallen into peril: embattled, ousted from the sanctuary of his castle of black Roman stone and driven from the capital northwards to this low Tuscan hill, to be his own sentinel, a lone watcher, menaced on every side yet nothing daunted, scanning the shrouded lowlands stretched all about him, preparing his strategies, biding his time.

The reality, as even he could not but acknowledge, was distinctly more mundane than the fantasy it had pleased him this afternoon to fashion about himself, like a coat of gleaming mail. He had quitted the Palazzo Roccanera, his principal place of residence, out of necessity and by his own choice, in order to escape the rigours of a particularly torrid Roman summer, and had moved north happily enough, to Florence, his beloved Florence, and to these quarters in the old house on the hill of Bellosguardo where in former times he had lived for a considerable number of years after the death of his first wife. When he had married a second time and settled in Rome he had kept up the lease—sadly soon to lapse, however—on the big dim shabby apartment that constituted almost one half of the long low abode, with its jutting roof and forbidding windows and muddied-yellow walls, that stood now at his back. Most of his things, his pictures and other precious items, he had carried away with him to Rome, so that the old place, bereft of its treasures, had about it an abandoned and even, at times, a sadly aggrieved air. Nothing, however, could mar the magnificence of the position and prospect of the house, set four-square as it was here on its hill above the soft splendours of the broad Val d'Arno.

He was waiting, was Mr. Osmond, watching and waiting, for one or other of two anticipated arrivals, and now he spotted, far below, along the windingly ascending road, a moving plume of dust that betokened, so he guessed, the progress of a carriage and pair. He had issued a summons to his sister, the Countess Gemini, which he had every certainty of being obeyed with more or less promptitude; she might delay her arrival, out of dread of what she would imagine awaited her when she reached her brother's hill-top eyrie, but arrive she would, and this ragged, honey-coloured cloud swirling in the distance now was most likely the mark of her approach. The traveller could be, however, someone entirely other. Mr. Osmond had been left hanging for some weeks in expectation of the return of his wife from her exploit to England to visit her dying cousin, which he had reprehended so adamantly and, indeed, with such a monitory note of finality that had she been other than she was he might have doubted she would come back at all to him and her Italian home. But he was confident that Isabel's inflexible sense of duty, that spiritual affliction inherited from her Puritan forebears, which he had found increasingly tiresome and which had grated on his nerves with a particularly abrasive sharpness in the latter years of their marriage, would not allow her to abandon him and all that he represented in her life and in her fate. She had written to say she would be returning.

It was not the question of her return that had been preoccupying him for some time now, but rather the puzzle of what it was that had delayed her for so long. Her cousin had at last expired not long after her arrival at his deathbed, so how was it she had stayed away for all this time, and in what place?—for he was not even sure of her precise whereabouts. It had been his expectation that for the duration of her time away she would remain in England, biding at Gardencourt, where Ralph Touchett was engaged in the quickening process of his dying, or with her friend the ineffable Miss Stackpole in London; but then her letter had come, bearing a Paris postmark, and written on the stationery of that impossible, dingy hotel she insisted on lodging at when she was visiting the French capital. What cause had she to be in Paris, he demanded of himself sourly, when she could have been at Gardencourt busy meddling in and perhaps even managing to spoil her erstwhile suitor Lord Warburton's impending marriage? The tremendous news of His Lordship's sudden engagement to a noble and notable lady had seemed to reach Italy almost before it was announced, setting so many expatriate tongues wagging, and causing so many languishing female hearts finally to abandon hope of capturing one of the most eligible bachelors in England, if not indeed in all of Europe. And if Isabel was being detained not by Warburton, the nonpareil prize she had once spurned yet had never quite let go her grasp upon, was not that fellow from Boston, Caspar Goodwood, the Tweedledum to Warburton's Tweedledee, still hanging about in London? The notion that Isabel would not have been dallying with one or other of these preposterously persistent beaux at every opportunity that offered itself, reclining her cheek upon one or other manly bosom with sorrow for the death of her cousin as a pretext, Gilbert Osmond was incapable of entertaining. And compared with those two champions, who was there in Paris to entice his wife across the English Channel? The likeliest possibility, to Osmond's mind, was that she had gone there to conspire with her friend, that frump Lorelei Bird, whom the Prince d'Attrait, a by no means distant heir to the French throne, had been fool enough to marry—for her money, of course, though even that fabled fortune could hardly be thought to justify the match—thus making himself the laughing-stock of half the continent. That his wife must be conspiring against him Gilbert Osmond did not doubt for a moment, given the previously secret matters that she had been apprised of in the days immediately prior to her wilful and precipitate departure from Rome, to attend on his deathbed that confounded cousin of hers who had made so celebrated a business of departing this earth.

"Damn the woman!" Osmond muttered now, wrathfully shaking his head.

This oath had been called forth not by the thought of his wife, but of his wearyingly troublesome sister. A little muscle in his left jaw was beating rapidly as he watched upon the road the furl of fawn dust, which seemed to be moving more swiftly now, and at the head of which could be discerned a pair of plunging horses and the open carriage they were drawing bumpingly along in their wake. The occupant of the carriage was as yet too indistinct to be identified, although by now Osmond was convinced it must be the Countess Gemini, that sister of his whom a moment before he had consigned to the Devil. When he was a boy he had wished he could have been an only child, and he still deplored the existence of his sibling, and would not have had her come today had he not a need of her.

It did not trouble him to any appreciable extent that his wife had been let in on his paltry secrets. In truth, he considered them not as secrets so much as—what? Discretionary withholdings? Pragmatic suppressions? Over the years he had as good as convinced himself that the things he had kept from Isabel he had kept from her for her own good, for her own peace of mind. What did it matter now, the mistake he had made with Serena Merle so many years ago, egregious though that mistake had been? Time not only heals, he believed, it also in the end exonerates, by a process of enervation if nothing else. And, anyway, had he not paid the bounty due upon his carelessnesses? Had he not, as the priests would say, atoned for his sin? Yet it was a pity, to say the least, that the seal of the confessional should have been broken, and Isabel made privy to what it had kept decently concealed from her for so long. The strict maintaining of secrets had, Osmond firmly believed, an ameliorating effect similar to that wrought by the passage of time. This gentleman was one of those fortunate beings who are more than capable of imagining that a misdeed kept sunk out of sight for sufficiently long—some two decades, in this case—is not a misdeed at all; that it is, by the slow action of erosion, assuaged and neutralised and rendered harmless, like a shard of glass on the seabed worn smooth by the turning and tumbling of the tides. Was it not the case that his wife would have been happier, or at least less unhappy, than she now undoubtedly was, had she been allowed to remain in ignorance of certain hitherto hidden facts, which had been so mischievously hauled up from their hiding place and thrust abruptly into her hands? The truth, if there were such a thing, was cruel and disruptive, more often than not, in Osmond's estimation. Besides, what of the sacrifices he had made, the risks he had run—what of the deeds he had dared?—in order to put matters to right and preserve the necessary, the aboundingly necessary, appearances? The things his wife had lately learned of were as nothing compared to some further things she did not know, and never should, if he continued to have the guarding of them.

Her letter had puzzled him, and, yes, had alarmed him, too, a little; what was puzzling was always alarming to a man such as he, who prized clarity and control above so much else. He had never found his wife enigmatic—if anything, he had, almost from the start, despised her for her transparency—but the Isabel who had written to him a matter of days ago from the Hôtel des Étoiles was a person he felt he hardly knew. The letter might have been penned by a notary, so dry and stiffly formal was its tone. It was also peculiarly sparse in content, communicating only the fact that she intended to return to Rome, without specifying a date, and announcing that there were certain proposals—or was "propositions" the word she had used?—which she intended to put to him for his consideration. She had enquired after Pansy's health and happiness, but had offered him no personal greeting at all, not even the formulaic "Dear," a thing hardly surprising, given the atmosphere of their final encounter before her departure for England. Their exchanges of that occasion, brief but sharply to the point, had seemed little less than a declaration of war, and the silence that had reigned during the weeks of her absence—of course, he had not written to her, not a line, and her solitary missive to him had been a letter only to the extent that it was written on a sheet of paper and enclosed in an envelope—had the ominous suggestion of troops creeping quietly up the lines, of cannon being drawn forward over strewings of straw, of snipers being allotted their hiding places. He must be on his guard, therefore; he must not allow himself to be outflanked through an hubristic lack of vigilance and preparation.

He narrowed his eyes now against the hotly glowing haze and, leaning far out over the stone parapet, knew at last the occupant of the approaching carriage; it was, as he had grimly anticipated, his sibling, the Countess Gemini. He turned back, removing his straw hat, and entered the house and paced through its shadowy coolness and came out at the other side on to the crooked little grassy piazza that extended over this flat portion of the hilltop. The countess's carriage was already drawing to a stop here, and the lady herself got down at once, with all her avian, querulous quickness, complaining of the dust and the heat and the roads, firmly avoiding the while her brother's impassive and unblinking eye.

"I thought you were in Rome," she said, fluttering past him and making towards the house. "You could at least have told me you were here." These last words were wafted to him from the dimness of the doorway through which she had entered, folding her parasol with a violent small tug, a movement reminiscent of that of a hunter dispatching some wounded half-dead creature. He waited a moment before following after her. She had halted in the middle of the tall gaunt room, and now she turned and looked at him at last. "I suppose you've brought me here to shout at me," she said.

Osmond laid his hat down on the seat of a venerable oak chair with carved armrests and a lyre-shaped back—it was said to have been sat in by Savonarola—and slipped his hands into the tight front pockets of his trousers and surveyed his sister with a deliberate absence of enthusiasm. "When, my dear Amy, have you ever known me to shout?"

"Your softest murmurs are a sort of yelling," the countess responded spiritedly, with a lift of her chin, or at least of the place where her chin should have been, for this was a feature in which the lower part of her face was distinctly deficient, a lack which, along with a downwardly curving nose and darting and slightly protuberant bright little eyes, gave her all the more a bird-like aspect.

Osmond thinly smiled. She had determined, he could see, on a show of defiance; he would easily put paid to that, should it prove necessary. When they were children he had perfected a way of taking his sister's wrist, with seeming friendliness, between his long, slender fingers and proceeding to squeeze it until the bones and sinews inside it creaked, which invariably caused fascinatingly fat tears to form on the rims of little Amy's eyelids and plop on to the front of her bodice, making there a random scattering of coin-sized stains. Thus from earliest times she had learned to go in fear of him, and to keep her distance when she could, although when he called, she made sure to come, and quickly, too. Today, however, he was bent on treating her gently, for he had a project in view that would require at least the simulacrum of brotherly indulgence. For her part, she could not understand why she should be afraid of him still; she was a grown woman, after all; she had a husband, of sorts, to whom she had borne children that sadly she had promptly lost, one after the other, with distressing inevitability; she was a figure in society—even if, at times, a figure of fun, as she had sadly to acknowledge—while he, for all his airs, was nothing but her idle fortune-hunter of a brother, whose wife had probably left him for good, taking her fortune with her, if she was wise. She did not doubt he had ordered her here to make her suffer; she had wondered that the dread call had not come sooner, and had assumed the delay was due solely to her being in Florence while he was still in far-off Rome, an assumption in which, as was now all too alarmingly apparent, she had been mistaken. He had been here, on Bellosguardo, for a matter of some weeks; why then had he held off from commanding her into his presence? Why had he delayed exacting retribution on her?

She turned away from the quiet mockery of his gaze, and glanced about at the bare walls and the numerous pale rectangles where formerly his pictures had hung. It gratified her to note how distinctly diminished her brother seemed amid the absence of so many of his precious "things"; the image he presented, she thought, with spiteful merriment, was of a Christmas tree denuded of its bells and baubles when the festive days have passed.

"Why do you laugh, pray?" he enquired pleasantly, as if desirous of sharing in her private jest. She was not taken in by the lightness of his manner: it was when he was at his seeming mildest that he was most to be feared. Receiving no reply, and seeing her bite her lip to curb her amusement, he leaned his head a little to the side and smiled, showing the glinting tips of his fine small square but slightly tarnished teeth. "Perhaps," he suggested, speaking in the same playful tone as before, "you were thinking of the damage you inflicted upon me, and upon my marriage, when you last spoke to my wife, before her departure for England. That piece of devilment is still, for you, I have no doubt, a rich source of vengeful satisfaction."

The countess, as if she had not heard, went on with her slow survey of the room's bared and barren walls. She was aware, of course, of who it was that had betrayed to her brother the fact of her indiscretions. Serena Merle's gift for knowing what things went on—what confidences were exchanged, what secrets divulged—even within chambers most securely sealed against her, was as uncanny as it was impressive. Since that day at the Palazzo Roccanera when the countess, at the end of her patience, had drawn her sister-in-law aside and revealed to her the conspiracy that Osmond and Madame Merle had mounted against her and sustained over the space of years, she had often found herself pondering, at night especially, or lying a-bed restless in the hour after dawn while she awaited the coming of her maid-servant, what it was that had emboldened her to dare so blatantly to expose her brother's perfidious secret. She had no great regard for her sister-in-law, whom she considered insufferably vain and pitiably naïve, and who she was certain looked down on her for her lack of intellect—what *she* would consider intellect—and the notoriety of her love affairs; yet that day, when the young woman's cousin was dying, and Osmond, as was plainly apparent, had been so horrible to her, she had felt something for the suffering creature, a sort of irritated compassion—her heart, as it is said, had "gone out" to her, a venture which that tempered and well-tethered organ was rarely permitted to undertake, even in the most tragic of cases. Was she sorry now that she had spoken? If she was not, she had the strong foreboding her brother would soon make her so.

"I hope," Osmond said now, still with his head tilted, and smiling yet, "you will not have the effrontery to deny interfering between my wife and me." For all the menace of his words, the smooth and urbane manner of their utterance made it seem as though he might have brought himself to forgive or at least to discount the injury against himself that he was accusing her of. But could that be? The countess's alarm tightened another turn.

"I do not know," she responded, with a fair attempt at an insouciance she could not ever really manage in her brother's presence, "that the telling of a few home truths could be characterised as—what did you call it?—devilment."

"Home truths!" Osmond smilingly exclaimed. "And what, may I ask, would you know of truths, or of the truth itself—or of home, either, for that matter? Your own life is hardly a testament to honesty and domestic devotion." Relinquishing at last her pretence of carefree poise, the countess whirled about with a sort of strangled squawk and faced him. Before she could utter a word, however, he lifted a hand to silence her, quite easy still in his manner, and even laughing a little. "Oh, calm yourself, sister dear," he said. "Let me offer you some tea. I shall have a table laid for us outside, in the shade. There is a matter I wish to discuss with you."

She stood for a moment, her lips still a little way open upon the response he had prevented her from making, then moved a step backwards, narrowing her eyes suspiciously. "What matter is that?" she asked; it seemed that, remarkably, the subject of her betrayal of his secrets to his wife was to be set aside entirely, even if only for the present. Yet she was if anything more uneasy now than she had been before. The notion that her brother would deign to discuss with her anything at all in the world of any significance was so novel as to provoke in her a positive rush of trepidation. What new manoeuvre was he mounting against her—what fresh assault would she have to face, she who shrank so from facing the least of life's unpleasantnesses? Well, she would be more daunted than she was had she not a secret weapon of her own to hand, for there was something she knew that she was sure Osmond did not, a thing that she was certain would set even one as well-shielded as he reeling back on his heels in astonishment and shock.

XX

The day had indeed cooled somewhat. The sunlit mist in the valley had softened from glitter to glow, and even the crickets seemed less desperate in the flinging out of their nets of scraped and numbingly vibrant song. In the shade of the house's overhanging roof a little round wrought-iron table had been set up on the gravel beside the riotous rose-beds; it was covered with a linen cloth, and laid with all the implements requisite for the taking of afternoon tea. This delightful ceremony, so characteristically English, though gently anachronistic here, in the midst of so much southern vehemence of temperature and light, was one of Osmond's more recently acquired affectations; in fact, the custom had been instituted at about the time, as the countess had not failed to note, of Lord Warburton's appearance in Rome. That appearance had proved to be, to Osmond's well-disguised but bitter disappointment, lamentably fleeting, the cause for lamentation being the fond father's unfulfilled wish to marry his only daughter to the great man. Another well-gnawed bone of contention between husband and wife was Osmond's unshakeable conviction that it was Isabel who, with much subtlety and deceitfulness, had prevented the marriage of Lord Warburton and Pansy, out of her unresting jealousy, and a simple determination to subvert her husband's plans and desires wherever and whenever she lit upon them.

Tea was served by Giancarlo, the dustily frock-coated major-domo, whose rule here at the Villa Castellani had been well-established long before Mr. Osmond first took up residence in the house; such indeed was the aspect of venerable decay the servant displayed in his person that one might have been forgiven for thinking him not much younger in years than the *casa di campagna* itself, which, as a sheaf of yellowed parchments could show to a visitor's inquisitive eye, had been standing for the better part of a millennium. He mumbled to himself as he attended to the master and his guest—the countess he addressed as Signora Osmond, evidently mistaking her for Isabel—plying the teapot with a gnarled brown quaking hand, and managing to leave in both their saucers a substantial spillage of tea as pale as straw. Osmond was surprisingly tolerant and even to a degree solicitous of the ancient retainer: the intricacies and contradictions of her brother's personality were a recurring source of bafflement to the countess. In general she judged Osmond to be wicked, not in the magnificent manner of one of those figures from history whom she knew he so admired and matched himself against, a Machiavelli or a Lorenzo de' Medici—she was sure there were more apt examples whose names she was not acquainted with, for there were wide gaps in her knowledge of the history of this exhaustingly historical land—but in cautious and petty ways, never venturing beyond the secure boundaries of his powers. He might torment his wife, which without doubt he had been doing behind closed shutters for a very long time, or contrive by any and every means to smother the ordinary childish aspirations and yearnings of his daughter, enclosing her under a cloche, like a bed of blanched asparagus, but before the likes of Lord Warburton, to take a recent instance, he was careful to display a veneer of yielding smoothness; even that Massachusetts mill-owner, Caspar Goodwood, who had courted the countess's sister-in-law back home when she was a girl—and who as everyone knew had not given up his romantic hopes of her even yet, these many years later, when she was already a married woman—had been a welcome visitor at the Palazzo Roccanera, where Osmond had treated him to such a convincing show of interest and amiability that the poor fellow had not realised how elaborately he was being mocked. Yes, it was one of Osmond's many skills to be capable of calibrating to the last decimal point how far he might permit himself to go in displaying his rich disdain of the world and what he considered its crowding complement of intermingled boobies and barbarians.

Over their tea the talk between brother and sister was all of the city shimmering below them in the effulgent light of the latening afternoon. The countess, through twenty and more years of assiduous application, had made herself into a specialist in the subject of the Florentine *alta società,* in particular its seamy underside. Like a busy blackbird, she hopped about in the undergrowth of society, nudging fallen twigs aside and twitching at dead leaves— not a few of them fallen from the fig tree—to delve deep down beneath them into the rich dark humus and pluck up what tasty morsels were to be found lurking there. The troves of titbits she brought to light were never less than toothsome. She knew which marriages had failed and which were faltering, which hitherto virtuous lady had succumbed to the operatic blandishments of one of the city's notoriously numerous Lotharios; she could tell you which husband was a dupe and which strategically complaisant, which daughter compromised, which son a rake in the making, or already made. Although Osmond maintained a pretence of deprecating his sister's bright salacious chatter, closing his eyes and pursing his lips and on occasion going so far as to mime the putting of his hands over his ears, the countess knew perfectly well how deeply it delighted him to hear of the low deeds of high folk: a predilection for exchanging choice scurrilities was the single point at which the sensibilities of this ill-assorted pair of siblings coincided. While they were engaged in this pastime Osmond had a way of luxuriously leaning back his head with nostrils distended, as if to draw in and savour a forbidden musky fragrance, turning down the corners of his mouth and complacently stroking his throat below the level of his beard with the backs of his fingers, chuckling the while so softly as hardly to make a sound. And nor did he only receive, but gave, too, and in abundance, although he produced each sullied nugget from his store of gold seemingly with the utmost unwillingness and moral abhorrence, shaking his head and sighing with feigned sorrow at the wicked ways of the world. The countess marvelled that he should be privy to so many secrets, given that he went about so little in the world.

"Ah, yes, people are so very bad," he said now, sitting back with a contented sigh, his elbows set on the armrests of his chair and his tanned bony fingers formed into a tall steeple, the top of which touched the sharp end of his carefully trimmed spade-shaped beard. "One finds even the most righteous-seeming among them, those whom one had taken to be the very models of virtue, ready at the least temptation to descend to truly astonishing depths of depravity. But I suppose that is how things are, how they have always been, and always will be." He paused, nodding sagely, gazing out over the valley with half-closed eyes. "Indeed, in this regard I have been asking myself for some time now if I was wise all these past years to shield my daughter so assiduously from the spectacle of society's sins and their consequences.

I sought to bring her up in the old way, as you know, according to the old customs, but have I thus perhaps left her unprepared and unprotected against the moral trials she will inevitably be forced to face as she makes her way through life, especially when the time comes for her to do so without a father's care and guidance?"

The countess, who had become very still, was regarding him with a brightly eager eye. What had he in mind, she wondered, what plan or plot had he in preparation? It was when, as now, he was at his most magisterial and most richly vocal, keeping up at the same time a studied vagueness of manner, that inwardly he was most intent upon some particular purpose; this she knew of old.

"You have made her into the daughter you desired she should be, that's certain," she said, with a dry flatness that was uncharacteristic of her—she had no wish to disturb him in his comfortable calculations. "She is a nun in all save the wimple."

He turned slowly his slightly grizzled but finely handsome head and bent upon her a keen and searching look. "Is it so extreme as that? It is not how I meant it to be. You don't think"— for a second his eyes betrayed what might even be a genuine doubt—"she might imagine herself to 'have a vocation,' as they say, for the religious life?" He looked aside from her once more. "I should be very sorry, if that were the case," he murmured, with less a worried than an ominous note; he did not for a moment doubt his power to banish with only the slightest effort whatever pious delusions as to the future course of her life his daughter might be foolhardy enough to entertain in secret.

The countess gave one of her piercing sharp little chirrups of laughter. "You fear she might take the veil? On the contrary!" she cried. "For how many years did you consign her to the care of the nuns? After such a sentence, even a girl as meekly biddable as Pansy pretends to be would surely be cured of any notion of spending the rest of her days on her knees, even if she thought that was your dearest expectation of her."

He remained silent for some moments, still looking down frowningly upon the view from under hooded lids. "'Pretends'?" he said softly. "Do you consider my daughter duplicitous? Do you think her insincere in her devotion to her father and her readiness to fulfil his wishes?"

"Oh, come, Osmond!" the countess impatiently replied—it was the only name she ever addressed him by. "She's twenty years old, she's not a child. I know you sent her back to the convent this time as a punishment for favouring poor little Ned Rosier over the much more desirable Lord Warburton—desirable to you, that is—but there is a limit to what even a Pansy Osmond will tolerate without rebelling or at least putting up a struggle!"

She stopped herself, pressing two fingers to her lower lip. Had she overstepped the mark? Her brother, no less than his daughter, had his limits, which along certain of their stretches were dangerously narrow and all too easy to cross accidentally by way of an ungoverned word or a thoughtless jest. He was a man to be approached with the greatest caution, keeping one's lines of retreat open and clear of hindrance. She watched his bearded, fine but somewhat decayed profile with a renewed sense of anxiety, as he sat there beside her for a long moment without uttering a word. However, to her relief he only sighed again, and again nodded.

"Yes," he said, sounding almost weary, "I fear have made a mistake. Oh, not a grievous one—I cannot think I need chide myself for exercising a father's duty to train and educate his daughter in a fit manner. But perhaps the time has come to—how shall I say?—to have her be shown something of the world, and to have the world in turn be shown something of her."

At that the countess began to have, though all indistinctly, the beginnings of an inkling of what her brother was about. She recalled how, for one usually so guarded, he had been incapable of masking his surprise and satisfaction, in fact his positive delight, when Lord Warburton, on a series of visits paid to the Palazzo Roccanera in the spring, had given unmistakable signs of wishing to woo his daughter. Like the entirety of Roman society, Osmond had been incredulous that Warburton, of all men, suzerain of vast estates and an eminence before whom the statesmen and parliamentarians of his own land bowed low, should put his eye on a wisp of a thing such as poor Pansy, of whom the most that could be said was that she was perfectly pliant and unfailingly polite. Her father, as everyone knew, had over the years ground the child steadily in the mortar of his will until her spirit, what there had been of it to start with, had been reduced to the consistency of a smooth, bland paste. No, the world said, it was not on the girl at all that His Lordship's sights had been set, but upon her step-mother, whom he had aimed slyly to approach by way of the useful conduit of her husband's pallidly nubile daughter. The Englishman, according to the common consensus, which prided itself on knowing such things, had never reconciled himself to and indeed had never fully accepted the spurning, years before, of his proposal of marriage to Isabel Archer, as she was then, and on the strength of rumours of conjugal discontent emanating from the Palazzo Roccanera had lost no time in making his way to the Italian capital with the aim of winning on this occasion by subterfuge what before he had forfeited in open competition: he would marry the girl and thereby secure the woman, the true and continuing object of his unfaltering passion—that, after all, was how the English were, supposedly so phlegmatic and sensible but in reality hopelessly lost to romance. That the deluded peer did not seem to realise what a ridiculous figure he was making of himself in his pursuit of Pansy only added to the muffled merriment of those avidly watching every twist of the pathetic little affair. When Warburton's enthusiasm for the match he had himself mooted evaporated suddenly, for whatever reason—her husband was not alone in believing that Isabel herself had fatally interfered in the thing, for her own ends—and he quietly withdrew and hied himself home to England, Osmond had been as disappointed as he was vexed. However, he had found consolation in the thought that, since Pansy had once come close to securing so great a prize, there was nothing to prevent her succeeding on a second occasion, or a third, or, if need be, a tenth. There was one quality in which Osmond abounded, namely the capacity to be patient and impose a calm restraint upon even his most urgent urges. So he had contented himself with letting his wife know that he knew she had spoiled his plans by exerting her sway over Warburton—she had of course denied the charge—and then had sent Pansy off for another extended spell at the convent, where she might bethink herself and her annoyingly persistent fondness for the wholly unwarrantable Edward Rosier.

After a long pause had elapsed Osmond spoke again. "Did I mention that my wife has written to me? Yes, I received a letter from her some days ago." He leaned forward and took up the teapot and proceeded with studied deliberation to replenish their cups. "An odd missive, with a peculiarly musty odour to it, suggestive of a lawyer's rooms."

"What—has she applied for a divorce?" the countess exclaimed, failing quite to suppress her all too obvious delight at the prospect of what surely would be a horribly entertaining tussle.

He shot her a wryly condescending smile. "Certainly not. How your mind leaps at once to the squalid!"

"Then what *did* she have to say?"

He considered, holding up his teacup and saucer at the level of his chin.

"Precious little, in the way of words," he said. "The true import of her meaning, I could see, lay between the lines. She has developed a subtlety, or at least an opacity, of expression I did not think her capable of." He stopped, and scratched his bearded cheek with a flexed index finger, producing a small dry crackling sound. "I wonder if she has found someone to tutor her," he murmured thoughtfully.

On this the countess ventured no comment. Had they been speaking of any other woman—herself, for instance—she would have known exactly the kind of tutor likely to have been engaged, but her sister-in-law was so determinedly, so tediously virtuous that the possibility of her having taken a lover, even if only to exact revenge upon her husband, was so remote as to be considered only in the realm of the absurd.

"She mentioned Pansy," Osmond went on, putting down his cup and brushing some invisible specks from his lap. "That she did do."

"Oh, yes? Mentioned her in what connection?"

"Well, there, you see, again, it's difficult to make out her meaning, or what she imagines her meaning to be. Despite the straightforward clarity of the lines in which she wrote, I suspect she is in a state of some confusion, which is hardly surprising"—he cast at his sister another sidelong glance, arching an eyebrow—"given the recent turbulence to which she has been subjected." He rose from the chair, stretching his legs that, even within the coarse cloth of his trousers, were visibly thin to the point of emaciation, so much so that they might have belonged to a much, much older man. These meagre limbs, a less than fortunate inheritance from the male Osmond line, had been the bane of his boyhood, when they were more frequently and more mockably on show; it gratified his sister that for her part she was gracefully endowed in her lower extremities, being possessed in particular of a comely calf, as she had been gallantly assured on more than one occasion, and in more than one bedchamber. Now Osmond slipped his hands into his pockets again—he had a particular and curiously jaded way of performing this common action—and, forsaking the table, paced across to the parapet and stood there once more to look out over the valley, leaning a hip against the mossy, sun-warmed stones, with his hands in his pockets still. His sister remained seated for a time, watching him, then she rose too and went forward and joined him where he stood. She looked out upon the sunlit prospect with an indifferent eye; she had long ago grown thoroughly tired of the supposed delights on offer from the Tuscan countryside, a land so bounteous, languid and lush and yet, to her, so gaudily insufferable. Frequently the fancy came to her of casting everything aside, including her irredeemably hebetudinous husband, and returning to her native land, but she had only to recall the Baltimore winters of her childhood to find herself reconciled, however ill-temperedly, to Europe and the insistent, sun-bleached south.

She examined again her brother's composed and inexpressive profile. "I must say, Osmond, you're being annoyingly mysterious," she said.

"Am I? More so than usual, you mean? For don't you find me an unsolvable mystery at all times? So you claim, at least. Whereas really I'm very simple, very simple and plain. Certainly, in this instance, it is my wife who is making mysteries."

"What did she have to say regarding Pansy?"

He put back his head a little and lifted his face to the sun, which, obscured in a glowing haze and resembling a flat gold coin, was poised upon the tip of its hardly perceptible late-afternoon decline.

"She seemed determined to make some manner of a claim upon her."

"A claim?"

"Yes. I confess it's quite beyond me. Pansy, as you are all too well aware, is no daughter of hers, save in the most tenuous and contingent fashion. What after all is a step-mother but a sort of accident, and not always a happy one, as the folk tales attest?"

"Does she aim to—to attempt to take the girl away from you?"

The countess felt as if she had been set the task of peeling away layer upon layer of an integument so delicately friable and precious in itself that the thing wrapped inside it could only be a disappointment when at last she should succeed in uncovering it to view.

Her brother, who had been pondering her question with his lips set into a tight knot at one corner, sighed now and shook his head, to emphasise an ongoing state of puzzlement.

"It is almost as if," he said, "she would descend upon us like a maharajah, and purchase my daughter for a lakh of rupees and carry her off to somewhere far and strange, there to feed her exclusively on sherbet and sweetmeats while the girl—the princess!—dabbles her fingers idly in great pots of precious things."

"I take it those are not the terms in which she expressed herself?" the countess satirically queried. "It hardly sounds the authentic note of Mrs. Osmond as I know her."

Her brother showed a pursed smile, shrugging; for one so measured, it was notable how on occasion it amused him to embroider; words, for him, the language itself, were mere modes of play, when they were not being put to serious employ as weapons of war.

"Whatever her intentions may be," he said, "I mean to frustrate her in them. She shall not have my daughter, at any price. What a thought, indeed!"

"And you, what do you intend?" the countess asked. The excitement she had felt a moment ago—for all that she deplored so much of him, her brother battle-ready was a spectacle thrilling to behold—had given way to simple curiosity. She did not understand the struggle that was under way between Osmond and his wife; that Isabel should desire to prise Pansy loose from her father's unyielding grasp and have her for herself was as novel and as improbable as had been Lord Warburton's short-lived wooing of the girl; yet something tremendous was afoot, some contest between titans, of that she was certain, and she herself, it seemed, was to be a part of it, for otherwise why was she here, on Osmond's hilltop redoubt, engaging with him in the charade of "afternoon tea"?

"What do I intend?" he said now, pensively repeating the enquiry she had a moment since addressed to him. He turned to her. "Rather, I think, we should ask the person in question what she would wish me to intend for *her*." He sauntered back to the table and took up from the tea tray a little bell with an ivory handle and shook from it a silver sound. At once Giancarlo appeared, tottering and vaguely mumbling, and Osmond, speaking in a slow, loud voice, for the servant was hard of hearing, requested him, *per favore*, to summon *la signorina* to their presence.

XXI

Pansy came forth from the house with the promptness of an actress responding to her cue. She wore a plain black dress with a scrap of white lace showing at the collar. Some few weeks short of her majority, she moved within a fixed aura of abstracted melancholy, as if she were to be for ever more in mourning for the shelter and security of a childhood that by season's end would have officially elapsed. Her dress, so severe in line, and starkly unsuitable in the summer light surrounding her, seemed not quite to fit her, and was suspended a little crookedly upon her slender figure. But then, the countess reflected, nothing Pansy ever wore looked exactly the right size for her, the consequence, so her aunt supposed, of the fact that when she was still in her teenage years and her father had not yet come into the benefit of the bounty his second marriage would bring to him, the few items he could afford to put upon the child's back required periodic adaptation at seam and hem in order to accommodate the succeeding stages of her growing girlhood. She stood now before her father and her aunt in her accustomed attitude of placid and slightly vacant acquiescence, absently turning one black slipper back and forth on the edge of its heel in a half-circle in the gravel beneath her. The countess, studying her, could as always see nothing in her of her mother, except perhaps a certain calculating coldness of expression, carefully veiled, which she might be thought to have inherited from Madame Merle, the serene chill of whose gaze was never more in evidence than when she was smiling. Nor, for that matter, did the girl display any ready resemblance to her father; she seemed, as it might be, a sport of nature, a self-sustaining thing, grown independent of the stock from which it had sprung. Her features, her aunt noted, had lost some of their former porcelain delicacy; she had begun, at last, to look something like a woman, a process that unfortunately could not be said to have wrought, as yet, any profound improvement in her looks. Pansy herself seemed unaware of the transformation she was undergoing—either that, or she was determined to resist or at least to disguise the marks of a burgeoning maturity, by maintaining, with a convincingness worthy of her father at his most dissembling, an appearance of demure blandness and childlike docility. Despite such efforts, the countess, with her keen sense for these things, was certain that somewhere about her niece's person there was the stub of a fuse waiting in eager readiness for the first incandescent application of a match.

"Come, my dear, join us, and take some tea," her father said.

Pansy greeted her aunt in passing with a vague unfocused smile. "Oh, but, Papa," she said, "the tea must be cold by now—let me make some more."

She reached for the teapot but Osmond stayed her hand with one of his. "Please, no," he said gently. "Let us summon Giancarlo, and have him do it for us."

The young woman, still with her hand outstretched, looked at him uncertainly; the preparation of this innocent beverage was an accomplishment on which she prided herself, and was the sole social ceremony in her father's world at which she had succeeded in making of herself the presiding priestess: Was she now to be dismissed even from this humble sphere of authority? Dutifully she stepped back from the table, lowering her eyes and setting her face into its accustomed mask of filial obedience. Osmond noted her chagrin, however, and, still seated himself, took her by the wrist and guided her forward to a chair. "Please, sit," he said, "and let us leave the tea-making to the servants, and to little girls. Yes?" He smiled up at her, with an encouraging nod, and, having hesitated for the merest instant, she did as she was bade, and took her place between her two relatives.

The countess had watched this curious passage between father and daughter with the deepest attention and interest; Osmond, few of whose actions were unpremeditated, had marked the moment as one of ritual significance, and furthermore had ensured that it should be recognised as such not only by his daughter but by his sister also. What, this sister now asked herself, *what* was he up to? She had believed at first, and feared, that she had been brought up here to Osmond's hill—she always thought of Bellosguardo as being her brother's exclusive domain—so that he might exact retribution on her for having dared to inform on him to his wife, but by now it was apparent, if from nothing other than his equable and smiling demeanour, that this was not so, and that something far more subtle and far more fascinating was to be played out here today, as upon a stage, within the broad and lofty proscenium of the Tuscan sky.

Osmond again picked up and agitated the little bell, and again the major-domo answered its tinkling peal, and was dispatched to the kitchen to fetch a vessel of boiling water and fresh leaves for the pot. *"Subito, signor barone,"* the old man said, employing the peculiar honorific by which it was his custom to address the personage whom he, like the countess, considered to be the rightful master of Bellosguardo, disregarding the fact, or perhaps forgetful of it, that this gentleman had long since ceased to live here, and now had his permanent residence in Rome. Osmond sketched a gracious gesture of dismissal, and the servant departed, shuffling backwards, bowing and droning.

A tense little silence fell on the table, although the tension was exclusive to the two females present, for Osmond continued to appear entirely at his ease; indeed, he was looking positively genial, as if a programme he had set in place for the afternoon were proceeding with gratifying smoothness and in steady accordance with his plan. "Well well!" he said now, with a cheerful sigh, and clapped his palms lightly on his knees and stood up from his chair and made his way forward amid the rose bushes and positioned himself yet again at the parapet to survey the valley's vista stretched out in the day's sun-struck stillness. The heat-haze of earlier was much dispersed by now, and the city was coming more clearly into view, in all its delicately varied shades of umber and amber, of ochre and old gold. Faintly through the dense unmoving air came a ponderous and quavering vibration of successive slow bell-notes from the tower of the cathedral of Maria of the Flowers, the terracotta-coloured dome of which sat high above all that surrounded it. Osmond raised an arm and swept it in a wide and generously commanding gesture, like a conductor at the close of a particularly fine performance drawing the orchestra before him to its feet. "Ah, but look: what would an artist of genius not make of a view as characteristically picturesque as this!" he exclaimed. "It would take a Turner, let us say, or a Bonington, to do justice to our Tuscan splendours." He beckoned to his daughter. "Come, dear, come and see it as if you were such a one, and with your eye fashion a contained scene out of Nature's sprawling spectacle.

One must do more than look at pictures if one is to learn anything of the art of painting."

The girl rose and went and stood beside her father and gazed down upon the landscape and the shimmering city with an expression of earnest application. Osmond draped an arm lightly upon her shoulders, which made her flinch: she was not accustomed to being embraced. On returning home from her most recent confinement in the convent, which she longed to think would be the last she would be made to endure, she had found awaiting her a handsome and, as she supposed, costly volume of prints by the latter of the artists her father had just mentioned, who, she discovered, with a not quite explicable small soft shock, had died when he was not many years older than she was now. She had gone to her room and sat by the window with the big book open on her knees, turning over slowly the heavy stiff pages. The scenes depicted seemed to her very pretty, and even she, who knew so little about paint or painting, could not but see that they were executed with dazzling skill and artistry—how was it one so young should have done so marvellously much?—but her view of them was in part obscured by a kind of misty unease. Gifts from her father were as rare as his paternal caresses, and the one no less than the other caused her to shrink back into herself apprehensively, like a snail into its delicately spun shelter. She had the obscure yet indubitable sense that this sumptuous portfolio was something at once more and less than a gift, and that eventually the bill for it, in bulging figures, would be presented to her, and that most likely she would be required to settle it in kind, although what that kind might be she could not guess. By now she knew well her father and his ways; she loved him, she supposed, as the world and the nuns assured her she must; he was the only parent she had known, until the coming of the second Mrs. Osmond, who seemed now to be gone, and gone for good, or bad, rather, to the girl's sad distress and deepening sense of grievance—her step-mother had pledged not to abandon her, though Pansy's hold on that pledge had become so tenuous as hardly any longer to exist—but she was well aware that nothing her father said or did was to be taken exactly as he offered it, with his practised candour and assumed simplicity of manner and intent. There was always, with Papa, an attached extension, a length of invisible elastic by which the thing given might be instantly snapped back. Hence, over the years, she had learned to be wary, to take nothing for granted, to doubt the face value of everything that was presented to her. She did not think her father underhanded, or deceitful: he did not lie, not in so many words. It was simply that, behind the lively attention he made a great show of bestowing on those around him whom he considered worthy of the effort—including herself, his daughter had to assume—there was always a calculation being made, another matter under consideration, another motive at work. She did not resent this in him: it was merely the way he was, the way things were; besides, it was not for a girl to resent her father, for such resentment, as the reverend sisters had taught her, would be a grave sin. But what was this painter, this Richard Parkes Bonington, who painted so skilfully and who had died so young—what was he to her, that Papa should suddenly wish her to know him and his works?

Osmond, leaning there beside her with his arm resting about her shoulders, was speaking of the painter even yet, lavishly extolling the charm of his scenes, the richness of his tints and textures—"those cerulean silks, those crimson brocades!"—and lamenting the fact that so few products of his genius were to be seen in Italy, for of course the Italians, with their inveterate insistence on extremes, were incapable of a true appreciation of an art as quiet and devoid of sensational effects as that offered by this supreme yet always modest master.

"How I envy my old friend Lord Lanchester," Osmond exclaimed, with a sigh, "who at Fernley Hall possesses one of the finest private art collections in England, including a dozen—no, more like a score!—of Boningtons."

He stopped, and removed his arm from around Pansy's shoulders—to the countess's eye his hold on the girl had seemed that of a constable apprehending a miscreant, or a gaoler restraining one of his charges—and walked back to the table and resumed his seat, just as the major-domo, as if at a concealed signal from his master, arrived with a jug of water, and a pinch of tea-leaves in a little silver pot.

No one, as it turned out, had a thirst sufficient for a second round of tea, which was as well, for the water the servant had brought was hardly lukewarm, and the leaves were a variety of Assam, while before they had been drinking Lapsang. Osmond leaned back once more on his chair, crossing a slender ankle on a skeletal knee, and again joined his fingers and thumbs at their tips to make a triangular cage of air, humming to himself and idly scanning the white-gold sky. He maintained this attitude of contented vacancy for some little time. His sister, sitting very still, with her small pink mouth pursed and her scant chin tucked in, watched him with fixed attention, as she had watched him for the duration of the little performance he had just now put on— extolling the beauty of the landscape and the city in its midst, summoning his daughter to his side and drawing her to him in an ostentatiously close embrace, all the while expatiating on that painter, Donington or Bonington, or whatever the fellow's name was—while the inkling that had begun to stir in her a while past continued to strengthen, although even yet she could find no certain form for it. She knew he was conscious of her scrutiny, which seemed only to amuse him. In their young days he had delighted in games of hide-and-seek, in which, no matter how closely she might stalk him, he always managed to elude her, and would stay crouched in his place of concealment until he judged the moment ripe to leap out at her and make her scream.

Now he frowned, though, and gave a little start, as if a sudden thought had struck him, and letting his hands fall to his lap he leaned forward, with his eye upon his daughter. The girl was still at the parapet, with her back turned to them, holding herself motionless in a stiff and oddly unnatural fashion, like a laggardly pupil who for her slowness had been made to go and face the wall and remain there and not stir on pain of worse punishment. However, when her father called to her, bidding her return to the table, she showed no sign of feeling herself happily released, but on the contrary turned back with what seemed reluctance, putting on a smile with the effortful care of an actor in an antique drama about to "go on" and fitting to his face the stiff plaster mask suitable to his part. Osmond extended a hand to her once more, and she approached and suffered him to enfold both of hers in the cage of his long and slender fingers. She stood above him, gazing gravely down into his brightly beaming countenance. His sister, meanwhile, watched this further piece of pantomime with a *moue* of disgust, feeling the sting of deliberate exclusion; it was as if her very presence had been cancelled, as if she had been elided from the action, like a stage corpse, visible but inconsequent, required only not to move and to try not to breathe.

"Tell me, how would you like it," Osmond asked of his daughter, "if I were to send you to England to pay a visit to my friend, and stay a while, perhaps, at his country seat?"

"Which friend, Papa?" the girl enquired, in a mechanical-sounding voice.

She knows! the countess thought, with a grim sort of thrill. She knows, or has guessed, at least, the sly plot Osmond has all along been developing.

"Why, Lord Lanchester—who else?" Osmond exclaimed, laughing. "I'm proposing to you a visit to Fernley Hall—it's in Kent, if you know where that is—so that you may see the Boningtons there. I believe among them are the originals of two or three that are reproduced in the volume I gave you." He waggled his head humorously. "Wouldn't you like to view them, in the flesh, as one might say?"

"You would take me there?" The girl sounded at once tentatively hopeful and afraid.

"Oh, no, not I," her father said, with another gaily dismissive laugh.

"But, Papa, I've never been anywhere," the girl protested, with awful simplicity.

"Ah, but you would not be alone," Osmond replied. "I have no doubt there is someone who could be found to escort you, some suitable duenna." He did not so much as glance in his sister's direction, though she was fixed upon him with narrow-eyed intensity, her look as piercing as the beam from a burning-glass. "You would enjoy such a trip, I am sure," he said, still addressing his daughter, "and derive much benefit from it besides." Now at last he allowed himself to turn to the countess. "Don't you think so, Amy?" he asked. She saw the hooded gloating behind the large bland innocence of his look. She could make no reply, and he turned up his face once again to his daughter, where she stood gazing down at him with a fascinated glassiness of expression, quite still and yet seeming somehow a-tremble. "You might even

make some additional side-visits, for Lanchester cuts a mighty figure in England, you know"—here there occurred a caesura, brief
as the intake of a breath, as the name of another English nobleman hovered for an instant in the air above the table—"and I have
no doubt he would be happy to provide you with introductions to
other houses just as grand as Fernley, with just as many lovely pictures to look at." The countess, mesmerised as she was by the sin-
uously gradual unfolding of her brother's tawdry scheme, could
not but admire the stealthy skill with which, for his own ends,
he was making Pansy seem an art enthusiast of long standing.
"The sons of English gentlemen," Osmond was saying, "are wont
to make the Grand Tour of foreign places, so why should not we
respond by packing you off on a little tour of England? And then,
my dear, England would be much preferable to the convent, yes?"
His fingers still enfolded both her hands, and now he gave them
a gently encouraging squeeze. "Much, much preferable, I'm sure
you'll agree."

The girl said no more, and for some moments Osmond
sustained the tableau of the two of them there, the one smiling
upwards and the other looking down at him in mute bewilder-
ment. He dismissed his daughter then, in a kindly fashion, urging
her not to delay in considering what of her things she should need
to assemble for the impending journey, which in his airy way he
had already made into a generally accepted intention, the realisation of which waited only upon the packing of trunks and the
summoning of a chaise.

XXII

When Pansy had gone away to her room, there followed an extended interval of silence between the two persons remaining at the table, a silence perfectly placid on one side and sharp as a shriek on the other. The countess sat with her back very straight and her head lifted high on its slender pale neck—another of the physical attributes that was often remarked upon approvingly by her admirers—gazing before her, seeing nothing save the fact of her brother's insolent deviousness. The joke he had played on her was plain: he had summoned her with frightening unexpectedness, knowing she would believe she was "for it," then had lulled her into thinking herself safe and perhaps even forgiven for her indiscretions, only to spring upon her at the last all fang and claw, like a grinning beast. Oh, how clever he was, and how heartlessly gleeful in his vindictiveness! Her punishment for past sins was to be the future care of his daughter, for an extended period, the possible duration of which she had not as yet the courage to contemplate. The antipathy she felt towards her niece was of the mildest order—the limp little thing did not have it in her to be much more than dismissed for the much that she was not—but it could alter under the action of prolonged proximity to the girl's damply vacant personality. The countess saw herself processing through the drawing rooms of England with the drab creature trailing behind her like a scrap of something that had attached itself to the heel of her shoe—or else she would be "it" in that dreary game they played in Britain, the object of which, depressingly vacuous though it seemed, was to pin a sheet of paper to the back of one's gown in the pretence of its being a donkey's tail. Yes, she would be laughed at and pitied and resented, in equal measure; the English had a special gift for mocking one mercilessly from behind a perfectly maintained straight face. And what would Gemini do, what would he say, when she relayed to him the news that her brother had commanded her to England, for who knew how many weeks or months, there to act as guardian and match-maker combined to his hapless and, so it seemed, suddenly superfluous daughter, as the girl made her bedraggled pilgrimage from one great house to another? It was certain her husband would give her no money—Gemini never gave her any money—and even if he were to fling a few coins at her feet, she had no intention of spending a cent of her own on this calculated caprice of her brother's. No: Osmond must be made to pay for every last item of expenditure the trip should involve, from two or three appropriately costly gowns for herself to the safety pins the girl's few scraps of apparel would require to keep them from finally falling apart.

She had felt a touch of pity, the merest pluck upon her heart-strings, at Pansy's plaintive cry of protest—"I have been nowhere!"—but after all, might she not say as much of herself? The places *she* had been to she could count on the fingers of her gloved right hand—and grubbily gloved, as now she noted with an irritated sigh: Osmond's precious hilltop was just as dusty and dirty as anywhere else in this incorrigibly begrimed yet inexplicably lauded land. No doubt to the eye of America she would seem the typical expatriate and international "type," but what did America know? Her life thus far had been horribly confined. Tears of rage and resentment pricked at her eyelids when she thought of what she might have done and where she might have gone to—where she might have *lived*, in the broadest and richest sense of what it meant to live. Baltimore had been her birthplace but not a "place" in the sense that Pansy had meant when she spoke of having been nowhere, and New York, where as Amy Osmond she had been sent "to be schooled," as her father had menacingly put it, was nothing more in her memory than the clang of streetcars and the smell of horses, and a cold schoolroom on 14th Street and the glint of her teacher Miss Sweeney's eyeglasses and the twitch of her long and narrow, purplish nose, as this wizened shrew-like spinster, a native of the County of Cavan, raised a ruler high past her shoulder preparatory to bringing the edge of it down swiftly and with a sharp and agonising crack on her recalcitrant pupil's chilblained knuckles. In Paris she had met her count, whose title had dazzled her to the same extent that his person—swarthy, stunted and shinily perspiring—had repelled her. She was staying in the city by the Seine with a dull cousin and the cousin's duller husband, the latter of whom had made Gemini, despite his furtive eye and glistening upper lip and curiously childish sallow little hands—he fancied himself a veritable Bonaparte—seem at least acceptable as to manners and deportment. For a week he had wooed her, employing his inaccurate and comically earnest English, and a month later they were betrothed, to his family's consternation and her brother's irritation—he was living in Naples at that period, and did not appreciate that his sister should, as he put it, "pile in upon him" by marrying an Italian and moving to Italy—and her own dawning sense of having awoken not into daylight's muted reality but the blinding glare of a conscious nightmare.

"What, Amy?" her brother said now, breaking in upon her reverie. "Is there to be no word of gratitude for the splendid prospect I have opened before you? Think of the opportunities England will offer—think of the adventures you shall have! You like an adventure, I know; you're famous for it. I grant I may have been somewhat abrupt in putting my plan to you, but I assure you, I have been thinking upon it for some time, first in Rome, then here, on good old Bellosguardo—"

"Where you have hatched so many of your dark schemes," his sister bitterly interrupted.

"Oh, come. I would have spoken to you earlier, but I was in Rome, and then up here, while you were"—he gestured dismissively towards the hazy valley below them—"down there."

He hooked his thumbs in the pockets of his brightly embroidered waistcoat—even he, most carefully conventional of gentlemen, allowed himself a certain leniency of dress when it was summer and he was at a safe elevation above the teeming city—and hitched his feet with ankles crossed on a rung of the little table; he was, his sister indignantly reflected, the very picture of ease and self-satisfaction.

"My husband will object," she observed.

"Your husband? I care nothing for your husband—and neither do you, so don't pretend." He rested his eyes upon her for a moment, with a cold smile. "Do not seek to thwart me in this. I am not a man to be thwarted." The countess looked away, tensing her nostrils and holding her head to the side, like a toddler at table disdaining its nurse and her insistent spoonful of gruel. The dress she wore, of a light pale gossamer stuff, was sewn at intervals all about with blossoms of pink batiste, which when she bridled set up a busy fluttering, like so many butterflies clustered on a bush. "It's all arranged, you know," Osmond went on, studying the dusty toes of his boots. "I telegraphed to Lanchester, who replied at once, saying he would be more than delighted to welcome my daughter and her aunt to Fernley Hall—you're to stay for as long as you wish."

The countess gave a stiff and furious little nod, still with her eyes turned to the side. "And what, pray, is there at Fernley Hall," she asked, in a distant, measured fashion, "besides the score of pictures by this painter you're supposedly so admiring of?"

"There is," Osmond said, "a son—a son of a suitably marriageable age."

The countess was poised to reply to this with an exclamatory protest at her brother's overweening presumption, both of Lord Lanchester's easy willingness to relinquish his heir into Osmond's clutches—Pansy would be of the least consequence in the transaction—and of her own preparedness to facilitate his sordid plan by acting for him as marriage broker. She paused, prey to a sensation she could not at first identify, though mingled in it were surprise and puzzlement and a curious disquiet. Then she realised that it was, simply, embarrassment. There was no man more studiously subdued than her brother; even as a youth he had stifled in himself youth's natural impetuosities. He had always prided himself on his reticence, his capacity to keep hidden from the outer world his inner wants and wishes. He had grown into the image of himself he had fashioned long ago—man and mask had merged, at least so far as the world was allowed to see. What had happened just now that he had lapsed into transparency? A year, six months, six weeks ago indeed, he would not have shown his hand to her so freely, so—yes—so shamelessly, as he had done today. Her brother had many attributes she would have wished curbed or suppressed, but his calm and quiet self-containment was not one of them, sinister though it might seem at times. When

Lord Warburton at the Palazzo Roccanera had put his eye on Pansy, her father had been a model of restraint and urbane discretion, even after the peer had departed and left the girl to her foolish and fruitless passion for Edward Rosier. However, the father's naked eagerness now to see his daughter married off, to Lord Lanchester's son or another, any other, it seemed, was as vulgar as it was surprising. Osmond—vulgar! She had never thought to find her brother guilty of descending into such bad taste. The spectacle disturbed her, and made her not a little ashamed for him. Was it the letter from his wife that had wrought this transformation?— a temporary one, surely? Was there some menace in it that had caused him to panic and lose his usually unassailably resolute nerve? He had said his wife had made a claim on Pansy, but had she also threatened to take away her money? He could easily assert possession of his daughter, and even if he were forced to hand over the care of her to her step-mother he would do it, provided he could turn a profit on the exchange; but the money, ah, the money would be an altogether different matter. For years, in polite penury, he had persuaded the world, or the major part of it, the part that counted, that he was sublimely indifferent to Mammon and all the supposed good things that gilded demi-god had to offer, but his sister knew how sharp was the pain it caused him to be poor, a pain that his pose as a man of flawless taste and a disdainer of mere cash could not assuage or entirely mask. Should his wife abandon him and take her fortune with her, he would become again the polished nobody he had been before he married her and her money. It was, his sister felt sure, this insupportable, this horrifying prospect that was making him so giddy, so transparent, and afraid.

He was watching the countess now from the corner of his eye; had he guessed that she had guessed the hidden source of his sudden unsteadiness? He had always had an uncanny ability to read her thoughts.

"So you're determined your daughter shall have a lord," she said. "It will not be so easily brought off as you seem to imagine."

"I have every confidence in your abilities in this particular theatre of action," Osmond lightly pledged.

"If that's a reference to my reputation as a woman skilled at snaring men," she returned, with deliberate crudity, "I would point out, though it's so obvious I should not need to, that I am not Pansy, and Pansy is most decidedly not me."

"Well, you must do your best," he said, with brisk cheerfulness. "And I do wish," he went on, "that you would soften that sour look, and stop pretending that you are anything other than delighted at the prospect of an excursion abroad. I have no doubt whatever that you will wring every last drop of enjoyment from it." She looked away, biting her lip. It was true, she could not deny it, not to him or to herself: the prospect of spending the remainder of the summer in England, perhaps extending her stay into a mild soft autumn, stirred in her an irresistible excitement and sense of anticipation. "And don't worry," Osmond resumed, "you need not approach that coxcomb of a husband of yours—I shall put money in thy purse."

"Oh, yes? But whose money will it be?"

Once again she broke off, alarmed at herself and the unheeding quickness of her tongue. Osmond, with no more than the shadow of an abstracted frown, was looking steadily at his boots where they were still hooked on the rung of the table before him. "I wish you to return home now," he said, "and inform Gemini of my munificence in sending you on what will be, after all, an extended vacation, with no duties other than to look after my daughter, and after that instruct your maid to commence packing for the journey." She made to interject a protest, but he held up a hand. "You did grievous injury to my marriage, and to me. Be glad that I am letting you off so lightly—more than lightly."

The countess gave a decidedly unladylike grunt, throwing up her head. "I declare, Osmond, I am heartily weary of you!"

Osmond nodded, as if it were the merest pleasantry she had uttered.

"Better you should be *wary* of me," he said, and smiled for pleasure at his word-play.

"Oh, I'm that too!" his sister replied, in a tone of tired resignation.

She rose, gathering up her parasol and plucking at two or three of the rosettes on her gown as if to refresh them. Together in silence the two walked back through the house. Osmond's gaze was cast downwards, and he had put his hands into his pockets again. Coming out into the piazzetta, they surprised the countess's coachman, in his shabby livery, lounging on the stone bench that ran along the wall of the house, smoking a cigarette, which, at the countess's glare, he guiltily dropped into the dust and trod upon with the toe of a scuffed brown boot. He went hurriedly to the carriage and positioned himself between the heads of the pair of horses, holding on to their cheek-straps to steady them, while his mistress, with the unenthusiastic assistance of her brother, mounted the step and settled herself on the dark leather seat under the shade of the canopy. It was time to spring her long-withheld surprise.

"By the way," she said to Osmond, drawing on her begrimed muslin gloves and looking down at him with a smile that might have been a smirk, "you are not the only one to receive a letter from a lady on her travels."

"Oh, yes?" he said, and a wary light came into his eyes.

"Yes—Serena Merle has written to me."

"How so?" He stared. "I understood she was on her way to America, if indeed she is not there already."

"No, no, she changed her mind on that or, rather, had it changed for her. In fact, she is returning to Italy, and will soon arrive in Rome."

Osmond by now was fairly scowling. "Rome? I believed we were to be rid of the woman."

"Well, we are not. She is coming back to stay—to live."

"To live in Rome?"

"To live in Rome." The coachman had taken his place behind the horses and held his whip at the ready.

"What was the cause of such an extraordinary *volte-face*?" Osmond demanded.

"Not *what*, but *who*," his sister lightly said, regarding him with a vengeful sweetness of expression.

"Who, then—who was it persuaded her?" Osmond asked, in a voice grown thick from the force of anger and foreboding.

"Why, your wife," she said, then leaned forward and poked the coachman between the shoulder blades with the point of her parasol. *"Andiamo!"*

XXIII

The Palazzo Crescentini was disproportionate to the narrow street—named for a famously war-like family of the Quattrocento—which it might have been said to dominate, had it been susceptible of being viewed in the entirety of its imposing brown bulk. However, wedged as it was among a jumble of edifices almost as large as itself, and facing its opposite neighbour across a span of hardly more than the length of two outstretched arms—one had inevitably the thought of doomed lovers, their families separated by an immemorial feud, yearning vainly towards each other from one high balcony to another, their fingertips destined never to meet—it presented itself to the eye of the dwarfed passer-by as the skewed and beetling frontage of an urban fortress, or even a place of dread incarceration. Its windows were guarded by heavy black bars, like neatly spaced racks of spears, while the front door was studded with iron spikes that might have been the tips of cross-bow bolts shot through the wood from within. The interior of the mansion fulfilled the promise, or rather say the massed threat, of its outer aspect. The rooms were unrelentingly square and high and dim, and communicated a sense of centuries of haughty, ill-humoured brooding. As one penetrated more deeply into the house, however, one became aware of a steadily burgeoning glow,

like that of the fabled light at the end of the fabled tunnel, until
at last one came gratefully in sight, through a series of tall triumphant windows, of a garden rife with plantings in multitudinous
hues of green and gold, of azure and indigo, of plush pink and vel-
vety white and countless shades of rosy red, where now, in summer, the unalloyed daylight was a steady soft blaze and even the
shadows seemed luminous. It was into these bright precincts that
Mrs. Osmond was shown by the man-servant who had answered
her summons upon the front-door bell. She stood a while quietly before the large glass panes, gazing into the heart of the garden's sumptuous profusion. She was pleased to recognise, strung
between two ancient fig trees in a sunny corner by a tawny wall
of warm brick, the canvas hammock where her cousin Ralph had
liked to doze of a summer afternoon, not minding the fiery glare
of the Roman sun beating upon him through the dappled foliage.
In the eye of remembrance she could see him there even now, his
sleeves rolled and his shirt unbuttoned on the deeply shadowed
hollow above his shockingly sunken chest. Although his mother
had made the palazzo more or less her permanent home, Ralph
had been willing to spend no more than a week or two with her
there each year. On one of the numerous upper floors there was
an apartment—Isabel had never been inside it and was not even
sure of its exact location—which had always been reserved exclusively as the quarters of the *signorino;* so gauntly funereal was this
chamber, as Ralph had confided to Isabel, that each night when he
stretched himself to sleep on the canopied bed, he had the disqui-
eting sensation of having been "laid out," his nightshirt become
cold cerements and the bed itself a bier.

Sighing now over these melancholy recollections of her late
cousin, Isabel stepped away from the window and seated herself in what looked the least uninviting of the numerous heavy

chairs placed about the room. Anticipating that Aunt Lydia, in accordance with the custom of a lifetime, would keep her waiting well beyond the hour appointed for her visit, Isabel had brought a book with her, a neat and closely printed volume of Mr. Emerson's essays, which she produced now and opened at the place, marked by a ribbon, where she had closed it last. However, she had progressed through no more than a paragraph or two of the sage's ruminations on the personality and genius of the poet Goethe before her mind strayed back irresistibly to her own preoccupations. It occurred to her to recall that she had been seated like this, albeit in altogether other surroundings and other circumstances, though with a similarly improving book open on her knees, when she had for the first time encountered her aunt, or when, rather, her aunt had encountered her, in Albany on that rainy afternoon not much more than half a dozen years ago. And at once, inevitably, the old question struggled to rise up in her, so that she had to push it down, with prompt force, as by a shove with the heel of her hand, the question, that is, of what might have been had her aunt not lighted upon her that day and on the spot proposed to carry her off to Europe and to a new and infinitely richer life than she could ever have realised in Albany—but no, she told herself now, no, she would not, she would *not* entertain yet another self-interrogation of the kind, specious and dispiriting, that had so tormented her these past weeks.

It felt strange to her to be in Florence again; in truth, it felt strange for her to be anywhere, so vague and aimless was her mood this morning. She had been gone from Italy hardly two months, yet so many and so momentous were the tests and tribulations she had undergone in that time that she was hardly recognisable to herself, but seemed a sort of Rip van Winkle, one, that is, who had grown old while her world remained as young as it had been when she was last awake to it. She had delayed her return for as many weeks as seemed conscionable, travelling in a wide slow loop that stretched eastwards from Paris to cross the south German lands and then turned south to Geneva and over the Alpine passes, until one day the thought came to her with a jolt that her husband might imagine it was fear of him that was keeping her so long abroad; this was enough immediately to stimulate her step, and straight away, in Milan, she boarded an early train bound for Rome. At Florence, however, she had changed her mind, or something had changed her mind for her, she did not know which, and despite her maid's scoldings—Staines disapproved of the slightest alteration to even the most rudimentary of plans—they emerged, in the middle of the morning, from the thunderously reverberant station of Santa Maria Novella into a city that was already shrouded in a throbbing and barely breathable miasma of heat and dust. It was only then that she thought seriously to ask of herself why, perversely, she had chosen to pause here rather than proceed directly to Rome. She was not afraid of her husband, or of the confrontation with him that assuredly awaited her at the Palazzo Roccanera; on the contrary, she felt before that prospect a pervasive and almost narcotic sense of calm, of a kind that puzzled as much as it pleased her. It was as if she were falling, the way that often in her dreams she felt herself to fall, slowly and in some way caressingly, wafted about by soft airs, safe and gently sustained upon nothing but a kind of silken emptiness. She could not account for this singular, drifting state of respite, except to think it a form of reward she was bestowing on herself—but what had she done to deserve being rewarded, by herself or by anyone else? Or was it that this serenity was being granted to her in return for a thing she had *not* done, indeed for that particular thing from which she had desisted, namely the wreaking of revenge on Madame Merle for the enormities that lady had committed against her? She could have broadcast to the world a sensational tale of the woman's baseness and treachery, but she had not, and her mind, if only for that act of forbearance, was at peace.

Yet there were, as she was compelled to concede, a number of immediate and practical questions to be dealt with. She had directed Staines to deposit their trunks and bags at the station's left luggage office, while she repaired to a café in the nearby Via della Scala, and ordered for herself a simple late breakfast of coffee and bread rolls; here at least she could make a little space in which to reflect and formulate a plan for the day or days ahead. However, it did not take very much reflection for her to realise that no plan was likely to present itself to her, since all her attention had been focused upon Rome and what she would have to face there; by stopping in Florence she had created an arbitrary hiatus, which, should she allow herself to luxuriate in it, would surely dissipate her energies and blunt the force of her determination to bring to a head the hitherto seemingly irresolvable crisis her life had arrived at. She had written to her husband from Paris, setting out proposals and informing him of what she considered the minimum required concessions from him for the conclusion of a truce in the undeclared war into which their marriage had degenerated; should she not be confronting him now, thrusting pen and parchment before him and demanding that he put his signature and seal upon the treaty of peace? *Was* she fearful after all of encountering him, and unable to admit it to herself? But if that were the case, the thing she was afraid of was not her husband or what he might say or do but, much more horribly, a kind of inchoate and unmanageable mass, like a congealed ball of mud, stuck with snapped twigs and bristling thorns and bits of broken leaf, that had rolled down a hill and come to rest, repellent and unavoidable, at her feet. She had thought to dodge the worst of the world's filth, but here it was, waiting for her only to pick it up in her hands and bear it with her, to wherever she was bound.

She had been hardly conscious of what she was about when she hurried to her feet and left the café and summoned a cab and presently found herself, in a daze of startlement, at her Aunt Lydia's daunting doorway in the vermiform and narrow confines of the vicolo degli Albizzi. Was it for this that she had stopped in Florence, to consult the one person she knew she could depend on to speak even the harshest truths?

Now, as she sat half lost to herself in the brightness of the garden room, her thoughts, or what there was of them, were interrupted by the soft sound of a door opening behind her. She shut the already disregarded volume of essays and put it aside, and rose from the chair and turned to greet her aunt's entrance. Mrs. Touchett wore a gown of unadorned brittle black satin with a high collar and cuffs closely buttoned. The severity of her attire was only relieved, and hardly that, by a pair of gleaming pince-nez suspended on a fine gold chain about her neck. She showed less of the effect of bereavement than she had the last time Isabel had seen her, after Ralph's death, standing impassively in the front doorway at Gardencourt, as Isabel's carriage set off for the railway station in a shower of summer rain that was thronged with countless tiny rainbows, a gesture of valediction and consolation, as Isabel had chosen to think it, conveyed to her by her beloved lost cousin.

"So you have come back," Mrs. Touchett said now. "I'm told all Rome was betting that you wouldn't."

Isabel had never been able to decide if the old woman's habitual rudeness was intentional and deliberately aimed, or merely the result of her not caring a whit for the world and what might be the world's opinion of her. She wished to believe the latter to be the case, but instances such as this, when her aunt in her first remark should have as good as likened her to a bolting racehorse and the course of her misfortunes to a steeplechase, caused her to wonder if this person too, like so many, so very many, others, held within her a deep well of vindictiveness and spite, of which her pose of indifference was no more than the cleverly camouflaged cover.

"Good morning, dear Aunt," Isabel said, with ironic formality.

In her person Mrs. Touchett appeared much as she always did—to Isabel's eye she never changed—except that she seemed hollow, somehow, in fact quite hollowed out and weightless, like a replica of herself fashioned from carefully cut, thin translucent paper; also she carried a cane, although it seemed, in her pale-knuckled hand, less an aid to walking than an implement of menace.

"We did not expect you," she said. "I must say, your suddenly appearing like this is a surprise."

"A pleasant one, I hope."

"That remains to be seen."

They considered each other then for a moment, wordless and guarded—like a pair of fencers, Isabel thought, peering through the mesh of their masks—then Mrs. Touchett went forward slowly, passing by her niece, and stopped before one of the tall windows, the height and sunlit splendour of which made her seem even more insubstantial than she had when she first entered.

"I have never understood the glorification of nature," she said. "Look at this garden—so crazily profligate. Old Tonio, my man, grumbles at the waste of so much good ground, says I should clear it out and cultivate melons. Perhaps he's right. What are flowers for, anyway?"

Isabel came and stood beside her. "It would be a pity, surely, to forfeit so much colour, so much gaiety."

"Gaiety?" Mrs. Touchett said. "You call it gaiety? It looks like riot, to me." She turned her head and peered closely at her niece, going so far as to lift up the glass on its gold chain to aid her in her scrutiny. "You are pale," she said, "pale and worn. Are you suffering?"

"From what should I suffer?" Isabel asked, calmly smiling.

"I fear you were born to suffer. I did not think so when I first encountered you, that long-ago day in your grandmother's dreary house in Albany."

"Have I been a great disappointment to you?"

"You have not been great in anything—that's the trouble. I expected more of you."

"So did everyone, I'm afraid."

"Including yourself?"

"Oh, but of course!" Isabel exclaimed, with a sort of rueful cheeriness. "I expected to do wonders, to perform miracles! *That*'s the trouble; *that*'s why I suffer."

Mrs. Touchett moved away and seated herself on the lower end of a chaise-longue upholstered in faded gold brocade, resting her cane against her knee. She patted a hand on the place beside her. "Come," she said, "come and sit by me."

Isabel, after the briefest hesitation, did as she was bade. It came to her that, posed there side by side, they might be a pair of watchers at a wake, and for a moment the sunlight surrounding them seemed a heartless mockery. Her aunt was alone in the world, having lost her husband and, perhaps more grievously, her only son. On the day Ralph died she had said to Isabel, with all the force of her desiccated vehemence—she was not a woman who wept—that her niece should count herself fortunate she had no child, thus forgetting, or choosing to ignore, that Isabel had lost a son of her own, though of a much younger age. Isabel did not often think of the poor little creature, born weak and bound to die. Her husband had taken the death badly, but only, Isabel could not but suspect, from seeing it as a dereliction on the infant's part, and an affront to Osmond's legitimate expectations as a father. Or was she being too harsh to think so? She must beware a hardening of the heart such as her aunt had undergone over the years.

"When did you come to Florence?" Mrs. Touchett enquired.

"Why, just now, this morning."

Her aunt turned her head again and stared. "And you came straight to me? I am doubly surprised. You know your husband is here, of course, in Florence." She saw from Isabel's look that on the contrary she had known no such thing. "Ah, then you are not in communication with each other. So matters between you are as grave as that. I see." She nodded. "Well, you can be assured it's safe for you to return to Rome and the Palazzo Roccanera. Mr. Osmond has come up to Florence for the summer and resumed his former lodgings in that perfectly hideous house out at Bellosguardo."

Isabel required a moment to absorb this information. "That is ironic," she said, managing a not quite steady smile.

"Is that the word you would apply to your situation, yours and your husband's?"

"Ironic, I mean, in that I had intended to ask, in the humblest fashion imaginable, dear Aunt, if I might lodge a day or two here with you at Palazzo Crescentini."

"So you stopped at Florence out of fear of having to confront your husband in Rome, is that the case?" Mrs. Touchett enquired, sounding a note of sly satisfaction.

"I don't know," Isabel answered. "Fear is not the word—I don't fear him. But the prospect of him daunts me." She cast about her, frowning. "I seem to be daunted for much of the time, nowadays. I wonder if I might be ill."

"You are not ill," her aunt countered briskly, "but only unhappy."

For some moments neither spoke, as if to allow the old lady's assertion to settle between them. Isabel thought to protest, but in order to do so she would have had to lie; she *was* unhappy—how could she deny it?

"You tell me," Isabel said then, "that all Rome is laying wagers on me and my affairs. Am I so common a subject of speculation? What do people know of me that so stimulates their interest?"

"They know you went to England to be with my son in his last days, although your husband had forbidden it."

"My husband never forbids," Isabel said, smiling at the matter-of-factness of the thing. Then she asked: "Is that all that's said, that I went away against my husband's wishes?"

"Oh, how should I know all that's said, or even a fraction of it?" Mrs. Touchett snapped. "I go into society less frequently now than I ever did. Besides, they say so many things, it makes a deafening clamour. And Florence is not Rome—down there they go about their gossiping and their back-biting with an energy we are no longer capable of, up here."

Isabel, with pensive eyes downcast, was smoothing the stuff of her gown across her knees. "Do they speak at all of Madame Merle?" she quietly asked.

"Madame Merle? What would they have to say of her? She's gone—driven out, so I have heard, by you, or by your husband, or by both of you together. The matter is of no interest to me."

"Well, she's coming back," Isabel said, in the same remote quiet fashion in which she had couched her question. "Is that not known?"

"Coming back to where? To Rome?" Mrs. Touchett's eyes gleamed like two black bright little beads. "Why did she bother going, if it was only to return? It was said she went to America— she sold her house here, did she not?"

"Yes, she did; when she returns she will live not here, but in Rome."

Her aunt was looking at Isabel now with an expression of large surmise, in the fashion of one suddenly seeing craft and cunning where before there had seemed dullness only. "How do you know these things?" she asked.

"I chanced to meet the lady, in Paris," Isabel answered, still with her eyes calmly lowered, still smoothing her hand upon the tautened silk of her gown. "She was about to take ship for New York, or Brooklyn, that is, where I believe she has some family members surviving—you know she was born there, where her father was something in the navy. We spoke. I urged her to abandon her plan and come back to Italy and resume her old life."

Mrs. Touchett considered that she had long ago put herself beyond being surprised, but for a moment now she fairly gaped. "*You* urged Serena Merle to—?" She stopped, and drew in a thin breath. "Might I ask what your motive was, in doing such an extraordinary thing?"

"My 'motive'? You make it sound as though I had committed a criminal act."

"You told me, at Gardencourt, that Madame Merle had made a convenience of you—those were your words. I remember them because they struck me as indicative of a deep grievance. I didn't ask in what way she had wronged you—I make a point of leaving other people's business alone—but I understood it was connected with your marriage, and that the wound was deep. Therefore I thought it would be nothing but a relief for you to see the back of her. Why would you wish her to return?"

"She too was wronged. I didn't see why she alone should suffer for it."

"Pish!" the old lady exclaimed. "No one is so tolerant as that, not even you." She paused. "But wait. I think I see it." She nodded slowly, narrowing her eyes. "You would have her here as an enduring affront to your husband—is that it? Have I guessed correctly?" She leaned back a little on her chair. "It occurs to me to wonder, Mrs. Osmond, if I have underestimated you, all along."

XXIV

For many weeks, since the day indeed when her husband's perfidious secrets had been revealed to Isabel at last, a question had
lain deep in the thickets of her consciousness, like a sprung steel
snare, a question among the many questions she did not wish
to know the answers to, and would have preferred not even to
address. She was well aware, as how could she not be, of the pru-
rient delight society took in nosing out the egregious misdeeds
of which it had no doubt all who were human were at all times
capable; she also knew, however, that her husband and Serena
Merle were unmatched for the cleverness and subtlety of their
conspiring. That they had deceived her so thoroughly and for so
many years was hardly a wonder—she had been the world's most
unfortunate fool—but from how many others had they managed
to keep their indiscretions dark? At one of the Thursday evening
"at homes" that in latter times she and Osmond had instituted at
the Palazzo Roccanera—for no other reason, as she sadly acknowledged, than to dilute with the presence of others, if only for a few
hours, the stultifying intimacy of their lives together—she had
overheard someone declare, with a burst of brash laughter, "Oh, if
the Countess Gemini knows it then so does all the world!" What
in this particular instance the "it" might have been she would

not stoop to speculate upon, for it had mattered to her not at all at the time. Now, however, the remark haunted her; she heard it repeated in her dreams at night, word for word, accompanied by the same gloating guffaw. Was she to believe that her sister-in-law would have been capable of keeping hidden through so long a time—twenty years and more!—all that she knew of her brother's affairs, and of his erstwhile lover, and of Pansy's true parentage? It seemed inconceivable, save for one starkly significant fact, namely the fear that Osmond inspired in his sister, which was the chief component of his power over her. Yet in the end the countess had broken her silence and blurted the truth—and Isabel that day had not for a moment doubted that what she was being made aware of was the truth—and furthermore had blurted it to the one person her brother would have most urgently desired it to be kept from. In the watches of many a night these past weeks, in London, in Paris, in Munich and on the shores of Lac Léman, Isabel had started from sleep, hot and perspiring, to find herself imploring of the darkness: *What, oh, what if everyone knew?*

Was it for this that she had jumped up from the table at the Caffè della Ferrovia and hurried here, so she might know from one at least of the spectators to her ugly little tragedy how numerous was the audience that sat, invisible to her, out there in the gloom beyond the limelight, watching in avid enjoyment as she strode upon the stage, reciting lines devised for her, did she but know it, by a pair of minds possessed of an unsurpassed genius for plausible artifice?

The span of Mrs. Touchett's interest in the affairs of others was exceedingly narrow. Having had her moment of insight into the nature of the clever coup, as she considered it, that Isabel had effected in persuading Madame Merle to return to Italy and be a poisoned thorn in Gilbert Osmond's side, her thoughts had veered vaguely elsewhere, and then settled, with bathetic abruptness, upon the notion of luncheon. She professed to having long ago lost her appetite in general, but there was an *osteria* on the other side of the Arno she had recently chanced upon—"modest in price, and the staff are civil"—which she had got into the way of patronising, and now she suggested they might go there, while it was still early and the ravening tourists would not yet be out in quest of *bistecca alla fiorentina,* which was, according to Mrs. Touchett, the one thing visitors to the city insisted upon, for lunch and dinner, and probably for breakfast too, if they happened to hail from Texas, or some other place of hearty eaters on the wild frontier. She called up her carriage, which, it being too wide to enter the *vicolo,* they had to reach by traversing the garden along a narrow pathway that led to the coach-house. Isabel, pacing behind her aunt, was assailed by the intensity of the day's heat and the mingled multitude of fragrances all around her, and grew dizzy and even feared for a moment that she might faint. Mrs. Touchett, ahead of her, having despite her years the constitution and sureness of foot of a chamois, never faltered for a moment, even though she had left her cane behind and carried instead a rather shabby lace parasol. She had changed into cream-coloured tulle—"I don't know why I should bother with mourning weeds, since it's the custom nowadays for every woman of fashion over thirty to wear them"—and sported a large straw hat, of questionable vintage, with a faded pink band and a haphazardly swooping brim. She spoke without turning, and Isabel, light-headed and distracted, caught little of what she said.

Isabel found herself wishing now, and in the agitations of the moment it was a fervent wish, that she had not been so capricious as to stop at Florence, but had gone on to Rome as she had at the outset intended; she would enquire at the restaurant for a railway timetable, and find a suitable evening train to take her southwards. Then she remembered—she was amazed to have forgotten it, even for a moment!—that her husband was here in Florence; he was the object towards which she had been aimed, and therefore there was no necessity for her to proceed onwards to Rome. Yet the thought of encountering him here, rather than in the capital, was oddly unnerving. Perhaps, then, she should press on to Rome, and wait there for his return. Yet if she were to leave, and he discovered she had been here, he would assume she had fled because her nerve had failed her. It would give him much satisfaction to think it, she had no doubt of that. But who was there who would tell him she had been here and gone? Only her aunt would know of her having stopped in Florence, and there was little likelihood of that lady being in communication with anyone at Bellosguardo. All the same, it would be cowardly to go: Fate, who was wiser far than she, had intervened to place her and her husband in the same city, and who was she to flout the goddess's crafty contrivances?

In the carriage she still felt feverish and unsteady, and at a point in her brow mid-way between her eyes there was a pain, as sharp as if she were being pierced by the point of a needle, that made her yearn for a soft cool cushion to lean her forehead on. Again she wondered if she might be "coming down" with something: perhaps she had contracted one of the mysterious maladies to which this city, in its unhealthily low-lying river valley, was notoriously prone, and which each season felled as many of the visiting consumers of *bistecca* as would fill a fleet of charabancs. Mrs. Touchett, who regarded all illnesses short of the killing kind as mere self-indulgence, sat forward on the carriage seat with the hook-like fingers of both hands entwined on the crook of her parasol, taking in the passing scene with an expression of lively disdain; she had lived in Florence for very many years but had few acquaintances here, and fewer friends, either among the city's native population or its extensive community of Anglophone expatriates. Formerly Madame Merle had been for her the *ne plus ultra* among women, a person of unparalleled accomplishment, learning and manners, who could play Scarlatti and *scala quaranta* with equal skill and gracefulness, the glowing grandeur of whose presence enlivened the dullest soirée, and whose wit shone with a brilliance equal to that of the most brilliant of dinner-party guests. "She has been everywhere, and she knows everything," her admirer would declare, and cast about with a gimlet eye to know if anyone should be rash enough to contradict her. The door at Gardencourt was ever open to Serena Merle—Ralph Touchett used to say he had once been in love with her, although Isabel had taken it as no more than another of her cousin's gnomic jests— and annually the two ladies would spend a month or six weeks in each other's company at one of the more exclusive European spas, where it was understood by hoteliers, restaurateurs and bath attendants alike that all accounts should be laid, without comment or question, to Mrs. Touchett's name. However, after the favoured one's precipitate departure from Italy—or desperate scramble, as some preferred—her star in Mrs. Touchett's sky had not waned so much as plunged through the ether in a burning blur.

Overheated accounts of the exact cause of Madame Merle's going, as propounded by the knowing ones of Florence and Rome, ranged from the unexpected acquisition of a goldmine bequeathed to her by a prospector uncle in the far western states of her native land, to a squalid but expertly managed escape from a jostling throng of creditors, all waving fistfuls of unsettled bills and angrily shouting her name. At the same time, those who thought they knew the lady best contented themselves with a meaning smile and the fleeting light tap of a finger to the side of the nose; among these wise ones the watchword was a murmured *"Cherchez l'homme!,"* since Serena Merle, for all that she was not beautiful, and furthermore had slipped by a ledge or two down the far slope of the peak of her prime, still maintained intact the greater part of that smoothly enigmatic magnificence—as sheer and shining as the Matterhorn itself—which yet could cause a *uomo suscettibile* to contemplate kicking over the traces of a marriage, and even of a career, to follow in her entrancingly fragrant train. Mrs. Touchett, while she would not have dreamed of stooping to such vulgar speculations, found her curiosity piqued by the confounding fact that Madame Merle should have changed her mind, at the urging of a woman she had wronged, and agreed to return, and to return not to Florence but to Rome, at that, a city she had always claimed to consider ugly, provincial and uncouth.

"Tell me, if you care to," the old lady asked now of her niece, "by what means you persuaded her to come back—for I should have thought so strong-willed a person not at all persuadable." What she had refrained from adding, as Isabel was well aware, was that she could not think how such a one as Madame Merle could be persuaded by such a one as *she.*

They were crossing a bridge; below them the river was the colour and, at least to look at, the texture also of stale mustard, a sight that, along with the day's flabby heat and the awful brown scent of their horses wafting back over her, caused our heroine, feeling already less than robust, to feel more queasy still. This river, so flat and sluggish as to seem not to be moving at all, had often struck her as the aptest emblem, for her, of the city where her fate had been sealed, and where her life had been printed with the insidious watermark that she had only recently made out, against the merciless glare of the unwelcome enlightenment that had been forced on her by the Countess Gemini. It was here in Florence, at the Palazzo Crescentini, that she had been introduced, by Madame Merle, to the man who, not by Destiny's agency, as she had thought, but by craft and infinitely careful manoeuvre, was to become her husband. It would be foolish, she knew, to resent a city for a misfortune that had befallen one within its walls, yet she could not but rue, even again, the impulse that had led her today to disrupt her journey and step down from the train into a place that was rife with morbid memories. But then, she reflected, what was Rome, the day's original destination, if not the place where she would be compelled to recall the slow and painful dissolution of her fondest assumptions, her happiest expectations? Her home, the Palazzo Roccanera, was well-named, for it was there that she had run up against the immovable black rock of failure—the failure of her marriage, the failure of herself, *her* failure—like the engine of a steam train rounding a bend and colliding full-tilt with a boulder fallen on the track.

It was not until they had arrived at the humble and pleasantly muddled little Osteria del Fiume, and had been seated, by the great-girthed and gloriously beaming *padrone,* at a plain square table with a red-and-white-checked cloth, that Isabel at last gave her aunt an answer to the question she had posed in the carriage all of a quarter of an hour ago.

"I made her a threat, and a proposition," she said.

Despite the interval that had elapsed, Mrs. Touchett had no difficulty in knowing to what and to whom her niece was referring.

"Well, it certainly proved an effective combination, if what you tell me is the case, and Madame Merle is to come back to us," she said, in her accustomed dry and matter-of-fact fashion. "May one enquire as to the sweetness of the carrot, and the rigidity of the stick? The latter, I guess, was an offshoot of your marriage."

Isabel, staring absently at a carafe of suspiciously cloudy water that had been set in front of her on the table, was slow to respond. "My marriage?" she said vaguely.

"I am assuming that your husband and Serena Merle were—how should one say?—conspiring against you. Am I mistaken?"

Isabel looked at her with an expression of deep perplexity, as if she were unable to comprehend not only the question, but even the meaning of the words in which it had been couched. "What conspiring?" she asked.

Mrs. Touchett lifted up the gold nippers and set them on the bridge of her pinched little nose and peered through them long and searchingly at her niece. Could the young woman be so dim, she asked herself, or was it a clever pretence? If she was pretending, then her sister's youngest daughter was blessed with a histrionic gift that no other member of the family, not even her feckless father, had shown the least suspicion of possessing.

"The conspiring, my dear niece," Mrs. Touchett said, with as weighty an emphasis as one so light and spare as she could muster, "that a woman so subtle and silvery of tongue as Serena Merle and a man so conceited and susceptible to flattery as your husband might be expected to engage in. Are you that innocent? Should you need to see Mr. Hawthorne's scarlet letter daubed on Serena Merle's handsome bosom before crediting what she is capable of? And don't imagine yourself singled out—she has ruined many a marriage besides yours."

"I thought you were her friend."

"I admired her, I admire her still, and may admire her again, when she returns to Italy—and what of it? If one were to choose one's intimate acquaintances on the state of their morals one should lead an exceedingly isolated life. I must say," she went on with a thoughtful frown, "if she settles in Rome I shall see very little of her, which may be for the best. But why Rome, anyway?"

"That was the carrot, as you called it, that I offered her," Isabel simply replied.

Her aunt eyed her again with a sharp surmise. "No," she said at length, shaking her head, "I don't see it. What of her oft-stated aversion to Rome?"

"That has been cured."

"Oh, yes? And what was the remedy?"

"I offered her an allowance—I bribed her, if you like."

The old lady evinced no surprise; it was one of her private satisfactions to be unshockable, and to show herself so. "You *bribed* her? To what end, may I ask?"

"To the end that she would agree to live in Rome, where her presence will be, as you guessed, a standing rebuke to my husband and a constant reminder of his base actions."

"Ah, yes—*she* will be *his* scarlet letter, for all to see."

"I don't care who sees or doesn't, so long as *he* does."

"I doubt it will be a great penance on him."

"He must not think he can so easily banish inconveniences from his life," Isabel said, with earnest insistence. "Besides, there are aspects of the matter of which you are not aware, of which no one is aware, except—" She stopped; she would not allow herself to introduce the gaudy figure of the Countess Gemini into the exchange, even if it were only by the uttering of her name. She looked at the tablecloth. "Is Pansy with my husband, at Bellosguardo, do you know?"

"I have not heard otherwise. Why do you ask?"

"The last time I saw her he had sent her back to the convent."

Mrs. Touchett nodded. "He has become a true Italian papa,

locking his daughter up on the slightest pretext. What was her crime this time?"

"She lost her heart to a person of whom my husband did not approve."

"You mean Mr. Rosier? Yes, I had heard something of that. The gentleman was going about pressing everyone he could think of to plead his cause. I believe he even approached Serena Merle. As well ask Herod's wife to intercede on behalf of the Holy Innocents." She raised a quizzical eyebrow. "What's Pansy to you, anyway? You were not permitted to be any kind of mother to her, were you?"

"She's an unhappy creature, a suffering creature," Isabel said, in her plain, precise fashion.

Her aunt sat back on her chair and gave her a considering look, so lengthy and so keen that it made Isabel fidget; she still felt unwell, and her brow was hot.

"Does it not occur to you," Mrs. Touchett asked, "that in launching out your numerous shafts of sympathy you may sometimes aim wide of the mark?"

Just then their host appeared, in all the glory of his jocose rotundity, flashing menus at them as a samurai would his sword. Isabel had wished to interrogate her aunt as to the meaning of her curious challenge—who more than Pansy Osmond was deserving of heartfelt pity?—but the old lady had donned her pince-nez again and given herself up so thoroughly to the *carta delle vivande* that she might have retreated behind a wall. The young woman put a hand to her burning brow. She could not think what she might eat—the very idea of eating seemed hardly tolerable—and the words on the menu swam before her eyes, as incomprehensible as hieroglyphs. There rose then in her mind, like some ghastly clay-encrusted thing pushing itself up from underground, a youthful recollection, one that came back to her with dreadful and persistent frequency. She and her sisters had been with their father on one of the ruinously profligate dashes to Europe that he undertook compulsively when the fancy seized him. Stopping in some Swiss or Austrian city, Lucerne, perhaps, or Graz, she could not remember which, they had gone on a day's outing to a preposterously picturesque schloss—pinnacles, pennants, pines—and were travelling through the outskirts at evening on the way back to their *pension,* when a carriage, smaller than theirs and painted a peculiarly unsettling deep lacquered shade of shiny black, came scuttling, as it seemed—with its taut domed black hood, the thing resembled nothing so much as a grotesquely overgrown beetle— out of a side road and veered into their path. Their horses shied wildly, and for a perilous moment it seemed that father, daughters and driver all would be pitched out upon the road. The other carriage did not slow in the least, but plunged past, swaying on its springs. Despite the speed and confusion of the moment, Isabel caught a glimpse of the driver, seeing him starkly and, as it might be, in utter stillness—it was as if time had been halted for an instant, in order that she might be afforded this clearest possible view of the creature, a view that stamped itself for ever on her young consciousness. He was slight of stature, and wore a black coat and an old-fashioned stiff white stock at his throat. For all that he was presented so vividly to her eye, she could not have guessed his age; he might have been a man of middling years grown prematurely old, or a youth even, a sort of ancient, wizened boy. His cheeks were sunken, and his skin was of a faded, yellowish cast; his hair, swept back from a high pale forehead, was also a soiled shade of yellow, and coarse, like so many twists of straw. It was his eyes, however, black and shiny as wet coal and aglow with what seemed to her malignant mirth, that struck her with most force and fearfulness. His lower teeth were bared to the utmost extent—she had the impression that she could see the very ridge of bone in which they were set; indeed, it appeared to her that the flesh had receded entirely from the lower part of his face, exposing the bare structure of his jaw, which looked as dry and pitted as a cuttlefish bone.

The encounter had lasted no more than a few moments, and then the bug-like carriage had sped on, and her father was cursing the demon driver for a blackguard, while their own horses flung up their manes and snorted, showing the whites of their eyes. Isabel was convinced that it was she alone to whom the creature had shown his ravaged visage, and that the others in the carriage had seen nothing of him, save his coat and his stock and one small white fist brandishing aloft a long black slender whip. But she, yes, she had seen him, and did not forget him, and never would. Why had he singled her out? What had he discerned in her that was not in her sisters? And what frightful message had he meant to convey to her? It was as if one corner of the fabric of the world had been lifted so that she might glimpse the darkness that lay underneath, the darkness and the dark things that were always there, waiting to crawl out and cling to her, and against which all her bright complacencies could offer no protection.

She had ordered soup and now it was brought to her, but for the moment she could not bring herself even to taste it. Her aunt glanced at her and enquired if she were unwell, and when she said no, that she was only tired from the train journey, the old lady, whose appetite, despite her claims to the contrary, was remarkable and consistent, returned her attention to her plate of *salume*, the drifting odour of which Isabel tried not to inhale. She felt as if the entire back of her skull were stuffed full of hot wet wool. She drank some water but it tasted stale, and was tepid besides.

"Do I take it from your silence," her aunt enquired mildly, "that you prefer to dispense with the subject of your unhappy marriage?"

Isabel tried to smile. "It's a subject, dear Aunt, upon which there is not very much to say. In fact, I wonder if there is much of it at all—my marriage, I mean."

At this the old lady looked up once more from her meat. "Has the thing gone so far as that?" she asked, and, upon receiving no reply, continued: "In that case why have you come back to Italy?"

"There are matters to be—settled."

"And do these matters include your step-daughter?"

Isabel was struck that her aunt should fix upon Pansy so readily, and with what seemed a certain sharpness. "Pansy?" she asked. "Why do you mention Pansy?"

"Why did *you* enquire of her and her whereabouts a while ago?" Mrs. Touchett swiftly returned, with the air of a compact, elderly cat, still spry for its years, pouncing on its prey. She rested her wrists against the edge of the table, with her knife and fork suspended at a vertical angle. She sat for a moment in this pose, seeming to ponder, and when she spoke, a stony coldness had come into her voice. "I shall tell you something I have never told to anyone before. When I do, I may regret it, and so may you, but that's a risk to be taken, I think, in the circumstances." She paused, and turned her head to the side, frowning and moving her lips a little, as if she were rehearsing in her mind the matter she was about to relate. "I once found myself in a position similar to that which you are in—at least, I assume it was similar, unless I have misinterpreted the things you have said today, and the many more things you have not said."

XXV

There is a universal truth which the young are all too infrequently
surprised into acknowledging, and then with a sense of having
been violently brought up short, which is that, as they are now, so
too were the old, once. We may figure it otherwise by proposing
that every generation considers itself unique, and that each batch
newly entered upon its adult estate believes itself to be enjoying,
or enduring, experiences, discoveries and difficulties that are all
novel, all singular, and all exclusive to them and their coevals. The
world of the young is ever a brave new world, populated by brave
young people like themselves. They are prepared to entertain the
possibility that their parents may once have lived and loved, have
rejoiced and suffered, as they themselves do, although they would
have done so in a paler, weaker way, of course, and by now would
have forgotten most if not all of what it was they used to know;
the children of these vague amnesiacs look upon them and smile
or scowl, depending on the degree of cordiality that has survived
the rigours of twenty or so years of intimate family life, and, like
ushers in the interval of the play, helpfully point them in the direction of the exit. The old, whom the young regard as an entirely
separate, prehistoric species, as the aurochs, say, or the California
redwood, are, in terms of experience, considered blandly discon-

nected from the doings and dramas of the current day, while their lives when they were young, in an impossibly distant, immemorial age, were surely as slow, serene and uneventful as they seem now to be; having passed from primordial youth to frictionless old age without the slightest inner disturbance or alteration, they exist as superannuated innocents, harmless, affectless, anciently virginal. It was therefore with the deepest astonishment that Isabel listened to her aunt's tale of age-old betrayal, passion and pain.

The young woman recalled the summer when she had first arrived in England, and the tranquil afternoons she had spent on the long, burnished lawn at Gardencourt, in the company of her elderly and, as sadly it was to prove, dying uncle Daniel, Mrs. Touchett's husband. It had been a remarkably fine, long-lasting summer, and it was the old man's fancy to sit in a wicker armchair out on the grass, with a rug over his knees despite the warmth of the day, facing the grand and venerable house of which he pretended not to be proud, tranquilly conversing with whatever desultory visitors might drop by, or serenely absorbed in his own thoughts and memories. He had "taken to" Isabel from the start, and often they were to be seen together in relaxed and intimate colloquy, the old man holding in both hands a big, brightly coloured teacup that was specially reserved for him, and the girl seated by his knee on a blanket of her own spread upon the grass. She could recall little of what they had talked about, but the hours they spent together had left her with the impression of having been the recipient of a deep fund of wisdom bestowed upon her with warmth, humour and an endearing diffidence. Could this have been the same man whose actions of long ago, which seemed well-nigh incomprehensible to the young woman, her aunt was describing to her now?

"At that time he was not yet a banker, but a junior partner in a Manhattan accountancy firm," Mrs. Touchett was saying, in her unvaryingly spare and measured manner. "It is no dishonour to his memory to say that without the money I brought to the marriage, money I had from my father, who died young at the height of his success as an investor in the railroad, we should have found life considerably less agreeable than we did. We were not many years wed—Ralph was hardly more than a babe-in-arms—and I imagine I was guilty of that complacency to which young wives are prone." She paused to drink some water from her glass; by now she had before her a dish of *ravioli del plin,* while Isabel had managed to force herself to take only three or four spoonfuls of her soup—twice already it had been necessary to fend off the worriedly deprecating *padrone,* who even yet was hovering nearby, with his lips pursed and shaking sadly his large smooth head. But how could she hope to eat, feeling so fevered and hot, and so dazedly incredulous of the amazing tale the details of which her aunt was calmly setting out before her? "The woman in question was some years his senior," this lady now went on, deftly stabbing one of the little pinched parcels of pasta with her fork. "She was the wife of another partner in the firm. We saw them socially on occasion, her and her dunce of a husband—as I say, I was young and much taken up with the care of a sickly infant, but surely *he* should have been mature and worldly-wise enough to have seen what was going on under his nose. But, then, perhaps he had similar private business of his own to attend to—New York in those days was as wild and unlicensed as they say the western reaches of our country still are today. At any rate the thing had been going on for some considerable time before I learned anything of it. Perhaps I should never have known, and it would simply have dissolved, as such things usually do—I believe it was no more than an infatuation, an *amour fou*—but there was a child, you see. Oh, yes, a boy. I never saw the creature, of course, but he was the cause of Daniel confessing to me, at last." She broke off and, with fork suspended, leaned forward to peer closely at her niece. "Are you sure you're not unwell?" she asked. "You look distinctly queer."

"It's nothing," Isabel responded, though her voice was weak and feathery. "I think I may have a touch of fever, that's all."

Mrs. Touchett shrugged, lifting her eyebrows in the lightly dismissive way that she did when there was a question of the well-being of someone other than herself. She had finished her pasta, and now she set to mopping up the residue of oil in the dish with a fragment of bread held between two fingers and a thumb. Isabel looked on with heavy-lidded fascination, as if she were witnessing an exotic and arcane religious ritual. "They call this the *scarpetta*, the slipper," her aunt said, showing her the soaked wad of bread. "Did you know that? They have so many curious and telling words to do with food."

"The child," Isabel prompted, effortfully pressing on, "what became of it—of him?" Her eyes had begun to scald under their leaden lids.

"Oh, Daniel wished to keep him, and raise him as his own. He yearned for a son, and it seemed Ralph would not live. You know what a thing it is with men, wanting their name perpetuated and all that. Vanity, vanity and nonsense, a trick to allow themselves to think they'll never die. I refused to have the boy, of course— the idea! The mother consigned the poor thing to an orphanage, and moved with her unhappy husband to Manitoba. Manitoba! Punishment enough, I suppose, for a creature of her sort."

She moved her plate aside and summoned the portly attendant and requested of him a *tazza di cioccolata* and, as an afterthought, a selection of *biscotti*. The fellow bowed and beamed and backed away, wriggling his fingers before him in a comical gesture of fawning servitude. Isabel, to whose hectic gaze everything had taken on a slightly fantastical aspect, watched him with a sort of uncomprehending wonderment. His scant hair, heavily pomaded and of a conspicuously deep shade of black, seemed to swarm athwart his expansive skull, and came to a point in a perfectly circular curl plastered to his forehead high up on the left side.

"But then," Isabel said, drawing her eyes back to her aunt, "but then Ralph has a half-brother, who most likely is still living, somewhere in the world."

Her aunt lifted her eyebrows again, in surprise this time, seeming mildly disconcerted. "I certainly never thought of it in those terms," she said. "And now that I do think of it, I don't at all like the notion." Her chocolate and her biscuits arrived and were set before her with lavish ceremony, which she entirely disregarded. She was watching her niece. "Do you not wonder why I've recounted to you this sordid and disreputable tale?"

"I fear I may know the reason," Isabel responded, in a small faint voice, hushed by misery. At least they only put Pansy in a convent, she thought, with a pang of pity—*they* being, of course, the girl's father and her clandestine mother.

"You must be cautious, you must go carefully," Mrs. Touchett said. "It would be very easy to make a tremendous mistake, at your age, in your circumstances."

"Yet Pansy is—" she began, in a plangently pleading tone, but the old lady seated opposite her at once held up the spoon she had been stirring her chocolate with and brandished it before her face to silence her.

"If you please, I will hear nothing of your husband's daughter—I will hear nothing of anything that is your husband's. It is one thing to exchange chitchat about the likes of Serena Merle, a person of the smallest consequence, I have come to see, for all the high esteem in which she holds herself, and in which I used to hold her. But all *that*, involving as it does a child, all that is quite another matter."

"But, dear Aunt," Isabel broke out, "I have no one, no one to advise me!"

"Then count yourself fortunate," Mrs. Touchett implacably replied, presenting to her niece the blank aspect of a sphinx. "Advice is another term for mischief-making, and anyone who asks for it deserves the consequences. One cannot be told how to live, my girl—and one shouldn't wish to be."

"And yet," Isabel said, with an unsteady and melancholy little smile, "would it not have been better if I had paid heed to those voices, including yours, which years ago, when I was hardly more than a girl, advised me against the course I had set myself upon, and the man I had chosen to be my husband?"

"You mix words, you mistake your terms. To warn is not the same as to advise. I *warned* you against a person I knew to be unworthy of you—not, frankly, that I considered you worthy of so very much. I warned you once and afterwards held my peace. About the things I suspect you to be contemplating now, I have nothing to offer you." She paused, still withholding of expression. "You said you threatened Serena Merle; since you mentioned it, I feel I am at liberty to ask you what was the nature of the threat. And before you answer, permit me to remind you that she is not a lady easily frightened."

Isabel was gazing again at a patch of the tablecloth, and some moments passed before she had collected herself sufficiently to resume speaking. "I reminded her there were things that, if I chose, I could publish abroad, in society, and in those places, even in America, where she could count on having a safe haven—"

"Where she can count on board and lodging at no expense to herself, you mean," the old lady sharply interjected.

"—places where, if I spoke out, or others were to speak out for me—"

"*Voilà* a certain countess!"

"—her reputation, and the universal welcome she is accustomed to enjoy, could not but be compromised."

Mrs. Touchett, waiting for more and realising more was not to come, sighed and shook her head, letting her thin shoulders droop. "My dear young woman," she said, "what are you thinking of? Do you imagine Serena Merle will be intimidated by the prospect of being made the object of gossip? Do you think there is anything you can say about her that has not been said already, time and time over?"

Isabel, raising her head with almost a jerk, had suddenly the look of a hitherto meek young miss who has been pushed beyond her limit in the school playground. "She is Pansy Osmond's mother!" she flashed out and, as if it were not merely a variation of the announcement already made but an extension of it, "Pansy is her daughter!"

If she had expected this revelation to produce a tremendous effect, as surely she had, then on the contrary, and to her puzzled consternation, she was startled to find that it had no effect at all, save that of causing Mrs. Touchett to look upon her pityingly.

"And Mamie Winthrop," this lady now said, "was the mother of what you refer to as my son's half-brother, and she went to Manitoba and for all I know lived out her life perfectly at peace with herself and her witless husband." She paused, and glared at her chocolate cup as if it too, like her niece, might be expected to say something vexatious. "Tell me this," she went on, "how many of Serena Merle's acquaintances—I doubt she has any *friends*, to speak of—how many, do you imagine, would be shocked or even surprised to learn she had been your husband's mistress and mother to his child? The world, *our* world, takes from people what it wishes to have of them—company, amusement, diversion—and blithely ignores the rest. You imagined Serena Merle to be your friend and mentor, you took her with you on your travels over half the world—paying every cent along the way, I have no doubt. Am I expected to believe that, in all that time and over all those miles, you never once had so much as a glimpse of a side of her that was less polished than the one she presents with consummate artistry to the public view?"

"Why should I not have taken her for what she seemed?" the young woman pleaded, twisting her napkin into knots in her agitation and distress. "Everyone sang her praises and said she was a wonder. Even Ralph confessed to having been in love with her once"—here Mrs. Touchett interjected a derisive "Ha!"—"while *you* said there was nothing in the world she didn't know and couldn't do."

"And was I not right? Have you not discovered, to your cost, that there is nothing she's not capable of?"

"Ah, you didn't mean it in that way!" the girl softly cried—for in the course of this exchange the married woman had become as a chit of a thing again, defenceless, lost and alone. "You didn't mean it as a warning to me."

"I didn't know you needed warning, then. I already told you, some time ago, that in those days, when I could see you had become a gleam in Osmond's calculating eye, your Madame Merle assured me that if there were to be the slightest danger of that gleam catching fire, she would make it her business to extinguish it herself."

Isabel at once seized on this. "And you believed her!" she wellnigh whooped. "You were as easily taken in as I was myself!"

"I am *never* easily taken in!" Mrs. Touchett magisterially pronounced. "And that I was deceived, quite calculatedly so, on that occasion, is only proof of the woman's skill—"

"As a liar?"

"—as an arranger of matters to her own advantage, and to the advantage of those few around her whom she chooses to favour!" She stopped, and allowed some moments of silence to pass, during which interval she sat and coldly contemplated the suffering creature seated before her at the table. "I repeat, you said to me she made a convenience of you. Do you remember what I replied? I said it is what she does—she makes a convenience of everyone, in one way or another."

The table was quite cleared of the remains of their repast— Isabel's soup, hardly touched and with unsightly congealings floating on the surface, had been snatched up and borne away in a flurry of wordless reproach—and now Mrs. Touchett signalled for the bill. While it was awaited, the two women looked about the low brown room in the vague, distracted way that people in restaurants often do, when the little drama of luncheon has come to a close and the afternoon looms vacantly ahead. Then Isabel stirred herself and asked: "But if she's not afraid of a scandal—if she's not afraid of *me*—why did she allow me to persuade her to come back?"

Once more her aunt bent upon her a sharply compassionate, yet also disparaging, look. "I doubt she required much persuading. Consider what you were offering her."

"You mean—?"

"I mean Rome! You tell me she has dropped the pretence of despising the place, a pretence I never believed in, anyway, for she often remarked, in that pointedly wistful way she affects when she is dropping a significant hint—she always had hopes I would give her money—that she would far prefer to live in a 'real' city, as she said, to rotting away in our poor Tuscan backwater, if she could have afforded to. Which now she can, thanks to your munificence." The account was brought on a little earthenware plate, and the old lady leaned forward and perused it closely with the aid of her glass. "So you see, my dear Isabel," she murmured, not lifting her eyes and still carefully computing, "she considered herself condemned to durance vile, and you have as good as bought her release."

XXVI

The pair had no sooner returned to the Palazzo Crescentini than Isabel's fever intensified alarmingly—she could feel it shoot up inside her, like the thin red thread in a thermometer. Mrs. Touchett, having no intention of exposing herself to the risk of contagion, assigned the patient a big room, light and airy, but daunting in its dimensions, high up at the far back of the house, and it was to there that the young woman, flushed and trembling, was straightway dispatched. Fortunately Staines was on hand to care for her—the maid's first action was to dismiss, on the spot, with one of the more fearsome of her basilisk stares, the trio of female servants who had helped her mistress up the many and wearying zigzag flights of marble staircase—and ordered her at once into the unaccountably high four-poster bed, a thing so broad and long it occupied fully a third part of the entire room. It was on this vast pallet that Isabel would lie for many days, drifting in and out of hot and fitful sleep, like a log borne on the back of a tropical river through steaming jungle depths. At times she was delirious, and imagined she was back in America, in the Everglades, or the savannah, or some other southern swampy place that she had never visited in her life but only read descriptions of. She suffered also passages of fantastic clarity, when there bore

in upon her painfully, with what seemed the profoundest significance, the most minute and trivial things—a loose thread in one
of her soaked and reeking bed-sheets; the black and pitted head of
a spent match lying in the trough of a candle-holder; a fly clamber-
ing over the Alpine expanses of her pillow, pausing now and then
to wash its face, as it seemed, with vigorous rubbings of its front
paws. Two tall windows to her left gave on to a scene of jumbled
terracotta roofs and the campanile of a church or cathedral she
could not identify; in the middle hours of the day the scorching
sunlight pouring in upon her through the glass made her feel like
a damned soul in one of the circles of Dante's hellish regions, and
she would call weakly for Staines to draw the drapes and deliver
her into a sort of blissful twilight. The sounds of the city came to
her as the buzzing of a myriad of distant beehives, although at
other times what she seemed to hear were the mingled voices of
an angelic choir, and she would feel herself carried softly upwards
into an empyrean of glowing blue and shimmering gold—on
one occasion, to be recalled with disturbing vividness when she
had recovered, she saw herself afloat in the upper reaches of the
Duomo, under Brunelleschi's wondrous dome, sustained upon
nothing but empty air, the stray strands of hair at her temples
stirred by chance elevated breezes.

Her aunt, of course, would not visit the sickroom, but Staines
brought up with her regular bulletins of news from downstairs.
The maid and Mrs. Touchett had, it seemed, forged between them,
to Isabel's surprise and intense interest, a strong bond of mutual
regard, and often of a morning the lady of the house would linger at table after breakfast and, before repairing to the cubbyhole
off the *piano nobile* that she had designated as her office, the two
women would converse together for as much as a half-hour. Isabel
was ever eager to know what they talked about—what they could

possibly talk about—but under interrogation Staines maintained a front of tantalising vagueness, and even at times appeared to hint at detecting a degree of prurience in her mistress's attempts to pry into what were, after all, private exchanges between two independent persons. At the Palazzo Crescentini the maid felt at liberty to seize for herself a degree of autonomy she would not have dreamed of claiming in any other establishment, not in Italy, not in France either, and certainly not in her native land. So the mystery of these morning tête-à-têtes remained sealed, to be added by Isabel to the ever-lengthening list of life's insoluble puzzles.

One afternoon, on a day when Isabel had begun to mend, her fever having much abated, the maid, herself in a somewhat elevated state, bore to her mistress's bedside a rectangle of white pasteboard on which was printed, in modestly small type, the name of one Myles Devenish, a correspondent, so an even more minuscule line announced, of the *London Clarion*. This was a journal that neither woman had heard of. They gazed at the *biglietto*, the two of them, like young ladies at a ball puzzling over the appearance on a dance-card of a fascinatingly unfamiliar name. Had Mr. Devenish offered a clue as to his circumstances, or to the purpose of his calling upon Mrs. Osmond? that lady enquired. He had not, the maid confirmed, except that he had mentioned a name with which mistress and maid were both acquainted, which was that of Miss Florence Janeway, the lady at whose hard-to-find home in far-off Fulham Isabel had partaken of a memorably, indeed an unforgettably, verdurous luncheon, one sunny afternoon several weeks previously. But how had the personable young man—that he was of an appealing aspect was attested to by a certain suspenseful quickening in Staines's manner—known where Isabel was to be found? He had also mentioned, the maid supplied, besides Miss Janeway, Isabel's friend Henrietta Stackpole, to whom Isabel, as she now remembered, had written from the telegraph office in the railway station at Florence, on the day of her impulsive stopping off there, to apprise her friend of the interruption in her itinerary, and of her intention to seek temporary shelter at the Palazzo Crescentini. Now Isabel turned over the card in her fingers, but the back of it bore no message, being entirely blank. "He does not say where he himself is staying," she murmured. So the two women, the maid leaning down by the shoulder of her mistress, where she reclined against a bank of pillows on the great high bed—an observer with an eye for such things might have remarked how uncanny a suggestion they made of a scene by Metsu, as might be, or the sublime Vermeer— continued pondering in silence the small but not unfascinating fact of Mr. Devenish's unforthcoming card. Perhaps he would call again, Isabel ventured, but the maid shook her head. "He said as he would be taking the sleeper to Paris this evening, ma'am, on his way back to London."

"Ah, then I imagine his call was no more than a politeness," Isabel said, "made at the behest of Miss Janeway." She put the card aside, propping it against the candle-holder on the commode beside the bed; there it stayed, and although it remained an enigma, her eye returned to it frequently, in vague but persistent surmise.

That night she enjoyed, for the first time in many nights, a sound and dreamless sleep, and woke late in the morning feeling rinsed and refreshed, as if she had been lifted up out of a viscous immersion into calm air and clean clear light—she was still of a young enough age that a minor malady such as that through which she had passed was less an illness than a curative in disguise, a process of cleansing and refining and reinvigoration. She had hardly opened her eyes before it came to her, as if a commanding voice had spoken in her head, that this was the day on which she would take hold of the staff of self-assertion and, like a doughty alpinist, ascend the hill of Bellosguardo and confront her husband. Confront: the word gave her pause. Gilbert Osmond was not a man to make himself amenable to confrontation; he would not stoop to anything so tasteless as domestic disputation, and abhorred the tedious "tennis match," as she had once heard him describe it, of charge and counter-charge, between defensively obdurate husband and implacably shrewish wife. In the refined yet savage circular stalking of each other that their marriage had become, he had always the soft sure-footedness of a panther, while she was as a goat tethered to a post. Now that she had shrugged herself free of the rope, how was she to defend herself against his sinuous ploys? She could not win against him by direct engagement: he was master of the sudden switch, the diversionary feint, the flawlessly executed outflanking manoeuvre. If there was a smudge in the burnish of his armour it was his slowness in adapting to surprise; before the onrush of the unexpected he could lose his footing and find himself in danger of being undone, though invariably it took him no more than a moment to be right again and fully in charge of his forces— Here Isabel, rueful and amused, broke off the military metaphor; if it was a battle she was marching into, should she not have done with it and fortify herself with a musket?

Scarce half an hour later, feeling remarkably refreshed after her bath, and seeming to herself like a vessel fashioned from glass of the finest and most fragile consistency, she made her way down through the layered maze of echoing staircases and deserted corridors—the palazzo had always for Isabel the odd air of having been recently abandoned in precipitate haste and disorder—and after a search found her aunt seated at breakfast on a sunny terrace, in front of which, beyond a low marble balustrade, the garden disported itself in abounding brilliancies and deep patches of lurking, limpid shadow. The old woman looked up at her quickly, and seemed almost to shrink away in frank alarm. Mrs. Touchett feared nothing in life save the prospect of departing from it, and regarded those tainted by even the mildest infection as potential and unconvincingly disguised agents of her extinction, and it was only good manners, which she prized as intensely as she deplored death, that induced her to bid Isabel now to join her in her repast. Isabel sat down beside the balustrade on a peculiarly unaccommodating iron chair—she often suspected her aunt of taking pride in the fact that only an anchorite could have considered comfortable those items of furniture in her house that were meant for sitting, reclining or sleeping on—and said that she would take only a cup of black tea and a slice of dry toast, since she felt as weak as a kitten. Mrs. Touchett mumbled words to the effect that perhaps her niece should have kept to her chamber until she was entirely certain she was fully recovered. "Oh, I'm perfectly well, really," Isabel lightly insisted. "The fever is quite gone, and any lingering infirmity is surely the result of lolling in bed for such an unconscionably long time." And she added, because now and then she liked to tease the old lady, "Don't I look a great glowing romp of a thing, dear Aunt Lydia?" To this show of facetiousness Mrs. Touchett made no reply, and presently Isabel was brought her tea and toast, which she drank and ate, and afterwards the two sat together quiet for some minutes in the morning's garden freshness. Then Isabel requested the use of a means of transport—"a dog-cart or fly will suffice"—for she wished to make a journey that would take her a little way beyond the city gates.

Mrs. Touchett gave her one of her sharp swift glances. "So you're going to Bellosguardo," she said.

Isabel smiled at her. "Yes, Aunt, I am going to Bellosguardo. It's time I did."

The old lady was watching her still, with a little gleam as of amusement, or else of malice, or of both combined. "You are not apprehensive?"

"On the contrary, I am *extremely* apprehensive," Isabel answered, in her simplest and most straightforward fashion. "I fear my weapons are inadequate to the encounter that awaits me; they are lacking in reach."

The old lady produced what with her passed for a smile. "Then keep in mind," she said, "what the Spartan mother replied to her son when he complained of his sword being too short: 'Step closer.'"

"Ah, but, dear Aunt," Isabel gaily countered, "that sounds to me very much like advice, of the kind you say you make it a point never to dispense."

XXVII

The day was delightfully fresh and clear under a sky of unblemished blue that bespoke the coolly lucid north more than it did the varnished south. Mrs. Touchett had insisted that Isabel must have a carriage and pair, and her coachman in charge of it—"Did you propose to drive yourself up that impossible laneway calling itself a road?"—and it was from the deep back seat of this elegant vehicle that Isabel, in the shade of her, or rather Miss Stackpole's, parasol and with a light veil arranged about her face to ward off the dust, was free to gaze all about her at the low mild hills strewn with unmoving flocks of sheep and dimpled with shaded valleys, at cinnamon-coloured tracks that seemed to wander hither and yon according to their whim, at slender cypresses set in strict lines like shrouded sentinels—at the entire Tuscan scene, which was innocently unaware of its own loveliness, as shy and simple and finely detailed as a background by Piero. How incongruously at odds it seemed, this tranquil prospect, with the task and the sure trial that lay ahead of her today. But then, she reflected, doubtless the Louvre loomed as peacefully at rights with the world, to the eye of one borne past it in a trundling tumbril, in the sparkling sunlight of a revolutionary morning, as did to her these easeful Italian splendours.

The carriage stopped at the purblind rear of the house, which gave by way of a courtyard on to the public piazzetta. Giancarlo, the major-domo, opened to her the big square door of time-darkened timber, a portal so broadly accommodating that Mrs. Touchett's pair of carriage horses might have passed side by side straight through into the living room of what in former days had been Mr. Gilbert Osmond's principal, indeed his sole, domicile. The old servant at first did not know her, confused by his recollection of the Countess Gemini's recent visit, then fell into mumbling effusiveness, addressing her as *signora baronessa*, and forming his hands into fists and beating them silently together before him in a gesture of heartfelt welcome. The *signor barone* himself, he informed her, had gone to visit his *amico americano*, Mr. Boott, who with his daughter and her sculptor husband occupied another apartment, at the far end of the portioned-off house, but he would send word to him of her arrival *immediatamente*.

As she stepped over the threshold Isabel registered a violent quick vibration within her breast, as if an arrow had come flying full-tilt out of the past and struck her quiveringly to the core. She took in, with a sort of soundless gasp, the mingled odours, instantly familiar, of oiled wood and damp stone, of polished brass and faded tapestries, of the must and dust of old damask and, behind all, the darker note of those little black cheroots, crooked and thin as twigs, that her husband had always favoured. She noted, as had her sister-in-law before her, the ghostly blank spaces on the walls where Gilbert's pictures, a few of them executed by his own hand, used to hang; she looked for, and found, below the middle one of three tall windows aglow with blond light spilling in from the courtyard, the deep marks in the floorboards made by the castors of her husband's massive writing desk of English oak that it had taken a full day's labour by four hulking workmen to transport down the hill to the Palazzo Roccanera and its new place at the centre of the high cool chamber there that he had picked out to be his study. She had lived at Bellosguardo with her husband in the first months of her marriage, and to her the old place would be for ever associated intimately with the happiness she had felt then, that happiness a hidden component of which, as she afterwards came to think, must have been her ignorance of how fleeting it would prove to be. Yet however brief, how lovely, too, it had been, that precious time. What she had prized most was the calm and isolated life up here on "the Hill," as it was known familiarly to its denizens. Looked down upon from this tranquil height, the world seemed far-off and indistinct, its angles and edges blurred under a dusting of soft Tuscan sunlight. Garibaldi's tremendous unifying venture had been, so far as the blessed ones of Bellosguardo were concerned, of no more moment than the defection of a servant, who had run off to join the Prussian offensive against the French, and another who had broken some fine pieces of Limoges from Gilbert's collection, and had to be let go under suspicion of harbouring revolutionary tendencies. Even Isabel, whose heart when she was young had been stirred to its deeply beating extremity by President Lincoln's war of emancipation against the secessionist South, had been content to let her radical ideals lapse, which, as she would presently be made to understand, was well for her, since had she attempted to uphold them, her husband would have made it his business to strike them down.

There was no sign yet of Gilbert's returning from his nearby visit—she thought it probable he had been informed of her presence, as Giancarlo had said he would be, and that he intended his delay to be taken as a conscious and deliberate slighting of her—and she set herself to pacing slowly among the rooms of the apartment. As she went she revisited in her mind scenes from that old time, scenes that were for her as distant as the battles of Bull Run and the Wilderness and, like those titanic and desperate engagements, graspable by her only through an effort of imaginative figuring. Hollow and depleted as the place seemed, she felt herself to be a phantom presence in it. Her husband, before her coming, had been happy on the hill, but the space he had to make do with, out of financial considerations—rentals on Bellosguardo, even by the standards of Italy, were irresistibly modest—hardly constituted the storeyed ivory tower to which he considered his talents and his taste should have entitled him. Isabel recalled the perverse pleasure he had derived from taking her on a tour of what he referred to, with high ironical disdain, as his "quarters." He had brought her up here to the house with the express aim of acquainting her with the pains and privations he had been compelled to endure before the advent of her and her money— they were not yet married, but the wedding was a matter of days off, and, as she imagined now, he was sure enough of her to risk disclosing to her a harsher side of his peculiar humour than she had yet been exposed to. "It is an old house, and you must see it entirely, front and rear, in all its splendour and its squalor," he had said to her, with steely jocularity, pressing a finger to her elbow and leading her lightly forward. Far at the back somewhere—she had never again returned to the spot—they had entered through a low doorway into a dim, dank and horridly noisome cell with a slit for a window and wet moss on the walls, and limp black pod-like things suspended from the ceiling that Isabel suspected were the birthing-cauls of bats. In one corner an open sluice of rough stone was set at a falling angle into a hole cut in the wall, and to this her fiancé drew her particular attention. "As you see, my dear, there are all the conveniences a medieval *casa signorile* could be expected to offer." And he had smiled, compressing his greyish lips and moving them a little against each other, as if he were rolling a tiny morsel of something between them, such as a hard little seed, or a grain of sand. She had looked at him in wondering uncertainty; never had his grizzled beard seemed so artfully sleek, or the waxed and upturned tips of his moustache so menacingly sharp. For all his devotion to the proprieties, for all his exquisite discriminations and wounded reprehensions, for all his genuflections at the unsulliable altar of art, there was a seam of coarseness in his character to which, as she belatedly acknowledged, she should have paid closer heed. She was young when she first knew Gilbert Osmond, but she was not an innocent, she was not a hothouse bloom; she did not avert her gaze, or her consciousness, from the fundamental circumstances of being human, from the base and sad necessities that life imposes upon mortal creatures; she was a woman of her time, or perhaps of a better time that was still to come; yet for all that, she saw no reason to immerse herself willingly, indeed to revel, in suffocating mire, in darkness and dung. Her fiancé's insistence that she should be made to descend into that long-disused cloacal den at the back of the old house was but one among several glimpses he had afforded her of what most likely he would claim to be a fearless candour, a frankness admirable and unflinching. But he was more than frank, he was more than candid: he took a malignant satisfaction in turning up the world's stone so as to expose to the light of day the foul things swarming and squirming underneath it. That which was disgusting he savoured in the same way, it sometimes seemed to her, as he delighted in his possessions, as though the value of the latter were enhanced by the proximity of the former. As to herself, insofar as she was possessed by him, the reverse had been the case: his proximity had left her besmirched.

She could not now remember exactly what she had expected

being married to a man such as Gilbert Osmond would entail; she supposed it was the point, that her expectations had been savingly inexact. She had presumed that his passion—although passion was not a word she judged applicable, in the circumstances— would be exquisitely judged, meticulously calibrated. He would comport himself so delicately, with such gentle insistence, that she would register him as hardly more than a disembodied sensibility, a mind afloat in the fineness of its own distinction. She had a vague notion of herself enveloped in a sort of soft sea-mist, inside which an essential aspect of her would remain untouched, unbreached, unbroken; instead, he had turned out to be not the mist but the sea itself, a violent element surrounding her on all sides and pressing irresistibly upon the shell of her very being. This was the great surprise, the great shock. She had thought a deep part of herself, an essential part, a part as polished and impenetrable as a pearl, could always, must always, be shielded from him, and that by his nature he would allow it to continue so; on the contrary, that essence, that allness of herself, was precisely what she was required to give up. What she discovered, with an awful thrill, was that nothing could be kept from him, that he would have everything of her, and the surprise and the shock of it were the swooning completeness of her surrender, the moaning abjection with which she prostrated herself before him. Of course, once he saw how it was with her, he saw too how to turn the thing to his advantage. *Her* passion was the question, and it would be *his* power. Now came the exquisite judgement, the meticulous calibration, in the matter of giving and withholding. There were occasions—drowsy dawns, shuttered noons—when as she knelt before him, a palely glimmering, suppliant form, he would gaze down at her for a while through half-closed eyes, in that way he did, and then would rise with a sigh and a cold smile and, brush-

ing aside her imploringly outstretched hand, would stroll away to
his books, or his china, or his easel, and leave her there, trembling
in frustration and shame. Assailed now by such recollections, and
worse—she tried, oh, how she tried to fend them off!—she shud-
dered inwardly, and shut her eyes. When, a moment later, she
opened them again, she turned her head and looked out through
an open doorway into the garden, and saw her husband there.

He had paused on a pathway, under a trellis of vines, and was
patting his pockets and frowning—he must have forgotten something at his neighbour's apartment, his cigar case, most probably,
since it was a thing he frequently mislaid and left behind. He wore
a pale loose linen suit and a cambric shirt with a soft collar; his
waistcoat was unbuttoned and his straw hat was pushed far back
at an uncharacteristically casual and what for anyone else would
have been a comical angle, although it nevertheless gave to him,
with his narrow face and tapering beard, the look of one of El
Greco's haloed, white-clad saints. Although they were separated
only by some yards, he would not yet have seen her, so bright was
the sunlight surrounding him and so dimly shadowed the doorway within which she stood. She made no sound or movement,
only stayed still and watched him. He was usually so sharply self-
aware a man that, caught there in the glare of noonday and not
knowing he was observed, he appeared to Isabel unwontedly a figure of the ordinary sort, distracted, agitated, vexed both at his own
forgetfulness and the stubborn way that supposedly inanimate,
taken-for-granted things have of making themselves infuriatingly
elusive. A moment ago she had been thinking of him and recall-
ing his spiteful cruelties with a bitterness of her own, but now,
seeing him so prosaically there, a man she had once convinced
herself she adored, she felt a sort of softening towards him, a
weary resignation in the face of his misusing of her. He had done

her grave wrong, but he too in his way had been tricked and disappointed, not by her, it was true, but by his own mistaken assumptions, his assured expectations—she had not been the person he had taken her for, she had not been the wife he believed he was in want of, the wife he imagined Madame Merle had found for him. Isabel, the real, actual Isabel, had defied him, or so he would have it; she had set out the charter of her rights and demanded they be respected; her ideas—her *confounded* ideas, as he declared them—he had taken as an affront to his husbandly authority; most recently, as we know, she had chosen to fly to her dying cousin even after he had warned her, with unmistakable directness, of the consequences for the harmony, or what remained of it, of their marriage. Appearances meant much to him—meant everything, as it might be—and she had violently put a rent in the veil. In Rome, in Florence, in London and New York and many places besides, for all he knew, they spoke behind hands of her desertion; spoke of it, and snickered, so he was convinced. By disobeying him, and leaving him open to the world's mockery, by that, above all else, he considered his wife to have traduced him. And now here she was, come to add to his injuries, as he would see it, and as, indeed, she supposed would be the case. What would he say, what do? He had turned about, as if to go back by the way he had come, and retrieve whatever it was he had lost. She stopped him, however, by stepping forward quickly, into the sunlight, and uttering his name.

XXVIII

She was distracted at first by a curious optical phenomenon, which she could not account for except to think it must be somehow, to the eyes of one lately recovered from fever, the effect of the abrupt transition she had made from the gloom of the doorway into the day's full dazzle. At the sound of her voice her husband had stopped and turned about, and stood somewhat awkwardly before her, listing a little, framed within the arch of vines, as if he had been required to pose there by a photographer and instructed to remain motionless for the taking of his portrait. The strangeness was, to Isabel's appalled yet obscurely fascinated eye, that he looked a shade reduced in stature, that he was smaller by an inch or so than he should have been. She really was unable to see how the thing could have come about—he seemed to have been "taken in" a size, in somewhat the way that formerly, as we remember, the growing Pansy's dresses used to be "let out." Was it possible that in a mere space of weeks she had forgotten his true proportions? It was not only that he appeared shorter than she had remembered him to be; no, the reduction, if that was truly what to call it, had been effected all round, so that his face, his beard, his arms and legs and hands and feet, all were a slight yet, to her, perceptibly miniaturised version of what they had been when she last saw him. She blinked rapidly to dispel the illusion, as illusion it must be. Yet for his part was he not looking at her in equal perplexity, as if to his eye she too were altered, as he was to hers? If so, was he seeing her diminished, or increased?

"You might have sent word that you would be coming today," he said, taking off his hat and peering irritably into the crown. "You know how I dislike being required to deal with the unexpected."

"Yes, forgive me," she replied, and immediately regretted the meek-sounding words; she should not have started out apologetically, since it was not how she intended to proceed.

"I had your letter," he said, after a pause. "I confess I could make little of it. You do not usually obfuscate to such a degree."

She smiled. "I don't know how you would know, for I can't remember the last time I wrote to you, it was so long ago, although seemingly you do."

"Oh, I remember your letters well, brimming with schoolgirl gush as they were. Anyway, I wasn't referring to your epistolary style. You convey your meaning clearly enough, on the whole. I hope that's what you've come here to do."

Still with a faint smile fixed in place she turned from him, and walked to the stone parapet and stood looking down upon the long valley and its molten meandering river.

"Have you been long away from Rome?" she asked. "I didn't know you were here."

"It will be the last time—the house and lands are to be sold entire."

"Ah. You'll be sad, then."

"How did you find me, if you didn't know I was here?" he asked coldly, still standing in the shade of the vine leaves and addressing her back.

"I learned of your presence from Aunt Lydia."

"Ah, the immortal Madame Touchett," Osmond said, with violent disdain. "I suppose you've told her all there is to tell. She doesn't receive me, these days."

She turned her head to look at him. "That surprises me. She doesn't judge people, except by her own eccentric standards."

"Judge?" he said with a sniff. "By what right should she think to judge me—she, or anyone else?"

"I employed the wrong term," Isabel murmured, and turned back to the view, which for all that she looked at it she did not see. She felt tired suddenly; a thought had come to her, an insight so weighty it wearied her just to sustain it, for it seemed to her of sufficient force to have a universal application. What she saw was that it had not been Osmond she had fallen in love with, when she was young, but herself, through him. That was why he was no more to her now than a mirror, from the back of which so much of the paint had flaked and fallen away that it afforded only fragments of a reflection, indistinct and disjointed.

She turned and walked back to where she had stood before, facing him on the gravelled pathway. He held his hat in his hands, fingering the brim. He still had that strange appearance of being somehow reduced, yet the effect seemed to her now not one of diminishment, but rather of concentration, as if he had drawn the belts and buckles of his armour tight the better to do battle with her.

"The sun is so strong," she said. "Do you think we might go inside?"

She could see him turning over the question, judging if it would not be to his better advantage if she were to be kept standing here in the midday's fierce glare and blinding glitter. He relented, however, and gesturing with his hat invited her to step through the doorway, where he followed after her. Within, Isabel seated herself on a straight-backed chair beside the table, feeling in need of the comfort and support of the venerable wood, while Osmond took to a big deep sofa below one of the three cross-barred windows that looked into the courtyard, half reclining with his hat beside him and his legs thrust straight out in front of him and his narrow, his emaciated, ankles crossed. In a further room a clock marked the hour with a rapid brassy chime, as if appropriately to signal the beginning of the bout. It was Isabel who made the first pass.

"I encountered Mr. Rosier in Paris," she said. "We found ourselves by chance in the Louvre at the same hour one day."

Osmond lifted a disdainful eyebrow. "Hardly to be counted a happy chance, I venture. How is the paltry fellow? Still pining for my daughter, I suppose."

"No, indeed, he has quite cured himself of her, or claims to have. He is to marry."

"Is he, now," her husband drawled, affecting to suppress a yawn. "And who is the lucky maiden he has fixed his soft-boiled eye on this time?"

"A Miss Rothstein, native of Paris."

"So he has got himself in with the Jews! I was not aware of them being native to anywhere, save some steamy warren beneath an escarpment in Palestine. Who is she? What is her father, banker or merchant? I'll wager he's one or the other."

"He is a dealer, one of the main ones, I believe, at the Hôtel Drouot."

"But of course a dealer, and a successful one, no doubt— I think I've heard of him. Rosier's type will have none but a man of means for a father-in-law."

"He would have had *you*," Isabel said, with a quickness and sharpness she had not intended, or had not been aware of intending—in her dealings with Osmond she always felt that there were two versions of her engaged: herself, and a hardly recognisable, fearsome other whom she strictly monitored but who nevertheless broke out on occasion. Her husband, leaning sideways on one elbow and with the fingers of both hands intertwined and resting upon the fob-pocket of his pale satin waistcoat, drew his head far back and looked at her long from under halfway-lowered lids. "I mean," Isabel hastily distinguished, "he would have had Pansy, even if she were poor."

"Oh, I know what you mean," Osmond said, with a silky softness.

They were silent then, and the sounds from without, near and far, asserted themselves upon the air of the room. Isabel looked at her hand where it rested on the table, and saw it for a moment as an alien, creeping thing that had without her noticing attached itself to her wrist. Everything was suddenly hideous and horrible. Why had she come here, to this place that held in it so much of the lost and sullied past?

"Is Pansy still at the convent?" she asked.

"No, she is not."

"Then she is here, with you?"

"No, not here, either."

In the dimness of the room the long rectangle of the doorway open on to the garden seemed an overly vivid, framed depiction of conflagration and motionless turmoil. Isabel could not quite make out her husband's expression, where he lolled lazily among shadows on the other side of the room. Now he stirred himself, and rising from the sofa crossed to a high old polished oak cabinet, and took up a goose-necked flagon and poured a measure of tawny wine into a goblet of carved Venetian glass. She had often noticed, when they confronted each other in one of these exchanges—not that this exchange was quite like any they had ever engaged in before—how deliberate and carefully measured his every word and gesture seemed. Acutely self-aware as he was, on this occasion he did not entirely convince. For all the deceits she knew him to be guilty of, it did not suit him to pretend to be what he was not—his true self he considered sufficiently formidable. That was Lucifer's saving grace: the Lord of Lies was never other than authenticity itself. Whereas Osmond, the Osmond she was seeing today, being uncertain of her and her intentions and consequently uncertain of everything, carried himself with too much of a ponderous swagger, like an actor miscast in his part and hiding behind an exaggerated style.

"I could not at all grasp the sense of the lines about my daughter in your letter," he said over his shoulder, lifting the goblet level with his eyes and scrutinising the tint and texture of the wine. "I am assuming there *was* some sort of sense to them, and that they were not mere rambling"—he bestowed on her a smile broadly arch—"for you do tend to wander, you know, on the occasions, happily few, when you take it into your head to put pen to paper."

It should have seemed to her more remarkable, she reflected, more perverse, indeed, than it did, that they had from the outset passed over in silence the only truly momentous thing that had occurred since they had last conversed together, namely the disclosure to her by the Countess Gemini of the secret that he and Madame Merle had kept concealed from her so carefully yet so brazenly, and for so long. She had no doubt that he knew what she knew, for the languid impudence of his manner, if nothing else, told her so. Madame Merle had straight off recognised in Isabel's expression the evidence of her newly acquired knowledge, that day in Rome they had by accident come face-to-face when Isabel, bound for England and her cousin's deathbed, had stopped at the convent in the dispiritingly narrow street hard by the Piazza Navona to say her painful farewells to Pansy. It would be hard to conceive that his former lover, and not incidentally Pansy's mother, would not have dispatched a note to Osmond to inform and warn him of what she had guessed of Isabel's new state of enlightenment. He would not even have had to confront the Countess Gemini with her betrayal of his secrets to his wife. And Isabel now could not but marvel at his actorly self-control, however flawed his performance; in her letter to him from the Hôtel des Étoiles she had been deliberately vague as to the extent of her knowledge of the web of fiction he had spun for her, and vaguer still on how she intended to act upon that knowledge; surely he must be on tenterhooks to hear the details of the famous "proposals" she had given the merest sketch of in her letter. Yet there he stood, leaning back against the cabinet, holding his wine aloft in one hand and resting the other in the crook of his elbow, gazing down at her in amused defiance, daring her to embark on the assault, in whatever form she chose, the assault that he was in no doubt she had come here to launch against him. Well, then, what else was there for her to do but to rise to meet him, and on his own terms?

"You're right, of course, I wasn't clear in what I wrote to you," she said, managing a smile she judged as audacious as his own. "I did not intend to be clear. I wished to leave you to speculate and guess."

In response to this he produced a large and passably convincing laugh, the ring of which had a crack in it, though, to match his eyes' faint flicker of disquiet; it was apparent he did not like the daring of her smile, and even less the tenor of her tone, which bordered on the bantering.

"All the same, I suspect you are being disingenuous," he said pleasantly. "I'm sure it did not take much trying for you to make, in your letter, a muddle of your meaning."

This she let pass; his insults were least effective when most openly delivered; he might be many things, but he had not in him the makings of a mere brute. He was never less than subtle, and subtly persuasive, as she remembered from the early days of his courtship of her. She rose from her chair now and went and stood in the effulgent doorway, not for the sake of looking at the garden's glorious riot—the noun, if not the adjective, was her Aunt Lydia's—but of not looking at her husband. She was a little like, she thought, the executioner who places the hood over the condemned man's head, to spare not his victim but himself a dreadful sight. She was about to subject to surely the worst hour of his life a person whom she had once thought the most honourable, the most admirable, the most beautiful of men. On the Day of Defiance, as in Biblical terms, not wholly ironic, she figured it to herself, the day when, in the face of the gravest warning her husband had ever yet laid upon her, she had left the house they shared together and flown to England and to Gardencourt and her dying cousin, she had experienced her intensest moment of weakness and wavering when Osmond, palely palpitant with the force of his conviction, had declared her to be committing a shameless and scandalous breach of the rules of right behaviour, those rules by which he, and she, too, or so he had thought until now, had determined life should, and could only in any decency, be lived. He did not seek to deny the pass their union had come to—there were depths of hypocrisy to which even he would not descend—or to pretend the damage done to it could be mended. But they had contracted to a marriage, and marriage was much, so he averred, was more even than the sum of their mutual unhappiness combined, and not a thing to be capriciously ducked out of. Yes, they had suffered, and were suffering, and likely would continue to suffer—but that which cannot be cured must be endured, and courageously and uncomplainingly accepted. For it was imperative, he declared, to accept the consequences of our actions, even those in which we were grotesquely mistaken, for by that only—and here he grew paler and intenser still—only by that are we to value the most valuable of all we possess, which is *the honour of a thing.* In that moment, as she listened to him and looked at him, herself pale and trembling, she had caught again a flash of that magnificence, that splendour of spirit, which she had originally discerned in him, and which had made him seem the worthiest object of her love that she had yet encountered. And even when, not five minutes later, as she was making her blundering way out of the house, too choked for tears, and Osmond's sister had drawn her aside and "told her all," as the forgers of melodramas like to phrase it, something still lingered of the magnificent glow she had just now glimpsed in her husband's passionate avowals. What, after all, she asked herself, had those two done between them, her husband and Madame Merle? They had secured for the former the means of living the moneyed life he felt to be his due—the matter of his having to marry a wife in the process would have been the least of it—and for the latter the assurance that her daughter should "have something" and so be made to seem if only a little bit more eligible to some prowling but impecunious *prétendant,* preferably one possessed of a title. The acknowledgement of the mundanity of the couple's crimes had been not the least of the factors in her deciding to return to Italy. And had she now the right to play the avenging angel, and with the flaming sword of her self-righteousness drive the unhappy pair of sinners, not naked into the fallen world, but all too suitably apparelled into a hell that was largely of their own devising? So moved was she by the contrary and revisionist logic of the rigorous if brief examination of conscience she had just performed that she was on the point of whirling about, with a muffled moan, to face her husband and pour out to him an inarticulate jumble of contrition, justification and denial, and was prevented only by his speaking first.

"By the by," he said, with exasperated levity, "what I am impatient to hear, indeed I hardly know why I haven't yet shaken it out of you, is what you did with that tremendous cache of our money—*our* money—that you extracted from the bank in London and took away with you."

XXIX

The bank had written to him, of course—that was only to have
been expected—first by way of a flustered terse telegram, and then
in a very much more extensive and painstakingly circumlocutory
letter. It was indeed a very large and, to a banker, frighteningly ill-
secured sum that Mrs. Osmond had withdrawn; as such it should
not have been difficult to keep track of, had it been directed along
the usual channels. Discreet enquiries had been circulated among
the financial fraternity—one might think it unlikely that such a
collaborative alliance could exist, in so uncompromisingly compet-
itive a market, yet it does, it does—but no such commensurately
considerable a sum had been deposited at any of the city's, indeed
of the country's, changing-houses, and certainly not in a common
leather satchel, by the hand of an unescorted lady. In the closing paragraph of his letter, Mr. Grimes—or perhaps Mr. Goresby:
Osmond had not bothered to note the name of the signatory—had
permitted himself cautiously, and so lightly as to have seemed to
be hovering in upper airs, to enquire if Mr. Osmond could say as to
what possible purpose or purposes Mrs. Osmond might have put
the amount in question. The banker duly noted the trite little story
Isabel had artlessly spun for him about the urgent requirement of
funds for the purchase of a house, but he had discounted it even

as it was in the course of being elaborated. Then, at the very close of the missive, there had come an inspissatedly expressed and barely scrutable conjecture, which Osmond, having succeeded in cracking the code of it, had at once taken up. "The fellow assumes you are being blackmailed; I'm rather inclined to think him not mistaken."

Isabel drew in a long deep painful breath. Her abstracted gaze, directed through the doorway at the garden, had at that moment settled upon a rose, the biggest blossom on a bush that sprawled in a twined and knotted confusion of gnarled limbs and crowding leafage against the base of the mossy parapet opposite, and now the thing seemed to transform itself before her eyes, as had her hand a little while past when it lay before her on the table, so that it seemed no longer a flower but a cluster of bulging crimson tongues stuck out at her in obscene mockery. She turned away hurriedly, and faced back into the room. Her husband had returned to the sofa with his glass of wine, and was stretched there at his ease, propped again upon an elbow.

"Ah, Gilbert," she exclaimed, in a sort of stricken gasp, "to think that I once thought you had so fine a mind!"

"While I thought you, if nothing else, were to be trusted."

"'If nothing else'?"

"What else is there to a marriage if not trust?"

He sighed, and put aside his glass and drew himself up to a seated position and leaned forward, placing his feet wide apart on the stone-flagged floor and setting his hands on his knees, looking a little askance with his head inclined as if he were listening for some far signal; it was an unselfconsciously characteristic pose, and seeing him there, in his well-cut coat and his pipe-clayed narrow summer shoes, with the ribbon of some order or other pinned to his lapel, she almost pitied him, not in anticipation of the hurt she had come here to inflict on him, but for what he was, a spiteful, disappointed man, lost in the arrogance of his delusions. He was silent for a long while, reflecting and calculating. Then, without turning his head, he looked at her sideways with narrowed eyes, and spoke. "Tell me, madam, what am I to think? I issued you a warning, the day of our last interview, but you cast it back in my face defiantly, indeed insultingly, and departed my house—"

"*Your* house?" Isabel boldly interjected.

"You left and travelled to England against my express wish and best advice," her husband pressed on, his voice sinking in timbre but intensifying in force. "Even after your cousin's much-heralded and wearingly long-delayed death, you stayed away for—what is it now, two months?—without a word of explanation or excuse; the next I hear of you is a cry of alarm from the bank, and news of a terrifyingly large and unaccountable withdrawal of cash; then at last you send a letter, on the notepaper of a shady Paris hotel, written in your usual quaint approximation of the English language, conveying a mixture of vague threats and impenetrably phrased propositions regarding, among other matters, my daughter. And now here you are, with a light in your eye and a menace in your step such that, were I of a less settled disposition and you a more formidable opponent, would have me positively quaking in my boots. Therefore I ask again: What am I to think?"

"I do not oppose you," Isabel wearily objected. She had returned to sit once more by the table, which by now had taken on for her the impersonal but sustaining solidity of some humbly living thing, a venerable donkey, say, or a dependable dog.

"You *do*, madam, you *do* oppose me. From the very start of our marriage the spirit of opposition has informed your every action. Do you dare deny it?"

She shook her head, not, indeed, in denial of the charge, but as a sign of fatigue, and a jaded refusal to engage in the dispute he was attempting to foment; she would argue with him no more. She looked about the room; its denuded and diminished aspect struck her as sadly expressive of the essence of the occasion, when the split and swaying edifice of their marriage was being finally dismantled, like a condemned building.

"Why did you hate him so?" she asked, her melancholy gaze still roving the room.

Her husband now turned full to face her. "What?" he demanded.

"My cousin—why did you hate him? You always did."

"You are mistaken; there wasn't man enough there for me to hate."

"How base, to speak so of the dead," she quietly protested.

"What—should I dissemble because the fellow finally attained that state he had been aimed towards throughout his pitiable excuse for a life? Do you expect me to sigh and sympathise and sound a mourning note? *There* would be baseness for you!"

She drew her face aside quickly with a grimace, as if he had struck her and she were avoiding a further blow. She had once proudly declared, to whom exactly she could not now recall—it must have been Lord Warburton, or Caspar Goodwood, she supposed: it hardly mattered which—her readiness to be unhappy and to suffer pain, if that was to be the cost of living her life to the fullest. The thought, when she revisited it in memory now, seemed a whistling past the graveyard in which the corpse of her defeated self was laid. What to Osmond had seemed her wilful and capricious opposition to him was in fact a necessary assertion of her independent self; he had sought to kill off in her all ideas that ran counter to his conception of the right order of things;

her mind must be made dull, must be neutralised, in order that his own opinions and pronouncements should shine out all the more brilliantly. Caspar Goodwood had been scandalised by what he saw as her pledging of allegiance to Europe by "marrying into it"—possibly he comforted himself for the loss of her by holding to account an entire continent, conveniently overlooking the fact that the man she had married was, at least originally, an American—yet deny it as she might, there was a bitter place in her heart where she part-way agreed with him. As we have already noted, that she had been betrayed by Americans long resident in Europe made it seem that Europe had connived in her betrayal, as if the place had prepared her downfall in advance. In entertaining such a thought she was, she knew, being every bit as unreasonable on the subject as Caspar Goodwood—more so, perhaps. She had long ago acknowledged that Europe had been her fate from the moment her Aunt Lydia lit on her that day in Albany. When she looked back now the road behind her was as smooth and straight as it had seemed it would be when it was still before her; Fate, she had come painfully to realise, allows of no deviations, but carries us inexorably forward, blinkered, between the traces.

Her husband had risen from the sofa and, after another vain patting of his pockets, was rummaging irritably here and there in search of a cigar; finding none, he poured himself another glass of wine—his not offering her a glass, Isabel realised, was a measure less of rudeness than of his discomposure. He set himself to stand before the fireplace, which was as tall as he, with his wine in one hand and the other braced at his back, and looked down upon his wife with frank displeasure. "Are you going to tell me what you did with the money?" he demanded. "I apologise for the crudeness of the question, but your inscrutability in the matter leaves me no choice other than blunt directness."

"I put it to a good purpose," she replied, in a placid tone she knew would increase his annoyance; it was a thing she could not help.

"And may we know the nature of this purpose? Did that dry stick from Boston whom you nearly married, the stern-faced Mr. Goodwood, discover a hole in his fortunes that required filling? Or perhaps you laid an injudicious wager on one of Lord Warburton's racehorses—though I grant you that could hardly be considered a good cause. Please tell me you did not give it to some home for stray cats and dogs—for I know you to be capable of any folly that will warm your Puritan heart."

She met his angry baiting with a long and level look. "Question me no further," she said calmly. "I've told you the purpose was good, and you must content yourself with that."

He took what amounted almost to a gulp from his glass, violently; his hand, she did not fail to notice, was not entirely steady.

"What would content me," he said, in a voice so restrainedly soft as to be almost a purr, "is that you should say you have the money safely kept somewhere, and intend to return it, sooner rather than later, to its rightful place deep in the vaults of Messrs. Touchett and Teddington." He waited, staring steadily. "You can give me no such assurance? Then the flames of my suspicions flare up again, more fiercely than ever. I believe you had no intention of informing me of your extraordinary deed, not realising the bank would write to me—though how could you think they wouldn't?—and therefore I assume the worst. And no, please, do not insult me with more talk of good works and pious donations." Again he waited for her to speak, again in vain. He shook his head, and tapped the toe of his right shoe rapidly three times on the hearthstone, an action that, by seeming merely petulant, was all the more revealing of his anger. "I believe you to have a lover," he said, with unrestrained directness. "Or that you did have. This is why you stayed away so long. I believe you threw him over, or injured him in some way; that he threatened to betray you in public; and that you needed the money to—what do they say?—to pay him off."

"Gilbert, Gilbert," his wife murmured, closing her eyes against him. "Please stop, I beg you. You disgrace yourself, and when you're cool again you will regret your words."

What shocked her most was not the wildness of the allegations he was flinging at her, like so many handfuls of dripping filth, but the shabby indecency of the thing. The man before her, trembling with the force of a barely suppressible rage, was a person she hardly recognised. Where was that delicacy of judgement, that subtle balance of tone, that graceful restraint, which were among the qualities she had loved him for? It was almost a physical pain to her to see him fall so far below his own standards. Now he swung about on his heel and set to pacing back and forth in front of the fireplace with a tense, tight tread, gesturing with his nearly emptied glass.

"Or perhaps it is something more subtle, and even more sensational." He gave her a brief, a sort of sliding, glance, showing the sharp tip of a tooth; she had the sense of him as an animal, ruffled and raging, pent in a narrow cage. "Those scribbles it pleases your friend Miss Stackpole to call her 'writings' hardly attain the Sapphic heights, but perhaps there are other ways in which her inclinations point in the direction of Lesbos. Has she seduced you into her *cénacle*, and demanded a mighty entrance fee?"

Isabel sprang to her feet. "For shame!" she cried, and stood swaying, her fingertips pressed to the table-top to steady herself. "Is there nothing so foul you will not say it?" She faltered, and lifted a hand to her brow; when she spoke again her voice was strained and faint. "I feel I have not known you before now. You delight in what is nasty, and call it sophistication."

"Oh, yes, and you are so pure," he returned, with biting scorn. He had ceased to pace, and stood confronting her again with his back to the fireplace. "Your money, you imagine, buys you sanctity. But did you ever pause to ask yourself where it came from, this famous fortune of yours? You will say your uncle willed it to you, at the urging of that fool of a son of his, who was so laughably in love with you. But where did old Touchett have it from? The bank, yes, of course. And how did it come to be in the bank, so much of it, all those mounds and mounds of gleaming gold? Do you think it floated down like manna from above to fill the vaults of Touchett and Teddington? No, my dear wife, it did not fall from Heaven: it was hard won, and hard fought for, and much innocent blood was spilled in the getting of it. The bank was set up on your aunt's inheritance of her father's railroad fortune. The railroad—ah. Think of the hundreds, the thousands, of Chinese coolies whose backs were broken in the laying down of those relentless tracks; think of the labourers who fled from famine in Ireland only to die of malnutrition in the sweltering western deserts; think of the tribes of Redskins who were slaughtered, their lands stolen, to make way for the iron road. You think your fortune pure? Your money is filthy, like all lucre. The bank is that very temple from which Christ drove the money-lenders with a scourge."

"And you, what of you?" Isabel enquired, mustering all her reserves of bravery and defiance. "I never heard you speak of these things when you were scheming to marry me. And when your scheme came good you were happy enough to take my 'filthy for-tune' and play at being the shrewd investor."

" 'Play'? I would remind you, madam, my 'play' at investing made half as much again of your fortune for you."

"For me? Ah, Gilbert, I have gone far beyond believing your mythologies."

He was still preparing a riposte when abruptly she turned from him and strode out into the garden, for she felt she would suffocate if she were to spend another moment in that room. Outside, however, the heat struck her a great stifling blow and made her throat constrict, and she was compelled to flee into the sheltering shade of an ancient fig tree, and there she stood, gasping a little, feeling the clammy dampness gather under the band of her straw hat. She looked about, somewhat desperately. Above the flowerbeds the air shimmered. She felt faint; she wondered if her fever might be returning. She touched one of the tree's big leaves; its underside felt wonderfully cool and fresh to her fingers. There used to be an old wooden seat hereabouts, she remembered, but it was gone now. In the early days of her marriage, when she and Osmond lived here at Bellosguardo while the Palazzo Roccanera was being got ready to receive them, she and Pansy used to sit together in the tree's friendly shade, reading to each other, or busying themselves with their needlework. She had been so happy—or so she had believed, for did she not sense, even then, a faint pre-echo of the heartsickness that was to come?

She heard the patter of light steps behind her, and turned to see a barefoot boy approaching through the garden. He wore loose knee-breeches, and a calico shirt much too large for him, so that as he walked he had to keep throwing back from his shoulders and his arms the floppy collar and the flowing sleeves. His smooth skin was tanned by the sun to the texture of oiled wood, and glistening thick black curls tumbled on his forehead. He greeted her with the broad white flash of a smile, and produced from a pocket of his breeches a small leather case polished from use— she recognised it as the receptacle in which her husband kept his cigars—and asked her if she might convey it to the *signore*, who had left it behind him after his recent visit to *la casa Boott*. This latter formulation, the uttering of which made the lad's cheeks bulge comically, sounded so charming and innocently droll that despite her agitated state she smiled, and when the *ragazzo* turned to go she bade him wait while she searched for a coin with which to reward him for his errand. Then he went off, skipping, with his bit of copper clutched in his brown little fist, and looking after him she experienced a pang of faint yearning and regret. All was not, was *not* vile and corrupt, as Osmond figured it to be; his version of the world was a place she could not live in.

He came out of the house now, and, having paused in the doorway and glanced about the garden in search of her, approached at a slow and pensive pace, with his hands in the pockets of his trousers and his eyes on the ground. When he stood in front of her he was as a visitor idling in a museum who has stopped to view a not particularly striking exhibit. "You seem an allegory of something," he said disparagingly, "posed like Eve in her full-fruited arbour, anticipating the appearance of the serpent."

She gazed back at him unperturbed, having succeeded in regaining, or reasserting, her composure, and determined not to be so foolish as to follow him into the treacherous tangles of his metaphor. "Will you tell me where Pansy is?" she asked.

He looked down again, smiling somewhat, and scuffled about in the gravel a little with the toe of one of his pale shoes.

"Well, she is in England," he said.

"England." Isabel had spoken without emphasis, in a flat dull tone, expressing no surprise and certainly no dismay, for she was neither dismayed nor surprised. She had long ago developed a carapace resistant enough to shield her against the small soft bombshells her husband devised and dropped upon her with exquisite timing and perfect aim.

"Yes, England—Kent, to be precise," he said. "I judged it a nice piece of symmetry that she should journey to that pleasant but enigmatic land while you were departing from it."

"Do you care to tell me why you sent her away?"

"I did not like the implications regarding her in the letter you wrote to me. I felt that she—well, that she needed protecting, and where better to sequester her than in a far-off green and pleasant land?"

"Against whom or what did you judge her in need of being protected?"

"Why, against you, my dear. By the way, is that my cigar case you are clutching so fiercely to your bosom? I take it Mr. Boott sent it round, for I hardly imagine you went yourself to fetch it for me."

She handed him the case, and he selected a cigar and lit it; the match-flame was unreally pale in the sunlight, and as she looked at it, for the moment of its flaring, Isabel had a new sense of inexplicable unease. Osmond watched her through a pale-blue and dispersing small flaw of smoke. "Don't you think it's time for you to lay your cards on the table?" he said, in what seemed a perfectly agreeable fashion. "I worry about the hand you're holding; it seems to me it is the upper hand, if I may so put it."

"What cards?" she asked. "What do you want me to tell you?"

"Tell me of the *money*, my dear," he said, leaning his face close to hers and waggling his head, an action at once menacing and horribly comical. "You hold it all, so I may neither bet nor bluff. Tell me, then: What is your wager?"

She hesitated but half a moment, long enough for her to draw in breath. "I want my freedom from you," she said, "mine, and Pansy's too."

XXX

Afterwards, what she recalled most clearly was not the ugliness of their exchanges, although certainly there had been a deal of that, but the oddly muted manner in which they were conducted. The two of them might have been attending the reading of a will, or meeting in the bankruptcy court to wind up finally a business that had long since failed. They had remained indoors, and Osmond had cast the stub of his cigar into the fireplace and the pair had seated themselves opposite each other at the table, and all that was missing on the bare board between them was a strew of documents done up with tapes and sealing wax, with an inkhorn and a quill standing by. Isabel had rehearsed her terms so thoroughly, in the deeps of countless wakeful nights, that she rattled them off with the dispatch of a Queen's Counsel anxious for his luncheon. In all of it there was one word that neither of them uttered, the most momentous word, the initial of which was a big bulging hateful D, that an unhappily married couple may hear, though it loomed over the table with all the awful potential of a reserved judgement. The arrangement she proposed to him was as simple as it was stark, and she left him in no doubt, if not by spoken terms then assuredly by tone—she would not have thought herself to be capable of such measured dryness—that she counted on him to accept it without quibble, since she would not alter or revise it by one whit. They were to part, never to see each other again, at least not by design; she would allow him to continue to reside at the Palazzo Roccanera—although it was Osmond who had found the place, who had bedecked and adorned it according to his exquisite taste, hers was the sole name on the deeds, in accordance with the strong, indeed the irresistible, advice of her English lawyer in Rome, the cautious Mr. Pettigrew—while she, along with Pansy, would take up residence elsewhere, in France, perhaps, or England; as to money, she would make over to him that portion resulting from the shrewd and profitable investments he had earned by the use of her original fortune. Osmond, who had sat stiffly upright, listening to her, at this last point stirred himself and delivered a sharp sidewise smack to the table with the palm of his left hand. "Oh, there's munificence!" he exclaimed, with a high sort of laugh. "I suppose you consider yourself the soul of generosity, to be granting me what is, by any standard, my own money."

"I don't know what your 'any standard' could be," she responded with calm restraint. "You made what you call 'your' money on the back of mine—without my fortune behind you, your financial skills would never have been tried. By the strictest standards, which obviously are not yours, the profits you made are mine."

He sat with his shoulders squared and his head set back and gazed at her stonily for an extended moment, during which she waited, genuinely interested to know what he would say next. A certain dreadful fascination, she had to acknowledge, attached to the unique exchange in which they were engaged, and when Osmond spoke at last it was apparent that he was experiencing the same dispassionate interest as she.

"My dear Isabel, I did not think you had it in you," he said, with a mildly wondering and rueful admiration. "Had you shown such spiritedness from the start, who knows what might have been saved between us?" He drew the leather case from the breast pocket of his coat and selected another cheroot. Isabel, frowning, begged him not to smoke, since the acrid smell of the tobacco would be sure to give her a headache; he ignored her, however, and when he struck a flame he did so with a vindictive little flourish. Then he leaned back on his chair and crossed an ankle on a knee and hooked a thumb again in the pocket of his cream-coloured waistcoat and, throwing back his head once more, regarded her along one side of his nose. "Putting from us, for now, the disagreeable topic of money, may I ask what is your interest in my daughter that you would take her from me, my only child? I never knew you to be so fond of her."

"No, you didn't," Isabel blankly replied. "There are many things about me you did not know, and many you didn't know about her, either." She moved her chair a little way back, in order to be out of range of the cloud of blue tobacco smoke that he had set lazily turning above the table. "I judge it best to remove 'your daughter,' which you ever made a point of calling her in my hearing, to remove her, Pansy, as far as I may, from under the weight of your influence, and that of her—her mother."

"Ah, her mother," Osmond echoed her, nodding. "I wondered if you would ever work yourself up sufficiently to say it outright."

"How should I have said it before now, outright or otherwise, since I was unaware the relation existed?"

"Would you have been better off knowing? Are you better off now?"

"You lied to me."

"My dear woman, you lied to yourself—which of us is the more culpable?"

It struck her, as it often had in the past, how he could shape so persuasively the twisted logic of his vision of the world and its ways; he managed it, she judged, by stating the most doubtful propositions with the least emphasis, smoothly, a touch wearily, as if he were rehearsing truths that no one ever, anywhere, would think or have thought to question.

"The strangest thing is," she said, and was surprised to catch the curiously wistful note in her own voice, "I almost admire the skill with which you kept your secrets from me, you and—and that woman."

Osmond rose from his chair and crossed to the hearth and knocked the ash from his cigar, then remained there, turned so as to face her, with an elbow propped on the high mantelpiece and the heel of one shoe hooked on the brass rail at the grate.

"I'm told you persuaded 'that woman' to abandon her sinner's penitential flight to America and instead return to Italy. May I ask what your motive was for such a bizarre and quixotic action? Did you figure her a repentant Magdalene and yourself a forgiving Christ?"

"I believe that only you, Gilbert," his wife said, again with a tinge of bitter admiration, "would be capable of deriving amusement from the predicament we find ourselves in."

"Yes, yes, you're right," he said, with a sigh, holding up his cigar and studying it. "I do find the oddest things droll, even quaintly comic. Although I have my limits. Money, for instance, does not make me smile, when I'm in the way of losing it." He blew very gently on the tip of the cigar and thus imparted to it a sullen brief glow. "How am I to live, do you imagine, on the pittance you propose to leave me with?"

"I would hardly describe it as a pittance. I recall how proud you were when you reported your achievement to me—'a tremendous return,' was how you described it. Besides, you will not have the expense of me, or of Pansy. I should think you will do very nicely, and if things should go hard for you, why, you can always sell off a picture, or an Etruscan vase—I shall not be claiming my share of the treasures you amassed with the benefit of my fortune."

He looked at her long. "And you accuse me of finding humour in the situation," he said quietly, with the faint lisping sibilance that came into his voice when he was at his angriest.

Isabel rose to her feet. "You married me for my money," she said, making of it no more than a matter of fact. "Now our marriage is at an end, and I am taking the money back."

"Take it, then. I wish you well of it. But as to the break between us that you insist on, be warned, I will not make it easy for you. I shall put every obstacle in your way that it's in my power to do— and my power is not to be underestimated, as you, dear wife, very well know."

"I have directed Mr. Pettigrew to draw up the papers," she said. "He knows what to expect from you, and you, I trust, know what to expect from him. Do not be deceived by his dusty frock-coat and his stoop—he is adept at clearing obstacles."

She could feel how hard was the face she was setting against him, harder than it had ever been before in her life, harder even than it had been that day when she heard the truth from the Countess Gemini; harder than it would ever have to be again, or so she hoped, fervently but with not much conviction.

Osmond turned to the fireplace and dropped another half-inch of ash on to the polished hearthstone.

"Then I bid you good day," he said shortly.

She waited silently and in the end he was compelled to turn back to her. They faced each other, standing there, she by the table and he with the tall black recess of the fireplace behind him; no more than yards separated them, though it might have been the deepest chasm, at the bottom of which she seemed to hear, distantly, oh, how distantly, the shattering of a small frail discarded thing that once she had deemed so precious.

XXXI

All through that long hazed-over afternoon the heat of the shrouded sun beat steadily upon the air, until an entire half of the congested sky had been pounded into a swollen lead-blue cloud in the shape of an anvil, tinged along its lower rim with a delicate, sore-seeming redness, like an incipient rash. Isabel, in concert with the day, came down from the hill of Bellosguardo feeling once more feverishly inflamed, with the dust of the road on her lips and a throbbing ache behind her temples. When she arrived at the Palazzo Crescentini she found it deserted, the entire household seemingly having succumbed to the airless languor of the atmosphere and retreated into shadow and coolness; the ground-floor apartments, as she moved through them, had the aspect of vigilant unease that takes over in a house during those intervals when the accustomed human bustle lapses into stillness. She made her way up the many flights of stairs to her room, where she was grateful to find the shutters drawn against the incendiary intensity of the sky. She removed her outer attire and lay down on her bed to rest, her spirit stilled, her mind bathed in a welcome balm of vacancy. It was strange how lightly the recent encounter with her husband weighed upon her. She was like a climber of high places who, returned for respite to the lowlands, recalls the peaks as little more than a chimera of blue air and blown snow.

She fell briefly into a kind of sleep, from which she woke and peered about her in the hot gloom, prey to nameless fright, not knowing for a moment where she was. She rose from the bed and poured water into a basin and wetted her fingertips and pressed them to her eyelids and to her aching temples. The water, though it made a fresh little plash against the bluish-white enamel of the bowl, was half warm and somehow thick, and afforded her little relief. She went to the window and drew open the shutters; the anvil-cloud of earlier had by now swollen to the point of entirely filling the sky, which loured over the rooftops like an inverted sea, brimmingly, bodefully still. She felt a movement of sluggish air against her face—it was as if the city itself had let go an exhausted gasp—then all reverted to heat and heaviness. She had much to do, and many matters awaited her attention, but lassitude enveloped her like a shroud of sodden warm sacking. Her life, it seemed to her, had rolled ponderously to a halt. She had steamed along for such a time, driven by a fiery determination to bring to a head the crisis that her marriage had turned into, but now her energy all was spent. What was to become of her? The prospect she had flaunted before Osmond of herself and Pansy setting out together, like a pair of caped and booted venturers bound for the Golden Horn—what was it but a fantasy worked up into a prop to sustain her in her confrontation with her husband and, through him, with her fate? It occurred to her that in all her planning and plotting she had never once paused to consider whether Pansy might not have her own plots and plans, if the girl—the young woman!—might not be preparing, even now, in some grand English parlour, among lofty lords and brilliant ladies, to affront her own fate. Poor Isabel! Having scaled the heights of Bellos-guardo and planted there the ensign of her independence, was she now to be brought tumbling down by mere inertia and infir-mity of purpose? At just that moment, as if in gargantuan affir-mation of her doubts, there rolled across the pendulous and livid sky, with bangs and rattles and colossal bumps, an extended peal of thunder, at once portentous and wholly absurd, followed by the slowly swelling swish of rain.

She dressed quickly and engaged in a careless essay at the arranging of her hair—suddenly so many things seemed not to matter any more—and made her way down through the house. The usually less than lively air was suffused with the perfumes of the garden, which the rain had freshly released. Passing by the *piccolo salone*, she heard voices from within, and paused and tapped lightly on the door, and her aunt's voice bade her enter. This dim and rather seedy room, cramped and peculiarly overpowering, was reserved by Mrs. Touchett for the receiving of visitors, and was therefore very much neglected. Mrs. Touchett's guest this evening was a young man, although perhaps he was not quite as young as his youthful appearance made it seem. He was slight of stature, with hair of a striking dark-red hue, a broad unwrinkled forehead, and lively green eyes that made Isabel think of a friendly cat. He wore grey trousers and a black frock-coat, and was balancing on his knee a scuffed and decidedly rusty silk top hat. He could not have been described as handsome, but he had about him such an aura of balanced ease and energy that the question of anyone at all being handsome or otherwise seemed an irrelevance. Isabel guessed at once he must be that Mr. Devenish, correspondent of the *London Clarion,* who the previous day had called upon her and left his card. He proved her surmise correct when he rose hastily now, inadvertently overturning his hat and spilling it on to the floor, and proceeded to introduce himself. He had a pleasant light English voice, the pleasantness of which was not marred but on the contrary curiously enhanced by a slight stammer. Isabel proffered her hand and smiled; she was conscious of her aunt's dark little eye fixed on her with accusing acerbity. "I told Mr. Devenish you were resting," the old lady said. "We expected you down before this."

"Yes, I was about to give you up and leave," the young man said genially to Isabel, keeping his green gaze fixed upon her. "Very glad I didn't."

"You left no address here in Florence," Isabel, still smiling, replied.

"Didn't I? Oh, that's me all over—no brain whatever, I'm afraid."

"You're a relative of Miss Janeway, I think?"

"Yes, I'm her nephew. She had me positively swear an oath that I should not fail to call on you. Our friend Miss Stackpole was able to tell me of your whereabouts—I was bent on seeking you out in Rome, but happily here you are!"

"Is your work in Florence?" Isabel enquired. "I mean, are you the paper's Florence correspondent?"

This provoked Mr. Devenish to issue a high mirthful hoot. "Ah, my dear Mrs. Osmond, if only we could stretch to that! I'm afraid we are a very humble organ, and can barely afford to keep an office in London—I say 'office,' but in truth it's no more than a lightless basement in the Gray's Inn Road."

"Then you are on vacation here?"

"On holiday, you mean? I suppose you might call it that. I have been here a week, perched in a garret in an establishment, calling itself a *pensione,* at the back of the main railway station, living on a convict's rations of bread and water."

"Oh, well, in that case we must offer you some sustenance," Isabel said, laughing. "Miss Janeway would never forgive me if you were to perish of starvation."

"I have asked for tea to be brought," Mrs. Touchett said tartly. "If we are patient we may have it within the hour."

Isabel, bethinking herself, turned her attention guiltily to her aunt, conscious of having so far entirely neglected her in favour of Mr. Devenish. The frail old lady was hunched in the depths of her chair, as if she had been folded carefully and set aside there, out of the way. She held her cane propped upright before her, with her papery hands clasped one over the other on the ivory knob. "Shall I go and see to it, dear Aunt?" Isabel solicitously enquired. She glanced back at Mr. Devenish. "They don't at all understand tea here, and cross themselves before they go about the brewing of it, as if they had been commanded to engage in an act of witchcraft."

"Well, I would forgive them much for the quality of their coffee," the gentleman affirmingly responded.

Isabel smiled at him again; indeed, it came to her that she had been smiling well-nigh continuously since she had entered the room—Mr. Devenish's good humour was catching. She had got out of the way of being treated pleasantly, and of being pleasant in return, in the ordinary human fashion; for a long time, for years and years, she had crouched inside herself, holding her breath and ever on the watch, like a child hiding in a cupboard from a capriciously cruel parent. What had she done, what had she ever done, to deserve the life of caution, watchfulness and dread to which she had been condemned these recent years? Yes, she had been proud; yes, she had prized her own counsel over that of others; yes, she had allowed herself to be married for her money; but did these sins, grave as they might be, deserve the retribution that had been wreaked upon her? Yet it was foolish, she told herself, foolish to skulk and be afraid. Today, in at last confronting her husband, she had pushed open the cupboard door a chink; outside, the room was bright, the floor swept, the crockery safe on its shelf, and no one was there, waiting with switch in hand for her to show herself. It was time for her to step forth and stand up straight and live—and *live*. She heard in the distance the thunder rolling.

Their tea was brought, along with bread and biscuits and slices of sweet cake. Mr. Devenish proved himself possessed of a hearty appetite, and partook with unabashed freedom of all that was on offer, expatiating widely the while on a broad range of topics, at times with his mouth nearly full. The *Clarion*, the "dear old rag," as he fondly called it, was robustly committed to the hottest causes of the day, including electoral reform, Home Rule for Ireland, liberalism, trade-unionism, disestablishmentarianism—indeed, he mentioned so many "isms" they seemed to swoop about the room like swallows—and, of course, universal suffrage for women. When he touched upon this last, he directed at Isabel an especially warm and meaning glance. "My aunt, as you know, Mrs. Osmond, is a leading campaigner in the cause." He turned his attention to Mrs. Touchett, bent in her chair, who was watching him with a bright beadiness that Isabel feared he might mistake for approval of the views he had been so freely expounding. "Recently my aunt has not been well," he said, addressing the old lady, and frowning and lowering his voice, "but she carries on the struggle regardless, though there are occasions when she is reduced to directing operations from her sick-bed."

Isabel's aunt, unmoved, glared at him.

"Oh, yes," Isabel interjected hastily, with the urgent air of one anticipating an imminent volley of gunfire and attempting to draw it off. "Do tell me of the state of her health, although I must say that when I met her at the beginning of the summer and we had lunch together, she seemed in very strong spirits."

"Ah, well," Mr. Devenish said, "as far as spirit goes, nothing daunts her, but, in bodily terms, I fear I must tell you she is failing fast." He looked down, and fixed his gaze a moment on his already knocked-about hat, which for the sake of safety he had set on the floor beside the leg of his chair. "The doctors give her but a month or two."

There was a silence. Behind the hush could be heard the steady drumming of the rain outside, and thunder, too, was still grumbling away, up behind the hills. Then Mrs. Touchett stirred herself. "Perhaps the lady in question would have been better advised to conserve her energies in the cause of her own well-being," she coldly pronounced, "and leave the great matters of the world to those fitted to engage with them." She rose slowly and with much effort from her chair, leaning her scant weight so heavily on her cane that it vibrated visibly throughout its length. Painful though it was to watch her, Isabel knew better than to offer assistance, and so too, by instinct, did Mr. Devenish. Upright at last, the lady looked from one of them to the other with an expression of angry defiance. "I have household matters to attend to," she said shortly. "Young man, I shall bid you good evening."

"And good evening to you, ma'am," Devenish responded, with his brand of eager politeness. "Thank you for receiving me—it was an honour to meet you."

They stood upon the moment there, all three, and the silence stretched between them. Isabel could see that the young man fully expected that it would be Mrs. Touchett who would depart, leaving him alone with her niece, and she could think of no practical way to disabuse him of the idea. Then Mrs. Touchett spoke, directly and to the point, though the words she employed were innocuous enough. "I hope, Mr. Devenish, you have brought your umbrella with you, otherwise I fear you are in for a drenching."

"Oh, I have my hat," the young man replied. "That will do well enough to shield me from the elements." He turned to Isabel, not without a flicker of rueful amusement in that remarkably virescent eye of his. "A great pleasure, Mrs. Osmond," he murmured, offering his hand. "I hope we shall have the opportunity to meet again, if not here in Florence, then somewhere else—London, even, for I know my aunt would be very happy to receive you again in Fulham. She recalls your luncheon together there with much warmth."

"As I do, also," Isabel replied. She could feel her aunt's stare boring into her, like the glinting tip of a sharp little metallic implement. "If you should see her before I do, please convey my friendliest greetings to her, and my concern for her sad condition."

She walked with him to the front door, where he paused, with his hat in his hands. "I fear your aunt disapproves of me," he said under his breath.

"You shouldn't feel personally frowned upon," Isabel replied with a smile. "She disapproves of things generally—the world as it's constituted fails to come up to her standards, which are very high, I'm afraid."

"She is a formidable lady, certainly," Mr. Devenish said, laughing, and shaking his head. Then he paused, looking down again at his hat.

"You know," he said, with shy hesitancy, "I had intended to depart Florence the day I called on you and left my card."

"But you stayed."

"Yes." He lifted his eyes to hers. "I didn't wish to go without having seen you."

"I'm glad, then, that you waited," she said, in a determinedly neutral tone; she knew the mile a man might take if he were offered no more than an inch.

Still he lingered, frowning, with lips pursed. She attended upon him keenly, even with a certain suspense. She guessed he would know something of her recent troubles—Henrietta Stackpole ever considered it her duty to expose injustice and point to its perpetrators, at the cost, should it come to it, of disclosing a friend's private sorrows—and had he shown the slightest hint of compassion or commiseration, she would have bade him a brisk farewell, shut the door on him, and found his calling-card and torn it into fragments. In her present circumstances she would rather be mocked than sympathised with. However, it was another tack he took. "My aunt told me of your generous act of patronage," he said.

For a moment Isabel was confused, and then she understood. "Oh, yes—the banknotes. I feel I behaved in rather a foolish way."

Myles Devenish stared. "But how could that be? You made a great contribution to the cause."

"The cause?"

"Well, of suffrage—of freedom."

"Ah, freedom," Isabel murmured. "It's a word that has been much on my mind in recent weeks. I'm very glad I was able to help your aunt. She is an admirable woman."

"That she is, that she is," the young man declared. He seemed to have more to say, much more indeed, but he confined himself to a quick goodbye and made a gallant little bow, and was gone.

XXXII

The storm was still prowling sullenly in the hills above the city, and Isabel felt febrile and on edge, as if tiny charges of electricity were shooting along her veins in all directions, and she could settle to nothing. She wandered aimlessly about the great gaunt hollow house, cross at herself and the things she encountered, no matter how eagerly they pressed themselves to her attention. She was like a bored child, whose brightest playthings have lost their lustre, astray in the empty hours of a deserted Sunday afternoon. Mrs. Touchett had retired to her quarters upstairs, leaving word that she would dine there alone later; evidently a scattering of the disapproval she had directed at Mr. Devenish had become deflected on to her niece. If that was the case, Isabel was glad of it. Her aunt was aware that she had been out to Bellosguardo, and she would surely have sought, in her coolly detached fashion, to know something of what had passed between Mrs. Osmond and her husband, after such a lengthy and, so it had been reported, stressful separation between the ill-contented couple. The last thing Isabel could have borne this evening was one of her aunt's interrogations, which were always as pointed and probing as a surgical procedure.

She went to the garden room and selected a book from a

shelf there—a volume of Browning's verse, which she thought would surely be apt to her mood—and seated herself in a wicker chair by the window. She was soon distracted by the crestfallen aspect of the garden—the rain had left everything bowed down in disarray—and the garish light that made the panes of glass beside her glitter menacingly. At home, by which we mean Albany and its environs, since for her there was nowhere else now that merited the appellation, she had loved the twilight hour, invested as it was for her with a sense of vague, melancholy and yet always exciting promise; here in the south, each day was brought to a brusque, unceremonious close, the darkness falling almost with a clatter, like the grille in front of a shopkeeper's stall. She put aside the book, and rang for Staines and informed her that she too would take a solitary dinner, in her room. "Just some eggs will do," she murmured, turning her eyes once more to the dismal garden, where already there was hardly a glimmer of daylight lingering.

"Shall I light the candles, ma'am, or will you be going straight up?" the maid enquired.

"Yes, light them, please, but only one or two," Isabel responded. There was a time when she would have thrilled to sit like this of a darkling eve, after rain, but the darkness was thicker now, and there were things that moved in it, indistinct but unmistakable forms, like wild beasts at the mouth of a cave, which only flame could keep at bay. "And bring me something to drink—a glass of moscato, perhaps."

"Very good, ma'am."

"And, Staines—"

"Yes'm?"

"Thank you for caring for me, as you do."

The maid reddened a little. "Well, it's what I'm for, ma'am, isn't it?"

"But I thank you, all the same."

She found it strange that she should feel so little disturbance within her at the close of such a day. It was only now she realised for how long a time, in a deep recess of her mind, she had been arming herself, all unawares and yet diligently, meticulously, coldly, for the struggle in which that morning she had joined with her husband. And was she to have no sense of victory, was she to experience no satisfaction? No misgiving, even? No remorse? Was this all there was to be of aftermath? Why was she not upstairs prostrated on her bed, weeping, if for nothing other than the bitter relief of having brought the thing off, of having carried the day? For there was no doubt that she had prevailed. Osmond, as he had threatened, would make all the difficulties for her that he was capable of, and he was capable of much—he was capable of anything!—but it would avail him naught. She had read her Maistre, and knew from that dark-minded savant of the moment in battle when one side, even if the stronger in manpower and matériel, suddenly loses heart, or nerve, or will, or all together, and on the spot collapses. She had seen the realisation of defeat dawn in Osmond's eyes today. It was not a thing she had ever expected to have occasion to witness. Yet it had not been a rout; there would be no disorderly retreat, he would not turn tail and run. It was not his way to submit himself to indignity; nor was it hers to force him into such submission. He would, as he had warned her, do everything in his power to obstruct her—he had acquaintances in the bureaucracy, in the judiciary, in the Vatican, even—while she, on the contrary, would make the way easy for him wherever she could. She recalled again his speaking to her, so memorably, of how in his dealings he valued honour above all else, a precept to which, so she had discovered, he paid poor observance, it was true; but even if he were to stoop below his own standards, that was no reason for her to crouch alongside him. No matter by what means he might attempt to thwart her, she would honour—yes, she would *honour*—the terms she had set out to him when they faced each other today across the table in that high room in Bellosguardo, a site that already in her mind had taken on the trappings of a memorial to the culminating engagement in a long struggle for liberty.

The maid had lighted the candles, the flames of which had extinguished on the instant the last glimmer of dusk in the window, and Isabel had been brought her glass of wine—it stood on a little tray beside her—yet still the maid lingered, even though Isabel had released her to her own devices until she should be required to come again a last time, to her mistress's room upstairs, bringing her a bedtime *tisane*. Isabel watched her with curiosity, as she straightened a candle in its holder, and smoothed the wrinkles in a floor rug, and plumped up yet another cushion. It was clear the kind-hearted creature had something on her mind. She stopped by Isabel's chair now, expressing herself concerned that Madam had gone through such a long and, as was obvious, an exceedingly arduous day, especially as only last evening she had still been "afire with that awful fever." Isabel conceded that she was tired, and promised to go to bed directly after she had finished her dinner, which perhaps she would take here, on a tray, and not, as she had thought to, in her bedroom, the nocturnal gloom of which had been intensified by the memory of the days and nights of illness she had been compelled to endure there. A silence followed, or would have, were it not for the peculiar humming sound, like a vibration lingering on the air after the tolling of a church bell, that Staines emitted, unconsciously, so it seemed, whenever she had an inner quandary to grapple with.

"Is something the matter?" Isabel asked. "You seem agitated—I hope you haven't caught my illness."

"Oh, no, ma'am, no, I'm perfectly well. It's only—" Her voice trailed off. She cut a stark figure there, looming in the glimmering candlelight, all elbows and bony shoulders and long sharp jaw, wringing her hands and still distressedly humming.

"What is it?" Isabel gently urged. "Is there something you have to tell me? And please, sit, bring a chair, do. We're quite alone. My aunt has retired for the night, we shall not hear from her before morning."

"It's only, you see, ma'am," Staines resumed, making no move to accept her mistress's invitation to be seated, "I know you was out this morning to visit the master"—this was the mode by which she was accustomed to refer to Mr. Osmond—"and when you come back I could see you was upset." She paused, twisting her fingers so hard she made the knuckles crack. "Forgive me, ma'am, being so forward and speaking to you like this," she pleaded in a rush. "I wouldn't for the world, only—"

Again she paused on that word, "only," as if it were a shibboleth she could not get past. Isabel rose, and taking up a candlestick led her companion to a big ugly marble table in the middle of the room, and there they both sat down, with the candle before them. "Come, my dear, speak," Isabel said, in a soft and reassuring tone, though her heart shrank within her for cold foreboding.

The tale that Staines had to tell was from long ago, and when it was told, Isabel wondered at herself that she had not fainted clean away during its telling. At first she had tried to dismiss it as the fanciful gossip of below-stairs, the kind of thing parlourmaids delighted in making up to shock each other and themselves. But, as Isabel reminded herself, servants knew everything, and did not have to invent; the things that were not said in front of them they always found out anyway, from behind, so to speak. How often had not she herself, as a child, heard her nurse tell the housekeeper, or the housekeeper tell her nurse, of the latest "scrape" her gaily improvident father had got himself into; of the creditors who had come barging to the door and been rebuffed; of the pretty young wives who had wavered into his path, and the outraged husbands who had littered that same path with gauntlets? Those tales too she had tried to disbelieve—*how* she had tried, squeezing her eyes shut to hold back the tears!—but in her heart she had known, beyond all denying, that they were true, at least in substance, if not in the suspiciously colourful detail in which they were related. Then, as now, what convinced her was the very dreadfulness of the thing, although her poor late father, for all that he was a rascal, would never have sunk to perpetrating an act of such wickedness an account of which the maid laid out before her mistress, there at the table, in the silent house, under a dome of darkness that not a high altar's array of candles could have sufficiently illumined.

There was some comfort for Isabel, though hardly more than a crumb of it, in the fact that the thing had been done in a time before Gilbert Osmond and Serena Merle could even have heard of her name—in a time, indeed, when she was hardly old enough to have had a name sufficiently established for anyone outside her diminished family and her few friends to care to take notice of at all. Osmond was living in Naples then, a youngish man with a young wife. The first Mrs. Osmond was a daughter of that city's teeming aristocracy, although her family's title dated no further back than Napoleon, and its fortune, reputedly founded on plunder from the Peninsular War—the lady's grandfather had served as a marshal in the Grande Armée—had sunk in the rocky channel between the twin hazards of speculation and peculation, and hardly a penny of it remained. When Serena Merle came processing down the Campanian coast from Rome—in her morbid excitement Isabel saw her in a plunging chariot, a Brooklyn Valkyrie, blonde-braided and with a chained leopard by her side—she was already estranged from her husband, the Swiss gentleman of obscure origins whom she mentioned as seldom as decency would allow. She had immediately set her grey and calculating eye on the private scholar Gilbert Osmond, in the mistaken notion— it was a mistake for which the celebratedly shrewd lady was never to forgive herself—that this ornament of the expatriate American community in Naples was a figure not only of prodigious learning and exquisite taste but also of financial consequence. They met and, seeing the point of each other at once, they matched; what followed was, in the way of these things, inevitable, though less by the force of fate than the lady's persuasive charm and unwavering single-mindedness.

They were discreet, the lovers—they were discretion itself— but Nature, in her heedlessly bountiful fashion, can surprise even the most careful of couples. In due course it became necessary for Madame Merle to retreat into seclusion for a certain period, since her "interesting" condition, increasingly evident as it was, would have been difficult to account for, in light of the fact that Monsieur Merle had been nowhere in evidence during the months that had elapsed since his wife had first descended on the city under Vesuvius; in fact, the gentleman was in America at the time, pursuing a business project, which, like so many other of his speculative ventures, would prove not only fruitless but ruinously costly. The lovers looked about for a place the burgeoning mother-to-be might securely retire to, and fixed on the Salentine Peninsula as conveniently distant from Naples—not so far that the fugitive would be entirely out of touch, but safely beyond the furthest limit the frothing tide of gossip might be expected to lick at—and accommodation was sought for her, and found, in the pleasant city of Lecce, known to its inhabitants fondly as the Florence of the south, a conceit, we should add, which the ungenerous Florentines regard as at best a laughably fond delusion. In Lecce the lady occupied for the half year that remained of her term a compact but perfectly pleasant apartment in a fine old palazzo hard by the picturesque ruins of the Teatro Romano—Gilbert Osmond was acquainted with her landlord, a collector specialising in faience, a *gentiluomo* as fine, and seemingly almost as old, as the building itself, who had been given to believe that his tenant was Mr. Osmond's spouse, and that her husband had sent her south to take the benefit of the bracing air of the peninsula and be delivered of her child amid peace and tranquillity such as Naples, in its habitual social tumult, could not be expected to provide.

While Madame Merle was in exile, Mr. Osmond too absented himself for some months from his adopted city, when along with the first Mrs. Osmond he decamped to the obscure Piedmontese town of Alba, for reasons he did not consider it incumbent on him to share among his circle; however, by way of certain carefully placed hints, he left behind in Florence the suggestion that his family of two was presently to be swelled to three, with the addition of an infant Osmond. Alba was, and is, renowned for its truffles, its wine and its peaches, samples of all of which the couple no doubt enjoyed during their initially pleasant but, as it was to turn out, eventually tragic interlude in the remote northwest. Mrs. Osmond's health had never been robust—her family on the maternal side had from time immemorial been subject to an inescapable and enervating malady of the blood—and it so happened that in Alba, and in the surrounding province of Cuneo in general, a fever of unprecedented virulence had for some time been rampant. It was to this cruel predator that Mrs. Osmond, defenceless by virtue of her inherited weakness, inevitably succumbed. Through painful days and tormented nights she fought for life, attended by her extravagantly distraught consort—it was said he did not leave her bedside for more than the briefest periods, never sleeping and eating hardly enough to sustain his own constitution—until in the end her invisible assailant proved the stronger, and the valiant lady, bathed in her husband's extravagant tears, folded her hands upon her breast and consigned her soul to a better place. All Alba marked her passing—she had become known, with affectionate inaccuracy, as *la signora inglese*—and the bells of the Duomo tolled in mourning when her lifeless remains were placed in the funeral carriage preparatory to the long and doleful journey back to the city of her birth.

This was the account of his wife's demise that Osmond had given to Isabel when the sad topic was first broached between them, on one of their strolls in the Boboli Gardens in the delightful early days of their engagement—or, rather, a *version* of this account, an elaborated sketch, let us say, delicately limned and lightly varnished, like one of Osmond's own amateur exercises in the painterly art. He spoke of his bereavement as an occurrence in his life the memory of which he was honour bound to preserve and revere in public, but which for obvious reasons he did not care to dwell on over-much—his stoical cast of mind would allow of no morbid sentimentality or self-pity—especially at a time of joyful renewal, when his solitary state, which he had come to accept as permanent, was to be so unexpectedly and so happily transformed. Isabel had accorded equal respect to the fact of his loss and to the discreetly sealed vessel in which he had interred the memory of it, with the result that "the first Mrs. Osmond"—it might have been the title of a fashionable theatre piece of the day—

was not mentioned again between the couple, not in the time of their happiness together or in the years that followed. It was with feelings of constraint, then, indeed of constriction, that the second Mrs. Osmond sat now in a crepuscular glow of candlelight and listened to her maid, of all people, resurrecting for her this tale of long-ago loss and consequent sorrow. The largest wonder of the thing was that Staines seemed on terms of such easy familiarity with the conspiracy that Osmond and Madame Merle had entered upon in order to keep hidden the conception and birth of their daughter. Of course, the maid had not related the sorry tale in the forms in which we have cast it here, but stumblingly, by way of evasions and awkward euphemisms; nevertheless she had been clear enough as to convey that she knew all there was to know, and further, that she had known it for a very long time. When Isabel asked why she had not spoken before now, the maid had fixed on her a stricken look and said, "Oh, ma'am, it never seemed my place to speak of such things!" But why then was she rehearsing it now? Did she believe her mistress to be ignorant of the dreary trick that Osmond and his lover had played in order to disguise Pansy's origins? Isabel hoped it might be so, but it was a faint hope, and one that the maid's demeanour and tone of voice did nothing to support. Since Staines knew all, and from the tale she told it was plain she did, then surely she knew that her mistress knew it also.

The moment was, for Isabel, as difficult as it was delicate. How was she to behave, how was she to respond, sitting here while a menial drew back the bolts and opened before her the door to the farthest, final bloodied chamber wherein her husband had kept his secrets sealed? How, *how* could Staines imagine it appropriate *now*, if she had not thought it so before, that she should speak to her mistress of these terrible things? And if the creature knew so much, how much more might she know? Before this question Isabel's heart quailed. All along, during these past weeks, there had lurked within her, kept as far down as she could make it go, the fearful notion that for all she had learned so far of the clandestine dealings between her husband and Madame Merle, there were further revelations still to come, further horrors that sooner or later she would be forced to face—was that moment now at hand? Thunder rumbled distantly; the noise was like that of an enraged child stamping about the floor in the far reaches of an upper room.

Isabel drew herself upright, squaring her shoulders and clearing her throat. "For how long have you known these things, Elsie?" she asked, jolted a little to hear herself addressing the maid, without thinking, by her proper name.

"Oh, from the start, ma'am," the maid promptly replied.

"But from which start?"

"Well, from when we come here first, you and me along with you, all those years ago, from Gardencourt"—Staines had been released from service in the Touchett household, at Isabel's request, to take up duty as her personal maid—"and the master, Mr. Osmond, began his courting of you. I got to know a maid that Mrs. Merle had here in Florence, Gabriella was her name, though I called her Gabby. She felt sorry for me, seeing as how I was all at sixes and sevens with everything being strange and me not knowing a word of the language. She had a bit of English, though, and she set herself to help me get the hang of things, with the tradesmen, and so on." Here the maid paused, and looked down, with a wistful expression. "Poor Gabby," she murmured, "she was such a nice, simple creature. She got in trouble—she had a boyfriend, unbeknownst to everyone, including me—and her mistress of course put her out of the house. I missed her something awful, when she was gone. Then, later, I heard she died, having the little one. Arturo, that was the boyfriend, he had left her by then, of course." Again she was silent, then gave herself a shake and looked up at her mistress with apologetically rounded eyes. "It was Gabby who told me about the master's wife, the first wife, that is, and as how she didn't have a baby at all, before she died. You was aware of that, wasn't you, ma'am?"

"Yes, I was," Isabel answered, lowering her own gaze to the table-top. "I know whose daughter Pansy is. I didn't for a long time, until—until I was told, some weeks ago."

"Yes, and when the poor little thing was born, the master brought her with him to Florence when he come back from being in the north, giving it out that she was—well, that she was the child of his poor dead wife." Once more she paused, and sat for a moment tensely regarding her mistress where she leaned before her with bowed head. "I suppose it was for the best," she ventured then, "I mean, for the master to bring up Miss Pansy motherless. Well, when you consider—" But here her courage failed her, although both women knew what it was she had declined to offer for consideration, and for a long moment they sat in wordless and wondering contemplation of the notion of Serena Merle being called upon to observe her maternal duty in the nurturing of Gilbert Osmond's daughter.

Abruptly the rain came on again, in a rush and a gush, and soon was beating steadily upon the invisible garden.

"I think I shall take my dinner now," Isabel said, with a certain strained sternness, in the manner of a person marshalling her faculties in the wake of a cataclysm she had by some miracle survived. She had raised her head, only to witness the maid lowering hers. "Is there something more?" the mistress asked, with a renewed tremor. "Tell me, please, what it is."

The maid slowly lifted her eyes, with an expression of such anguish in them that Isabel thought to jump up from her chair and flee the room—the house, the city itself!—so as not to have to hear what she dreaded hearing but which she knew must be heard.

"Oh, ma'am, it's the worst thing," Staines whispered, in a hush of horror, "the very worst."

"And that's why you kept it until last," Isabel said, with a cool collectedness she would not have thought herself capable of mustering.

"Yes, ma'am," the maid responded, "that's why I kept it till last."

XXXIII

On a distressingly hot day less than a week after that night of tempest and revelation in the garden room at the Palazzo Crescentini, Mrs. Osmond had herself delivered by coach to the central railway station at Santa Maria Novella, where she boarded the express train to Rome. She was travelling alone, and had brought with her no other baggage than a small valise, which the porter handed up to her, after he had assisted her in negotiating the steps to her compartment, and which she placed in the overhead rack, and took her seat. She did not expect her business in the Eternal City to detain her long, and planned indeed to return to Florence on the morrow. She was far more composed than she considered she had any right to be, given what Staines had told her in the garden room, while the thunder in its tantrums strode about the sky above the palazzo, shivering the candle-flames and causing the timbers of the vast old house to quake. Her calmness, her coldness, even, Isabel could only think to attribute to the relief she felt at having been delivered what was surely the last of a long series of blows out of the dark past. As she listened to the thing Staines had forced herself to tell her that night—after so long a silence!—she realised that it was something of just the sort as she had been waiting for. The jigsaw puzzle that the Countess Gemini had impatiently assembled and thrust before her shocked gaze had lacked a final piece, and now it was in place. She did not know how she could have been aware that there was a gap in the pattern, a blank space throbbing to be filled, but she had; a vacuum asserts itself by the simple force of its being void.

In fact, that was precisely how she figured her own present state to be, a tense, expectant emptiness, a poised blankness immanent with potential. She seemed again as she had been long ago, in Albany, sitting quite still, with her hands folded in her lap, waiting for the world's engine to start up and sound its whistle and plunge off with her amid smoke and flying sparks into the future. She knew this fancy for what it was, of course; she could not be as she once had been; the years could not be unwound, the damage they had wrought could not be undone. And yet, was there not a life to be lived, a destiny to be fulfilled? She had been tripped up and sent sprawling on to the iron rails, yet she had managed to scramble to some sort of safety; she had survived.

Now the train, the actual train in which she was seated, set off with a sense of banners waving, of streamers flying. The heat in the compartment was great; Isabel hardly noticed it.

She arrived in Rome at the luncheon hour, that interval of the day when the city briefly suspends its frantic clamour and subsides into a languorous yet somehow restless torpor. Outside the station she hailed a carriage and directed the driver to the Hotel d'Inghilterra. The winding streets, bisected down the middle by wedges of hard-edged purple shadow, held a sinister stillness, and the rattle of the horse's hoofs struck ringing echoes from the walls of the shuttered houses on either side. The strong sunlight penetrated the sleeves of Isabel's light gown and made her shiver—she noted, as she often had cause to, here in the south, that strange phenomenon whereby intense heat had some of the same effects upon the person as extreme cold—and she was glad when the carriage came to a jingling halt under the hotel's taut blue-and-white awning. The marble-tiled lobby offered a balm of blessed dimness. She approached the desk and spoke a name to the concierge, who was tall and slim and silver-haired, and presented him with her card, which he held by one corner between a brown finger and a browner thumb while he scrutinised with an air of haughty interrogation the information printed upon it. *"Sì, sì, la signora è nella sua stanza,"* he said, with the merest shadow of a glacial smile. *"Le dirò che sei arrivata—un momento."* He clicked his fingers, and a young man in a blue satin waistcoat popped up, like a jack out of its box, was spoken to in a rapid and confidential-sounding undertone, flashed a gleamingly ingratiating smile at *L'ospite,* took delivery of her card, and bore it away in the palm of a white-gloved hand. The concierge withdrew his attention from the lady before him with the blank briskness of one pinching out a candle flame, and set himself to shuffling, with all the appearances of intense concentration, through those mysterious flimsy sheets of paper that members of his guild have ever to hand just under the lip of their desks. Isabel turned away, smiling a little to herself over the perennial and covertly vindictive rituals of those tasked with attending to the public, and paced slowly about, stopping to examine idly a framed map of the city, or a fancifully romantic engraving of the ruins of the Capitol, or an assortment of potsherds, of doubtful vintage, distributed upon the shelves of a glass-fronted cabinet. Whence came these fusty adornments, she wondered, and by whose decision were they installed here, by what sustained directive diligently dusted and dutifully maintained? It sometimes seemed to her that the chief aim of all inanimate objects was to hold themselves in hiding in plain sight and thereby go safely unnoticed; it was her aim, too. She was aware now, although she had been trying for some time not to be, of her heart's increasingly disquieted stirrings within its shrouded cage. She had a hard task ahead of her.

"Ah, my dear, so you have come," a honeyed, deep-toned voice said behind her.

"Yes, I have come," Isabel said, turning with calculated deliberateness towards the stairs, on the lowest step of which Madame Merle had paused, one hand resting on the newel-post and the other employed in pinching the skirts of her pale-blue gown so as to hold the hem suspended a protective inch above the carpet.

"I wondered if you *would* come, you know," this lady said with a smile, "so long were you about it. For myself, I've been here the best part of a week, awaiting you."

"But you had my telegram last evening?"

"I did, with relief—I worried that some mishap might have befallen you, since last we communicated."

"I had business to attend to. It took more time than I had anticipated."

"Ah, yes, business," Madame Merle said softly, with a feline sibilance. "For a person of means I'm sure it must be very time-consuming." She was all of her accustomed magnificent self, fair of hair and smooth of complexion, with her large handsome face, and shoulders that were nothing but impressive, if perhaps a shade too broad; with her candid grey eye and that elegantly lazy smile, wholly characteristic, that lifted her mouth a little at the left corner; with all, in a word, of her imposing if not to say daunting presence, before which the very prints on the walls seemed to lean a little more steeply forward in respectful acknowledgement. She gestured towards the *sala da tè*. "Shall you take some refreshment?"

"No, thank you. I lunched on the train."

"On the train! That was intrepid of you. I feel I should offer you an antidote, rather than further fare."

On the instant Isabel's gaze grew sharp—antidotes and their opposites were among the darker topics she had come here to raise—but the blandness of Madame Merle's manner reassured her that her intent had not been somehow anticipated.

"I should prefer a place where we might speak in private," she murmured.

"But of course—my suite here includes a very pretty little parlour, where we shall be sure of being undisturbed. Unless, of course"—she paused, and her smile again drew up her lips at one corner—"you fear I might be the spider, and you the fly?"

"Oh, I trust my wings have strength enough to escape any web you might fashion for me."

To this sally Madame Merle, still smiling, responded only by lifting a sardonically appreciative eyebrow. "Come, then," she said silkily, and side by side the two ladies ascended the broad staircase.

The room they entered was not so modest as might have been expected from Madame Merle's figuring of it. It had a sofa and a pair of armchairs, a low circular table with an inlaid glass top, and two fine, deep-embrasured windows side by side facing in the direction of the Piazza di Spagna. The sofa, upholstered in sea-green satin, had the aloof and dignified aspect of some grand elderly lady of a bygone age, and looked as if the last thing it expected was to be sat upon; the chairs, however, knew their place well enough, and extended humble arms in a gesture of commodious and well-padded accommodation.

"Oh, these Roman summers!" Madame Merle exclaimed— the atmosphere in the room had the texture of a tepid fog—going from one of the delicately mullioned windows to the other and throwing them wide. She glanced back at Isabel. "Is that better, or worse? One never knows, since often the air in the streets is stuffier than that indoors." She checked herself. "But I forget myself, and speak to you as if you were a stranger newly arrived in this infernal place—that's my name for it in summertime, you know, the Infernal City."

"Yes, and Gilbert's too," Isabel said. "I imagine you would be hard put now to say which of you thought of it first."

This, the barest shadow of a challenge, Madame Merle met with another of her distant, blank-eyed smiles. "Are you quite sure you won't take something?" she asked. "A cooling drink, or an ice, perhaps? I could ring for a dish of water-ice, they do it wonderfully here, especially the lemon-flavoured one. No? Ah, well then, let us sit, at least. One finds it wearying even to remain standing, in such heat."

They sat down in the armchairs, which had been set directly opposite each other at either end of the forbidding sofa, so that the two women found themselves starkly face-to-face with nothing between them save the glass-topped table. It was an arrangement that they both felt at once to be distinctly theatrical, and it was a question, their being thus histrionically disposed, as to which of them, lacking a cue, would be the first to speak. Through the wide-open windows there entered untrammelled the confused clamour of the street below, where twin concourses of tourists flowed and mingled in both directions, and there were the cries of souvenir-vendors, and the curiously hollow-sounding, weary hoof-beats of plumed carriage horses drawing their complements of sightseers back and forth between the Spanish Steps and the river. Madame Merle had opened a painted fan and was flicking it in front of her face with rapid, butterfly strokes; of the two women she was decidedly the ampler, and the temperature in the room therefore was more distressing to her than it was to Isabel. "You have an air about you of stern intent," the older lady said now, striving for lightness but failing to keep an edge of irritability out of her voice. "Have you changed your mind and come to rebuke me, as you so markedly refrained from doing when we chanced upon each other in Paris?"

"Ah, no," Isabel replied. "I am past the need to rebuke anyone, except, perhaps, myself. As I told you, on that occasion at the Princess d'Attrait's, what I seek is not revenge, but a reckoning."

"Between revenge and reckoning there is not such a great distinction to be made, is there? Anyway, I believe, rather, the term you used that evening was 'an accounting'—in fact, I'm sure it was, for I noted it well, and gave much thought to it, afterwards. It seems to me"—here the lady switched the fan to her left hand, the right one having grown weary from its efforts—"you have had a sufficient accounting, or reckoning, call it what you will, from the Countess Gemini, and who knows how many others?"

"Are there so many others who know enough to be capable of enlightening me as to your schemes, yours and my husband's?"

"Oh, for goodness' sake, woman, how should I say who knew what and who didn't? Do you imagine I kept a register? Do you think I had a cadre of informants who came to me each evening with word of what they had overheard during the day? I was above such pettiness—*we* were above it, *we*!"

It surprised Isabel with what equanimity, with what an extent of protective numbness, she had absorbed the blow of that *we*— for it had been meant to strike her full in the face with all the force of a wielded cudgel. She had been acquainted with Madame Merle for a long time; the lady, for all that she was Brooklyn-born, had been one of the first through-and-through Europeans she had encountered, after she had first stepped on to English soil, and was still Isabel Archer, late of Albany, in the state of New York;

they had stayed at Gardencourt together, in what by now could be called "the old days"; they had taken the Grand Tour in each other's company, with never a cross word exchanged between them; they had been each other's confidante and *les plus grandes amies* for years—for years!—but only now did it occur to her that she had never before seen her, Serena Merle, so highly wrought, so far beyond the run of herself, as she so plainly was, sitting here, flushed and furious and vainly fanning herself, in these absurdly genteel surroundings—the sofa! the cushions!—at the centre of a ruined empire overrun by latter-day barbarians armed with Baedekers and billfolds. Had she, had Isabel Archer, as in her mind she suddenly was again, had she come at last to her second moment of triumph, to her second time of, yes, reckoning? A week ago she had faced her husband, on that afternoon at Bellosguardo, and had faced him down; was she to do the same now with her husband's erstwhile consort? So it must be, otherwise how account for the bitter taste in her mouth, for the depth of darkness in her heart? In that instant, she almost hated herself.

"When Osmond took his wife away from Naples and brought her to Piedmont, many years ago," she said, in a voice that surprised her by being of a remarkable steadiness, "he knew she would die there, didn't he?"

It was not a question, but neither, in some peculiar fashion, was it a statement; it seemed to her, rather, in the manner of an hypothesis, the soundness of which she did not herself doubt, but which required to be put out upon the common air in order for it to be publicly authenticated. As to Madame Merle, her immediate response was the abrupt stilling of the fan she had been so vigorously manipulating, while her gaze fixed itself as if upon a mote in the middle distance. She spoke not at all for some moments, and Isabel was content to wait upon her without betraying the least sign of impatience. Indeed our heroine—and just then she was nothing if not heroic—permitted herself to take a modicum of pride in the control she was managing to exert over her own impulses and emotions. She was conscious of having stepped with awful ease over a boundary that before had seemed so high she would have surmounted it only at the expense of splintered fingernails and scraped knees; here, now, on the other side, she was in a new realm, alien and oddly featureless, a parched place, where a cold wind whipped up eddies of dust and sent soiled scraps of paper scudding over the level dry ground; it was, she realised, the blighted country where Madame Merle and her like had their abode. And Isabel herself, had she not been made to live there too, for years and years, without realising, or at least without acknowledging, the fact? Was that a real boundary she had seemed to step over, or a barrier her imagination had erected for her, so that she should not see for what it was the dead world into which she had been so subtly, so smoothly, inveigled? If that were the case, then today she would make her escape, no matter how solidly real the hurdle or how hard to scale, and return herself from that dead land, scuffed and bleeding, as it might be, to the domain of the living.

When Madame Merle stirred herself out of stillness at last it was as if a stone monument had come stiffly to life and turned its head with great effort on the pivot of its marmoreal neck. "My dear Isabel, I must say, one is never in want of surprises in your company nowadays. Gilbert Osmond do away with his wife? Wherever did you come by such a wicked notion?"

"I said nothing of his 'doing away' with her," Isabel evenly replied. "But I believe he put her in the way of mortal harm, as deliberately, shall we say, as *you* put me in the way of *him*."

To this Madame Merle returned a hard cold laugh. "Do you think of your marriage as having been a form of dying?"

"I would not put it so strongly as that," Isabel calmly observed. "Not *so* strongly. Anyway, it is no business of yours what my marriage was or wasn't, even if you were instrumental in the making of it."

" 'In the making of it'? You seem to have surprisingly scant regard for yourself as an active agent in your own fate. Yet you came to us flying the banner of independence, flaunting the reputation of a young woman who would not be *made* to do anything, by anybody, that she had not already fixed on doing herself."

"You saw exactly what my strengths were, and my weaknesses," Isabel murmured, "and weighed them judiciously in the balance."

She hardly knew what she was saying, and hardly cared: she had introduced a matter of grave moment, and each crabwise step away from it that Madame Merle effected convinced her all the more firmly, and all the more miserably, that the terrible tale that Staines had told to her, the source for which was none other than Madame Merle's own personal maid, was nothing less than the truth. She felt like one who, standing at a window, had witnessed an atrocity committed in the street below, from the sight of which the perpetrator's confederate was drawing her away, with an arm firmly linked in hers and speaking earnestly and volubly of everything save the corpse sprawled on the pavement below, and the blood trickling into the gutter. What Staines had disclosed was that the man who some fifteen years later was to become the husband of Isabel Archer had conveyed his first wife to Piedmont after word had come to him that there was an outbreak of typhoid fever in the region, and that the worst of the contagion was centred upon Alba. The deluded Mrs. Osmond had gone willingly enough, trusting her husband's assurance that the northern air would offer a welcome respite from the noxious vapours of the south—the uncommonly hot weather of the summer had persisted into autumn and showed no signs of abating—and would be a tonic greatly to the benefit of her delicate state of health. The Albanese city fathers had done all in their power to suppress the fact that sickness was rife in their streets—if the tourists stopped coming, what of the season's harvest of fragrant truffles and succulent peaches, and of that year's vintage of those opulent wines for which the region is celebrated by the wide world's palate?—but Osmond knew the truth of the matter, by way of that network along which the guild of true collectors discreetly communicates. Someone he was acquainted with had told him there was sickness in Alba; Madame Merle was in Lecce, about to bear his unlooked-for child; in Alba lay the possibility of a solution to his predicament, or at least an amelioration of it.

Over the years Isabel had learned many things about her husband that she could not have guessed at before she had married him. That was only natural, of course; indeed, successive discoveries, leading to a deepening of knowledge and an intensification of intimacy, was what she had looked forward to with the keenest anticipation when she had agreed to share her life with Gilbert Osmond, the extent of whose knowledge of the world and its wonders had so impressed her, and the subtlety and variousness of whose mind she had confidently expected never to see exhausted. She had soon learned that in all his aspects he had his limits, and that they were exact, and rigidly demarcated; indeed, the realisation of his narrowness of vision, of thought, above all of emotion, was the thing that most sorely disappointed and pained her. She believed she could have borne almost anything else; let him be a philanderer, a shameless cheat, a Byronesque transgressor—let him be anything other than the pinched vindictive spirit she had discovered him to be, and she would have found some way to reconcile herself to her life with him. But he was what he was, and what he was she could not find it in her to accept, try as she might, but now, suddenly, startlingly, there was manifest, in the tale Staines had told her, a version of him she had never glimpsed before. He was a gambler. Yes, a gambler; not a daring one, not one who would smash down his last handful of gold upon a single square of the roulette table and face disaster fully in the intoxicating thrill of the moment; but a gambler nonetheless. He had wagered that his wife would die in Alba, and he had won. The stakes were high: he would have risked the forfeiture of his reputation as a gentleman, as a person of the highest probity, as a paragon of honour, should his lover have returned from her sequestration in the south and displayed before the public, or at least that thin slice of the public whose regard he prized, the incontrovertible evidence of his deplorable foolishness in allowing himself to fall a victim to passion—passion, the affect of all the affects that, when it was evidenced in others, Gilbert Osmond lost no opportunity to mock! No, the thing could not have been borne; to lose face would have been, for him, insupportable, for what else had he other than the appearance of being what he was not?

Of course, Isabel reflected now, seated in the full insuppressible glare of Madame Merle's antipathy—intensified, as it was, by that lady's anxiety over her own security and interests—she would have had to grant Osmond a grudging admiration, however deplorable his actions, had he put himself, as well as his wife, in mortal danger by venturing north to that afflicted province. But he had not; no, he had not, for the dice had been weighted in his favour.

A muffled tap sounded on the door, and at a word from Madame Merle there entered, not the ephebe of the glossy curls and the blue waistcoat, but the silvery guardian of the reception desk himself, bearing a card, which Madame Merle took from his fingers, and, having produced a pair of pince-nez, which Isabel had not known her heretofore to be in need of, read the name printed thereon, at sight of which her eyes widened in pleasurable but, so it seemed to Isabel, exaggerated and not quite credible surprise. *"Sì, certo, fai entrare il signore,"* she said, and, when the servitor had obsequiously withdrawn, lowered the glass and sat for a moment silent, regarding Isabel with an expression of quiet yet not inexuberant satisfaction.

"Well, this is a day of visitors, certainly," she said. "Hardly have I settled to the pleasure of your company, when here is your husband come to join us!"

XXXIV

In her Albany years Isabel had read widely, if not deeply, into
the history of Rome, as much for excitement as for instruc-
tion, it must be admitted. Shockingly little of what she read had
remained with her, and she had sadly assumed her memory to be
singularly defective, until presently there was borne in upon her
the consoling fact that the majority of people, by the time they
attained adulthood, had forgotten almost the entirety of what they
had learned when they were young. With the approach of her marriage, and her husband's intention that they should live not in
Florence but in Rome—he had of course taken it upon himself to
decide the matter, as if by perfect right—she had viewed the prospect of residing in the capital as an opportunity to be reacquainted
with the glories she had read of and subsequently forgotten; deep
stores of knowledge shut up within her long ago would surely be
reopened to her, like so many tombs that for centuries had been
sealed by time; surely the city would bring alive the ancient past
by presenting to her eager gaze the very streets and squares and
palaces wherein the *Imperium Romanum* had been played out in
all its magnificence. Alas, though so much of antiquity remained
intact, the city of today was a far cry from the Rome as she had
figured it in her youthful imagination, an imagination fired by the

numerous densely printed volumes from which she had derived much of her education, and which she had impressed herself by being able positively to flash through, as if they were no more demanding than the lighter of the productions of Mr. Dickens or of Mrs. Oliphant. No restrictions were placed upon the works she should have access to—her mother, who might have been expected to impose a degree of shielding censorship, was deceased, and her father, as he generously expressed it, didn't give a hang what the girl read—and she had free range of the admittedly limited household library. It was in Gibbon, she thought, or in one of the contemporary recorders, Tacitus, perhaps, or Plutarch, that she had encountered a passage, in a chapter devoted to the reign of the Emperor Nero, describing, with a restraint that served only to emphasise the horror, the afternoon entertainments on offer at the Colosseum in those days. The cruelties enacted in that fell arena would have been unbearable to contemplate had they not taken place so very long ago; however, there was a detail that struck our young scholar with dreadful force, and that stayed with her when so much else had fled, which was that often one of the wild beasts, lion or tiger or the like, would, to the disgust of the howling spectators, pause a while in the midst of rending asunder and devouring some Christian martyr or Nubian slave girl, and relax on its haunches, the initial pangs of its hunger having been assuaged, and seem fondly to caress its half-dead victim with gentle pats and pushes, with licks and nuzzles, with even, sometimes, a clumsy sort of embrace. These endearments, as they appeared, were nothing of the kind, of course, no more than are a cat's toyings with a captured mouse. But had there been an audience present that day in the Hotel d'Inghilterra, when Mrs. Osmond sat at the mercy of her lately arrived husband and his erstwhile paramour, it too would likely have voiced a violent protest at the deceptive delicacy and considerateness with which the pair of predators circled about their captive prey.

In point of fact, it was Osmond alone who circled, while Madame Merle kept to her chair at the end of the sofa, calm and handsome as she always was, with her fascinatingly one-sided smile, and her head haught and her broad back held straight, in the attitude not of one who is party to the proceedings but, rather, of a disinterested observer settled comfortably in the gallery of the courtroom. "Your wife, Gilbert, believes you stood by and let your first wife perish," she said now, without the slightest adjustment to her majestically composed demeanour. "What do you say to that?"

It came to Isabel that she had never before heard the woman address Osmond with such easy intimacy; it seemed intentionally pointed now, like a sharp slap upon the cheek with a silk glove. Osmond, who wore a pale-cream suit and a blue cravat stuck with a silver-headed pin, had so far said not a word, but on entering the room had only stopped and stood, his hand still on the doorknob, and bent upon his wife a gaze lacking in all expression save what might be a certain faint disappointment—disappointment not at finding her there, she thought, but at the notion of her in general, of her being anywhere, at any time; he had imagined himself done with her, yet here she was. Or, rather, here *he* was. She had the impression that he had, as had she, lately arrived in the city— perhaps they had been on the same train. She pictured him, on arrival, hanging back on the busy platform, concealed behind a soot-blackened pillar and watching out until she had safely quitted the station. Madame Merle, having last evening received Isabel's telegram announcing that she would come to Rome this morning, would in her turn have telegraphed Osmond, bidding him to hasten to her side, and now here they were, the pair of them, in the arena, she a lioness, tawny and sleek, and he the grizzled leopard he had always been. He was padding about here and there in the half-part of the room behind Madame Merle's chair, picking up things and examining them with a show of interest, of absorption, even—as if, Isabel thought, with a flicker of amusement, there could possibly be anything in a room such as this that he would consider deserving of the least of his attention.

"I have always been aware of the vulgarity of your mind," he said now, in a controlled and level tone, addressing Isabel without looking at her, "but I confess I would not have thought even you should be capable of sinking to such a depth of cruelly bad taste as to utter such a *canard* about me and my late wife." He had stopped by the window, and was turning in his hands a Murano glass vase, purple in hue and of a remarkable ugliness. "How dare you," he said softly, and almost with a kind of mildness, "how dare you make reference to that lady, even if it were only so much as to utter her name?"

Madame Merle was watching Isabel, with an expression of keen attentiveness—she was openly and unreservedly savouring the spectacle of husband and wife in conflict—and Isabel met her now candidly, with not a trace of flinching or shrinking back. She felt no fear; they would aim to maul and maim her, they might aim even to devour her, in their sleek slow way, the pard and his partner together; they might succeed, might tear every strip of flesh from her bones; she did not care. Her safety, her very survival, were the least of it; her spirit, like the martyr's, would rise up from the blood and mire of the scorched arena, and be saved. She was glad Osmond had come: his precipitate arrival, which of course was Madame Merle's little *coup de théâtre*, had given her a moment's pause, no more than that; thereafter she had understood that it was right they both should be here, facing her, and she facing them.

Osmond had turned at last to look in her direction, still cradling the vase in his hands. "Might one enquire how you came to the preposterous notion—preposterous, disgraceful, disgusting: you find me lost for words adequate to the thing—how you arrived at the notion that—what was it?—that I *allowed* my wife to *die*? What do you know of these matters, madam? What *can* you know? My wife passed away a long time ago, in a far-off place, of a malignant fever. You and I had an agreement, tacit, I grant you, not to speak of her or of her tragic end. I honoured that agreement, though Heaven knows I might have used the fact of my loss to win your sympathy when I was in need of it." At this Isabel allowed herself to stare; when could he ever, possibly, have thought himself in need of her sympathy? Unalloyed admiration, due respect, a fit modicum of fear—these were some of the tributes that he had asked, that he had demanded, of her; but sympathy? Or was she wronging him in this? Was he more vulnerable than she had realised? The thought chilled her, not least for the fact that it had come to her too late. "Is it part of your vengeance on me, for what misdeed only you can say," Osmond went on, "that you have chosen now to break that sacred covenant? For I, at least, regarded it as sacred."

It interested Isabel to note how roundabout yet inescapable were the ways by which guilt was led to betray itself, and that often it was the care the guilty ones took to avoid acknowledging or even alluding to their wrong-doing that was the unmistakable sign of their culpability. Neither Madame Merle nor Gilbert Osmond had thought to issue a direct denial of the allegation she had raised against them—and it was against them both that she had laid her charge—but instead had bent all their efforts to diverging from the central issue; it was as if a defendant in the dock were to confine himself to criticising the manner in which the description of the deed he had been indicted for was couched. Had either of them shown signs, not even of outrage but of simple startlement, at the notion of the enormity she was accusing the one of having committed and the other of having countenanced, she would have paused a moment and obliged herself to entertain a doubt. How she had pressed Staines, that evening at Mrs. Touchett's residence, as the twilight gathered in, and the storm growled above them and the rain beat on the garden and roiled in the guttering, oh, *how* she had pressed, until big tears squeezed up to sit trembling on the rims of the maid's eyelids, and her voice shook, and she beat her fists upon her breast. She had got the thing from Madame Merle's personal maid, poor Gabriella, a simple Florentine *ragazza* "afeard of her own shadow," who had overheard her mistress and Osmond, on one of his infrequent and clandestine visits to Lecce, discussing the matter in what, for that circumspect pair, must have been remarkably direct and open terms. The lady had urged her lover against the venture to Alba, given the danger to himself, but he had dismissed her fears, for a reason that, whether Madame Merle knew of it at the time, Isabel was able instantly to recall. It had happened, during the time when he was paying court to her, that she and her urbane lover had found themselves, one unseasonably damp spring morning, sheltering from the peculiarly inconsequential yet decidedly wetting Italian rain in one of Florence's innumerable and, to Isabel, confusingly similar churches. They had strolled up the aisle at one side and, after pausing for a cursory glance at a markedly unremarkable altarpiece, were proceeding down the other, when Osmond had laid a hand upon the young woman's arm and drawn her atten-

tion to a mural—was it by Giotto?—in which the souls of a multitude of clay-coloured corpses were being escorted, in segregated
batches, by busy squadrons of angels and demons, either downwards towards the gates of a garish well of perdition, or upwards
into the glory of a gold-leafed firmament. Isabel, in her impetuous
fashion, had exclaimed at the majesty and frightening force of
the artist's vision, for she had a long way to go before she would
learn the advisability of waiting on Osmond's judgement on this
or that work of art before putting forward her own opinion. And
indeed, on this occasion, having dropped a discreet little cough
and allowing a moment or two of silence to pass, Osmond had,
with a less than convincing show of diffidence, ventured it as *his*
opinion that the piece, while doubtless possessed of a certain dour
force, and displaying an earnest aspiration towards the majestic,
was overall a clumsy thing. "It was merely for the subject that I
wished you to notice it," he had said, smiling, and pinching the
point of his beard between a finger and thumb. "Since I have been
so assiduously pressing upon you those aspects and attributes of
my personality, which in my estimation make me the ideal appli-
cant for your hand in marriage"—it was this brand of irony that at
the time she took for the chief sign in him of a high droll wit, and
even found endearing the laboured archness of his tone—"I think
it right to add to my list the happy fact that, should you consent to
be my wife, to become, in plain, mere Mrs. Osmond, you may be
assured that there is one form of pestilence to which you shall not
lose me, since I survived a bout of it in boyhood, and may therefore fairly consider myself sufficiently immunised against it."
However, she had hardly had time to enquire the name of the malady he meant, employing as she did so a to e of mock-solemnity,
in order to enter into what she judged the straight-faced frivolity of the exchange, before her lover's expression had darkened

and he had turned brusquely aside and set off at a grim stride towards the church doorway and the great dark leathern curtain overhanging it. At once it had come to her that the "pestilence" he had spoken of must be the same one to which his wife had fallen victim, and that this accounted for the sudden alteration in his temper. She had found him waiting for her outside, with his collar turned up against the grey and drifting rain, and instead of questioning him further—which of course she would not have dreamed of doing—she had linked her arm in his, and together in silence they had descended the marble steps, worn glassy-smooth by the feet of countless generations of worshippers, and stepped into the street, and back into their lives, and it had been like moving from oppressive shadow into the balm of bright sunlight. Was it only her fancy now, or had that been the moment when she had decided to accept his proposal and allow herself to become "mere Mrs. Osmond"?

Her husband now still had his eye on her, awaiting her reply; she could not recall what question it was he had asked. She felt, suddenly, the weariness of years descend upon her shoulders. What did any of this matter? What was it to her if her husband—it amazed her that she should still think of him by this formulation— what matter if he had taken his wife to Piedmont in the full expectation that she would contract the fever against which he knew himself to be almost certainly immune? What matter? She could no longer act, Isabel told herself, as if she were the appointed invigilator of the world's wickedness.

It was Madame Merle who spoke into Osmond's waiting silence. "She has been listening, I wager, to listeners at doors." Although her eye was fixed upon Isabel, she had addressed her words to Osmond behind her at the window. "How else should she know anything of what you and I only were privy to?"

Osmond considered this. "There is the Touchett woman," he said. "She is witch enough to hear through solid walls."

Madame Merle, still regarding Isabel with a sort of smiling frown, slowly shook her broad blonde head. "No, I think that is not the source. I detect distinctly the echo of a menial's whisperings. That maid I had—remember? The one I took with me to Lecce?"

"Remember?" Osmond snapped. "You expect me to remember some peasant girl from twenty years ago? I am not an elephant, I have not an elephant's gift of remembering, as you seem to have."

Isabel had been attending upon them, absorbed and appalled, as they batted the ball of their displeased and anxious speculations back and forth between them—it seemed all the uglier that one of them kept her back turned to the other, as if in compliance with a rule in some dreadful game. She felt herself to be a—how had Madame Merle expressed it?—a listener at a door, her presence disregarded. This was how they had discussed her, among themselves, from the start—she could hear in their voices the authentic ring of casual and amused contempt, could hear it as clearly as Madame Merle had claimed to have heard in hers the echo of the little Florentine maid's whispered disclosures, long ago, to her gangly *controparte inglese*. How shabby it was, the whole thing, how shabby, and soiled, and dispiriting. She could bear it not a moment more. She rose abruptly from her chair, fairly surging up, like one struggling against the threat of drowning who breaks the surface of the sea and gasps in great lungfuls of the saving air.

"I must go," she said, stammering in her distress and haste, "I must—I have to—" She stopped; she had the image of herself now not as a saved swimmer, but as a fish hauled up and tossed upon the river bank, agape and twitching. The two persons in the room with her had abruptly disengaged their attention from each other, and were staring at her in surprise. Osmond, with an uncertain frown, came forward and placed himself beside the seated Madame Merle; he had only to set a hand upon her shoulder and they should have seemed a couple posing for their portrait to be taken by a crouched and hooded photographer. When Isabel spoke again it was to Madame Merle she addressed herself. "My purpose in coming to Rome was to inform you of a decision I have made that concerns you," she said. "In Paris, when we met by chance that evening, you were surprised when I urged you to return to Italy. I was surprised myself. I had given no thought to the matter—I had believed you to be already in America, and that I should never see you again."

"There were others of us who thought the same thing," Osmond trenchantly interposed.

Madame Merle ignored the intended slight in his remark, and gave no sign of having registered it, except that her cheeks coloured a little. Isabel too ignored her husband; she wore a frown of agitated concentration, which made her seem suddenly very young; she was like a child in the classroom who has been summoned to her feet by the teacher and commanded to recite a lesson she had spent all of the previous evening striving, with much worry and effort, to learn off by heart.

"You asked then," she resumed, still fixed on Madame Merle, "where you should live, since you had sold your house in Florence. I assured you that you should have a place in Rome, if you would agree to live here, and a modest allowance to sustain you in your new place."

"Yes, and it was generous of you, I'm sure," Madame Merle coolly conceded, though with a movement of her handsome shoulders that belied any sentiment of appreciation her words might have seemed to convey. "Indeed," she went on, with a heightened emphasis, "so generous were the terms you offered that I could not but be suspicious." She smiled coldly, her lips lifting at the left and her eyebrow at the same side inclining sharply in response. "You speak of a decision: Are you about to confirm that I was right to be sceptical?"

This interruption too Isabel chose to bypass, as if she had not heard it, and pressed on. "This week I summoned my lawyer, Mr. Pettigrew—he has his offices in Rome, but he kindly consented to come up to Florence personally to attend me."

"Oh, yes, the old scoundrel knows on which side his bread is buttered," Osmond scoffingly observed. Isabel only shut her eyes against him, giving her head a quick little shake—she would not be deflected from her recitation, which she must finish and have done with before she could be gone.

"I gave instructions that he should bring with him the deeds to the Palazzo Roccanera and all documents pertaining to its ownership." She had opened her eyes, and now she turned them full upon her husband, lifting up her head in preparation for the delivery of a blow she knew full well would wound not him alone, but herself also. "I told you, Gilbert, when we spoke last week at Bellosguardo, that you might remain in residence there. It is your home, it's where you have your life, and so it must continue. The basis of your occupancy will change, however."

Osmond too had put back his head, and was regarding her, at an angle, from under half-lowered lids. "The devil," he exclaimed, "but if you haven't sold the place out from under me!"

"No, I have not," Isabel responded. "But I have transferred the deeds out of my own hands."

"Transferred them? To whom? To Pansy? Tell me you gave the place to Pansy."

Isabel slowly shook her head. How calm she felt all at once, how calm and clear of mind, how serene of heart. She might have been standing atop the tallest peak of a serried range of mountains, looking into an immensity of blue and limitless sky.

"Not to Pansy, no," she said, "but to someone who was once as dear to you as she, or dearer." She dropped her gaze and allowed it to settle upon Madame Merle. "You were mistaken to be suspicious of me," she said, addressing this lady. "You shall have— you *have*—your place in Rome, as I promised." She smiled, and nodded once, and turned aside to find her parasol—it was the same silly pink one she had inadvertently taken away with her after sharing her confidences with Henrietta Stackpole that day in Cavendish Square. She quickly found it, leaning against a bureau upon which she had set her hat and her gloves, and taking up all three of these articles now she moved towards the door. "Goodbye," she said, in the most casual fashion imaginable. "I leave for London tonight." On the threshold she paused, and glanced back into the room, at the man standing there, who had once been her husband, and the woman seated beside him, whom she had once thought her friend. The two were staring at each other, eye to eye—*a quattr'occhi*, as the Italians say, Isabel recalled with surpassing inconsequence—and in their looks were mixed so many meanings, emotions and calculations that it would be foolhardy to attempt to enumerate them here.

XXXV

Her faithful friend Miss Stackpole it was who next evening met Isabel on her arrival at the Charing Cross station. She had travelled via Turin and Paris, and the Channel crossing had been so sweetly calm that the sea, under a moonless sky, might have been a dark mirror on which an infinitesimally thin film of oil had been poured out. She had stood on deck for a long time, watching first the dim coastline of France recede, and then the glimmering cliffs of England growing near. She had the sense of her journey being far larger than it was, as if she were crossing not between countries but continents. Her forebears had been among the first to come out from the Old World to the New, and now she felt like one of them, gazing back with a detached sort of wistfulness, regretting that she had so few regrets, and looking forward in a balance between anxiety and hope. Hope: the word caught her up. Were there things she hoped for, any more? It seemed to her now that to be in a state of hopefulness for what was to come was in some way to hold in low esteem the things that were already here. What was the uncertain and beautiful future compared to the dear and dusty old palpable present? It was in the here and now that her life was to be lived; after all, were not the now and the here the shapers of what was to come?

"So, you've left him!" were the first, grimly gratified, words Miss Stackpole thought to utter, after the two ladies had exchanged joyful greetings and embraces amid the smoke and smuts on the station platform. "I knew you would, in the end."

"Henrietta, my dear, you are incorrigible!" Isabel exclaimed, laughing, and then, with an exclamation of dismay, "Oh, look, Staines is going to fight with the porters again! Come, we must prevent it."

Peace was quickly restored, or imposed, rather, following the stern intervention of Isabel, and the judicious distribution among a covey of indignant stalwarts of the station staff of a certain number of sixpenny pieces, which Isabel, having nothing but French and Italian money in her purse, was compelled to borrow from Miss Stackpole, and at last the maid, with the baggage piled behind her on a commodious carriage, was dispatched to Pratt's Hotel. When she was gone, and after an interval of nervous waiting to see if she might not come back—Staines had a strong inclination towards second thoughts—Isabel declared herself in urgent need of a restorative cup and a crumb or two of something sweet, and therefore she and Henrietta took themselves off to the station buffet, and there ordered a pot of tea and a plate of hot scones with butter and honey and marmalade. They were no sooner seated than Henrietta returned to the attack. "I suppose he was beastly to you, yes?" she said, with the undisguisably self-satisfied air of one who had "told you so."

"What a taste you have for the dramatic!" Isabel said good-humouredly. "There was no beastliness at all—you've met my husband, you know with what restraint and quietness he comports himself."

"But you have left him, I mean definitively?" Henrietta persisted.

"You may mean definitively, but what does 'definitively' mean, in your lexicon?"

"Why, that you told him your marriage, yours and his, was at an end!"

The tea was brought then, the waiter's ministrations providing, for Isabel, a welcome respite from her friend's relentlessness. In the intervals when she was away from Henrietta she tended to forget the at times raucousness of her manner, the blank American way she had of saying out, "at the top of her voice," things that more prudent souls would have hesitated to formulate even in thought, and would have made sure to mull over a long time before thinking to utter them aloud. What on earth did Mr. Bantling's sister, Lady Pensil, make of the young woman who was soon to be her sister-in-law? Henrietta may have learned to use terms such as "beastly," and how to butter a hot scone without making stains on the tablecloth, but surely her forthrightness would set the dovecotes a-flutter at Pensil Magna, and many another English establishment beside?

"So are you going to disclose anything at all of what you have been about, in these past weeks?" Henrietta demanded now, in an aggrieved and petulant tone. "Or will your deplorable sense of discretion seal your lips for ever on the subject of your escape from bondage?"

"Bondage!" Isabel breathed. "If that's how you figure marriage to be, I wonder at your intention to enter that state of servitude and suffering yourself. How is Mr. Bantling, by the way?"

"He's very well," her friend snapped back at her, "and don't try to change the subject."

Isabel bent her face over her cup, to duck for a moment below the level of her friend's fierce glare. The tea, in the proper English way, was as brown as winter bracken, and also had something of what she imagined would be the flavour of that hardy plant. She added two lumps of sugar to the brew, in the manner of a votary making an offering to her deity.

"I stopped at Florence," she said. "On the way to Rome, that is."

"What—then you didn't see your husband at all?" Henrietta exclaimed.

"No, no, he was there, at Bellosguardo, staying at his old quarters for the summer."

"And his daughter, where was she? Immured in some convent, I dare say."

Isabel sighed; she was weary after the journey, but she was more than a little tired too of her friend's seemingly endless haranguing. "As a matter of fact, Pansy is here, in England. Her father sent her to visit a titled acquaintance of his, at a castle somewhere—in Kent, I think."

Henrietta, blunt as she was, could on occasion be as sharp as a pin, and here her power of insight pierced straight to the heart of Osmond's motive. "I presume the titled acquaintance has a son, or sons, of an eligible age," she said, with a sort of sneering little laugh that Isabel found both irritating and faintly offensive. Her friend went on: "Your husband, I know, never got over the loss of Lord Warburton for a son-in-law."

Isabel quickly picked up her cup, and put it down again slowly. "You go too far," she murmured.

Here Henrietta immediately relented—the effect was somewhat like the sudden escape of all the air from a pneumatic tube—and reaching impulsively across the table she grasped her friend by the hand with a look of sorrow and remorse. "Forgive me, my dear," she cried softly. "I know, I know, I go too far, and say too much. Poor Edward—Mr. Bantling—tries his best to curb my excesses, and steer me upon a politer path, with what success you see today. *Will* you forgive me?"

"Of course, of course," Isabel said, striving to mask her impatience, "of course I forgive you"—*as I must always do,* she did not add. "I went to Florence, I saw my husband, I told him there was no possible future for us together—and here I am!" She forced her face to show a bright smile. "What more is there for me to say? What more would you wish to know? It's over. *Factum est.*"

Henrietta released her friend's hand and sat back on her chair and looked at her for a long moment, solemnly. "I'm glad," she said at last. "The failure of a marriage is not a thing that would usually gladden me, but in this case, I confess it does. I grieve for you, in what must be your distress, but I'm happy for you too. You're free."

"Yes, I'm free!" Isabel returned, her smile more bright, more brittle, more breakable than ever. She stood up. "And now I must go to the hotel. Staines will be fretting and, besides, I'm fatigued, and want my bed."

When they came out of the station Isabel was surprised to find the evening sky a dense gold glow—she always forgot, between one visit and the next, how long the twilight lasted up here in the north—and when her friend had left her, to attend a lecture on theosophy in High Holborn, she set off to stroll along the Strand, in the direction of Trafalgar Square. The setting sun dazzled her eyes, however, and she had gone only a little way when she was overcome by dizziness, and she turned back to the station and at the rank there requested one of the linkmen to call up a cab for her. Once she had ascended to the seat and settled herself she laid her head back and closed her eyes, hoping to lull her mind to rest, but in vain. Henrietta's words—*You are free, you are free*—rolled over and over in her head, insistent and monotonous as the circular rhythm of the wheels of the hansom grinding on the roadway beneath her. She did not feel free; but then, she reflected, she really did not know how being free should feel. She supposed it would be a negative sensation, not a positive, a matter of not having rather than of having—of not having to strive, of not having to resist, of not having to guard one's little corner, one's bit of shelter; above all of not having to insist, against the will of others, on the sovereignty of one's self. Once, long ago, she had thought, secretly, shamefacedly, that money would be a form of freedom, and the mover of her fate. She had soon come to see that only one part of this notion was the case: her fortune had sealed her fate, but in the process had made her the opposite of free.

That night she slept but fitfully, and woke late, half in a daze, with the sun on her face. When she had bathed and put on the costume of light linen that Staines had laid out for her, she went down and breakfasted in silence and solitude, the other guests having long since been and gone about their morning affairs. She had ordered a second cup of coffee when Mr. Pratt himself, the proprietor of the inn, as rotund and affable as ever, came to inform her that there was a visitor—indeed, two visitors—waiting on her in the parlour. She cancelled the supplementary cup and rose quickly and left the breakfast room, curious to know, and conscious of an unaccountable faint foreboding, who it was that should be calling upon her at ten-thirty of the clock on a sleepy London weekday morn. On entering the parlour she caught herself up momentarily at the sight of what, in her initial confusion of mind, she took to be Madame Merle's unmistakably straight and handsome back confronting her through the narrow slats of a small gilt chair set beside the fireplace. She was still staring when a second lady, standing in the bay of one of the windows that looked out on Dover Street, turned about swiftly and revealed herself to be the Countess Gemini.

"Aha, you thought to avoid us, did you?" this lady demanded, with a roguish brightness. "But see, we have tracked you to your lair!"

Now the seated person turned also, but even before she had done so Isabel had realised her mistake: it was not Madame Merle, but her daughter; it was Pansy, in all the pale reality of herself.

"I was not aware of being in hiding, from you or anyone else," Isabel said to her sister-in-law, with a smile, "and I'm very glad that you have found me out—though I should not think so public a place as Pratt's Hotel could be described as a lair." She transferred her gaze to Pansy, on whom it lighted with an instant softening. "My dear, how well you look, and—and how fine!"

It was not, in fact, the fineness, or the wellness, of her aspect that seemed to Isabel worthy of remark, but the change that had come over her, a change far more momentous than might have been expected to occur in the short time since Isabel had last seen her, at the convent of the Sacro Cuore di Gèsu in Florence. Then, she had been a girl of twenty: now she was a woman of twenty-one. It was not that she was so very much altered as to appearance, although her face, even in the short time that had elapsed since Isabel had looked upon her step-daughter, had lengthened, and her shoulders, in particular, had broadened; but there was about her a new air of determination, of self-possession, of— and here Isabel faltered, wishing to stop herself on the brink of the word—of a new hardness. She greeted her step-mother with a curt *"Buon giorno,"* and then, remembering where she was, changed, off-handedly, to an even cooler "Good day." Isabel, all at once overcome by a kind of happy anguish, went forward swiftly and took the girl—the woman!—in her arms and drew her almost passionately to her breast. Pansy suffered the embrace stiffly, then disengaged herself and stepped back, at which Isabel let her arms drop to her sides, and knew herself, in that instant, to have been abandoned.

"I thought," she said falteringly, addressing both Pansy and the countess, "I thought you were in—in Kent, was it?"

"Oh, we were, yes," the countess said dismissively. "At Fernley Hall, the home, or seat, I suppose I should say, of Lord Lanchester and his numerous sons—numerous, and dull. The entire place was the very definition of dullness, wasn't it, Pansy?" Pansy's only reply was the merest shrug, and the countess turned her attention to Isabel again. "We have been to other places too, of course. There was Fawns, an enormous and perfectly hideous mansion owned by that very rich American—what's his name? I've forgotten it—an acquaintance of Lanchester's, on whom his lordship pawned us off—you needn't look at me like that, Pansy, the folk at Fernley couldn't wait to see the back of us—and when our welcome *there* ran out, we had no choice but to seek refuge at Gardencourt—yes, my dear Isabel, Gardencourt—which was not at all what I expected, having heard so much about the place—*very* dreary, and with bathrooms that even an Italian would balk at— although there was the one bright spot, which was the absence of Mrs. Touchett—they say she will not return to England, and intends to put Gardencourt on the market. It was while we were there, at Gardencourt, I mean, that Osmond telegraphed to say he would sustain us here no longer, and that we must return at once to Florence—he's vexed at me for having failed in the mission he had tasked me with"—she directed her eye meaningfully in Pansy's direction—"so here we are, filling in the time as best we can before taking the train to Paris this evening—to Paris, and then onwards, to"—she grimaced—" 'home'!"

Isabel had attended patiently to this account—which in the telling was far more extensive and richly detailed than the version of it we have provided here—and now enquired how the pair had known that she was in London, and here at Pratt's.

"Mrs. Touchett sent one of her famous telegrams to me to Gardencourt—I have it, look."

She produced a small green envelope and extracted the scrap of telegraph paper from it, upon which was printed the terse directive:

```
My niece at Pratt's stop take yours to visit
her there stop Lydia Touchett
```

"Ah, yes," Isabel said, smiling and nodding, "that is the true stamp of my aunt. I'm glad she wrote to you; and I'm glad"—she looked at Pansy—"oh, I'm so glad you came!"

She bethought herself then to offer refreshments to the pair. The countess declared that she "would kill" for a glass of champagne, despite the unseemly earliness of the hour—"In England the best one can hope for is a thimbleful of sticky sherry as one is about to sit down to dinner!"—but added that Pansy wished to pay a last visit to the shops in the Burlington Arcade.

"Oh, Pansy dear, must you go?" Isabel exclaimed. "I should so like to hear your impressions of England, and—and how you found the English." She smiled apologetically for the lame manner in which she had couched her entreaty; she had turned a little aside from the countess and her avid eye. "Remember what you said to me, what you asked of me, the last time we spoke, at the convent?" Pansy stood impassive, with her hands folded before her, and said nothing. "You asked me," Isabel went on, "to promise to come back to you. Do you recall the moment—do you recall saying it, 'Tell me you will come back'?"

"Yes, I remember," Pansy said, in her new sharp cool manner. "But you didn't, did you? You didn't come back."

At these words Isabel had the sensation of some spurned thing inside her spreading wide its wings and launching itself sorrowfully into the desolation of the sky.

"Well, well, we all make promises and break them," the countess said briskly, with a glance towards Isabel that was not entirely lacking in sympathy. Then she turned to Pansy. "You should run along now and visit your shops, before the noonday crowds come in." She peered into her purse and drew out a sovereign. "Here is a little money to spend—it's all I have."

Pansy took the proffered coin with an air of indifference, and made to leave, ignoring the look of anguished imploring that Isabel bent upon her. At the door the young woman paused, and turned, and gazed a moment, through half-closed eyes, at the step-mother she was in the act so pointedly of spurning for ever. "And Papa," she said, "have you forsaken him, also?" And then, not deigning to await a reply, she was gone.

Isabel crossed swiftly to the window, and stood there, pressing a knuckle hard against her mouth and peering down into the street in hope, a hope that was to prove vain, of catching what she feared would be the last sight of her step-daughter. The countess, behind her, looked on, somewhat impatiently, with eyebrows sceptically lifted. Usually she was much diverted when one person was awful to another, thinking of the so many times when people had been awful to *her*; all the same, she could not but feel a little sorry for Isabel, who when it came to the conduct of life was really very stupid, for all her much-vaunted cleverness in matters of the mind. "Don't be affected by her cutting tongue," she said. "This is how she is, now."

"But she's so much changed!" Isabel, still facing the window, as good as wailed. "She's so like—"

"Her father? Yes, and her mother, too."

"But she was so gentle, so sweet!" She turned, and when she spoke again her voice was sharper, with the sharpness of an accusation. "What happened to her?"

The countess returned her an indignant stare. "I hope you do not mean to blame *me*?" she challenged. "What she has become is all her own work—hers, and her parents'. None of us can escape what we inherit, not even you."

Isabel, too shaken to bother questioning that last sally, walked across the room to the fireplace and stood gazing emptily into the empty grate. "Her father sent you with her here to make a match for her. He will not be pleased that you have failed him."

"Failed him? Ha! Osmond doesn't know this country and, more than that, he doesn't know his daughter. He thought to marry her, without mention of a *dot* to help her, into one of the great houses of England, imagining it would be he who does a favour to the realm by enriching it with the gift of a child of *his*. But he was wrong in every way possible. I can tell you, if one of Lord Lanchester's doltish sons had set his eye on her, he would have needed to be of a nature more complaisant than even the usual run of Englishmen."

"Complaisant?" Isabel asked, her distracted attention caught by the word. "What do you mean?"

The countess, with a sort of flounce of impatience, threw a quick glance towards the ceiling, then fixed again upon her sister-in-law.

"Don't you understand *anything*?" she asked, simply and slowly, as if addressing a child. "Don't you *see* anything? You should never have allowed that brute of a brother of mine to send the child to a convent."

"Why not?"

The countess gave an exasperated groan. "My dear, *everyone* knows what those places are like, and what goes on in them."

Isabel had turned her head and was staring at her with a frown of baffled interrogation. "What do you mean?" she demanded weakly. "I don't understand what you mean."

Again the countess turned her eyes heavenwards a moment, then shook her head and sighed. Isabel, although she had a good two or three inches in height on her sister-in-law, had the strong impression of being looked down upon.

"That creature would never have found a husband," the countess said, "for the very reason that a husband was the last thing she wanted."

"But Mr. Rosier," Isabel murmured, "she wanted *him*."

"Mr. Rosier?" the countess scoffed. "Oh, I grant you she may have *wanted* him, in some sort of way, but only for the reason that there was not enough of a man in him to be—well, to be a *man*." She stepped forward quickly and set both of her hands on the half-dazed woman's shoulders. "Don't you see, my dear," she said with unwonted softness, "don't you see how it is with her? It will most likely pass, in time—you know what young women are—but for now it is not men she cares for, not men at all!"

Isabel nodded, with the affectless regularity of a clockwork figure. She saw; she saw.

XXXVI

She had herself a visit to make this day, and the prospect of it had been much on her mind, although the events of the morning, which we have just related, had diverted her temporarily from any thought of it. After the Countess Gemini had left, however— Pansy had not returned from her excursion to the brilliant and bounteous Arcade, so her aunt had felt obliged to go in search of her, saying with high sarcasm that Osmond should never forgive her if she were to lose his daughter entirely—she got herself ready, a matter merely of putting on her hat and making sure she had British silver in her purse, and requested the hotel doorman to summon her a cab. The day had turned cloudy, though it was horridly hot, and the air had a dullish grey gleam to it, like the bloom on tarnished pewter, and the leaves hung listless on the trees in Green Park. Isabel paid only the vaguest heed to these meteorological effects; she was thinking of Pansy. Was the Countess Gemini correct in accusing her of having misjudged her step-daughter all along? Had the sweet and docile child she had thought she knew been not docile or sweet at all, but a dissembling little schemer quietly and craftily biding her time until the opportunity should come when she might kick over the traces and be her true self? It was not to be credited, really it was not. The suspicion the countess had imputed to Isabel, namely that Isabel considered it was the aunt's frivolous and irresponsible influence that had produced, in a matter of weeks, such a startling transformation in the girl, was not a suspicion at all, but a conviction. The countess had chided her for allowing her husband to put Pansy in a convent, but what, she might ask, had Osmond been thinking of to put his daughter into the care of his sister, of all people? Had he wished her to be made hard and careless and cruel? Throughout the child's life, until now, he had been unrelenting, to the point of tyranny, in his determination that she should be sealed off from the world and its ways; under his despotic authority she had known little else but cloisters and choirs. When she had reached an age at which it was natural for her to leave the convent, he had promptly enclosed her within the further confines of his steely vigilance, meaning to keep her there until he should judge the moment opportune, and the chosen candidate of the highest suitability and worth—suitable and worthy by *his* lights—to marry her off. Lord Warburton had been his ideal, his very dream of a son-in-law, but Warburton had prudently withdrawn when it was made clear to him that Pansy's affections had been bestowed elsewhere, on poor Ned Rosier—Isabel could never think of Mr. Rosier, even now, without that pitying epithet attached to his name—at which point Osmond had sentenced the girl to another term of corrective custody at the house of the holy sisters. And then, all at once, astonishingly, shockingly, the years of drilling and disciplining had been set at naught, and Osmond's daughter had been packed off under the care, if that was what to call it, of her notorious aunt, to rattle around the stately homes of England in search of a husband, any husband, with any sort of title at all. Had the countess disclosed to Osmond, as she had just a little while ago disclosed to Isabel, her conviction as to Pansy's true and secret nature, with the result that he had ordered her to take his daughter to England and find a match for her, on the assumption that no one there would dream such a thing could be true of such a young lady— Osmond, as Isabel knew, had a low opinion of the perspicacity of the Anglo-Saxon sensibility—or that even if the truth about Pansy's predilections were to be recognised, no one among that neutral and neurasthenic race would care a fig in the matter?

And now what was to happen? Pansy was returning to Florence husbandless; would she live with her mother? Would she live with her parents? Would they make the semblance of a family together? Impossible, surely. How should Gilbert Osmond, that paragon of proper appearance, that fanatic of convention, how should he display before society's gloating eye the living evidence of his past sins and present insupportable predicament? No, it could not be. Yet Pansy must live somewhere, she must have a home. Isabel looked back now, with a kind of detached self-sympathy, at the pathos of her plan, which that morning had been so definitively dashed, of being Pansy's provider and protector, of being her saviour and nothing less.

What if the countess should take the young woman under her once colourful and now decidedly dusty wing? This, however, was a thought far beyond Isabel's sustaining.

Her sister-in-law was the one confidante, if that was what she was, to whom Isabel had disclosed the fact of her having given over sole possession of the Palazzo Roccanera into the hands of Serena Merle. Why she had not told it to anyone else, to her friend Miss Stackpole, for instance, she was not quite sure, except of course that she knew Miss Stackpole would have informed her flat-out that she was a hopeless fool, and disgracefully irresponsible to boot, while others, had there been others to tell, would simply have laughed at her. The countess, who if not clever was certainly worldly-wise, had seen to the heart of Isabel's motives more quickly and more clearly than had Isabel herself.

"They are two condemned souls," she had said, "Osmond and the Merle woman, and you have devised a hell for them to torment each other in! Why, you cunning thing—who'd have thought it of you?"

"If they are condemned, then it's their own work," Isabel had protested, but the countess was not listening, engrossed as she was in contemplating the gratifyingly entangled implications of the thing that Isabel had brought about.

"I must say, my dear, it's an expensive revenge you have exacted. But you can afford it, and I imagine the palazzo is a poisoned place for you, now. She'll sell it, of course, and he'll be put out on the street. He may even be compelled to come to me for shelter." And she had given one of her gay little shrieks of laughter. "I shall enjoy that."

Now Isabel was jogged out of her disquieted reverie as the cab came to a stop at the neat little house in Cedar Street. The hollyhocks in the scrap of front garden were in full bloom, while the lilac trees had lost their lustre, but otherwise everything was as she remembered, including the faint rank smell coming up from the river. Her tug at the doorbell-rope produced no sound from within, yet after but a moment Daisy the maid appeared, cheerful and charming as ever. She greeted the visitor warmly, in a low voice, and explained that the bell had been muffled so as not to disturb the lady of the house. "She sleeps a great deal," the maid confided, "and as a matter of fact is resting now. But Mr. Devenish is here."

Isabel was shown into the sunny dining room, where indeed she found the said Mr. Devenish, he of the green eyes and russet hair, who put aside the journal he had been perusing and scrambled up from the stern little armchair where he had been awkwardly perched—the house, as Isabel knew, had not much to offer in the way of creature comforts—and came forward, smiling, with a hand extended.

"Mrs. Osmond, how delightful to see you!"

Daisy was relieving Isabel of her straw hat and Miss Stackpole's enduring pink parasol—at the latter of which Mr. Devenish had cast a quizzical glance—and now she enquired if the lady and gentleman might care for some refreshment. "A glass of elderberry cordial, perhaps?" she asked of Isabel, with a discreet but definite twinkle, a reference no doubt to the daunting fare on offer when Isabel last visited, and the fortitude with which she had faced it.

"Perhaps some tea?" Isabel ventured.

When the girl had departed, Mr. Devenish and Mrs. Osmond stood smiling somewhat helplessly into each other's faces, until Mr. Devenish at last, stammering a little, suggested that they might be seated, and went to the deal table in the middle of the floor and drew out a chair for the lady. They sat. They smiled at each other again. Mr. Devenish fidgeted with his hands. His eyes were of a truly remarkable shade of green, flinty and transparent, just like the sea, Isabel thought, on certain crisp sunny days in spring.

"Tell me how Miss Janeway is," she said now, dispensing with her smile, which had become altogether too strained and awkward to sustain.

"Very poorly, I'm afraid," Mr. Devenish replied, and he too assumed a grave look. "She keeps to her bed, and manages to get down for no more than an hour or so, usually in the evenings."

"As bad as that?"

"As bad as that. I fear the end cannot be far off. The doctors—"
He lifted his hands from the table and let them fall back, in a gesture of sad helplessness.

Daisy the maid came then with their tea on a silver tray, along
with a plate of arrowroot biscuits. The girl's good humour was so
artless and unfailingly infectious that Isabel felt cheered just to
look at her.

"Perhaps I could come back, this evening," Isabel said, when
the maid had gone. "Do you think that might be possible? I
should so like to talk to your aunt, before—" She left the phrase
unfinished.

"You could stay now," Mr. Devenish replied, and immediately
blushed—he was of that race of red-haired folk who colour easily.
"I mean, you could stay until my aunt has finished her rest."

Isabel smiled over the rim of her teacup. "That might be quite
a long time, if Miss Janeway is as weak as you say she is."

"Well, then, we might"—Mr. Devenish eagerly began, but then
got stuck in his stammer—"we might—we might"—and had to
stop and swallow heavily.

"We might go out, and come back again, you mean?" Isabel
offered helpfully. "In fact, there is a place I have meant to visit,
since my return—I was in Italy, until the evening before last." She
paused, struck in wonderment at the thought of all that had taken
place in her life in so short a span of time. "It's not a place of any
consequence," she resumed, "as you should see if you were to
accompany me there. Indeed, I'm sure you'd laugh at me as being
capricious to the point of silliness."

Mr. Devenish was already rising from his chair. "I'm always
ready to follow a caprice," he gallantly declared. "Just let me creep
up first and check on the patient to make sure she's at rest."

He fairly sprinted from the room, and returned hardly a moment later, panting and smiling, to announce that the ailing woman was sleeping soundly and apparently in no pain or distress.

"Well then," said Isabel, "let us go!"

They left the house, Mr. Devenish having informed Daisy of their, to him, mysterious outing, and walked together to the cab rank nearby. The day was still oppressively overcast. Isabel enquired of her companion how his journalism work was progressing, at which he sighed and launched into a droll account of the woes attendant upon anyone foolish enough to take up a cause along with a career—"The road to Socialism is long and winding, of that much I can assure you"—and at points in this litany she found herself laughing aloud, wondering, as she did so, when was the last time she had been given cause for simple and unaffected mirth. When they were in the carriage, they moved on from Mr. Devenish's affairs to the not unrelated topic of Miss Janeway's numerous projects and protests, which was the occasion for Mr. Devenish to rehearse that lady's heartfelt pledges of gratitude for Mrs. Osmond's bounteous generosity—he was speaking of that famously mislaid satchel of banknotes—but Isabel shook her head to stop him. He glanced at her sideways, struck by the sudden seriousness that had come into her manner.

"I don't think of it as bounty, or of myself as generous," she said. "I was, and am, embarrassed by the childish impulse that led me to withdraw such a monstrous sum of cash from the bank. Further, and even more shamingly, I must confess that I left that rather ridiculous bag of money at your aunt's house by mistake, and only afterwards thought to donate it to what I suppose I must accustom myself from now on to calling 'the cause.'"

Mr. Devenish had listened to this candid owning-up with

amusement more than anything else; his attention had been sharply caught, however, by the young woman's final words.

"You say you must accustom yourself to the term," he noted thoughtfully. "That would sound to some ears—to Miss Janeway's, certainly—as conceding that the first long step has been taken towards your *committing* yourself to the cause." He turned now and looked at her directly, and when he spoke, all traces of drollery had been banished from his voice. "Would it be a mistake for Miss Janeway, or for others—myself, for example—to imagine that is indeed what your words should be understood to have conveyed, whether intentionally or otherwise?"

Isabel turned away from him, and looked out at the hot grey pavements and the random pedestrians passing to and fro upon them.

"Many things have occurred in my life in recent times, things unexpected and often unpleasant—in fact, almost beyond bearing, some of them. I may tell you about them, some day, should our acquaintance continue long enough." She turned back to face him. "I have a fortune; not a great one, but a fortune, nonetheless, and I am"—she paused, and her lips twitched in an ironical small smile—"I suppose the word is 'free.' That being the case, there must be something to the service of which I can devote my freedom, and my fortune. I used to think my first and sacred duty was to myself, and to the working out of my 'fate'—another of those words I am no longer sure I know the meaning of, though it hardly matters, since I employ them now to myself only within the confines of quotation marks." She looked away from him again, and faced forward this time, over the back of their horse and into the oncoming light of afternoon. "I shall remain in London, and help you tend your aunt, if you will let me, until her struggle is over. Her end will mark, for me, a beginning"—she glanced at him quickly, almost fearfully—"or does that seem like my old self-ishness asserting itself again?"

Mr. Devenish said nothing for some time. His expression, grave and tensely pensive, was that of one unaccustomed to such flights of high seriousness as his companion had just undertaken, and who must have a moment in which to adjust his own plumage so as to be able to ascend sufficiently far to join her in those heady heights. At last he spoke.

"This is—and here I am going to employ a term which the world nowadays would put in quotation marks, but I do not—this is a noble offer, and one that I readily accept, and thank you for."

"I can see you are wondering if I will be equal to the task. I have attended other deathbeds, I have witnessed other deaths. My little son died—*there* was a fire to temper a soul. You may trust me. I shall not falter. I shall not fail you—I mean, I shall not fail your aunt."

"I believe it, dear Mrs. Osmond," he said, with almost an overflow of conviction. "I believe it." Here he frowned, taking on an air of deeper earnestness that made him seem all at once very young. "Do you think, if I were to ask you to address me by my first name, that you might allow me to address you by yours? I am aware," he hastened to add, "that this is only the second time we have met."

Isabel looked away. "I wonder if that might not be a little too much *tutoyer*-ing for one day," she murmured, but gently.

"Yes, of course, I understand," Mr. Devenish said, colouring, and frowning all the harder.

"But perhaps we may come to it," Isabel went on, to console him. "Who knows? These things must occur naturally, don't you think?"

"I do think so, certainly. But will you permit me, if only inwardly, to think of you as Isabel? In the way of practice, you understand." The lightness of this last was only a little marred by his getting stuck on the awkward plosive at the start of that word "practice."

Now all at once they had reached their destination, and Isabel tapped the roof of the cab to signal to the driver, perched high behind them, to stop. Mr. Devenish—Myles—craned forward to see where they were. "Why, it's Paddington!" he declared, and turned to the woman at his side. "Do you mean to take me on a journey?"

They got down from the cab and walked forward a little way, to the corner of the broad thoroughfare that led down into the dark depths of the station, which from here were impenetrable to the eye, and Isabel put a hand on her companion's arm and drew him to a stop. This was the place where the weeping man had stood, that morning when she had come up from Gardencourt after her cousin's death; she described now, to Mr. Devenish, how lost and desolate the unfortunate fellow had sounded, like a child bereft of its parents.

"You didn't expect him to be here still, did you?" Mr. Devenish asked, with an incredulous smile.

"No, of course not," Isabel answered. "I only wanted to see the place again, and I wanted you to see it, too. I did nothing to help the poor creature in his distress, and I have not forgiven myself for it." She turned to face him, animated suddenly, and unaccountably so, as it seemed to him. "Tell me, Mr. Devenish, what, had you been in my place, you would have done," she demanded gravely. "For I'm sure you would have done something."

The young man glanced this way and that, passing the tip of his tongue along his lower lip. He was conscious of the weight of the moment, as he stood there with Isabel's eyes earnestly fixed on him, but he could not have said what it was exactly that would warrant such weight.

"I don't know what there would have been to do," he said, struggling not to stammer. "Our task, it seems to me, is to look beyond the individual case, and aim to make a world that will not any longer allow of the wretchedness you witnessed in that poor man's plight." He stopped, irresolute; he could see, from the way the light faded in her eye, that he had given the wrong answer. "I mean," he said, ready to try again, "I mean I—" But it was too late.

They turned together and walked away from the station entrance. He thought to link his arm in hers, but then thought better of it. He told her, as they went along, how it was his aunt's wish to set up a radical journal in New York, with him as its editor, and, as Isabel heard it wordlessly implied, with her—with Mrs. Osmond's—fortune to support it.

"I should like to see it, the New World; I should like the challenge of it," the young man said.

He had meant his words, shy and tentative as they had been, to convey an explorative note, a note of invitation, even, which he hoped Isabel would meet, and answer; but Isabel said nothing, nothing at all.

LONG LANKIN

A collection of short stories from the early years of Man
Booker Prize–winning author John Banville's career, *Long
Lankin* explores the passionate emotions—fear, jealousy,
desire—that course beneath the surface of everyday life.
From a couple at risk of being torn apart by the allure of
wealth to an old man's descent into nature, the tales in this
collection showcase the talents that launched Banville onto
the literary scene. Offering a unique insight into the mind
of "one of the great living masters of English-language
prose" (*Los Angeles Times*), these nine haunting sketches
stand alone as canny observations on the turbulence of the
human condition

Fiction

ALSO AVAILABLE

Athena
Birchwood
The Book of Evidence
Doctor Copernicus
Eclipse
Ghosts
The Infinities
Kepler
The Sea
Shroud
The Untouchable

VINTAGE INTERNATIONAL
Available wherever books are sold.
www.vintagebooks.com